"Captain, this is Ambassador Kollos. My habitat is outside the rec deck, and I have a last-ditch plan."

Kirk raised the communicator to his face. "I'm listening, Ambassador."

"I wish to enter and let the Naazh see me. Do you understand?"

Chekov saw that Kirk grasped the proposal, and so did he. Kollos clearly hoped that the Naazh would be incapacitated by the sight of a Medusan.

"It's too risky," Kirk said. "We don't know how they'll react—it could make them *more* violent."

"That hardly seems possible, Captain. At least it would disorient them long enough for me to get the Aenar out."

"Assuming their helmets don't filter out the effect."

"Unlikely. Filters have to be designed specifically for that purpose."

"What about sighted personnel?" Chekov asked.

"You'll have to withdraw for your own safety. I assure you, my habitat is robust, and Medusans are difficult to kill. Trust us, Captain. This is the lateral move we need."

Chekov watched the decision play across Kirk's face. But he was James Kirk, so he arrived at his decision swiftly. "All right, Ambassador. Come in." He raised his voice. "All personnel! Retreat and form up on me!"

THE HIGHER FRONTIER

Christopher L. Bennett

Based on *Star Trek*
created by Gene Roddenberry

GALLERY BOOKS
New York London Toronto Sydney New Delhi Laikan

Gallery Books
An Imprint of Simon & Schuster, Inc.
1230 Avenue of the Americas
New York, NY 10020

First Gallery Books trade paperback edition March 2020

Manufactured in the United States of America

10 9 8 7 6 5 4 3 2 1

Library of Congress Cataloging-in-Publication Data

Names: Bennett, Christopher L., author. | Roddenberry, Gene, other.
Title: Star trek : the higher frontier / Christopher L. Bennett ; based on
Star Trek created by Gene Roddenberry.
Other titles: Higher frontier
Description: First Gallery Books trade paperback edition. | New York :
Gallery Books, 2020.
Identifiers: LCCN 2019036426 (print) | LCCN 2019036427 (ebook) | ISBN
9781982133665 (trade paperback) | ISBN 9781982133672 (ebook)
Subjects: LCSH: Star trek (Television program)—Fiction. | Star Trek
films—Fiction. | GSAFD: Science fiction.
Classification: LCC PS3602.E66447 H54 2020 (print) | LCC PS3602.E66447
(ebook) | DDC 813/.6—dc23
LC record available at https://lccn.loc.gov/2019036426
LC ebook record available at https://lccn.loc.gov/2019036427

ISBN 978-1-9821-3366-5
ISBN 978-1-9821-3367-2 (ebook)

To Shotaro Ishinomori,
for showing us the way to transform

Historian's Note

The main events of this story take place several years after the *Enterprise* stops V'Ger from destroying Earth (*Star Trek: The Motion Picture*) and several years before Khan Noonien Singh escapes from Ceti Alpha V (*Star Trek: The Wrath of Khan*).

2278

Prologue

Aenar Compound
Northern Wastes, Andoria

Sisyra could smell the city burning.

Few things were more frightening here than a fire raging out of control, a heat great enough to soften the crags of ancient, stonelike ice to which the Aenar's homes and structures were attached. The buildings were anchored deep enough that no normal fire could loosen them before it could be put out, but there was nothing normal about what Sisyra sensed all around her.

In a typical crisis, the mental cries of the Aenar closest to the scene would be immediately heard and responded to by the whole community. There were so few Aenar left in the universe anymore—fewer than a thousand of pure blood now—that every life was jealously guarded. Sisyra zh'Sakab was herself one of the community's main protectors, the chief physician these past few years since her mentor Shikis had passed away. She was unusually young for such a crucial role in society, but with so few left, many Aenar were obligated to rise to whatever responsibilities fell upon them. Whenever one of her neighbors had cried out in need, she had felt it and sped to the scene, along with the other emergency responders.

Yet this time, there had not been just a single cry for help.

Dozens had called out at once, sending mental impressions of the invaders that had suddenly materialized in their midst and begun attacking indiscriminately. All over the compound, Aenar were dying, the precious few being diminished even more. Loving family members were being cut down before their bondmates. A young *thaan* screamed as he was hurled through a window in one of the highest modules and plummeted toward the icy crags below. A much younger brother and sister were burning to death in their home. Their mental cries of terror and anguish filled Sisyra's mind, paralyzing her with indecision. Which of them could she help? Which way should she turn? How could she come to anyone's aid without being struck down herself?

Sisyra felt the same paralyzing helplessness in the familiar minds of the compound's other protectors. They were trained to deal with emergencies and accidents, but no Aenar had raised a hand in violence for more than a century, no matter the provocation. As a rule, it had never been necessary to employ means as crude as violence. The remoteness of the Northern Wastes and the maze of tunnels between the compound and the surface provided protection against routine visits from outsiders. The magnetic anomalies near Andor's pole created a natural damping field around the settlement, blocking most known forms of transporter, and a network of field amplifiers had been erected around the compound to block the rest. On those few occasions when intruders did come—Andorian radicals resentful of the Aenar's struggle for their rights, or offworld slavers seeking to exploit their telepathic gifts as the Romulans had done generations before—the strongest telepathic adepts had been able to confuse their senses and hide the compound and its occupants from their view, or to frighten them off with hallucinations of the caverns collapsing around them. Species that relied on vision were easily fooled.

Yet these attackers had appeared out of nowhere like the

phantoms of ancient myth, with no trace of a transporter signal to trip the compound's warning sensors. And something shielded their minds from telepathic influence. Sisyra could feel every emotion, every anguished sensation, from the invaders' victims, yet the slayers' own minds were voids to her. Oh, they were not silent; they laughed as they beat defenseless Aenar to death, as they shot them in the back, as they set their homes afire. *"Fan the flames,"* she heard them roar through others' ears. *"Crush everything!"* But neither Sisyra nor any of the others whose minds she connected with could gain any sense of *why* the invaders were so filled with hatred toward her people.

And she did not sense the phantom warrior coming for her until it was almost too late.

Just in time, as she ran down the rampway from the burning hospital module into the tunnel network carved within the ice crag that supported it, her antennae sensed the electromagnetic signature of an armor-clad figure approaching through an adjoining tunnel. She spun and dodged down another branch of the intersection just before the phantom lunged at her. She heard the *whoosh* of a heavy blade of some kind passing just a few handbreadths behind her head.

A sword. It must have been a sword, like those in the tales of the Aenar's ancient battles with the other, more populous subspecies of Andorians, before her people had embraced pacifism. These attackers had amazing technology; surely they had weapons that could have wiped out the compound in seconds. And yet they chose to hunt the Aenar down individually, to kill them with ancient blades or beat them to death with armored fists. Sisyra could not read their thoughts, but she could read their actions: sadistic, vindictive, personal. They were not here simply to exterminate, but to terrorize.

And at that, they were succeeding effortlessly. Sisyra's terror as the sword-wielding hunter pursued her was overpowering. Between that terror and the sensory overload of the suffering and deaths she felt from all around her, Sisyra lost her bearings and made a wrong turn. She found herself in a cul-de-sac, a path blocked by an icefall months ago and never cleared out because the population had shrunk so much that the part of the settlement it connected to was no longer needed.

And now it would be the cause of the population's reduction by one more individual.

Her resignation dissolved her fear, and she turned to face her attacker stoically, antennae coming to bear so that she could get a sense of the phantom's shape and body language. The tall, powerful, evidently male figure was entirely encased in faceless armor, rigid and metallic yet with an organic texture, and charged with energy as if somehow alive. But she could get no sense of the being within the armor . . . until he chuckled.

"Who are you?" Sisyra cried in outrage. "What are you, that you would do this to a race already dying?"

The phantom replied in a distorted voice. "Those who are about to die do not need to know the reason why."

Something welled up inside Sisyra in response to those cold words. Anger, defiance—but something more. It was like a long-sleeping part of her was starting to wake. *Fight*, it seemed to say within her. *If you do not fight, you cannot survive!*

She had been raised to believe otherwise—that it was better to die to preserve the Aenar's principles. But if the Aenar as a race were now dying, what was left to preserve? She had no chance of killing such an enemy in any case—but at least she could make a point.

Sisyra listened to the call of her heart, embracing the warming energy that grew within her. She stretched out her hands to direct it toward the phantom. She felt *something* emerge from her and push him back like a strong wind, making him stagger.

Her antennae reared back in surprise. *Telekinesis?* She'd heard tales of such abilities existing among rare, special Aenar in the past, but it was not a side of their psionic abilities that they had chosen to explore, preferring to use them for gentler things, for sharing thoughts and connecting souls. It was certainly nothing Sisyra had ever imagined herself capable of.

Again, he chuckled. "There you are. At last, this fight is getting interesting!"

She sensed and heard it as he raised his sword and charged her. She raised her hands again, blocking the swing with another telekinetic pulse. She felt the tunnel ceiling rattle in response, perceiving its instability and weak points more clearly than she had mere moments before. Her desperation, or her resolve, must have heightened her powers. Trusting implicitly in these new sensations, she directed a surge of energy upward, shaking loose the already unstable ice.

The debris fell between her and the phantom, for even now, she could not bring herself to attack him directly. Still, there were now tonnes of ice between them, blocking the tunnel almost completely. Sisyra was trapped within the cul-de-sac, but at least she was safe from his sword.

"Now I'm getting vexed," the phantom told her, his voice carrying through the narrow gap that remained. "I'm going to carve you up and see what lets you do that."

He raised a hand, and she felt a surge of energy around it, heard a crackle in the air. Suddenly he held a weapon that had not been there before, summoned as if by magic. Bolts of plasma flew from it and blasted through the pile of debris. Sisyra backed away, raising her hands to shield her face from the ice shrapnel. When she lowered them, he was stepping over the last of the debris.

"I know what lets me do it," Sisyra cried defiantly as she sent forth more surges from her mind to repel him. "I feel it inside me. My life burns brightly!"

The phantom held his ground, slowly pushing forward

against the psionic gale. "It's not your life," he declared. "And I intend to prove it."

At last, Sisyra could sustain the effort no longer. She sank to her knees in exhaustion and despair as the phantom strode casually up to her. Armored fingers closed around her throat.

"So," the phantom said, "shall we begin the experiment?"

One

U.S.S. Enterprise

"Was the Aenar massacre as bad as the news services are claiming?"

On the desk screen in James Kirk's quarters, Admiral Harry Morrow stared back grimly as he answered the captain's question. *"If anything, it was worse, Jim. Every last Aenar in the settlement was systematically, brutally murdered. And not from a distance, not cleanly with energy weapons—they did it with their own hands, and they took their time.*

"But they were thorough," the Starfleet chief of staff went on. *"The Aenar were already a dying minority on Andoria—less than a thousand left. Even so, they've resisted contact with outsiders, mistrusted Andorian and Federation offers to help them rebuild. There were only a few dozen who ever left their compound, mostly a group of political activists lobbying against the Andorian terraforming program."*

Over Kirk's left shoulder, Leonard McCoy crossed his arms. "Unbelievable that the fight over terraforming is still going on. After fifty years of arguing, you'd think they'd have found a way to balance the need to warm the rest of the planet with the need to preserve the Aenar's way of life. The Andorians' reckless disregard for the Aenar came close to being genocidal in itself."

"That may be, Doctor," said Morrow, *"but in an ironic way, it's the reason that any Aenar are still alive. There are fewer than seventy survivors on Andoria now, and they've all been placed in protective custody. Starfleet is tracking down some others who have gone offworld to appeal for aid from the Federation or NGO charities, and one group that was searching for a suitable ice world where they might relocate. We estimate there are now no more than ninety-five Aenar left in existence."*

At Kirk's right, Commander Spock shook his head. "Strange . . . to go to such extremes in the attempt to exterminate a subspecies already on the verge of extinction. It would seem more logical merely to wait and let nature take its course."

McCoy threw a glare at Spock and opened his mouth to argue—then paused, for even he could hear the muted anguish and disgust beneath Spock's words. It had been nearly four and a half years now since Spock's mind-meld with the vast cybernetic entity V'Ger and his epiphany that a life without emotion was sterile and pointless. Since then, he had come to accept both his Vulcan and human sides and found a comfortable synthesis between logic and emotion, giving him a greater serenity than he had ever possessed during his first five-year tour of duty under Kirk. Though times like this, it seemed, could challenge his equilibrium.

Instead, McCoy's anger when he spoke was directed at targets more distant than Spock. "Some people get a thrill out of destroying what's rare and precious," he said. "Like hunters going after endangered species, just to show that they can. It gives them a sense of power."

"While that is one possible motivation for such an act, Doctor, it is premature to presume it to be the underlying cause of this crime. Am I correct, Admiral, that the Andorians have not yet determined the identity of the attackers?"

"That's right, Commander," Morrow replied. *"The Andorian government has thrown its full resources into the investigation—*

as a response to allegations that they didn't care about the Aenar—and Starfleet Sector Headquarters in the Andoria system is providing full cooperation."

Kirk furrowed his brow. "But you contacted us for more than just a news update, Harry. What help can we provide from out here on the frontier? There are many ships closer to Andorian space."

"But you're not that far from Medusan space."

"The Medusans?" Kirk leaned back in surprise. He'd heard little about that mysterious, incorporeal species in almost a decade, since the time the *Enterprise* had ferried their ambassador, Kollos, back home to Medusan space as part of an experimental project to adapt their extraordinary navigational skills for Federation use.

He would certainly never forget Miranda Jones, the proud, beautiful human telepath who had been chosen to attempt to form a corporate intelligence with Kollos—a permanent mental link that would allow Medusan navigational senses to be employed by humanoid pilots. Given all the trouble that the *Enterprise* crew, Spock most of all, had endured in order to complete that mission, it sometimes troubled Kirk that nothing appeared to have come of it in the ensuing years. The Medusans had maintained cordial relations with the Federation, and Doctor Jones still lived among them as far as Kirk knew. But there had been little to no increase in their involvement with Federation society in the decade that the project had been underway, and they seemed to show little interest in changing that. Why, then, would they be involved in an incident involving a Federation founder world?

Naturally, Spock provided the answer. "Of course, it stands to reason. The Aenar were among the candidates considered for the Medusan navigational project. As powerful telepaths who are naturally blind, they would theoretically have been as ideal as Miranda Jones—able to join minds with a Medusan and immune to the severe psychological disruption that the Medusans' optical signature induces in most humanoids. Ultimately, Ambassador Kollos was unable to persuade the Aenar to overcome their isolationism and pacifism in order to cooperate with Starfleet. Yet he did become acquainted with a number of Aenar individuals during his time on Andoria. I recall from our mind-meld that he found them quite agreeable. It is no wonder that he and his people would take an interest in this tragedy."

"You're right, Spock," the admiral replied. *"Ambassador Kollos personally contacted us—through Miranda Jones—to request a Starfleet escort to Andoria to assist in the investigation. According to Doctor Jones, Kollos insisted on the* Enterprise *when he learned it was one of the ships in range."*

"Understood, Admiral," Kirk said. "I presume the Medusans will send a vessel to rendezvous with us en route?" Given most humanoids' inability to withstand the Medusans' appearance, interactions between the Medusans and other civilizations tended to be conducted at a distance from their homeworld.

"Yes, Jim. Set your course directly for Andoria, and the Medusan authorities will contact you with the specifics. We want to get the Enterprise *and Kollos there as soon as possible. We could use all the help we can get to find the ones responsible for this atrocity—and fast."* Morrow leaned forward urgently. *"Because we don't know if or when these monsters will strike again."*

"You know what really gets me about all this?"

Pavel Chekov's question prompted Hikaru Sulu to turn to his right to meet the younger man's eyes. The two of them and Nyota Uhura were standing on the balcony at the rear of the *Enterprise*'s expansive recreation complex, gazing out one of the aft viewports (just large enough for three to stand abreast) at the prismatic streaks of warp-distorted starlight cycling back past the streamlined nacelles that drove the ship toward Federation space at warp nine.

Sulu suspected he knew what Chekov was going to say—assuming it was the same thing he was feeling—but he respected the security chief's visible need to say it. "What's that?"

Chekov turned back to the port, unable to meet his friends' eyes. "I barely even knew the Aenar existed. A whole civilization that was already dying—right on one of the Federation's founding worlds—and I never really gave them much thought. They were . . . a footnote of history, nothing more."

"I know," Sulu said. "We didn't make the effort to think about them until this happened. And now they're all but gone. I feel terrible about it . . . but at the same time it feels like a sham to feel terrible about people I barely ever thought about in the first place."

On Sulu's left, Uhura nodded. "I hear a lot of people wondering if we allowed this to happen through our neglect. The Andorians and the Federation Council are insisting that it was the Aenar's own choice to stay isolated, that we were only respecting their wishes, but that rings hollow now."

Sulu shook himself and straightened, firming his resolve. "All we can do is find whoever did this and bring them to justice. Make sure it never happens again."

"Whoever did this," Chekov echoed despairingly. "A 'whoever' that left no traces of their passage, no DNA on the scene, no clue to their motives."

"That they've found so far," Sulu added. "Once we get there, I'm sure Mister Spock and Doctor McCoy will turn up something the others have missed. It's what they do."

Chekov tilted his head. "True. Possibly they even have an excellent chief of security to spearhead the investigation."

Uhura chuckled. "I'm sure Hikaru didn't mean to devalue your talents."

"Th-that's right," Sulu stammered, trying to cover for himself. "After all, that goes without saying."

"Hmp," Chekov replied, giving Sulu a mock-skeptical look.

The exchange brought some much-needed levity to the trio's somber mood. Over the past few years, ever since Sulu had gotten serious about pursuing the command track and been named the *Enterprise*'s second officer, he and Chekov had been in a friendly competition to see which one would make captain first. Typically, though, Chekov had pursued the competition more determinedly, striving to prove himself at every opportunity, while Sulu had been content to take it slowly and steadily, wishing to make the most of the opportunity to learn from an exceptional commander like James Kirk. As a result, Chekov had already earned promotion to lieutenant commander, matching Sulu and Uhura in rank for the first time in their careers. But this had not goaded Sulu to strive harder to surpass him, for he was too happy for his friend and pleased that the three of them were finally equals.

"Happy birthday!"

The cry from below and the ensuing laughter drew the trio's attention. They turned and looked down over the balcony rail to see a group of engineering personnel bringing out a birthday cake for Marko Nörenberg, a technician from damage control. The three officers exchanged a wistful look, reminded that life always went on in the face of tragedy. The crew was not insensitive to the magnitude of what had happened; but facing death and destruction was all too common an occurrence in the lives of Starfleet personnel, and this crew had learned the importance of keeping up their morale, the better to stand ready so that further loss of life might be prevented.

The three officers made their way down from the balcony via the side stairs, spent a few moments mingling and congratulating Nörenberg (though Uhura lightly slapped Chekov's hand when he reached for a slice of cake, reminding him that there was only so much to go around), then strolled through the main atrium, taking in the various activities of the off-duty crew. Rixil, the Edosian medtech, was playing a jaunty three-handed tune on his Elisiar keyboard, while the Megarite oceanographer Spring Rain sang along sweetly in her polyphonic voice. T'Nalae, a young Vulcan astrophysics specialist, was leaning her tall frame over the keyboard, grinning and moving her head in time to the music. Sulu was aware that T'Nalae was a member of the *V'tosh ka'tur* minority of Vulcans that rejected Surak's philosophies and embraced their emotions; but even now, two months after she'd come aboard, the sight of a Vulcan showing emotion so openly still induced the occasional double take. As second officer, Sulu was aware that T'Nalae could be defensive about the crew's reactions to her. The fact that she seemed to be enjoying herself, bonding with the others, was a good sign.

Meanwhile, Devin Clancy from flight deck ops was engaged in some sort of dance competition against Crewman Ki'ki're'ti'ke in time with Rixil's music, though Sulu had no idea how one would judge a dance-off between a bipedal human and an eight-limbed, centipede-bodied Escherite. Nearby, Rahadyan Sastrowardoyo from xenoethnography was putting on a show of magic tricks, and was apparently about to try sawing Joshua Vidmar from security in half with a plasma cutter. "This might tickle a bit," he advised. Sulu was afraid to watch what happened next. Although two of the audience members, Chief Onami and her girlfriend Ensign Palur, seemed to be cheerfully wagering on his survival.

"Aha! Let's settle this man-to-man!" The familiar chirping cry came from Hrii'ush Uuvu'it, the Betelgeusian petty officer, and Sulu moved toward it to see what his energetic friend was up to now. Uuvu'it had always been competitive; like most of his people in Starfleet, he'd enlisted in the hope of gaining achievements that would earn him status and mating rights in a Betelgeusian argosy. Within the past year, both of the other 'Geusians in the crew had achieved that goal and moved on, leaving Uuvu'it increasingly insecure and driven to prove himself. He'd recently transferred from sciences to security in search of worthy challenges, but that hadn't made him any less hypercompetitive in his everyday life.

To his amused astonishment, Sulu saw that Uuvu'it was facing off with communication tech Cody Martin in some sort of eating contest. Between them was a large plate holding a massive heap of some kind of rice-and-vegetable dish resembling Japanese *chahan*, a prodigious hill of food at the summit of which a small, colorful banner had been inserted on a long wooden skewer. The two petty officers were taking careful, calculated scoops from its sides with large spoons, and Sulu realized that the goal was to eat as much as possible without toppling the banner. It seemed an uncharacteristically subtle challenge for Uuvu'it, especially given how hyperactive he was these days, but the tall, hairless, blue-skinned semi-avian chirped confidently through his beak-like speaking mouth as he chewed with his fierce-looking eating mouth below it and positioned his spoon carefully for his next move in the game. "I will be the one to stand atop this hill," he boasted.

Despite his bluster, though, Martin's hand proved steadier, and it was Uuvu'it who toppled the banner a few bites later, forcing him to tip his spoon upward and concede defeat. "Too bad, Hrii'ush," Sulu said, clapping him on his wiry shoulder. "Maybe next time."

"Not to worry, Commander." His confidence unbroken, Uuvu'it stood and raised a finger skyward. "As my mother's mother always said: I am the one who . . ."

Sulu tuned out the rest of Uuvu'it's boast, partly from long practice, but mainly because his eye was drawn to the group that had gathered on one of the raised platforms near the front of the rec deck, in front of the display of past vessels named *Enterprise*. Four human members of the crew crouched there in white robes, holding hands and communing with heads lowered. Sulu knew them all, of course: Ensign Daniel Abioye from engineering; the burly, shaven-headed ecologist Edward Logan;

and Heidelberg Universities had developed a means of testing humans for psi potential, and over time, assessments of "ESP ratings" and "aperception quotients" had become a routine part of psychological and educational assessments—even though they were usually all but meaningless. Most humans, including Sulu, proved to have virtually nonexistent esper levels, while moderate test quotients often represented nothing more than heightened sensory acuity, spatial awareness, or synesthesia. Even those with high esper ratings had little more than heightened intuition or occasional faint extrasensory awareness. But a tiny fraction of humans had proven capable of genuine telepathy when properly guided to cultivate their potential—to the surprise of human scientists who had believed such phenomena to have been thoroughly debunked by previous experimentation. And so the testing continued, in the generally vain hope of discovering an extraordinary gift.

In all his life, Sulu had encountered only a handful of humans with active telepathic abilities. Two of them, his former crewmates Gary Mitchell and Elizabeth Dehner, had possessed fairly high esper ratings but no overt psionic gifts until the *Enterprise*'s encounter with the mysterious negative-energy barrier at the edge of the galactic disk a decade ago. That incident had somehow supercharged their brains, causing an exponential surge in their psi abilities to unprecedented levels—and leading to their deaths when they had proven unable to handle the temptations of their new powers. Sulu still got a chill at the memory of Mitchell's eyes glowing silver, his temples graying as if the carefree, boyish navigator had been replaced by some aloof Olympian elder looking down with scorn on the mortals below.

Aside from those two—and the similar case of Charlie Evans, a youth somehow imbued with psionic abilities by the incorporeal Thasians to let him survive on their world, and having even worse impulse control with his enormous powers than Mitchell—probably the only naturally powerful telepathic human Sulu had ever met had been Doctor Miranda Jones, the human prodigy who had needed to be trained on Vulcan to control the strong telepathy she had possessed since childhood. He had met her only briefly, but he had gotten the impression of a lonely, isolated woman who felt forever set apart from humanity—which might have explained her willingness to live the rest of her days among the Medusans, a species as far removed from humanity as he could imagine.

Those encounters had driven home to Sulu how rare true psionic ability was in humans, and so he'd come to think of esper ratings as little more than pseudoscience. The pride DiFalco took in her own moderately high esper rating of fifty-six, and her belief that her extrasensory potential gave her a special intuition as a navigator, was something he'd seen as merely an endearing personality quirk. So he wasn't quite sure how to respond to her question without slighting her obvious sincerity. There seemed to be a new excitement in her since she'd returned from shore leave on Deneb Kaitos IV, and it clearly had something to do with these "New Humans" she'd just mentioned.

Despite his best efforts, she caught his hesitation. "I know you're skeptical about it, Hikaru, but just hear me out. The people I met on Deneb IV were extraordinary."

"But you mean these 'New Humans.' Not the native telepaths."

"They were there to study with the Denebian adepts, but they were human, yes." She paused, taking her time to choose her words. "The New Human movement started to emerge a few decades ago among human espers. According to them, the number of humans with high esper ratings has been rising since we figured out how to measure the ability. Projecting backward, it's as if genuine psi abilities only started to emerge two or three centuries ago. Some people wondered if it was a mutation introduced in the Eugenics Wars or World War III, and there were a few paranoid musings about Vulcan experimentation . . . but the

New Humans took a more spiritual view. They believe that, by making contact with other worlds and achieving peace and unification among ourselves, humans have finally begun to mature as a species. To expand our minds and souls in new ways that let us make stronger connections with each other, and with the universe itself."

"Or maybe it's just a statistical artifact," Sulu countered gently. "We're finding more espers because we're improving our ability to look for them." He kept the other possibility to himself. Critics of the esper tests had long argued that wishful thinking had compromised their scientific value, leading to an erosion of standards that had allowed some of the old psychic pseudoscience to get mixed in with the genuine research, leaving the testing process increasingly susceptible to false positives.

"That might've been a valid possibility," DiFalco said. "Until V'Ger came."

Sulu was only momentarily startled. The advent of V'Ger nearly two years before had been an extraordinary, terrifying, profound event in the eyes of many. The vast alien probe—an altered and evolved form of the twentieth-century *Voyager 6* space probe, rebuilt by incredibly advanced cybernetic aliens into a sentient entity seeking to merge with the Creator it expected to find on Earth—had emanated a mental presence so powerful that telepaths all over the Federation had felt it coming. Its near-annihilation of humanity, followed by its spectacular ascension beyond its physical form and its departure to explore higher realms of existence, had been interpreted by many people on Earth and beyond as a religious or spiritual experience. The initial wave of cultish fervor was dying down now, but there were still those who made pilgrimages to Earth in hopes of feeling some spiritual or psychic connection to V'Ger, some trace it had left behind.

It was therefore no surprise to Sulu that these "New Human" spiritualists had latched on to the V'Ger mystique as well. Even their faint psi potential might have allowed them to sense V'Ger's presence in some way, so it stood to reason that they would feel influenced by it.

DiFalco must have seen the play of thoughts behind Sulu's eyes—in the normal way, not psychically—because she added, "Don't give me that look, Hikaru. This is a documented phenomenon. In the past two years, humans with esper potential have begun manifesting new abilities. Our ratings have been increasing. I got retested on Deneb—Hikaru, my esper rating's up to seventy-two, and my AQ's up to twenty over eighty-six! And the New Humans . . . I was able to sense their emotions, even hear their thoughts when we concentrated together as a group. I've never been able to do that with other espers before. *Something* has changed." She shrugged. "It's like . . . like V'Ger's ascension triggered something in us."

"In human espers."

"Yes. Maybe when it ascended, when it expanded its consciousness to a higher plane, the energies it sent out had an effect on esper minds. Sparked a new evolution." She gave a self-effacing smile. "I don't mean to suggest we're anywhere near ascending like V'Ger and Captain Decker did, but maybe we got a boost just from basking in their glow. And it's up to us to embrace it, to develop our new gifts and advance further." She leaned forward. "Since I got back, using the techniques the New Humans showed me, I've already been able to connect psionically to other espers in the crew, like Ed Logan and Jade Dinh. They've felt it too—this is something real. Human potential is infinite, Hikaru. And we're just beginning to unlock it."

Sulu suppressed a twinge of jealousy, reminding himself that he'd been ending things with her anyway. Edward Logan had always been a bit of a flake, professing to be a follower of Deltan spirituality and shaving his head to mimic their appearance—something that seemed more like appropriation than reverence to Sulu, though he had no idea what a Deltan would think of it.

He'd always suspected that Logan's true interest was more in the Deltans' sexual openness than their spirituality. But Marcella was her own woman, and her sex life was no longer his concern.

"Well," he said hesitantly, "I'm glad you've found a . . . connection. It makes me feel better about . . . stepping away."

She took his hand. "It's fine, Hikaru. You have your path to command, and I have mine to . . . I still don't know what." She grinned. "But exploring the unknown is why we're out here, right? And I really look forward to discovering where my path leads."

2278

By the time Uhura and Chekov rejoined Sulu, a small crowd had congealed loosely around the four white-robed New Humans on the platform—a tentative assemblage of people curious to see what they were doing but hesitant to intrude. But the four opened their eyes in eerie synchronicity, and Chief DiFalco turned her head to smile at the lookers-on. "It's all right," she told them. "We're doing this in public because we welcome participation."

Uhura took a step closer. "Is this a vigil for the Aenar?" she asked kindly.

"Partly," Edward Logan replied. "A commemoration of the lost, and a show of support for the survivors."

"We and they are family, in a way," Jade Dinh added.

"But it's more than that," DiFalco said to the growing crowd. "This is also a meditation on hope—the hope brought by the impending arrival of Ambassador Kollos and Doctor Jones. They're also part of the family of telepaths, but our differences with the Medusans have been a difficult obstacle to surmount. Now this tragedy has given us a reason—"

"A need," Daniel Abioye interposed, almost as if they were a single speaker.

"—to cooperate more closely," DiFalco finished. "It's an opportunity to come closer at last. So we wish to meditate on thoughts of welcome for the Medusan representatives, and on our shared commitment to resolve this threat to the peace."

"We invite all of you to join us in that contemplation," Logan finished.

Sulu traded a look with his fellow bridge officers, who both seemed game. It struck him as a good idea, in fact; even in a crew selected for xenophilia and fascination with the unknown, the literally maddening appearance of the Medusans was a source of reflexive fear and revulsion in many humanoids. Sulu admittedly shared that reflex, even though he'd worked with Kollos briefly nine years ago (or ceded the helm console to him, to be more honest) and had been in awe of the ambassador's navigational gifts. Encouraging the crew to focus on thoughts of welcome and acceptance in advance of Kollos's arrival seemed like a good idea.

"What is the point?"

The question came from Specialist T'Nalae, whose good mood from the music appeared long gone. The young Vulcan stepped toward the robed foursome, her mien confrontational. "Sitting around and thinking won't bring back the dead Aenar, and it won't protect the ones that are left."

DiFalco frowned at her, confused. "I didn't think you'd need help understanding the emotional need to grieve, T'Nalae."

"Oh, I understand all too well. And I resent that you're exploiting others' deaths to call attention to your own deluded belief system. Just because you share a similar aberration to the Aenar doesn't make you a 'family.' At least they had the decency not to impose their aberration onto others' attention."

Sulu moved in to put a stop to this, facing down T'Nalae (even though she was noticeably taller than he was) and speaking quietly but firmly. "Specialist, you're out of line. Whether anyone participates in this vigil is up to them, and it's not for you to judge. If you object, you're welcome to leave—quietly."

Anger and defiance flashed in her eyes, but after a few seconds, she calmed herself. "Yes, sir. Understood."

She turned and left briskly, leaving Sulu puzzled. Since she came from an unpopular minority on Vulcan, he would've expected her to feel more sympathy for other atypical groups.

In any case, the important thing now was to restore calm and positivity. Luckily, everyone else in the crowd seemed content to put T'Nalae's outburst behind them and join in the vigil.

As Sulu and his friends led the gathered crew in sitting cross-legged around the platform, he contemplated the look of serenity on DiFalco's comely face. He had long been skeptical of her affiliation with the New Human movement, but it seemed to have brought her greater self-assurance and inner peace. In some way, she really did seem larger than before. Could it be that this was the future of human evolution after all?

The next question that came to him sent a chill through him. *Was that what the Aenar's slaughterers were afraid of? And if so, who else might they come for next?*

Two

This time, Kirk and Spock did not need to wear protective visors when Ambassador Kollos and Miranda Jones beamed aboard. The radiation shield in front of the upgraded transporter console had been designed with built-in filters against the harmful optical frequencies emitted by Medusans—a feature reflecting Starfleet's anticipation at the time of an increased Medusan presence in years to come, though it had turned out not to be needed until now. Also, both transporter technology and Medusan mobile habitats had been refined to reduce the chance of stray emissions leaking through an incompletely reassembled habitat shell.

Still, Kirk was almost grateful for a barrier between himself and Miranda Jones, for he was uneasy about facing her again. When he thought back on their first encounter, he was embarrassed by the way he and his crew had behaved toward her and her partner Kollos. He hoped that he had grown enough since then to be a better host this time.

When the shimmer of the transporter energies faded, Kirk's eyes were immediately drawn to Doctor Jones. At first, her poised, regal beauty seemed unchanged by the passing years—though after a moment, he realized that she had simply matured gracefully, and that his own standards had matured along with him. Still, she had not changed her style very much. She still wore her hair long and elaborately braided, a fashion of the previous decade. Perhaps she'd been too long out of touch with shifting styles in the Federation—or maybe she simply wore her hair that way for her own pleasure. Now that he thought about it, he'd probably never met a woman with more disdain for other humans' standards of physical beauty. Although the diaphanous sensor web she wore to compensate for her lack of sight, with its lenses and emitters disguised as decorative gems, was still a sublime and elegant piece of tailoring.

By contrast, the ambassador's mobile habitat bore little resemblance to the simple hexagonal-prism box he had traveled in nine-odd years ago—a unit that some crew members had jokingly referred to as a "cat carrier" out of the ambassador's hearing (assuming Medusans had hearing). The new model was more upright and streamlined, equipped with inbuilt antigravs so that Kollos could move under his own power. It also appeared to have a pair of robotic manipulator arms folded up in recesses along its sides, and the lid had a domelike shape that vaguely implied a head. Perhaps the hint of anthropomorphism was meant to put humanoids more at ease toward the Medusan within.

As the captain and first officer moved out from behind the radiation shield, Doctor Jones and the ambassador's habitat moved forward off the platform in perfect sync, as if they were one being—which, in a real sense, they were. "Captain Kirk," Jones said, extending her hand. "And Commander Spock. It's a pleasure to see you again. Kollos and I thank you for your assistance with the tragedy on Andoria."

Kirk clasped her hand graciously, and Spock gave a nod of solemn respect. "Doctor Jones," Kirk said. "And Ambassador Kollos. Welcome aboard the *Enterprise* once again." His eyes darted between the human face and the featureless dome, unsure which one to address.

Taking pity on him, Jones smiled a bit wider. Her eyes turned in his direction when he spoke, but she no longer pretended to focus them on his. "You may address me when speaking to either of us, Captain. We are both in here." She tilted her head toward the habitat. "And both in there as well. Though there are no human or Vulcan words for what that's like."

She turned to take in her surroundings, spreading her arms to widen her sensor web, presumably for a better scan. Her head tilted in a listening pose as she did so. "Your starship has changed a great deal in the past decade. And your uniforms. Both more utilitarian than before."

"In some aspects," Kirk agreed. "But in others, I find them both more comfortable. May we show you around a bit before you see your quarters?"

Jones's face brightened. "Oh, we're in no rush to retire, Captain. Being on a Starfleet ship again is quite invigorating, especially one so new. I'm eager to see how you've advanced."

There was something different about her manner now, yet it was familiar as well. Spock caught it too, and as the party left the transporter room, he tilted his head and asked, "Are we now addressing Ambassador Kollos?"

She laughed. "If you prefer to think of it that way, yes. But you know, Spock, that the distinction is not so clear-cut."

"Yes, I remember. But my meld with the ambassador was for mere minutes. After nine point three eight years, I imagine the difference between the two personalities may be almost negligible."

Something shifted in Jones's features, and Kirk sensed that the doctor was in control again. "In some respects, yes, Mister Spock. In others not so much. It's similar to the Vulcan concept of *tvi-dah'es*."

Kirk stared. "Mister Spock?"

"Roughly 'inner duality,' Captain, though it is difficult to interpret the concept."

Jones grew thoughtful. "Let me put it this way, Captain. Are there times when the officer in you has one thought and the man another? And are there times when you set one aside so the other can take the lead?"

Kirk understood what she meant very well. He'd struggled throughout his career with the conflicts between the discipline of the officer and the passions and loneliness of the man. "I see your point. We all have different facets within us."

"Yes. Kollos is like a . . . a side of myself that I sometimes bring to the fore. A more relaxed, wise, and joyous side, so it's generally a pleasure to embrace it." Her speech became more animated again. "And Miranda is the same for Kollos when we interact with other Medusans. She is my more cautious and analytical side. Perhaps more reserved, and more vulnerable, but endlessly curious about aspects of my people I used to take for granted. I've gained so much from having that new perspective joined to mine." The shift in personality made it easier for Kirk to keep track of the shift in pronouns. And he doubted Jones would speak so freely of her own vulnerability.

Kollos was content to leave his Medusan self in the VIP guest suite while Jones toured the ship for both of them. While the new mobile habitat was far more secure against accidental opening than the original carrier, there was no reason to take chances when Kollos could see and speak through Jones at any time. Apparently it was more difficult to sustain the mental bond over large distances, but the range was sufficient to encompass the *Enterprise*.

The tour proved refreshing for Kirk. It had been a while since he'd had the opportunity to show the refitted *Enterprise* to someone who had known the ship only in its previous configuration. And the fusion of Jones and Kollos proved a far more engaged guest than Jones had been by herself. They were suitably intrigued by the ship's cutting-edge technology, and they were more eager to meet and interact with the crew.

"It's a shame that the joint navigation project hasn't borne more fruit," Kirk said as he and Spock escorted their dual guest down into the monitor station for the ship's main sensor array, located on the lowest deck of the saucer-shaped primary hull and accessed via companionway from the deck above. "We'd hoped to have multiple Medusans serving in the fleet by now."

The station was a toroidal room circling the cylindrical pillar of the saucer's central computer core, with four stand-up monitoring consoles evenly spaced around the pillar. The outer wall was covered in circuit panels and maintenance access ports for the wide variety of powerful detection systems filling the cross-shaped outboard sensor array that surrounded the room, while removable floor plates granted access to the planetary sensor dome beneath it. At the moment, the monitor station was crewed by two enlisted personnel, Chief DiFalco of the navigation department and Specialist T'Nalae from sciences. The arrival of three new people made for a tight fit, reminding Kirk why he usually didn't include the station in his tours for visiting dignitaries. But Kollos had not been able to resist a look at the *Enterprise*'s navigational sensors.

Miranda Jones's face beamed while her hand roved across the circuit panels for the forward stellar graviton detectors, and Kirk again sensed that it was not the doctor in control at the moment. "That's quite all right, Captain. It's true that the obstacles to integrating Medusans into Starfleet have proved more extensive than we hoped a decade ago. But our partnership has produced many improvements in the sensor systems you see around us—insights based on Medusan senses and navigational methods. To a large extent, those improvements have already achieved the benefits that we hoped to bring about with corporate bonds between Medusans and Federation telepaths." The smile returned to Jones's face. "And speaking just for ourselves, this particular corporate bond has provided numerous other benefits, so it was entirely worth the trouble."

"I'm gratified that you feel that way," Kirk said. He wished to say more, but the presence of the two crewwomen deterred him.

Glancing toward them, he saw that Chief DiFalco was gazing raptly at Jones/Kollos, while T'Nalae bore a look of irritation on her delicate features as she strove to remain focused on a circuit diagnostic. Kirk tried not to read too much into her reaction. He was naturally aware of T'Nalae's public outburst during the New Human vigil on the rec deck the other night, but per Sulu's report, it had not been serious enough to warrant disciplinary action, and the specialist had engaged in no other disruptive behavior since. Conventional wisdom among Vulcans was that *V'tosh ka'tur* were too irrational and unstable to be capable of the discipline of Starfleet, but in her brief time aboard, T'Nalae had done nothing to prove them right. She may not have been the easiest person to get along with, but then, neither was Leonard McCoy.

Jones/Kollos had noted DiFalco's attention as well, turning to smile at her. "We can feel you reaching out to us. You're strong for a human esper."

Kirk nodded to the navigator, giving her permission to approach. "Doctor Jones and Ambassador Kollos, this is Chief Marcella DiFalco, one of our navigators."

DiFalco shook the offered hand with reverence. "It's an honor to meet you. Both of you."

"Are you perhaps one of the 'New Humans' we've heard about?"

The chief flushed. "It's a pretentious title, I know. Especially in comparison to you. You achieved levels of telepathy in childhood that most of us have only begun to approach in the past few years, since V'Ger awakened our gifts. And what you and Kollos have achieved, that union of selves . . . our philosophers believe it's a harbinger of what we're starting to evolve toward. But we're still a long way from achieving that kind of collective consciousness." She hesitated. "If . . . if you had the time . . . I and the other espers aboard would love to hear about your experiences as a corporate mind."

"We would be delighted to, at the right time," Jones/Kollos told her. "Right now, though, we have a tour to continue and matters to discuss with the captain and Mister Spock."

DiFalco sobered. "The Aenar. What happened to them . . . it's hit everyone hard, but to us, as fellow telepaths . . ."

Jones's hands clasped hers. "We understand. The Medusans share that sense of community with the Aenar, and a deep distress and anger at what was done to them. I promise you, we will do everything we can to expose the perpetrators of this atrocity and ensure it never happens again."

"If anyone can, it's you, Ambassador—Doctor." DiFalco smiled at her superior officers. "And the captain and Commander Spock as well. I'm certain we're in the best of hands."

The deck above the sensor monitor station contained little beyond three observation lounges to fore, port, and starboard, each one containing four circular viewports on the sloping underside of the hull, plus the monitor station and backup memory banks for the main computer core. While Kirk showed Jones/Kollos the view from the forward lounge, Spock noted Specialist T'Nalae ascending from below, catching his eye. While the specialist may not have embraced Surak's teachings, she had been raised on Vulcan just as Spock had, and so he recognized her head gesture indicating a wish to converse. He moved aft into the computer room and beckoned T'Nalae to follow.

"You have a question, Specialist?"

"Was DiFalco right in what she said before?" the tall young woman asked. "That the emergence of human espers is a change triggered by V'Ger?"

"Not 'triggered,'" Spock told her. "Telepathic potential has been known to exist in a small percentage of humans for as long as the means to measure it in their species have been available.

Doctor Jones is herself a signal example, predating V'Ger's arrival by decades."

"But if an external influence such as V'Ger could amplify the ability, doesn't that suggest some artificial influence created it in the first place? There has been evidence of earlier alien visitations to Earth, has there not?"

Spock steepled his fingers before him. "To answer your initial question, Specialist, I do not believe that V'Ger's presence above Earth was responsible for the recent rise in human psionic ability—at least, not in the direct manner that Chief DiFalco postulates. After all, V'Ger's mental presence was sensed by telepaths on many worlds simultaneously—as I can attest from my personal experience while on Vulcan. And yet no similar increase in psionic ability has been detected in any species besides humanity."

"The New Humans on the ship believe it had something to do with Commander Decker merging his human consciousness with V'Ger's, or with the metamorphosis that resulted."

"I think it more likely," Spock replied, "that those events merely inspired human espers to seek each other out, enabling them to work together on developing and refining their latent capabilities. However, it is difficult to say for certain. As with the Aenar's telepathy, the origin and nature of psionic ability in humans is still a mystery to Federation science. Neither species is naturally telepathic, and their brains lack structures akin to the paracortex that enables psi abilities in species such as Vulcans, Deltans, and Denebians.

"Additionally, if a segment of the population had telepathic abilities, it would logically be an evolutionary advantage that would propagate species-wide over time; yet telepaths remain a tiny minority in both humans and Andorians. Granted, there are exceptions—for instance, the paracortex in Arkenites is underdeveloped, so that the metabolic cost of active psionic ability outweighs its evolutionary advantage. And the ancient priestess class of Argelius carefully regulated their breeding to ensure the gift remained exclusively theirs, thus leading to its virtual disappearance in modern times. Yet neither of these applies in the case of humans or Andorians."

T'Nalae frowned, the show of emotion on her Vulcan features seeming incongruous to Spock. "Permission to speak freely, sir?"

"Granted."

"You're not what I expected. I sought a posting on the *Enterprise* so I could learn from you—a successful Vulcan who had renounced the traditions of repression and logic above all. Who had accepted emotion and found ways to manage it more effectively than most *V'tosh ka'tur*. Yet now you speak of logic just like any other follower of Surak, and you hide your emotions the same way too. I . . . do not understand."

Spock narrowed his lips. "Regrettably, you have misunderstood my situation, Specialist. Despite what has been rumored about me among Vulcans, I have not renounced logic or discipline. I have merely come to recognize that emotion is an integral part of the cognitive process, and it is thus logical to accept its presence and employ it—to integrate it with one's reason rather than existing at odds with a part of one's own being."

T'Nalae shook her head, the fringes of her straight black hair barely brushing her shoulders. "But that still puts logic above all," she protested with some heat. "That's not—" She gathered herself with difficulty. "With all due respect, sir, I don't believe that's valid. Logic isn't a natural part of the Vulcan character. We are intrinsically, intensely emotional beings. That is what we evolved to be, and it's unnatural to change us into something else." She glanced toward the forward gallery where Kirk and Jones/Kollos were. "As unnatural as it is for humans to have telepathy."

Spock examined the specialist, troubled by the hint of purism in her expressed beliefs. He and his family had suffered in his youth from the fanatical purism of Vulcan logic extremists who had opposed the "tainting" of Sarek's family with human elements. And as the history of Earth, Sauria, and other worlds had shown, such purism could be still more destructive when paired with open emotionalism. In theory, Starfleet's training processes would weed out or cure such tendencies in its members, but they did not always do so successfully; Spock thought of Lieutenant Andrew Stiles, who had prided himself on his family's achievements in the Earth-Romulan War and who had thus felt mistrust and resentment toward Spock upon learning of the relationship between Vulcans and Romulans.

However, it was premature to assume that T'Nalae's beliefs were that extreme. As her superior officer, he had an opportunity and a responsibility to steer her away from such beliefs before they hardened.

"The most unnatural thing of all is uniformity," Spock pointed out gently. "Individual variations within any species are what give it the evolutionary robustness to adapt to changing conditions. Diversity of ideas within a population allows a similar adaptability and facilitates growth and innovation. This is the essence of the principle of infinite diversity in infinite combinations."

T'Nalae looked chastened but unconvinced. "I respect *Kol-Ut-Shan*, Commander," she said, using the Vulcan term for the IDIC principle. "I appreciate the uniqueness of every species. But that is *why* I believe each species should be true to its own inherent nature. Why it should be what the universe shaped it to be, instead of trying to deny its true self and become something else."

"As I said, it is the nature of every species to be diverse within itself."

"Up to a point. There are limits. Vulcans don't have wings. Aurelians don't breathe underwater. And humans don't read minds—not naturally."

"Clearly, some do. That is a fact we must accept."

"But why? Federation law prohibits the genetic enhancement of sentient beings beyond their natural abilities. So why is something like the New Human movement permitted to work on enhancing humans' mental abilities beyond the norm?"

"The law can only regulate artificial change. If the emergence of psionic abilities in humans is a new stage in their evolution, then it is part of their natural diversity, and attempting to outlaw or regulate it would be unethical, harmful, and ultimately ineffectual."

"Even if they come to dominate and replace non-esper humans, as you said they naturally would?"

"I did not express it in such loaded terms, Specialist. It is far too early at this stage to speculate on any such occurrence, which would presumably be millennia in the future."

Before T'Nalae could reply, Spock heard Kirk arrive at the entrance. "Everything all right in here? We're ready to resume the tour."

"Very well, Captain. I shall join you in a moment."

Once Kirk had moved on, Spock took a step closer to T'Nalae. "You say that you boarded the *Enterprise* to learn from me, Specialist. What I have to teach you may not be what you expected to hear . . . but that is the nature of true learning. I request that you ponder on that until we speak again."

Once Kirk, Spock, and Jones/Kollos settled down in the officers' lounge to discuss the mission ahead, the captain was relieved that this visit was so far proceeding more smoothly than the first. But when Jones turned from examining the simulated viewports showing a holographic view of the *Enterprise*'s engine nacelles and the streaking starlight of the warp effect beyond them, her face bore a probing, smiling look that Kirk could not readily pin down to either of the personalities within her. "I can sense what you've wanted to say since we came aboard,

Captain Kirk. We wouldn't intrude on your private thoughts, but strong emotions radiate clearly, so I have the gist of it." She sat across from him, her striking gray eyes turned patiently in his direction.

Kirk fidgeted. "I feel . . . embarrassed about the way I and my crew treated you during your first visit, Doctor Jones. We flattered and flirted with you like a visiting celebrity, not recognizing that the attention made you uncomfortable. We praised you for your physical beauty and thoughtlessly denigrated the Medusans' appearance in the process. It was . . . immature of us. Of me. We didn't make the effort to understand your unique perspective, to judge you for more than what was on the surface, and so we were unthinkingly inconsiderate."

Jones nodded. "I appreciate that, Captain. But you were far from the first to treat me that way. It was always difficult for other humans to relate to me, or vice-versa. My telepathy set me apart from an early age. I grew up barraged by the unfiltered private thoughts and dark, repressed urges of the humans around me, and they couldn't understand why it was hard for me to trust them, to open up to them. I, in turn, did not understand that they chose to keep those sides of themselves buried, that they did their best to keep them from harming or frightening other people as they did me.

"It became even harder as I matured and found others drawn to me for what they called my 'beauty'—something that, to me, was utterly meaningless and had no bearing on who I was, so how could I trust in their intentions?"

Kirk struggled to imagine what she must have felt, but Spock nodded knowingly. "It is difficult to grow up feeling alien among one's own people. To face struggles that none around you can comprehend—not even one's own family."

Jones's gaze shifted toward him in sympathy. "I know that about you now, Spock, since our meld. When we first met, I didn't understand you either, and I wrongly judged you a rival and a threat, when you could have been an ally." She sighed. "I suppose it helped me, growing up, that both my parents were espers, though neither of them remotely as psi-sensitive as I was. They had some understanding of what I was going through, and some ability to mask their thoughts from me—though not nearly as much as they would've liked," she added with a wry expression. "They took me away from our home on Deneva, and we wandered the outer worlds in relative isolation, until I finally found solace on Vulcan and was trained to shield myself from others' thoughts.

"With the help of that training, I was able to turn my telepathy into an advantage at last, using it in my work as a psychologist. But I still felt detached from other humans, set apart by my abilities. It didn't help that my blindness is due to a defect of the optic nerve, one not yet curable by implants. In this day and age, with disabilities so rare, humans are out of practice at understanding those of us who still have them—or taking our existence in stride without pitying us."

Kirk lowered his head, remembering her words from nine years ago—*Pity is the worst of all.* "We certainly could have stood to be more broad-minded. Not only toward you, Doctor Jones, but to Ambassador Kollos as well. A visiting diplomat aboard my ship, and I barely made an effort to get to know . . . you."

Kollos's relaxed smile came onto Jones's face. "At the time, it wasn't safe for you to be in the same room with my habitat. And I couldn't exactly speak to you over the intercom. Even today's universal translators still struggle with Medusan language concepts. It takes a sentient mind like Miranda's to interpret between us.

"To be honest, Captain, I feel I have much to apologize for as well—particularly to you, Commander Spock. I deeply regret the lapse in my attention that led us to forget your visor when we severed our meld."

Kirk saw Spock suppress a shudder at the memory. He still

recalled the incident vividly. When Jones's spurned lover, the engineer Lawrence Marvick, had attempted to murder his perceived rival Kollos, a glimpse of the Medusan had driven him mad, and Marvick had tampered with the *Enterprise*'s engines and somehow flung it into a mysterious extradimensional void, through means that remained unexplained to this day. The only way back had been for Spock to meld with Kollos in order to share in his extraordinary navigational senses. When the joined Spock and Kollos had neglected to don the protective visor during the dissolution of Spock's meld, it had exposed the science officer to the unfiltered sight of Kollos and shattered his sanity.

Miranda Jones had been the only one who could restore his mind, but Kirk had mistrusted her, believing her so envious of Spock that she might allow him to die. He had confronted her about it so viciously that even then, in its immediate wake, he feared that he had gone too far. She had proven him wrong, restoring Spock to full sanity, and had claimed to forgive him for his words; she had even thanked him for forcing her to confront a painful truth. But in the years since, he had been unable to think back on that mission without shame. This conversation was doing much to assuage his conscience. It helped to know that Kollos had his regrets as well.

"Our confusion was understandable," Spock said. "We were both overwhelmed by novel, alien sensations and experiences. To be perfectly honest, Ambassador, I have often suspected that the culpability for forgetting the visor lay more with me than with you. On some level, I believe, I yearned to know what you looked like, raw and unfiltered. My curiosity has always been my greatest weakness. In our meld, with our emotions and impulses blended, it is possible that we were unable to regulate that temptation sufficiently."

Jones's face took on a thoughtful frown. "And was your curiosity satisfied, Mister Spock? Do you remember the sight of me?"

"Indeed I do, though my ability to process what I saw is limited—my ability to verbalize it even more so."

"Fascinating. That should dispel the belief of many that the sight of Medusans is so horrific that even the recollection after the fact would induce madness."

"An illogical notion," Spock replied. "The neurological disruption is no doubt the result of direct exposure to the complex optical and electromagnetic patterns emitted by Medusans, analogous to how certain patterns of strobing lights can induce epileptic seizures, or certain magnetic fields can induce hallucinations or fear responses. Similar principles underlie the phaser stun effect, the neural neutralizer, the Klingon mind-sifter, and other neuroactive technologies."

Kollos/Jones took on a sour expression. "I'm not sure I like being so completely demystified."

Spock's slanted eyebrows drew together. "I admit, I cannot be certain my own reaction would be typical. Since childhood, I have been prone to a degree of spatial dysphasia, a condition known as *L'tak Terai*, which affects my visual perception, similar to dyslexia among humans. While it has created difficulties I had to strive to overcome, it has also, at times, enabled me to perceive and interpret sensory phenomena in ways that others could not. Perhaps that is why I was subconsciously willing to believe I could cope with the unfiltered sight of a Medusan. It is at least possible that it in some way enables me to cope with the memory of that sight."

"Remarkable," Jones said—at least, Kirk believed it was Jones now. "That explains so much—why you're so precise and disciplined even compared to the other Vulcans I've known. You had to be in order to cope with your disability." She gave a sad smile. "I wish I'd known before that we had that experience in common."

"There is much we did not understand about each other on that occasion," Spock replied. "It is gratifying that we finally have the opportunity to set that to rights."

"I think we've all grown since then," she replied. "Perhaps you most of all. You have a serenity, a self-assurance you didn't have before. It feels like you've finally resolved the inner struggle Kollos and I sensed in you when we melded."

"Indeed. My meld with V'Ger four point four years ago brought me much clarity."

"Much as my meld with Kollos has for me."

Spock tilted his head skeptically. "In my case, V'Ger provided only a negative example. It revealed to me that an existence of pure logic without emotion was sterile and purposeless. I came to understand that it was better to seek a synthesis of the two."

"And you seem to have succeeded."

"It is still a work in progress," Spock demurred.

"But so is life," Kirk ventured to add.

Kollos/Jones smiled. "Indeed it is. May we never reach the point where we have nothing more to learn." She, or they, turned back to Spock in puzzlement. "And that surprises us, Mister Spock. Kollos and I have grown so much through our bond, and we sense you've grown as well. Yet here we are, almost a decade later, and you're still in exactly the same place you were then, first officer of the *Enterprise*. By now you could have been a captain of your own ship, if you wished."

Spock's gaze in return was untroubled. "I have never sought command. I am a scientist above all; my first, best path is to provide knowledge to others."

"Then you could have become an instructor at Starfleet Academy, or a researcher at the Vulcan Science Academy. I'm sure universities on a dozen planets have courted you."

"I can learn more aboard a starship on the frontier than I could in those places. And I can learn more from serving under a captain like James Kirk."

"But what is there to learn from that, except how to command a crew yourself?"

"That question would take a long time to answer."

Kirk was flattered and gratified by Spock's reply. He had valued both of the first officers who had served under him on his first command, the scout ship *Sacagawea*; but he'd had Spock at his side for so long now that he could no longer imagine serving without him.

Still, this whole conversation had been about the importance of looking beyond the limits of one's expectations. Had he come to take Spock for granted? And was he holding his friend's career back as a result?

Three

Laikan, Andoria

The headquarters of Andorian Homeworld Security was shielded against transporter access, so the *Enterprise* landing party materialized in the wide octagonal plaza in front of the building. The Andorian passersby took the arrival of Kirk, Spock, and Lieutenant Commander Chekov in stride, for it was not unusual for Starfleet personnel to liaise with AHS; yet they evinced somewhat more curiosity toward Ambassador Kollos's mobile habitat, which hovered alongside Miranda Jones in her shimmering sensor-web gown. The civilians' surprise at the sight of the habitat reminded Spock of the regrettable failure of the effort to integrate Medusans into Starfleet. A decade ago, it had been hoped that their presence on Federation worlds would be more commonplace by now.

Spock took the opportunity to contemplate the scenery of Laikan, the Andorian capital. The city was built on a spacious plan, with wide pedestrian plazas filled with greenery and fountains, taking advantage of the urban heat-island effect created by its many high, angled towers. The terraforming efforts had warmed this part of the planet considerably over the past five decades, yet most of the surrounding continent of Zhevra was still cool even by human standards, let alone Vulcan. To the south, across the nearby Tezh'Lai River, Spock could see the blockier, more utilitarian skyline of the neighboring city of Laibok, a manufacturing city that had become Andoria's industrial capital through its proximity to the political capital. As the region had warmed, both cities had expanded to the point that they had all but merged into a single megalopolis, their names sometimes used interchangeably.

An Andorian Starfleet commander, no doubt the Sector Headquarters liaison they'd been told to expect on their arrival, came forth from the building entranceway where he had presumably been awaiting them. As he approached, Spock could see that he had craggy, aquiline features and an unusually pale complexion, more gray than blue. Spock's brows rose, and a traded glance with Kirk confirmed Spock's own certainty that they had met this *thaan* before.

Or rather, they had met a version of this *thaan*, during an ill-fated attempt to conduct historical research via the Guardian of Forever more than eight years ago. Both men schooled themselves to calm, for incidents connected to the Guardian, time travel, and parallel realities were strictly classified. Spock noted Jones/Kollos glancing at them curiously, sensing their recognition of the commander, but Spock sent a subtle thought impression invoking privacy. As he had melded with both halves of their corporate intelligence individually, some lingering vestige of the connection endured, allowing the message to reach them clearly. He felt that their curiosity remained, but they chose not to pursue it.

"Captain Kirk, greetings," the commander said in a reedy but strong tenor. "I am Thelin th'Valrass, from Sector HQ. You may call me Commander Thelin." He pronounced it *Thay-lin*, as Spock recalled.

"Commander Thelin—good to meet you," Kirk said, shaking the offered hand and maintaining his usual excellent poker face. "This is Commander Spock . . . my first officer." His voice hitched very slightly on the title. He went on to introduce the rest of the party, who greeted Thelin in turn.

As the commander led the group inside, Kollos (through Jones) regaled him with questions about the city and its architecture. Thelin seemed initially puzzled about which of the two he should address, but he quickly adjusted. Kirk took the opportunity to fall back next to Spock, while Chekov remained alongside the two emissaries—most likely a redundancy in the midst of Homeworld Security headquarters, but entirely in keeping with Chekov's relentless dedication to his duties.

"Thelin, Spock," Kirk said, pitching his voice for Vulcan ears alone. "I knew he must have had a counterpart in our timeline, but somehow I never expected to meet him. It's a big galaxy, after all."

"Yet one that contains numerous causal influences that lead certain individuals' life paths to converge," Spock replied. "In the divergent timeline we accidentally visited through the Guardian, I had died as a child and Thelin had become your first officer in my place, yet most other members of the *Enterprise*'s crew and even its specific mission at the time remained the same, despite thirty years of independent evolution of the two timelines. Which suggests that our paths through life are guided by numerous causal and probabilistic influences both direct and indirect, leading the same individuals to converge upon one another in many histories."

Kirk's eyes widened. "Why, Spock—I never thought I'd hear you say you believed in fate."

Spock raised a scathing brow. "I do not, Jim. I believe in causality. And I take it as a lesson in humility that my absence had comparatively little effect on the course of the *Enterprise*'s missions."

The captain studied him for a moment, then smiled. "I consider your presence over these past years to have been nothing less than invaluable, Spock. But it follows that Thelin was able to be just as invaluable to that other version of myself and my crew. That suggests he'll be a good man to have at our side." Spock nodded.

Once they rejoined Thelin and Chekov, Spock could see that, despite their restraint, Thelin had registered their curiosity toward him. However, he had formed his own conclusions about the cause of it. "If you're wondering, gentlemen, yes, I am one-quarter Aenar, on my *zhavey*'s side. It's why I requested this assignment. I have worked closely with the Aenar over the past decade, and I had friends and kin among the casualties."

"My sympathies for your loss, Commander," Kirk said. "Your *zhavey*?"

Thelin shook his head. "No, she died several years ago of natural causes. Yet two of her cousins were among the murdered."

"I'm very sorry, Commander. I know how it feels to lose family to violence."

"Appreciated, Captain. We are a warrior people who allow ourselves few sympathies, but we make an exception for family. In this time of despair, I am deeply grateful for my bondmates and our child." Kirk and Spock traded another meaningful look, acknowledging that this Thelin was very reminiscent of his double. Chekov glanced between them, appearing confused.

Thelin led the *Enterprise* officers and the two emissaries into a meeting room with large picture windows overlooking the plaza outside. Two Andorians rose to greet them—a lean, compact female with stern, dark eyes and a confident bearing, and a mature male with rounded features and a more uneasy manner. Thelin introduced them as Captain Thamizhan sh'Zava of Andorian Homeworld Security, heading the task force investigating the attack, and Keshemai ch'Hatharu, the minister for Aenar Affairs. Thelin recited the title with a hint of disapproval, which Spock surmised was due to the fact that the *chan* showed no visible sign of Aenar ancestry. Captain sh'Zava greeted the officers and emissaries with cool professionalism, while ch'Hatharu's body language and antenna movement evinced unease toward Kollos and Jones.

Sh'Zava invited the newcomers to help themselves to cups of *katheka*, the local coffee equivalent, which Spock declined but Kirk and Chekov accepted, grimacing a bit at the unfamiliar pungency but seeming to appreciate the stimulant effect. Jones/Kollos also accepted a cup and both winced and smiled, visibly intrigued by the novelty of the flavor.

The Homeworld Security captain took the emissaries from Medusa in stride, but did not appear to warm to them. "While we appreciate your concern in this matter, Ambassador, Doctor," sh'Zava said, "I recommend that you leave the investigation in the hands of experienced professionals. The involvement of civilians often creates more difficulties than it solves."

"As we understand Andorian law," Jones/Kollos replied, showing no offense, "a planetside investigation normally *would* be the purview of the civilian authorities, would it not?"

The *shen*'s jaw clenched. "Given the severity of the terrorist attack, and the possibility of offworld involvement, the presider authorized Homeworld Security's involvement in this matter."

"Then you should not be averse to offworld assistance. We have skills you could use. The skills of an expert psychologist could aid you in profiling suspects, and our combined telepathy could reveal—"

"Do you think we have no telepaths already involved? The Aenar are formidable telepaths, and several of the braver survivors have already been to the scene to search for any impressions." Sh'Zava lowered her eyes, the first time her stern façade had softened. "They had to walk among the ruins of their homes, the blood of their families, and yet all it did was make them suffer. We learned nothing of value from it."

"Perhaps," Kirk interposed, "you could tell us what you *have* learned so far, and we can work from there."

The security captain's antennae curled back in displeasure

as she answered. "We've learned very little. There's no trace of blood or genetic evidence from the attackers. Footprints and glove prints tell us they were andorianoid—or humanoid, if you prefer—but most likely encased in sealed environment suits or body armor."

Spock steepled his fingers. "Interesting. Perhaps, then, they belong to a species whose atmospheric needs are different from ours."

"Or one unable to bear the cold of the Northern Wastes," Chekov suggested. "So we can assume they were not Russian."

Sh'Zava frowned at the security chief's non sequitur. "Or maybe they were Andorian extremists who wished to leave no identifiable traces," she said.

"You believe this was domestic terrorism?" Kirk asked.

"We did find trace charges and molecular disruptions in the ground suggesting the use of a transporter beam of unknown type . . . but our planetary and orbital sensors registered no unidentified spacecraft at the time."

"Starfleet has encountered several transporter technologies with interstellar range," Spock replied. "The Providers of Triskelion have that capability, as did the ancient Kalandans." He declined to mention the mysterious organization that had beamed the operative Gary Seven to twentieth-century Earth from a thousand light-years away, as the *Enterprise* crew's involvement with Mister Seven was another classified matter of temporal security.

The response came from Thelin rather than sh'Zava. "Based on the *Enterprise*'s own reports, such transporters require massive amounts of energy and leave clearly discernible ionization trails in the interstellar, or in this case interplanetary, medium. No such trails or energy bursts have been detected."

Minister ch'Hatharu finally spoke up, his hands and antennae gesturing nervously. "That's true, that's true. Ah—but those energy signatures at the massacre site, the prints and such—

they're not like anything here on Andor," he said, using the world's local name. "So it must be aliens, mustn't it? They just have some kind of transporter beam we can't detect." He smiled at Jones/Kollos. "That's why I, for one, am grateful that you're here, Ambassador—Doctor—b-both of you. And you as well, Captain Kirk, and your crew. You are the experts at dealing with interstellar crises."

"Oh, stop it," sh'Zava barked. "You just want it to be off-worlders so you can wriggle out of responsibility. There are multiple active hate movements directed toward the Aenar right here on Andor. Movements that have been allowed to thrive because your 'Aenar Affairs' bureau has done nothing to protect the Aenar. You and the rest of the Visionists have sided more with the business interests chipping away at their territorial rights, emboldening the hate groups to believe the government is on their side!"

The minister was taken aback. "Now, that's uncalled for," he said, his voice quavering. "Do you think I benefit in any way from the extermination of nearly all the Aenar? Without Aenar, there is no Ministry for Aenar Affairs! Why, what would I do without my career?"

"The Ministry is a dead-end office for incompetents and political cronies. I'm sure your sponsors could find you another sinecure, one with more prestige. You probably welcome this."

"Now, that's just hurtful!"

Kirk began to speak up, but Thelin beat him to it, addressing sh'Zava. "Thamizhan, if you don't mind, I think our guests would like to hear more about these hate groups you mentioned."

Sh'Zava's dark eyes remained locked on the pouting minister a moment longer, then turned back to the others. "Yes, of course. There have been a number of vocal anti-Aenar extremist factions for decades now, ever since the Aenar began campaigning against the planetary warming program. Many Andorians felt that the desire of a tiny indigenous group to remain in its ancestral glacial lands should not outweigh the economic benefits of warming the entire planet, freeing more land and ocean for development and population growth, as well as tourism from warmer Federation worlds.

"When the Aenar's pleas for compassion, backed by the diplomatic efforts of the Federation Council, succeeded in bringing about a slowdown and reassessment of the terraforming effort, it was detrimental to a number of industries and business interests that had a heavy investment in the warming of the planet. Some of them began backing the small fringe of Aenar-haters, clandestinely funding them, helping them amplify their message and coordinate with like minds elsewhere on Andor, and encouraging them to become more radical in their beliefs. They even backed political efforts to weaken our legal prohibitions on the manufacture and import of heavy weapons, so that the ability of Homeworld Security to prevent these groups from arming themselves was undermined." Sh'Zava's antennae flattened in controlled anger.

"Then you think one of these groups may have bought some unknown, advanced transporter technology from an offworld source?" Chekov asked.

"Or some form of personal cloaking to allow them to infiltrate undetected?" Spock added.

It was Thelin who replied. "That is possible, Commanders. Some of the businesses suspected of backing the extremist groups have offworld ties, even beyond the Federation. Some of them have their own programs to explore the frontier, searching not for new life and civilizations but for exploitable resources or advanced technologies. Surely you are aware that many extinct civilizations have left behind artifacts of great advancement."

Spock traded a knowing glance with Kirk. "Indeed."

"That's why we mustn't blind ourselves to the possibility of a domestic threat," sh'Zava went on. "Some of these groups have hatreds extending beyond the Aenar—to other telepaths such as Vulcans and Deltans, or to offworlders in general. Some are so mad as to wish harm to other Andorians who wish to slow the terraforming efforts. For all we know, the Aenar massacre was just a trial run for something bigger."

Doctor Jones spoke angrily. "'Just'? So the Aenar matter less to you than your own people? Is that the only reason you're so diligent about this, because you think it affects your kind as well?" The familiar indignant tone left no doubt in Spock's mind that Jones was in control.

To her credit, sh'Zava looked humbled. "I apologize, Doctor, Ambassador. That wasn't what I meant to suggest. I merely mean that it is my responsibility to be alert to any threat to the people of Andor, regardless of their species. We failed in that responsibility toward the Aenar victims, so I am determined not to fail again in my responsibility to the rest of our people, *including* the remaining Aenar. We must explore every possibility."

"Then let's do just that," Kirk said. "The benefit of having more eyes on the problem is that we can divide and conquer. Captain sh'Zava, I'd like to assign Commander Chekov and a security detail to assist you in your domestic investigation. Meanwhile, I'd like Mister Spock, Doctor Jones, and Kollos to investigate the Aenar compound. Not that I doubt the thoroughness of your investigation, Captain, but a second look never hurts. And if the attackers *are* of offworld origin, a Starfleet team or a Medusan might be able to spot some evidence to that effect."

Sh'Zava nodded. "That sounds reasonable, Captain Kirk. I recommend that Mister Spock take Commander Thelin with him. In the years I've known him, I've found him to be a keen scientific mind." She gave a slight self-deprecating smile. "And a capable diplomat as well."

Spock studied the *thaan* who could have been the *Enterprise*'s first officer in his place. He had always been curious to know more about the alternate Thelin, whom he had known for a scant few hours. As Spock's own absence from the timeline had been the only readily discernible difference between that reality and this, it was logical to surmise that both Thelins' formative years had been the same up until the alternate had been assigned to the *Enterprise*. Thus, working with this Thelin might be illuminating.

"I would welcome the commander's presence," Spock said sincerely.

U.S.S. Enterprise

Chief Petty Officer Reiko Onami watched with interest as Specialist T'Nalae fidgeted in the comfortable chair across from her. In four years as the resident xenopsychologist of one of the most diverse multispecies crews in Starfleet history—not to mention a childhood spent as one of the few humans on Nelgha, a crossroad of interspecies trade and cultural exchange—Onami had witnessed an enormous range of different species' behaviors and responses. But even she had rarely encountered an openly emotional Vulcan. She'd met a few Romulans during her time on the *Enterprise*, but they were different. In their own way, they controlled their emotions almost as much as their Vulcan siblings did, channeling them through martial discipline and collective service to the state rather than through logic and individual meditation. By contrast, T'Nalae was an open book—yet at the same time, she was defensive in her emotionalism, expressing it defiantly while expecting to be judged for it.

"I've been trying to get you in here for a week now," Onami told her bluntly. It had never been her way to mince words. "Ever since—"

"Ever since I gave my honest opinion about the New Humans' so-called vigil?" T'Nalae sighed. "I admit I spoke out of turn. I may not have liked how the New Humans were exploiting the situation, but saying so at that moment was inconsiderate to the rest of the crew. I've kept my opinions to myself since then."

"But you still have them."

"I have a right to my beliefs."

Onami leaned forward. "Here's the thing about rights: If you're going to get defensive about your own rights, then it follows that you should defend everyone else's rights just as forcefully. Otherwise you're just being a hypocrite and abusing the concept for your own advantage.

"We're all members of a community here, T'Nalae. Considering each other's rights and feelings goes both ways. What you said was hurtful to your crewmates, and you haven't made any attempt to talk to them and hear their side. As long as you resist coming to an understanding, that tension's going to remain, and that's going to make it harder for people like Dinh and Logan to work with you."

T'Nalae's defensive expression did not soften. "It may not be an issue much longer. I'm thinking of applying for a transfer."

Onami's eyes widened. "That seems drastic. Do you always run away from your problems?"

The young Vulcan glared at her. "It's not as simple as that. I . . ." She let out a sharp breath. "I sought this posting because I wanted to learn from Commander Spock. I'd heard he was a *V'tosh ka'tur* like me. But I was wrong."

"Hmm." Onami stroked her chin. "Seems to me that you can't learn that much from someone who's already like you. That *might* just be why we're out here exploring strange new worlds instead of ordinary old ones."

"I've had my fill of lessons in logic." T'Nalae shot to her feet and started pacing around the office, towering over the dainty Onami. "Vulcans claim to celebrate diversity, but it's a lie. When I failed my maturity test, I decided that Surak's way was not for me. I sought instead to explore our true, repressed heritage, to embrace the emotion I was born with. But my parents refused to listen or support me. As soon as I was old enough, my father shipped me off to Gol so the *Kolinahr* adepts could 'correct' my thinking. I was forced to live like an ascetic, cut off from my friends and family. The more they pressured me, the more I realized that I was *ka'tur*. Eventually I left the monastery, left Vulcan, and never looked back."

Onami couldn't help but be moved by her confession, by her honest pain and anger. Her impulse was to share in it. But she still had a responsibility to the ship and its crew. "I'm sorry that happened to you. Your father shouldn't have been so intolerant. But you know what it feels like to be judged that way. So surely you can understand how it feels to other people when you judge them."

"I don't like cults," T'Nalae countered. "Surak's cult took over Vulcan and it's kept our spirits imprisoned for two thousand years. Now this New Human cult is spreading and it's more of the same. A minority trying to warp its people away from their true nature, turn them into something they're not."

"But you don't seem too fond of the Aenar either. They've always kept to themselves. And it's not like either they or human espers can *convert* anyone who isn't already born with psi potential." Onami shook her head. "So I don't get it, T'Nalae. What have you got against telepaths?"

"Telepaths in species that shouldn't be telepathic. Whose brains don't have the anatomy for psi sensitivity, but are somehow charged with psionic energy anyway. Where does that power come from? Nobody's ever explained it. So I don't trust it. Maybe someone, or something, *did* convert them into telepaths. Maybe it's some kind of infection—or infiltration."

Onami stared, troubled by the turn this was taking. She spoke carefully. "Do you have any evidence for that?"

T'Nalae caught herself. "I'm not paranoid, Chief, if that's

what you're thinking. And I wasn't telepathically abused. The monks never forcibly melded with me or anything like that."

"I'm glad to hear that," Onami said sincerely.

"I may not repress my emotions, but I'm still capable of thinking logically. And I have a rational mistrust for what can't be explained. Until and unless we can identify the basis for telepathy in species like humans and Andorians, we shouldn't be so quick to embrace it. It may prove to be a maladaptive trait. As suggested by the fact that the Aenar were nearly extinct even before the massacre."

Onami rose to confront T'Nalae. Her height fell significantly short of the other woman's, but she'd never let that hold her back. "Okay, then, what *do* your emotions say? What do they tell you about how it feels to have people assume the worst about you, to be unwilling to give you the benefit of the doubt?"

T'Nalae stared back. "How does it make *you* feel, as a human, to hear these 'New Humans' tell you that you're an evolutionary throwback? That they've grown beyond you into something bigger and better?"

The chief stifled a laugh. The truth was, Onami had never much cared for humans outside her own family. The other species among whom she'd grown up on Nelgha had always seemed more interesting and easier to relate to. In her opinion, most humans were pretentious and full of themselves, so the New Humans hardly stood out from the pack. So T'Nalae's attempted diversion had little effect.

Aloud, she merely asked, "Have you heard them actually say that to anyone?"

"It's implicit. Oh, they say that their abilities prove that all humans have unlimited potential, but since only a fraction of humans demonstrate any actual psi capabilities, it rings hollow."

The rest of the session proved similarly unproductive. For all that Onami encouraged T'Nalae to see a different point of view, the specialist remained committed to her dislike for those who, in her opinion, denied or perverted the intrinsic nature of their species. When asked how she would relate to the Aenar survivors if it became necessary, T'Nalae merely pointed out that her specialization in astrophysics made it unlikely that she would be assigned to any duties associated with them. Onami found herself thinking that Commander Spock and the captain would probably agree on her unsuitability for the task, though for a different reason.

That was the conclusion she reported to Doctor McCoy later in the evening, as they met in his sickbay office to discuss her casework. "I don't know how to get through to her, Leonard." Many officers would object to an enlisted person addressing them so familiarly, but McCoy was a civilian at heart, and their friendship had come a long way since its turbulent beginnings. "I'm tempted to say we should let her transfer off, but that would just make it some other crew's problem. We can't be the only ship with New Humans aboard. Or other kinds of people who 'defy their species' true nature.'" She sighed. "Besides, I understand her reasons for being so mistrustful. I don't agree with how she's acted on those feelings, but I get where they come from."

McCoy shook his head. "Unbelievable. An emotional Vulcan who's having problems with telepathic humans. Did we cross over into an alternate universe again?

"Frankly, I'm tempted to tell Spock that he *should* assign her to work with the Aenar. If she sees what they're going through, gets to relate to them as victims, maybe she'll learn something." He sighed. "But no. After the hell the Aenar have been through, it's not *their* job to help some arrogant kid have a learning experience. They're the ones who need our help right now. If she's not willing to be a part of that, then maybe she isn't Starfleet material at all."

Onami chuckled. "You know me so well that I can count on you to carry my side of the argument without me needing to do a damn thing."

"I just try to preempt being yelled at by a shrill tiny person."

"Hey, I am not 'shrill'!"

They chuckled together, and Onami then grew serious again. "So . . . any theories yet on who or what killed the Aenar? And why?"

McCoy shook his head, his shoulders sagging. "All we have are questions. But Spock's heading out to search the ruins in the morning. If there's anything there to be found, he'll find it." His angular eyebrows twitched and drew together. "This one . . . I don't know. I've seen some horrific slaughters out there on the frontier. Billions of people killed on Maluria, on Gamma 7A. But this . . ."

Onami nodded. "Right in the heart of the Federation. It's scarier when it's closer to home."

"It's not just that." He paused. "Spock once told me it was easier for us humans to understand one death than a million. He said if we could expand our hearts that much, feel those million deaths, it would've made our history less bloody."

"Do you think he was right?"

"It's a nice idea, but no. I think some tragedies are just so vast that we couldn't survive it if we could feel the grief in proportion. It's a mercy that they're beyond our comprehension. But of course," he went on sourly, "the downside is that seeing a million deaths as an abstraction makes it easier to inflict them too. Spock was right about that, at least."

She peered at him. "Amazing. You put the words *Spock*, *was*, and *right* together in that order without your head exploding."

"You tell him I said that and I'll make something creative happen to *your* head. Anyway, I'm bein' serious here, okay?"

"You're starting to cross over into maudlin. Remember, Leonard, I'm going to be counseling some of the Aenar survivors, trying to help them cope with this horror. I'll be dealing with enough of a burden from them without you laying your sorrows on me too."

"Well, you were the one who brought it up," McCoy protested, but she could hear the understanding and apology in his voice.

She sighed. "I guess I shouldn't ask what the chances are of saving the Aenar from extinction now. Don't want to get even more depressed."

"I plan to investigate that question thoroughly, don't you worry." But McCoy's attempt at confidence gave way to a worried grimace. "Though first we have to find out who did this—and stop them from finishing the job."

Four

Aenar Compound
Northern Wastes, Andoria

Thelin th'Valrass stared at the splashes of dried blue blood on the broken wall before him, wondering how many of them had belonged to someone he knew.

"Commander?" Spock's voice drew Thelin out of his reverie, and he turned to face the half-Vulcan, finding an unexpectedly solicitous look on his craggy face. "If this is too difficult for you . . ."

Thelin shook himself. "No, Mister Spock. The loss is painful, but it is the Andorian way to face our pain head-on. Our response to a loss is not passive grief, but the pursuit of retribution." He took a breath, then added, "Though of course, as a Starfleet officer, I wish that retribution to be achieved through the capture and trial of the perpetrators, if at all possible."

"I commend your discipline," Spock told him. "Yet I understand your anger. If there is one emotion whose value Vulcans have never denied, it is grief at the loss of life." The *Enterprise* science officer studied him. "Did you know many of the Aenar well?"

"I fear I did, Commander. For more than a decade, I have dedicated myself to improving relations between Andorians and Aenar. I have spent much time among these people."

"And done a lot of good," said Miranda Jones as she approached the two commanders, clambering gingerly over a low pile of rubble. The party stood on what remained of one of the city-block–sized, disk-shaped dwelling modules that jutted out on thick pylons from the central icy pillar of the cavern, not unlike the shape of a *Constitution*-class saucer and dorsal connector. The attackers had set the module on fire and blasted out many of its internal support walls, causing the roof of the module to cave in. Incongruously beautiful sunlight shone down in misty rays from the thin glacial roof above.

Jones continued to speak as she drew nearer, though Thelin was not entirely sure whether the speaker was the human psychologist, the Medusan diplomat sharing her body, or some amalgam of the two. Ambassador Kollos's mobile habitat was elsewhere in the ruined module, not currently in sight, but Thelin understood that their telepathic bond persisted across distance, at least on this scale. "As we understand it, you helped prove the viability of Aenar food production methods—showed that they could improve productivity in your fields without the need for further warming that could endanger the Aenar habitats. In the process, you even helped resolve a blood feud between the Aenar ruling family and the presider at the time."

"I merely helped others communicate the value of their knowledge," Thelin demurred. "But I am gratified to have been in a position to provide that help."

Spock examined him. "If I may ask, Commander . . . is that the reason you chose to transfer to a ground posting on Andor?" At Thelin's inquisitive expression, he elaborated, "I familiarized myself with your service record. You had an impressive career as a science officer on several starships."

Thelin smiled modestly. "The Aenar situation was only part of the reason. My goal back then was to continue rising through the ranks, perhaps even earn a captaincy." His antennae curled wryly. "Unfortunately, Starfleet has no shortage of exemplary science officers. All the postings I could have been promoted into were already filled, so my career stalled."

He gave a slight chuckle. "To a degree, Mister Spock, I saw you as an obstacle."

Spock's brows rose. "Me?"

"Of course, you were not the only science officer who blocked my path to promotion. But you remained in the same posting for an unusual length of time. Had you moved on, it might have opened a slot for me aboard the *Enterprise*."

Spock's expression was mysterious. "A plausible hypothesis."

"Or some other *Constitution*-class or comparable vessel, if their science officer had replaced you." He shrugged. "In any case, once Captain Kirk succeeded Captain Pike in command of the *Enterprise* and you remained aboard, I began to suspect that my prospects for promotion were not likely to improve. My prospects worsened when we lost the *Constellation*, the *Intrepid*, and others. Of course, my thoughts were with the officers who were lost with those ships—but as a practical reality, the reduction in the size of the fleet reduced the prospects for transfer or advancement."

"I understand."

"So I reevaluated my priorities and decided it was better to transfer back home—to remain in Starfleet, but devote my efforts to the service of Andor and its people." He smiled. "Please do not get the wrong impression—I am grateful that my starship career hit a dead end. For coming home has enabled me to help my people—of both subspecies. It has let me do my part in mending the rift between Andorian and Aenar. And it has brought me my greatest desire—a family." A few years after coming home, he had met the lovely Thali sh'Dani, and they had swiftly fallen in love and been betrothed. There had been some resistance from the Eveste Elders to approving her request to bond to a quarter-Aenar *thaan*, due to the prejudices inflamed by the political tensions over the terraforming project. That, admittedly, was part of what had motivated Thelin to work so hard to improve relations. Finally, their request to join with a carefully selected *chan* and *zhen* in a procreative bondgroup had been approved, their *shelthreth* had been successful, and Cheremis, the beautiful *zhei* who had resulted from their union, was coming up on her sixth birthday.

Spock's eyes showed appreciation for Thelin's sentiment. "It seems, then, that you have found your optimal path despite my presence on the *Enterprise*. I am gratified to learn that."

"Or perhaps because of it," Thelin allowed. "So I do not begrudge you the success you have had in your own path, or the opportunities you still have for further advancement in the service."

The Vulcan looked away at the suggestion. "I have never sought command. Had I wished it, I could have achieved it on more than one occasion in the past."

Thelin studied him. "It has always seemed to me that command is not about what you desire for yourself . . . but what you can do for others. With your skills—and your insight—I believe you could do much good as a starship captain."

Spock considered his words quietly for a time. Finally, he said, "We should return our attention to the investigation. The good of the remaining Aenar, or any other potential victims of these attackers, is our immediate priority."

Thelin looked outward, examining the bloodstained wreckage around them. "You're quite right, Mister Spock. My daughter is only one-sixteenth Aenar, but if someone hated them enough to do this, then no one with Aenar blood can be presumed safe until they are stopped."

"That is one puzzling thing about this attack," Spock observed as they moved through the rubble. "If the motive were simple race hatred, one would expect an attack of opportunity. It would have been easier to strike against the various part-Aenar individuals living within Andorian society, such as yourself, Commander. Indeed, such a public attack would likely have promoted an agenda of hate and fear more successfully than this more thorough, yet more distant, slaughter, leaving no witnesses to tell the tale. Though this loss is stunning, to be sure, it is remote enough to feel abstract to many."

"Which tells me," Thelin replied, "that the motive was not political. These killers did not wish to make a statement." His antennae folded back grimly. "They merely wished to exterminate the Aenar—swiftly, efficiently, and thoroughly. And they have come very close to succeeding."

"Regrettably, yes. Which makes it at once more challenging and more urgent to discern their motivation."

"For now, I'd be happy to start with knowing *how* they did it," came a new voice. Thelin turned to see the remaining member of their party, Lieutenant Mosi Nizhoni. The *Enterprise*'s deputy chief of security was a fairly young human woman with black hair and brownish skin, her uniform adorned with beaded decorations reflecting her heritage, an Earth people known as the Diné or Navajo. "The molecular disruption traces suggest they beamed in somewhere around here, but no known transporter could've gotten past the natural *and* artificial jamming fields around the compound. Not unless they were allowed in, which there'd be a record of in the defense computers. We've got the equivalent of a locked-room mystery."

"Perhaps we should focus on what we *can* learn from the evidence, Lieutenant," Spock told her. "We may be able to deduce something from that."

The team proceeded to scan the ruined compound methodically. It was easy to remain engrossed in the tedious work, for the alternative was to think about the events that had produced the many bloodstains, burn marks, blade marks, and further scars of violence. Thelin analyzed those scars with care, hoping the attackers had left some trace of themselves behind that would identify them—or at least, that one or more of the Aenar had lived long enough to leave some message identifying their killers.

Soon enough, Nizhoni called Thelin's and Spock's attention to something that might have been just that. "It was buried under a fall of rubble," the young human told them as she showed them the dried blue-black scrawl that some dying Aenar had written in their own blood. "Maybe if the first teams had found it, we'd already know . . ."

Thelin shook his head. "It tells us little, I think. It's one word, in the ancient language we and the Aenar shared."

"Can you read it?" Spock asked.

"It appears to say '*naazh*.' A kind of phantom from our ancient myths." He looked around at the bloodstained rubble in disgust and frustration. "I refuse to believe that this was done by ghosts."

"Indeed. More likely the description is metaphorical. Possibly a foe with some form of personal cloak?"

Thelin shook his head. "*Naazh* were not invisible like the phantoms of Terran lore. They were fearsome, demonic creatures. They took many forms, though, and struck in many ways, so the word alone tells us little. The one common aspect of the *naazh* was their savagery—and the fact that any who saw them clearly were as good as dead already."

Oresan Colony, Motar
Andor system

"Stop right there!"

Pavel Chekov could barely spare the breath to shout the order, for he was running at top speed after his Andorian quarry as the three of them fled pell-mell through the narrow, maze-like alleys of Oresan. The mining town had been built up over the past two centuries within a vast underground lava dome on

Motar, the second large moon of the gas giant Andoria orbited. Or rather, it had been built down, expanding into successively lower terraces as the floor of the domed cavern had been mined away layer by layer. The extremists Chekov pursued had already led him up two steep stairways in the course of this pursuit, and for once he was grateful for the diet and exercise program Doctor McCoy pushed him to maintain.

Nevertheless, running in security armor and a helmet made him sweat copiously. Wiping perspiration from his brow, Chekov glanced up at the arrays of artificial lights hanging from the rocky, domed ceiling and reflected that this was an ironic place to hunt down a fringe group calling itself "Blue Sky." But Andorian-supremacist groups like this one had often sought out recruits from isolated working-class communities such as this, where the inhabitants were used to mingling only with their own species and could be easily deceived into seeing non-Andorians as threats to their jobs and community values—never mind that mineral exports to other Federation worlds were what kept this town alive. A remote, offworld site like this was also a good place for extremist groups to hide out from Homeworld Security. Unless HS were engaged in a joint operation with Starfleet to track down the extremists wherever they went.

Unfortunately, the extremists knew this town's twists and turns intimately, and though Chekov had a whole *Enterprise* security team and a squad of Captain sh'Zava's HS officers with him, he'd managed to get separated from the rest as their quarry had split up to lead them in various directions. Chekov followed his three targets—who appeared to be two *thaan*s, roughly male, and a *zhen*, roughly female but big and strong—right down a short alley, then left into one of the narrow major streets running the length of the terrace. This street had less skimmer and pedestrian traffic than some, and in the straightaway, they were able to pick up speed. The *zhen* paused to topple over a food vendor's stand behind her, spilling dozens of some kind of small, tentacled crustaceans across the road in Chekov's path. The vendor's efforts to keep his stock from skittering away impeded Chekov's movement, giving the Blue Sky trio an even bigger head start by the time he got past the mess.

Raising his wrist communicator, Chekov opened the channel. "Chekov to Alpha Team. I need backup at these coordinates. My quarry is getting away!"

"Can't help you," sh'Zava's curt voice replied. *"They've started shooting. My teams are either pinned down or holding back to avoid risk to civilians."*

"Not to worry, Commander!" came a familiar, chirping bark on a different channel, and Chekov almost groaned that it had to be *him*.

A moment later, the three extremists pulled up short as an *Enterprise* security team stepped out in front of them. There were three of them as well: Crewmen Worene and Vidmar, and at their head, the distinctive dark blue, avian/feline hybrid features of Hrii'ush Uuvu'it. The Betelgeusian struck a cocky pose and spoke with the same chirping confidence Chekov had just heard over his communicator: "I . . . have arrived!"

The three Andorians looked around in panic, and Chekov allowed himself a grin. Both Uuvu'it and the Aulacri female Worene had somewhat fearsome, predatory appearances (as long as you didn't know them well), and these were racists conditioned to fear aliens. Just the sight of them was an effective psychological warfare tactic, and for once, Uuvu'it's bombastic need to show off may have been an asset.

Or maybe not—for the *zhen* now drew a phaser and aimed it toward Chekov. The bystanders cried out or ducked for cover, but near Chekov, a young *shen* who couldn't have been more than twelve stood paralyzed. As the radical fired, Chekov tackled the girl and shielded her with his armored back.

The Blue Sky group took advantage of the opening, dashing past Chekov as he shielded the girl. "Human weakling!"

the shooter cried. "Cower from us! Weep at true Andorian strength!"

Chekov wondered if the extremist had even noticed the girl she had endangered—or if, despite her group's pretense of esteeming Andorians above all others, she simply didn't care if she endangered her own people.

But someone cared. After the radicals ducked left down another alley, the girl ran to the embrace of a big, bearish Andorian male who'd come out of the adjacent *katheka* shop. "Airina!" he cried, cradling her against the wide expanse of his apron. His eyes met Chekov's gratefully.

Unfortunately, Chekov had no time to accept any thanks, just offering the *katheka* vendor a quick smile and nod before resuming the chase. The three *Enterprise* guards were soon loping alongside him, and Uuvu'it quickly outpaced him, going down briefly on all fours and cornering like a cat to enter the alley. "Let's go, let's go, let's go!" he cried. Worene followed a moment later, her prehensile tail whipping behind her, and Chekov and Vidmar were racing close behind.

Their speed almost cost them, for it was a trap. The *zhen* fired her phaser *forward*, and then the Blue Sky trio veered sideways with Uuvu'it and Worene close behind, moving too fast to swerve. Chekov had barely begun to register the partially disintegrated railing and the vast open space beyond when Worene attempted to skid to a stop and failed, going over the edge of the terrace—

—and stopping with a squeal of pain. Uuvu'it had caught a surviving piece of the railing in one hand and Worene's tail in the other, stopping her from going over the edge. Pulling her back to safety by her tail, he spun her around balletically and set her down on the narrow path along the terrace edge. "Mind if I reel you in?" he asked.

"Mind if I thrash you?" Worene hissed, more annoyed at her close call than grateful. The two of them had been a couple on a casual basis for a while now, but they were both from species that pursued romance very competitively, so it was hard to tell their flirting from their fighting.

Worene pushed herself away and resumed the chase after the extremists. "Now I'm getting angry!"

"Only now?" Uuvu'it countered, joining her in the chase. "I've been at peak intensity from the start!"

"Can't hear you!" teased Worene, who'd already outpaced him.

The *zhen* resumed firing as Chekov's people closed on them, and one of the *thaan*s now opened fire with what sounded like an antique plasma pistol. Worene ducked agilely, but a plasma bolt barely missed Vidmar. "Take cover," Chekov ordered his team, "and return fire, heavy stun." He gave the order reluctantly. Even this narrow street was not entirely free of bystanders, and phaser stuns were not always harmless. But the Blue Sky members were shooting to kill, making them the greater threat to the civilians.

His team took the nearest available cover and drew their phasers, taking careful aim. Before they could fire, though, something new entered the equation. A horde of townsfolk surged out of an alley into the extremists' path, confronting them angrily. The three radicals pulled up short, surprised. "No," Chekov heard one of them cry. "We're fighting for you!"

At the head of the group was the burly *katheka* vendor from before. "Tell that to my girl you almost killed!" He lunged forward, grabbing the *thaan*'s plasma pistol and wrenching it aside.

"Now!" Chekov cried, waving his team forward. They lunged ahead and took out the armed *zhen* and the other *thaan* with precision phaser fire before the extremists could recover from their surprise.

But Chekov was content to let the bearish vendor deal with the third extremist. Once the security team closed in, the vendor had knocked the *thaan* to the ground, where he lay dazed and gasping in pain.

The vendor traded an appreciative look with Chekov, then looked down at the extremist. "How about that?" he taunted. "My Andorian strength has made *you* weep." He pulled a *katheka*-stained cloth from his apron pocket and tossed it into the extremist's face. "Wipe your tears with this."

Homeworld Security Headquarters
Laikan, Andoria

"I refuse to bring them in," Kinoch zh'Lenthar insisted. The young, intense Aenar activist crossed her arms and continued, "Bringing us all together will just let them finish us off once and for all. Solve a lot of problems for the government."

Nyota Uhura took a calming breath as she faced the pale-skinned firebrand. She knew that the Aenar's antennae and ears could discern much about her emotional state even without eyesight, and the last thing she wanted was to provoke further mistrust from zh'Lenthar. The activist leader's angry rhetoric was already creating anxiety in the other Aenar survivors gathered here, in a makeshift dormitory in the Homeworld Security building's gymnasium. While many of the Aenar who had been away from their compound at the time of the massacre had been political activists like zh'Lenthar's group, the others were mostly individuals who had chosen to leave their insular community and assimilate into Andorian society. A number of those had married into four-person Andorian bondgroups, and a few were here with their part-Aenar children.

"Please, try to consider the best interests of your people," Uhura said, hoping her choice of words would encourage zh'Lenthar to consider her effect on the others, especially the children. "We can protect you better if we know where you all are."

"As if this government has ever cared about our best interests.

That so-called minister for Aenar Affairs can't even be bothered to show up. He's never cared about helping us, only keeping us quiet and docile while the Andorians crowded us toward non-existence."

"Separation won't protect us," countered Rukash th'Miraph, an elder among the assimilated Aenar, who seemed to have naturally gravitated toward him as a spokesperson for their group. Like most of them, he dressed in Andorian fashion and wore a sensor web similar to the one Miranda Jones employed. "In the past week, one Aenar living alone was killed in a suspicious skimmer crash, and another traveling in the Vezhdar Plain has disappeared. We fear they, too, may be victims of the unknown killers."

Uhura turned to th'Miraph. "Have any of you received any telepathic impressions to suggest that?" She had known telepaths to experience the terror and death of others of their species over great distances, as when Spock had sensed the destruction of the Vulcan-crewed *Intrepid* some years before.

He shook his head. "Such things have been known between immediate family members, but those of us who have chosen to integrate into Andorian society generally do so because we have few or no surviving kin among the Aenar." His antennae sagged. "That is . . . even more the case now."

She touched his hand. "I'm sorry. You all should know that we've still received no word from the Aenar group that was searching for a new homeworld, or the ship of petitioners to the Federation Council. Starfleet is searching for them both, but nothing's been found."

The Aenar elder absorbed the news with more resignation than shock. A moment later, he turned to zh'Lenthar. "You see, Kinoch? Something is picking us off, and it evidently prefers to strike unseen. If there is any safety left for us, it is in a group."

Zh'Lenthar sneered at him. "If you thought unity would protect us, you would never have left our community. You and the others have already resigned yourselves to Aenar extinction and have fled the sinking ship."

"Expecting us to be able to survive as we were is a lost cause, now more than ever. If we wish any part of our genes and culture to survive, we must share it with our fellow Andorians and merge it with theirs."

"By abandoning everything we are? Hybrid children are never telepathic, rarely blind. If we interbreed, we cease to exist."

"Those are not the only things that make us Aenar. The important thing is to preserve what we can of ourselves, to leave a legacy."

"Our way of peace is what makes us Aenar. Do you think the warrior Andorians would allow it to survive?"

"The 'warrior' Andorians ended their wars a century ago and joined the Federation in peace."

"And helped to found Starfleet, which still wages war."

"Starfleet's job is to protect life," Uhura told her. "We fight when we have no other way to protect the innocent, but only as a last resort."

"Then you lack the courage of your convictions. I would die for mine."

Uhura sharpened her tone. "It's one thing to say that when it's only your own life you're putting on the line. Do you have the right to make that decision for others as well? How will you feel if your friends die because you refused to let us protect them?"

The young activist's expression wavered, but only briefly. "You still presume we would trust Starfleet or its friends in Andor's government to care about our survival."

"Then what about the Medusans? What about Ambassador Kollos, who personally requested that the *Enterprise* bring him across hundreds of light-years so he could help you in your time of need? Who's personally surveying the ruins of your compound this very moment, searching for any clue? Do you doubt that he truly cares?"

Zh'Lenthar's eyes widened and her antennae reared back in surprise. "Kollos? I . . . I remember him. He came to our compound when I was young. I sensed . . . such beauty and warmth from him."

"He tried to help your people, didn't he? Even after his attempt to recruit you for his navigation project fell through."

"Yes. He still tried to advocate for us. He was one of the only offworlders who really seemed to care."

Uhura placed a hand lightly on the young *zhen*'s shoulder. "I assure you, he's not the only one. Perhaps we have cared less in the past than we should have, but that's not a mistake we want to repeat." She paused. "If you doubt it, search my mind—search my feelings. I give you my consent."

Zh'Lenthar's fork-tipped antennae swiveled to bear on Uhura, and she felt a form of scrutiny she knew no Earthly words for. She summoned her memory of the recent shipboard vigil on the rec deck, focusing on the New Humans and their sense of oneness with their fellow telepaths. She didn't shy away from her own sense of guilt at paying the Aenar so little attention in the past. She had to be honest to earn the young Aenar's trust. Thus, she also openly shared the memory of T'Nalae's hostility toward the New Humans—as well as the rest of the crew's firm rejection of such negativity.

At last, the scrutiny faded, and zh'Lenthar tilted her head, contemplating Uhura. "I had not expected such . . . gentleness . . . from a military officer."

"Militaries can support and protect as well as fight. Sometimes nothing else is powerful and organized enough to make a difference when it's needed." She touched zh'Lenthar's shoulder again. "Please . . . let us try to make a difference for you. Your people's story doesn't have to end here."

After a moment's thought, the activist leader nodded. "Very

well. I shall advise my group to assemble here—provided that *you* remain to supervise."

Uhura smiled. "I'm not going anywhere."

Aenar Compound
Northern Wastes

After several hours spent examining the wrecked compound, Thelin, Spock, and the others gathered to review their findings. "As we have detected only five distinct footprint and stride patterns, it appears probable that all of this was done by five individuals," Spock concluded.

"Five." Nizhoni shook her head. "To kill nearly a thousand people. I mean, since they were pacifists, I suppose it's feasible. But still . . . what kind of person could kill that many people, one by one, up close and personal?" She grimaced. "Oh, I'm getting sick just thinking about it."

"Even by Andorian standards, this was savage," Thelin replied. "Note also that we have found traces of thirteen distinct bladed, projectile, or energy weapons. Meaning that each of these 'phantom' killers possessed two to three different weapons. It feels . . . like this was sport to them."

"There's no sport in killing pacifists," Nizhoni countered. "Especially blind ones." She flushed. "Oh, I'm sorry, Doctor Jones! I didn't mean—"

"It's nothing I haven't heard before, Lieutenant," Jones told her patiently. "But keep in mind that the Aenar were far from helpless in their own homes. They knew every centimeter of this place, and their living environment was adapted to their sensory abilities. Recall that Andorians, Aenar included, do sense electric fields with their antennae."

Nizhoni frowned. "Since we're on the subject, I've been wondering . . . but it seemed crass to ask such a banal question . . ."

"Go ahead, Lieutenant," Thelin told her. "Any distraction should be welcome at this point."

"Well, why is it that the Aenar's buildings . . . the partly intact ones I've seen, anyway . . . why do they have windows? And indoor lighting?"

Thelin chuckled. "Simple enough. Most of these structures were built to Andorian designs. When the Aenar were rediscovered, near the start of the twenty-second century, there was an initial attempt at cultural assimilation, under the guise of modernization. The Aenar welcomed the improved technologies and conveniences at first, but the Andorian contractors brought in to build the new structures unthinkingly built them to Andorian standards, designed for sighted individuals, with only cursory attempts to adapt them to the blind. To the Aenar, that was one of a number of warning signs that the Andorians intended to colonize their territory, even supplant them. In reaction, they reverted to their traditional isolation, a policy that they have maintained to this day." His antennae sagged in sorrow. "Perhaps it was an overreaction. I believe the contractors' error was more one of thoughtless habit than deliberate intent. But if they had simply been more attentive to the needs of the Aenar, then, maybe . . ." He trailed off into a sigh. There was no point dwelling on hypotheticals; this reality was the only one Thelin or the Andorian people had.

"In any case," Spock said after a moment, "the Aenar's isolation was itself a defense mechanism. Part of their reason for locating their primary compound this far north was to take advantage of the hostility of the surrounding environment, and of the natural interference fields near the pole, to deter easy access."

"Which they supplemented with their illusion powers to confuse intruders," Thelin added. "And with the aforementioned transporter damping fields."

"We may have a theory for how the attackers got through

those," Miranda Jones said, tilting her head toward the Medusan's hovering habitat beside her. "Kollos has been reviewing the sensor data of the molecular disruption patterns you detected earlier. We thought a Medusan's sensorium could perceive something humanoids couldn't."

"Intriguing," Thelin said. "You believe you—he—has found something?"

If Jones, Kollos, or both were bothered by his confusion at their compound identity, no sign of it showed on the woman's face. "To the Medusan eye, so to speak, the molecular disruptions in the floor surface look less like thermal damage or quantum-interference spillover than like a geometric translation—as though the particle lattices had been partially rotated through a higher dimension."

Thelin had pulled out his tricorder before Jones had finished speaking, and Spock had done the same. Thelin assumed that Spock was programming in the same type of simulation parameters that he was, for rotating the lattice patterns through various multidimensional shifts. Before long, Thelin's tricorder produced a pattern match. It had been easy to miss. Some subtle rearrangement of surface particles was common with transporter beams; normally, the interference patterns created between the coherent carrier beam and the modulated signal beam created the quantum assembly matrix that guided the transported particles to revert to their original pattern, but fringe effects on the edges of the beam could create pattern echoes that altered the quantum states and positions of particles in the arrival surface. This was on top of the simple thermal and electromagnetic disruptions resulting from the sheer concentration of energy in a transporter beam. Thus, it was common to look for molecular disruption as evidence of transporter use, but Thelin would never have thought of examining the specific geometry of the molecular rearrangement. He began to understand why Starfleet had been so eager to ally with the Medusans.

Looking up at Spock, he saw that the Vulcan had reached the same conclusion. "I see what you mean," Thelin said. "If the transport passed through a higher dimension, it would explain how it left no ionization traces *and* how it circumvented the damping fields."

Nizhoni stared at him. "Commander, are you telling me that we're dealing with an enemy that can beam clear through shields?"

"That is far from certain," Spock cautioned. "Even normal transporters operate partially through the dimensions of subspace, which is what enables them to transmit through solid matter. This may simply be a variant application of the confinement beam principle.

"However," he added, "under the circumstances, we cannot afford to ignore more . . . pessimistic interpretations. Until we know more about these attackers, we cannot rule out the possibility that they could strike anytime . . . and anywhere."

"Naazh," Thelin said, remembering how the dying Aenar had christened them in blood. "Phantoms. Truly, it is a fitting name."

Five

U.S.S. Enterprise

"So what's your reaction to T'Nalae's attitude?"

Reiko Onami studied the four New Humans who sat with her in the forward observation lounge on H deck, a favorite place for them to gather and meditate together. Onami hadn't wanted to call them into her office for a formal session, since they had been the recipients of the bad behavior—and since this meeting was as much out of curiosity on her part as any kind of formal counseling. Her title was "xenopsychologist," and these were her fellow humans; but from Onami's perspective, humans had always been as "xeno-" as anyone else, and New Humans in particular might even represent the dawning of a new subspecies, like the Aenar. As a scientist, she couldn't pass up investigating that phenomenon, if only on an informal basis.

Daniel Abioye, Jade Dinh, and Edward Logan traded looks, but deferred to Marcella DiFalco to speak for them. Abioye was an ensign, the only officer in the room, yet the soft-spoken West African acted no different from the other enlisted New Humans when he was among them.

"It's nothing we haven't faced before," DiFalco said after finishing her silent exchange with the others. Onami wondered how much of that was genuine telepathy and how much was just groupthink. "Rarely here in Starfleet, of course, since most of us embrace the new and different. But other New Humans on Earth, Deneb, and elsewhere have encountered the occasional few who didn't understand us, or didn't want to."

"Humans today take pride in our common humanity," Abioye added in a soft, deep voice, "but we can be inflexible about what 'humanity' means. The Eugenics Wars were long ago, but the Augment crisis last century reawakened old fears."

"There's mistrust of people who have more power than others," said the shaven-headed, tough-looking Logan. "We celebrate egalitarianism, which can create mistrust of exceptionalism."

"Not that we think we're better than anyone else," added Dinh, who wore her silky black hair loose when off duty, letting it fall clear to her waist. "We learned to strengthen our powers through commitment and meditation. It's just about unlocking our latent potential."

"Are you sure?" Onami countered. "I did some digging—the vast majority of rated espers haven't had the same increase in psi abilities as those of you who've adopted the New Human label. Hell, I have a thirty-nine esper rating myself, and it hasn't budged since V'Ger came."

DiFalco spoke with the tone of someone trying not to sound pitying. "We don't fully understand yet why only some of us have been able to unlock our potential. But our numbers grow every day," she assured Onami, reaching out to touch her hand. "I'm sure you'll have your awakening in time."

Logan leaned closer and gave her a flirtatious smile. "We'd be happy to meditate with you, try to help you unlock your gift." Behind his back, Dinh and Abioye rolled their eyes. Onami was pretty sure Logan was sleeping with both of them; New Humans tended to be open and casual about such things, as part of their philosophy of communal love and unity. So they showed no sign of jealousy, but they did seem amused by Logan's blatantness.

"I have a partner already, thanks," Onami said. "If I could just look into someone's head and *see* what the problem was, it'd take the challenge out of it. And yes, I know it's not that simple," she added when DiFalco opened her mouth. "I was kidding."

"You are curious, though, right?" DiFalco asked. "You came to us informally, not because you had to, but because you wanted to." At Onami's stare, she added, "I wasn't probing your thoughts, but emotions kind of . . . shine through."

"Yours shine very brightly," Logan added with what he thought was a charming grin.

Dinh socked his arm. "I'd say it's more like a glare."

"Sure, I'm curious," Onami told them. "But scientifically. I'm interested in how different cultures mix and bounce off each other, how they blend or how they clash. You're building a new culture as we watch, splitting off from regular humanity."

DiFalco's eyes widened. "We're not—is that how it seems to you, Reiko? We don't want to isolate ourselves."

"We want to reach out and share what we've gained," Abioye finished for her.

"Maybe," Onami said. "But you four have become pretty much inseparable. You spend all your free time together, and that does set you apart from the rest of us. You share something we can't."

"Is that why T'Nalae mistrusts us?" DiFalco asked.

"I'll tell you what I told her: The best way to get that understanding is from the source. I hope you and she can work out your differences; I'm just trying to nudge you the right way."

Dinh looked around at the others. "I guess we have formed kind of a bubble around ourselves the past couple of years. We get so caught up in each other we lose track of other connections."

"That's not always so bad," Abioye said. "I'm glad I got past the artificial hierarchy of officer and enlisted."

"But on the other hand," Logan teased, "Jade hasn't remembered to get a haircut in four years."

Dinh stroked Logan's carefully maintained, Deltan-smooth scalp. "I'm just balancing you out, Ed the Egghead. The Law of Conservation of Hair."

Onami left the meeting with most of her questions about the New Humans still open, but she had gotten one answer, at least: despite their increasing mental bonds, they were still as imperfectly, irritatingly human as ever.

Homeworld Security Headquarters
Laikan

Arashiki ch'Rushima crossed his arms and gave a sullen shrug, fidgeting slightly under the piercing stare of Captain sh'Zava. "Exterminate the Aenar?" he asked, then scoffed. "Why bother? The terraforming already did most of the work. The rest is only a matter of time."

From his vantage point to the side of the interrogation room table, Kirk studied the Blue Sky leader's reaction as the Homeworld Security captain leaned over him, no less intimidating for her dainty size. "Maybe you got impatient and decided to help the process along," sh'Zava said. "Wanted to be able to see their extinction within your lifetime."

"You don't understand Blue Sky's philosophy if you think we'd do that. We serve the pure will of Uzaveh the Infinite, as handed down to Thirishar at the beginning. The dwindling of the Aenar is Uzaveh's hand at work, and we would blaspheme against Her by usurping the task for ourselves."

"Well, if your wonderful Blue Sky organization is so philosophical and hands-off, why have its members been implicated in multiple attacks on offworlders? Why were all of your cells heavily armed when we raided them?"

"Why have Vulcans and Romulans and Earthers and Klingons been heavily armed when they came to face the Star Empire? Uzaveh made us warriors, so we fight in defense of the Whole." He glared at sh'Zava's HS insignia. "Even against Federation lackeys among our own people. But Aenar do not fight, so it is not for us to fight them. They are merely an aberration in the process of being corrected."

Ch'Rushima's gaze hardened. "Whoever struck them down came from outside. That makes this an alien attack on Andor—something that your vaunted 'Homeworld Security' is supposed to protect us from. Most likely, they struck at the Aenar first as a test run, before daring to take on foes who could defend themselves. We should be on the same side in this, hunting down the violators of our world so we can stop them before they attack again." He threw a glare toward Kirk. "Instead, you work *with* pink skins to persecute fellow Andorians."

Kirk took the Blue Sky leader's xenophobic rant as his cue to step forward, placing a data slate on the table before ch'Rushima. "If you're so hostile toward aliens, then how do you explain this correspondence we recovered from your computers? You managed to erase a lot of it, but we recognized the contact codes and message protocols of the Redheri Trade Consortium. Oh, yes," he added as ch'Rushima stiffened in surprise. "We've encountered the Redheri before, and they're about as alien as they come. But we know your group has made overtures to them, seeking access to exotic technology."

Sh'Zava picked up the thread. "What technology were you bargaining for? Was it, perhaps, an advanced form of transporter? One that could penetrate the Aenar's damping fields undetected?"

Watching the extremist leader closely, Kirk couldn't deny that he seemed genuinely surprised by the suggestion. "Is that how it was done? If they have such a transporter, all the more reason we need to unite against these invaders!"

Kirk traded a look with sh'Zava. After a moment's wordless communication, he let her ask the next question. She sat opposite ch'Rushima and moderated her tone. "Very well, then. If you wish to convince me you're on my side, then reassure me of your intentions. Tell us what technology you sought from the Redheri."

The extremist winced, his antennae folding back in what seemed like shame. "We . . . hadn't gotten that far in our negotiations yet. We just wanted . . . *something*. Something advanced, something beyond Federation science, something from a civilization distant enough that its origins could be obscured. They said they had access to ancient ruins, relics from civilizations millennia ahead of ours."

Sh'Zava frowned. "If you didn't know what you wanted, why were you seeking it?"

"So that . . ." His embarrassment was more obvious now as he wrestled with himself, then finally spat out the words. "So that we could take credit for its invention! So that we could prove Andorian superiority with some breakthrough beyond anything the pink skins or green skins had ever achieved."

Kirk shared another look with the HS captain, but it was clear they'd already arrived at the same conclusion. For all its bluster, Blue Sky was far too pathetic to be the threat they sought.

". . . And Blue Sky was our best lead," Thamizhan sh'Zava concluded as she reported to the group gathered around the conference room table, including Kirk, Spock, Chekov, Jones, Kollos, and Thelin. "Their overtures to the Redheri made them the only domestic radical group that could have had access to unknown transporter tech."

"And even that was tenuous," Kirk added. "My crew and I have dealt with the Redheri more than once. Their values are different from ours—they're willing to interfere with pre-warp cultures to open trade with them, and they can be reckless in their efforts to exploit advanced relic technologies—but they see themselves as benevolent, engaging in free commerce for the betterment of everyone. The Aenar massacre was big enough news to reach beyond the Federation. If they'd heard about it and recognized the use of a technology they'd sold to Blue Sky, I believe they would've come forward."

"Indeed," Spock affirmed. "The Trade Consortium would perceive it as a breach of contract and a stain upon their reputation—such as it is—and would have sought to exact financial penalties upon the parties involved."

"So that's a dead end," sh'Zava said. "And none of the other pro-terraforming groups are promising as suspects. They all seemed genuinely horrified at what happened to the Aenar. They may have opposed their politics or seen them as an economic threat, but wanting them driven to extinction is a radically different matter. And they all volunteered to submit to verifier scans to confirm it." She sighed. "Granted, that's not as reliable a technology as it was believed to be a decade ago, but many laypeople still don't know that, so the fact that they were willing to volunteer is telling."

"There is one other key data point to consider," Spock put in. "Ambassador Kollos?"

The Medusan spoke through Miranda Jones, whose face and voice conveyed some of his usual enthusiasm and curiosity, now tempered by solemnity and sorrow. "I took detailed psionic scans of the Aenar compound using the sensors built into my habitat. It took me a while to analyze the readings, since there was so much psionic residue left on the scene by the Aenar. But I can now say with high confidence that there were non-Aenar psionic signatures involved in the massacre."

Sh'Zava stared. "Can you explain how you know this?"

"Well, psionic phenomena aren't magic. They involve a class

of exotic particles called psions, which interact using psionic energy fields, much like how electrons interact through electromagnetism. Certain sentient brains are able to resonate with the quantum wave patterns of psionic fields, enabling them to use those fields for communication, or to manipulate psion particles for telekinetic interaction with normal matter."

"You can scan for these psion particles?"

"Yes, and for the residual psionic field charges they leave in affected matter. Each telepathic or telekinetic species emits its own characteristic psionic signature, similar to its electromagnetic brain-wave signature and shaped by its distinct neural anatomy in corresponding ways. I became familiar with Aenar psionic signatures during the process of testing them for the Medusan navigational program. That familiarity enabled me to filter out those signatures and confirm the presence of additional, non-Aenar signatures. I'd estimate four or five distinct patterns, which agrees with the five distinct stride patterns we found on the scene."

The HS captain sighed. "If any of the extremist groups had psi abilities, I presume we'd know about it."

Thelin folded his hands on the table in front of him. "Psionic abilities are all but unheard of in non-Aenar Andorians. I am a quarter Aenar myself, but my psi rating is essentially zero."

"And there's no chance, Ambassador, that these extra psi signatures could be Aenar? Perhaps if some of the Aenar went mad, lashed out in violence against their own kind, it would alter their telepathic spoor?"

Jones's head shook as Kollos answered through her. "It would not alter their signatures that significantly. Nor would it explain the evidence of telekinetic abilities being used. While telekinesis is not unheard of among the Aenar, it's never been recorded to this extent."

Kirk frowned. "What about . . . I know it's a crazy idea, Spock, but what about kironide poisoning? You and I discovered on

Platonius that kironide injections can induce telekinetic ability in humans and Vulcans, at least briefly." *And not without cost*, he added to himself, feeling a moment of psychosomatic nausea as he recalled the unpleasant aftereffects of kironide toxicity and the similarly unpleasant chelation therapy he and Spock had endured for a week after their departure from Platonius. It had been the only way to escape imprisonment and torture at the hands of the sadistic Platonians, but the consequences had been almost as bad as the torture.

Spock shook his head. "While it has been difficult to experiment with kironide-induced telekinesis due to the hazards of heavy-metal poisoning, simulations have proven unable to replicate the effect outside the specific environmental conditions of the planet Platonius. Evidently the high proportion of kironide in the planet's crust and biosphere turns the entire planet into a psionic resonator, which beings who absorb and metabolize sufficient quantities of kironide are able to connect with. Kironide is found only in trace quantities on Andor, insufficient to produce a comparable effect."

"It seems," said Thelin, "that we are left with nothing but the name we found scrawled in blood. *Naazh*, or phantoms. Vicious, seemingly supernatural killers. If they were psionic, at a level well beyond the Aenar, it could explain that description."

"And maybe their motive," Chekov suggested. "Some kind of grudge against rival telepaths. Vulcans or Betazoids could be in danger too."

"Everything we learn makes our job more difficult," sh'Zava said, grimacing. "How do we protect against an unknown, outside enemy that can penetrate our defenses undetected? One whose motives are as obscure now as when we started?"

Kirk thought for a moment. "I recommend moving all the surviving Aenar to the *Enterprise*. We know they can penetrate transporter damping fields, but that doesn't mean they can beam through a starship's full shields."

Sh'Zava's piercing, critical gaze fell on him. "And if they can? You would put your crew in danger."

"My crew is trained for danger, Captain, better than any Andorian civilians who might end up in a crossfire. If there's an attack coming, let's control the battlefield as much as possible. On the *Enterprise*, at least we'll have the home-court advantage."

The slim, strong *shen* hissed through her teeth. "I hate to concede that I can't protect my citizens on my own world. But my personal pride is not what I've sworn to protect. I'll begin arrangements to transfer the Aenar survivors to the *Enterprise* at once."

"Thank you, Captain," Kirk said, holding her gaze to convey his sincere appreciation. Then he turned to Thelin. "Commander, I'd like you to come aboard as liaison to the Aenar. They need someone they know and trust, now more than ever."

"Thank you, Captain. I was about to request exactly that." He gave a tight smile. "I had hoped my first visit to the *Enterprise* would be under better circumstances."

Kirk blinked, remembering a different Thelin on a different *Enterprise*. He realized he'd unconsciously started thinking of the *thaan* as a member of his crew already.

"We make do with the reality we have, Commander," he said. "So let's get started."

U.S.S. Enterprise

"I know it's a bit crowded with this many people," Nyota Uhura said to the sixty-eight Aenar who stood assembled in the main atrium of the *Enterprise*'s recreation deck, turning their heads and waving their antennae in all directions to take in the sounds and sensory impressions of the large, two-story chamber. "But it's the largest single space on the ship that has the facilities to take care of so many."

It left her somewhat staggered to think that she might be gazing upon the entire surviving Aenar species, save for a smattering of Andorians with partial Aenar heritage, in small enough portions that they had not considered themselves under threat and had declined the offer of protective custody. But five of the Aenar who had assimilated into Andorian families had brought their part-Aenar children of various ages with them—only one child each, as was apparently usual for Andorians these days. Commander Thelin also stood alongside her, holding the hand of his five-year-old daughter, Cheremis. Though she was only one-sixteenth Aenar and showed no outward sign of it that Uhura could discern, the commander had not wished to take any chances with her safety.

"Rest assured," Thelin told the group, "that even though this is a makeshift facility, it is as secure as any location aboard the ship. This class of starship has a dual shielding system: the standard, directional deflector grid within the hull and an advanced force-field screen that surrounds the entire vessel like a bubble. The aft saucer deflectors are being kept up at all times to shield this area of the ship against transporters, even when other portions of the deflector grid are lowered to allow the crew to beam to and from Andor. If a threat is detected, then both shield systems will be fully raised. Additionally, we have equipped this entire facility with transporter dampers a generation more advanced than the ones around the Aenar city."

Kinoch zh'Lenthar tilted her head skeptically. "We thought our dampers and natural disruption fields were good enough to protect the city. We were wrong."

"As you can perceive, we do have an additional line of defense." Thelin gestured toward the armored security guards who stood vigil at all entrances to the deck, armed with hefty tri-beam phaser rifles. "Multiple guards will be on duty at all times."

"Will we have no privacy?"

"There are private alcoves and facilities on the balcony level above, and a couple of semiprivate lounges on this level through the side archways," Uhura explained. "We're converting the upstairs rooms into dormitories right now. The stairs are through the rear doorway on your right, or you can take either of the forward turbolifts up one level."

"But let us face the facts," Thelin told the Aenar activist, his voice pitched toward the others as well. "You are all under threat, and isolation is a luxury no Aenar can currently afford."

"We have always preferred to keep to ourselves. Can we be promised that your crew will not intrude on us in our grief?"

The elder th'Miraph stepped forward to confront her. "Be realistic, Kinoch. All of us here are more gregarious than the Aenar norm—it is why we are still alive, because we chose to leave our city for whatever reasons. Even in our isolation from the Andorians and the Federation, we still valued community and connection among ourselves. And now that there are so few of us left, is it wise to deny the company and support of whoever is willing to offer it?"

Uhura picked up on that. "Indeed, we have a number of telepaths among our crew. Kinoch, you know of them from my mind. They feel kinship with you and would welcome the opportunity to spend time with you, to support you in any way they could. We'll respect your privacy if that's what you wish, but I hope you'll consider letting them in."

Zh'Lenthar's antennae waved, and many of the others' wiggled in response. Uhura got the impression that they were communing telepathically. "Very well," the activist said a moment later. "The telepaths, at least."

"And your crew has our thanks," th'Miraph added pointedly, "for surrendering their recreational space for our comfort."

"You're very welcome," Uhura replied. She declined to mention that the crew would still have the arboretum in the secondary hull and the officers' lounge just behind the bridge as fallbacks. A crew of nearly five hundred people spending five years in deep space needed all the recreational facilities they could get for the sake of their morale and mental health, but to these refugees, it might seem like an overindulgence in luxury.

"And rest assured," Thelin added, "that we are doing everything in our power to identify and neutralize the threat, so that you can return to Andor as soon as feasible."

"And what then?" asked another member of zh'Lenthar's activist group, a lanky *thaan* named Shinai. "What then? We have no home left. Not enough of us to repopulate. How can we hope to rebuild?"

Thelin stepped forward to confront him. "I cannot guarantee that every problem has a solution," he said. "But I can guarantee that giving up is never a solution. My advice is that you do the same thing in this situation that we all do in every situation: Strive. Adapt. Learn. Persist—until it ends. Solve one problem at a time. That is life. Do you understand?"

Shinai blinked several times, then nodded. "Yes. Yes, I understand."

Zh'Lenthar moved to stand beside him, contemplating Thelin with new appreciation. "Yes. We all do."

When Leonard McCoy arrived at Specialist T'Nalae's quarters with Nurse Liftig at his side, he found the young Vulcan scientist lying flat on the floor, clad in a white bathrobe. Standing beside her was Barbara Attias, the engineering tech whose quarters shared the bathroom with T'Nalae's. "I found her passed out in the shower when I got in," Attias explained. "After I called you, I had it materialize a robe for her and . . . I hope it's okay."

After reassuring her briefly, McCoy scanned T'Nalae, reviewing the data as it showed up on his medical tricorder screen. "Funny . . . surprising amount of activity in the—"

T'Nalae opened her eyes and sat up abruptly, making Attias yelp and almost knocking McCoy over until Ron Liftig caught his shoulders and helped him up. The specialist turned her head sharply back and forth, taking in her surroundings. "Explain."

McCoy gestured to Attias. "Barbara there found you unconscious and called us. Do you remember passing out?"

She blinked. "Yes. There were . . . headaches. Since . . . the Aenar arrived."

"Yes . . . it does look like your paracortex has been unusually active. There's a residual psionic charge there. We've been seeing a lot of headaches, anxiety, and so forth in our psi-sensitive personnel over the past few hours. The Aenar . . . they're powerful telepaths, and they're in a lot of pain. They don't intend to project it onto others, but it's so strong that it's hard not to. The other telepaths on board are all affected—though you're the only one so far to lose consciousness from it."

Her gaze sharpened upon him. "Why?"

"Maybe we can find that out once we get you to sickbay."

Despite McCoy's recommendation that she wait for a stretcher, T'Nalae insisted on walking to sickbay, and indeed she showed no ill effects from her bout of syncope. An examination on the micro-diagnostic table showed her to be in excellent health, even surpassing the results of her physical on first joining the crew. According to the detailed brain scans on the full-length wall screen next to the table, the heightened paracortical activity was the only anomaly in her readings.

"Can you explain it?" T'Nalae said, studying him closely.

McCoy crossed his arms. "Well, I can't find a physical cause, which makes me wonder if the difference is psychological. The other telepaths in the crew feel acceptance and affinity for the Aenar. So when they feel the Aenar's grief being broadcast, they let it in. They're willing to sympathize—in the most literal sense of the word.

"But you've made it clear that you're not comfortable with the Aenar and the nature of their telepathy. So maybe when you felt their grief and pain in your mind, you resisted it. And by doing so, you put your mind under greater strain. Maybe that made the pain or anxiety severe enough that you passed out. Maybe your brain even shut itself down as a defense mechanism."

"I see," T'Nalae said. "Tell me—how are the others coping with the distress?"

"Most of them have gone to visit the Aenar on the rec deck, commiserate with them. They seem to think it makes it better. There's a human saying—sorrow shared is sorrow halved."

"Then by going to the rec deck—by reaching out to the Aenar—I will get better?"

"I know it's not what you want to hear, T'Nalae. But I hope you'll at least consider—"

"Say no more." She rose abruptly from the diagnostic table. "You're right, Doctor. This is a wake-up call. If my resistance to the Aenar is hurting me, then it's time for me to change. I should seek them out, as the others have done. They're still on the recreation deck?"

Her sudden epiphany seemed too good to be true. And since she'd awakened, she'd seemed unusually intense—though judging from what he'd heard about her from Reiko Onami and others, she'd always been intense. He glanced back at the diagnostic screen, confirming that there were no signs of neurological imbalance beyond what could be accounted for by the Aenar's influence.

Besides, he'd seen on Sarpeidon, in that time when Spock's emotions had been somehow unleashed by his travel to the past, that Vulcans without logical reserve could be volatile and mercurial in their moods. Maybe, in some cases, that could be a good thing. *Maybe it's the logic that makes them so damn stubborn, so sure they're always right.*

"They are," he said. "But I suggest you take it slow. Maybe just sit with the others and listen for a while. Think about what you hear, and what you feel."

Her lean body strained toward the door, as if she were impatient to pursue her new goal. But she turned back to him and offered a confident smile. "Good advice, Doctor. Don't worry—they'll hardly know I'm there."

Six

"Ready or not, here I come!"

Marcella DiFalco uncovered her eyes and began to search the rec deck for Getran, the four-year-old son of one of the Aenar refugees. The boy's Aenar mother—or rather, his *zhavey*—turned her way and chuckled, taking care not to give away her child's location. The Aenar seemed to find it endlessly amusing that a human like DiFalco was so dependent on her sense of vision that merely covering her eyes rendered her unaware of the actions and movements of the people around her. She had wondered—belatedly, after already starting the game—if choosing an activity so dependent on vision would be seen as a slight toward the Aenar, but if anything, it had turned out to have the opposite effect.

Indeed, DiFalco had initially been the one hiding from Getran, on the assumption that her esper intuition would give her an unfair advantage if she were the seeker—for hybrids like Getran never seemed to inherit their Aenar parents' telepathic gifts. But she'd failed to account for Andorian antennae and their sensitivity to electric fields and motion. The boy had been able to find her in mere moments, no matter where she hid on the rec deck. Once the positions had been reversed, the game had become far more challenging. Even though she could get a general psionic sense of the boy's nearness, he had proven unusually creative in finding and exploiting hiding places she never would have considered. Observing their youngest child so completely outmaneuvering a crack Starfleet navigator was a further boost to the frightened Aenar's morale, so DiFalco made a show of it and didn't try very hard to follow her intuition. "Oh, where are you this time? Where could you be?"

Of course, she also had to put up with the laughter from her crewmates as they watched her humiliate herself. In addition to the multiple security guards (who *mostly* contained their amusement at her expense), Daniel Abioye, Jade Dinh, and Edward Logan were here too. Commander Spock had granted all four New Human crew members dispensation from their normal duties so they could assist the Aenar, bonding with them and trying to reassure them that, while they may have lost the majority of their own people, they were still connected to the greater whole of the galaxy's telepathic community. Just about all of the telepaths on board had visited the Aenar at least once, including Spock, the telekinetic Crewman Zabish from Kazar, and Ensign Palur, an Argelian descended from the planet's ancient priestesses and inheriting their rare empathic gift. DiFalco even noticed T'Nalae hovering in the background now. She hadn't tried actively engaging with the Aenar yet, but at least she was here. DiFalco was glad she'd finally started to overcome her resistance.

Reiko Onami had been spending a lot of time with the Aenar as well, offering one-on-one counseling to those who wished to talk out their problems instead of seeking psychic solace. The dainty, pretty xenopsychologist was currently in one of the side lounges, in a group session with the four oldest part-Aenar children—save only Getran and Commander Thelin's daughter, Cheremis, who were still too young to cope with the issues being discussed. DiFalco hoped the boy hadn't snuck in there to hide. The emotions she felt emanating from that lounge were rather fraught.

But no; as she reached out with her mind, trying to feel

the boy's bright, pure emotions, she caught a familiar whiff of amusement from the upper level. She made her way to the forward turbolifts, exchanging a friendly smile with the security guards th'Clane and Vidmar as she passed them, and rode up one deck to begin searching the small, individual game rooms, holotheaters, and privacy lounges that flanked the main atrium on the balcony level.

Her sense of Getran's mixed anxiety and anticipation at being discovered intensified as she moved aft, and she grinned. "I'm getting closer!" she lilted. "There's no getting away from me now!"

Someone screamed.

More screams followed, and a surge of terror from multiple minds nearly overwhelmed DiFalco. Gathering herself, she sent an urgent thought Getran's way: *Stay hidden. No matter what.*

The sound of phaser fire joined the screams as DiFalco made her way to the rear balcony. She heard Worene above the Aenar's cries: "Security to bridge! Intruder alert! An unidentified lifeform has appeared in the rec deck! It is hostile, repeat, hostile!"

A transparent, two-story planter in the rear corner of the atrium provided cover as she peered through the leaves at the scene below. The first thing she saw was Shantherin th'Clane trading blows with a dark bipedal figure, his burly, armored frame blocking her view. The other guards were shielding the terrified Aenar as they backed away, and she could feel the minds of community leaders th'Miraph and zh'Lenthar sending out calming thoughts to their people, though in differing ways; the elder broadcast reassurance and trust that Starfleet would protect them, while the young activist radiated defiance, urging her followers to remain true to their Aenar unity and pacifism no matter the provocation. DiFalco hoped the mixed messages would not undermine the intent of calming the group.

From her overhead vantage point, she could see that Logan and T'Nalae were working together to herd some of the Aenar into one of the side lounges, trying to hurry them and calm them at the same time. DiFalco caught T'Nalae's eye and nodded her thanks, moved that the young Vulcan had come through when she was needed. T'Nalae returned the nod briefly before she disappeared from view.

This close to the rim of the saucer, DiFalco could hear and feel the surge of the force-field generator coils that ringed it as they were promptly activated in response to the alert, forming a defensive bubble around the *Enterprise*. Yet she knew the stronger, hull-hugging deflector shields had already been in place around this section of the saucer the whole time, as had the transporter damping field around the recreation complex. So how had the intruder gotten aboard?

The "unidentified life-form" shot out a fist with enough force to knock th'Clane down and send him tumbling, and DiFalco finally got a clear look. The figure was humanoid, of moderate height and lithe but strong build, its gender indeterminate. It was encased from head to toe in streamlined body armor, deep scarlet in hue with black upper arms and legs and a textured black strip around the waist with a large red crystal in front fringed in silver, suggestive of a belt. The helmet's face was smooth and featureless, a crimson cabochon held in its black setting by four claw-like silver prongs in an X configuration. The armor's textural details and joint structures appeared almost organic, suggesting the chitin of an insect, but the material looked more like a mix of crystal and metal.

A phaser beam struck the intruder from somewhere below DiFalco's vantage, but it merely sparked off the armor and briefly staggered the humanoid. The intruder then cupped a hand in front of the red belt crystal, which glowed—whereupon a shield materialized on the intruder's left forearm, seemingly of the same material as the rest of the armor. The warrior used the shield to deflect another phaser beam as it strode forward.

Then, to DiFalco's horror, an actinic flicker of light shone through the side archway leading to the lounge where Logan and T'Nalae had retreated, followed by screams and the sounds of violence. She recognized one of the screams as Logan's, feeling his terror and confusion in her mind—before both his voice and his emotions cut off sharply in a final surge of agony, staggering her with loss and grief.

A few of the Aenar inside emerged through the archway, fleeing back out in a shrieking panic, despite the imminent danger outside. Even the jumbled final sensations from Logan had made it clear that what was happening inside the lounge was far worse.

Then there was another flash right alongside DiFalco on the balcony. She toppled back onto the deck and stared in shock at the whirling ball of light, which faded to reveal another armored humanoid, this one clad in white with dark gray highlights. Its helmet was also faceless, but textured with gray striations that suggested an insect's compound eyes and mandibles. Atop the helmet was a pair of long, forward-curving protrusions, like a mockery of the Aenar's antennae.

The thought of the Aenar galvanized her. As the invader got its bearings and began to turn toward her, she shot to her feet and lunged past it. It whirled more swiftly than the armor should have allowed, its metallic fingertips digging painfully into her shoulder even in the brief contact before she slipped past. She ran, thinking only of leading it away from Getran.

"It is hostile, repeat, hostile!" Worene's report over the bridge speakers was accompanied by the sounds of screams and phaser fire.

"Chekov, mobilize Beta Team now," Kirk ordered, then turned his chair to face the science station, where Commander Thelin stood beside a seated Spock. "Any idea how they breached our shields?"

"I find no evidence that they did, Captain," Spock replied. "No external signals, no energy drains or disruptions to the shields themselves. The only energy readings are from within the recreation deck itself."

Kirk rose. "Then we'd better get down there." He moved toward the port turbolift. "Chekov, Thelin, with me. Spock, you have the conn."

As the turbolift descended, Thelin clenched his fists, trembling with emotion. "Not even here. We couldn't stop them even here. We just gathered them all in one convenient place!"

Kirk put a hand on his shoulder. "My guards are protecting them. We're moments away."

Rather than using one of the turbolift exits inside the rec room—a perfect bottleneck that the intruders could use to pick them off as they emerged—they met up with Beta Team in the G-deck corridor outside the main entrance. Lieutenant Nizhoni led the team, backed up by Petty Officer Uuvu'it and Crewmen M'sharna and Lance. All were armed with large, two-handed phaser rifles, and the deputy security chief handed Chekov a spare rifle-grip attachment for him to plug his pistol phaser into while she addressed him and Kirk.

"Commander. Captain. At least two more intruders have materialized. Alpha Team is engaging them. Chief Onami just reported that she's managed to sneak the four older children out through the port exit, but the two youngest are still unaccounted for." Nizhoni glanced toward Thelin. "Including your daughter, Commander. I'm sorry."

Kirk turned to Thelin. "Maybe you should hold back."

The sharp-featured Andorian gathered himself. "No, Captain. I am a warrior and a science officer. My passion is undimmed, but I will direct it with discipline."

Taking him at his word, Kirk nodded to his security chief, letting him take the lead. "Chekov?"

"Phasers on heavy stun," the Russian ordered, "but use discretion. Our priority is to protect the Aenar. And the remaining children," he added with a nod toward Thelin.

"And Worene," Kirk heard Uuvu'it mutter under his whistling breath.

Chekov clasped Uuvu'it's shoulder. "Don't worry. I've got a feeling this will work out."

The Betelgeusian rallied himself. "Of course, sir. This is the fight I've been waiting for to earn my name at last." His lower mouth snarled. "Right now, I feel unbeatable."

Kirk nodded to Chekov. "Go."

The security chief glanced back at Kirk, his expression a condensed form of their familiar argument: He wished his captain would stay behind in safety, but was resigned to the knowledge that it wasn't going to happen. Still, Kirk had learned to accept going in second.

He did so now, following Chekov through the doors into the starboard entry hallway and then out into the rec deck's large atrium. In the near ground, security guards Worene, Vidmar, and Sakamoto were engaged in hand-to-hand combat with two armored intruders. Both wore similar body armor—all-concealing, blank-faced, seemingly semiorganic, with belt-like waist sections framing central crystals. The one on Kirk's right was in red and black with four claw-like protrusions framing its mask and pointing in toward its center, giving it a hostile, frowning mien. The other, slightly smaller one wore golden-brown armor with mask, belt, and boots in brighter gold, its helmet smooth and nearly featureless save for two small, tapered bulges at the temples, suggesting stubby devil's horns. That one had apparently just emerged from a side lounge . . . and was holding a pronged dagger covered in blue and red blood.

Naazh indeed, Kirk thought, recalling Thelin's name for them. He didn't know what the ferocious phantoms of Andorian myth looked like, but these warriors certainly seemed to be reasonable facsimiles.

Beyond the Naazh and the guards, Kirk saw several other personnel forming a defensive line in front of the Aenar refugees: the New Humans Daniel Abioye and Jade Dinh, the Kazarite Zabish, and the Argelian Palur, who was standing guard over an unconscious Shantherin th'Clane. The Aenar themselves huddled together to the rear of the rec deck behind their leaders th'Miraph and zh'Lenthar, before the array of viewports looking out on the *Enterprise*'s starboard nacelle. Unfortunately, the battle was between them and the exits, so they were trapped for the moment. He saw some of them straining hesitantly toward the archways to port. If they could reach the side passageway, they could follow it forward to the port exit hallway, getting out the same way Onami and the children had. But the red Naazh was in position to spot them through the open archways as they passed, so they did not dare to try.

Movement caught his eye on the balcony up above. He spotted Chief DiFalco fleeing from a third, white-armored Naazh with a vaguely insectoid visage, complete with antennae. Kirk promptly raised his phaser pistol and fired at the white Naazh, who merely stopped and turned its eyeless helmet toward him briefly, then resumed its pursuit. Kirk only hoped he'd given DiFalco enough of an extra lead.

Kirk's shot had drawn the attention of the red Naazh. Seemingly in reaction, it broke free of Sakamoto's grip and struck him with a forceful blow, sending him flying into the translucent lift shaft to port of the forward viewscreen. The guard hit hard and fell to the deck, apparently unconscious.

The Naazh then turned to face Kirk, who shouted, "Stand down and identify yourselves! Why have you attacked the Aenar?"

"Do not question me," the red Naazh replied with a filtered voice. "This is not your concern, nor are you ours."

"You've attacked and killed Federation citizens. That makes it my responsibility to stop you."

The red-armored figure laughed. "You can try. But it will end in despair."

Accepting the invitation, Kirk nodded to Chekov. The two of them, Nizhoni, and M'sharna opened fire on the red Naazh with their rifles, while Uuvu'it and Lance flanked the gold Naazh who was facing off with Worene. Thelin stood his ground, analyzing the scene carefully.

"Here's an advance warning," Uuvu'it called to the gold-armored figure. "I'm fairly strong."

The gold Naazh said nothing, merely slashing its vicious-looking dagger toward the Betelgeusian. He twisted away from its swing, and the Naazh took the opportunity to spin around and launch a kick at Worene, who had been lunging at it from behind. Even the lithe Aulacri could not change course fast enough to evade the kick, which knocked her back and over a toppled chair.

Meanwhile, Kirk saw Chief DiFalco emerge tentatively from the side stairwell at starboard aft. Spotting the fallen, semiconscious th'Clane on the deck near her, she moved to help him to his feet. There was no sign yet of her pursuer; Kirk hoped its armor would impede its descent of the narrow spiral stairway.

Chekov and M'sharna had moved to flank the red Naazh, while Nizhoni hung back with Kirk. Their rifle fire failed to overcome the red Naazh, even when Vidmar joined in from behind. "Hand to hand," Chekov ordered, gesturing M'sharna forward. The bulbous-eyed Saurian laid down his rifle and dove into the fray, landing several blows. The Naazh gave as good as it got, but M'sharna's exceptional strength and endurance served him well, keeping him in the fight.

Meanwhile, the recovered Worene clambered onto the fallen chair and gave a feline yowl as she leaped toward the gold Naazh, who had just knocked down Casey Lance with an acrobatic kick. The force of the Aulacri's lithe body landing on the Naazh from behind before it could fully recover was enough to knock it over, and Uuvu'it joined Worene in trying to pin the struggling figure to the deck.

Kirk spotted a small blue figure moving among the cluster of white Aenar faces to the rear. He touched Thelin's shoulder to get his attention. Taking advantage of the red Naazh's distraction, young Cheremis was slipping into the portside passageway, out of the enemies' sight. The other Aenar could have followed, but instead they simply huddled together fearfully in front of the entranceway. Even the firebrand zh'Lenthar was acting too paralyzed to move. Kirk immediately understood what they were doing. If more of them tried for the side passage, it would draw the Naazh's attention to the girl. They were choosing to remain in harm's way so Thelin's daughter would have a chance to escape. For once, both zh'Lenthar and the elder th'Miraph were acting in total harmony.

Determined not to let their courage be in vain, Kirk nodded subtly to Thelin. "Go," he whispered. The pale Andorian nodded thanks and began edging unobtrusively to port.

Breaking free of M'sharna's hold at last, the red Naazh jumped back and placed a curled hand in front of the crystal on its waist. The crystal glowed, and to Kirk's amazement, the Naazh *drew a sword from it*. The blade was as long as its arm, impossible to contain in a fist-sized crystal, yet the scarlet-armored hunter drew it out as if from a magic portal.

The sword flickered with energy as the unknown being struck at M'sharna, slicing through his body armor. The Saurian spun and fell to the ground, trembling. The Naazh turned away, no longer concerned with its opponent, and Chekov and Nizhoni moved forward to drag M'sharna to relative safety.

The red Naazh strode toward Abioye and Dinh, who stood their ground in front of the huddled Aenar, even though they were unarmed. DiFalco came to their aid by picking up th'Clane's fallen phaser rifle and firing it at the red Naazh. The weapon's multiple beams slowed it only slightly.

But then the Naazh staggered back, and Kirk saw Zabish stretching his hands toward the armored figure. Kazarite telekinesis was not very strong as a rule, but Kirk had heard that they could sometimes intensify it *in extremis*, at considerable metabolic cost. The Naazh was only briefly affected, though, continuing to stride forward with minor difficulty as Zabish persisted.

Abioye and Dinh flanked the Kazarite, joined their hands with his, and closed their eyes. Somehow, they managed to amplify Zabish's psionic push, forcing the Naazh slightly backward. Seeing this, DiFalco returned the rifle to the recovering th'Clane and moved to join her fellow New Humans.

Meanwhile, the gold Naazh had regained its footing, but Worene and Uuvu'it's teamwork and fierceness were keeping it fully occupied. Kirk allowed himself to hope the tide was turning.

Just then, the white Naazh emerged from the side stairs. It touched its white belt crystal with its left hand, and a sidearm materialized out of nowhere in its outstretched right hand. Kirk immediately opened fire on the antennaed figure, hoping at least to draw its attention away from the others. It had little effect, though; the white, insectile Naazh fired on the Aenar, instantly felling the elder th'Miraph with a searingly bright plasma bolt. Kirk felt the other Aenar's grief and terror surge across his mind.

The distraction broke Zabish's concentration, and the red Naazh lunged forward and knocked the Kazarite back with a kick. DiFalco, Abioye, and Dinh toppled back with him, staring up in fear as the red Naazh raised its sword to strike them down. "Now," it intoned with finality, "count up your sins!"

"Nooo!" Even as the glowing, crackling blade descended, Joshua Vidmar threw himself into its path. The blade pierced him clear through his upper back just below the neck, and he trembled and convulsed horrifically as its energies discharged into his body. The Naazh yanked its blade clear, and Vidmar fell limp to the deck, unquestionably dead.

The gold Naazh stared, then finally spoke, its filtered voice angry. "He was not our quarry!"

"He chose to intercede," the red one replied coldly. "I did warn them."

Kirk's next order was just as cold. "All personnel—set phasers to kill."

"Vidmar is dead," Commander Chekov reported over the bridge speakers. *"Three other guards are down, along with one of the Aenar leaders. The intruders are . . . materializing weapons out of thin air! The shields have no effect!"*

Spock rested his elbows on the command chair's arms and steepled his fingers, frowning in concern. By his side, Doctor McCoy was his usual unhelpful self. "Damn it, Spock, we've got to do something!"

By his other side stood Miranda Jones, whose shared consciousness with Kollos offered a more helpful observation. "Could they be drawing these weapons from extradimensional space?"

Spock raised an intrigued brow toward her—or rather, them. Medusans did appear to have extensive expertise in higher-dimensional physics, which Spock had long suspected was an element in their navigational skill. "It would explain how they got on board despite our shields. Rather than going through them, they simply went around them in a higher dimension."

"Please tell me that actually helps us," McCoy said, "and isn't just some curious mathematical conundrum."

"I think it does," Jones/Kollos replied, their animation suggesting that the Medusan persona was currently dominant. "If we go to warp, the continuum distortion might disrupt their access to whatever dimensional domain they're drawing from."

"Indeed it might," Spock replied. He used the arm controls to tap into the open comm line to the captain, relaying the ambassador's suggestion.

"Worth a try, Spock," Kirk replied. *"Take us out of orbit. Engage warp as soon as we're clear!"*

"Acknowledged. Commander Sulu, break orbit and ready for emergency warp."

Executing that command, even in an emergency, took more time in Andorian orbit than it would have in many cases, for first Uhura had to notify Andorian Space Control of the emergency departure, while Sulu had to wait until the navigator charted a safe path clear of local traffic. Still, it was a mere forty-three seconds before Sulu managed to launch the *Enterprise* into warp. Spock did not bother to report this to the captain, for the jump to warp would have been clearly visible through the recreation deck's aft windows. He merely sat and waited to hear if the tactic had any effect.

Alongside Captain Kirk, Pavel Chekov concentrated his rifle fire on the red Naazh, controlling his aim carefully. He understood the captain's order to escalate to the kill setting, even with civilians present; the risk to their lives from the enemy was imminent enough to outweigh the risk of friendly fire. Still, he could never live with himself if his aim slipped.

At least he could take comfort that Commander Thelin's daughter was safe. The science officer had taken advantage of the red Naazh's distraction to coax her forward through the side passage and had slipped out of the rec room with her moments before. Meanwhile, Ensign Howard had reported that the last part-Aenar child, Getran, had been found crawling through a Jefferies tube on F deck. All the children were safe—now it was just a matter of saving the fifty-odd adult Aenar who remained.

Meanwhile, Uuvu'it and th'Clane were pinning down the white Naazh with rifle fire, desperate to keep it from killing any more Aenar. Nizhoni had moved to join Worene in fighting the gold one hand to hand. The amplified phaser fire finally seemed to be taking its toll on the other two, leaving glowing gouges in their armor.

But then the red Naazh touched its belt crystal again, the white following suit. In tandem, both their upper torsos were cocooned in white light, which faded to reveal new, heavier body armor. The new armor's thick crystalline plates simply swallowed up the multiple rifle beams without being affected, like the reverse of how the red Naazh had drawn its sword from its belt crystal.

Chekov glanced at the rear ports, seeing the streaked starlight of warp space beyond. "It didn't work!" he said to the captain.

"Follow my lead!" Kirk called, then raised his rifle to strike at the red Naazh's opaque helmet. Chekov saw his goal: even if they couldn't penetrate the armor, at least they could attempt to block whatever the intruders were using for vision.

To aft, th'Clane followed suit with the white Naazh, and Uuvu'it rashly took the opportunity to duck in under the rifle beams and wrestle the alien firearm from the intruder's hand. "Ha!" the Betelgeusian crowed, turning the gun on its owner as th'Clane held his own fire. "Not so effective when you can't see, are you?" Catching himself, he glanced over at the Aenar. "Uh, no offense."

"You're starting to vex me," the white Naazh growled at Uuvu'it.

"You'll be more vexed when I finish you!" Uuvu'it pressed the firing stud.

The white Naazh laughed as it held out its hand. With a flicker of light, the gun vanished from Uuvu'it's grip and reappeared in its own. "You talk too much," it said, and fired.

The bolt drilled through Uuvu'it's breastplate, blasting its gray-and-brown material apart in a spray of incandescent fragments, mixed with dark violet Betelgeusian blood. With a piercing, hawklike cry, Uuvu'it convulsed and fell to the deck, the impact dislodging the helmet from his bald, dark blue head.

"Hrii'ush!" Worene cried in anguish. The gold Naazh had frozen at the sight, giving Worene an opening to leap to her fallen friend's side. Even the red Naazh had paused to observe the scene.

"Was that necessary?" the gold Naazh demanded.

The white one tilted its antennaed head dismissively. "A sacrifice for the greater good."

Worene cradled Uuvu'it's head in her lap, her feral features twisted in grief. But Uuvu'it gasped a chirping laugh, seeming pleased with himself. "At last," he wheezed. "This will . . . finally . . . earn my name."

Uuvu'it slumped, and Chekov knew that the vivid, intense, frustrating Betelgeusian who had been a welcome thorn in his side for so long would never move again. "You Cossacks!" he cried, resuming fire on the red Naazh, and taking advantage of its distraction to circle around it closer to the New Humans and the Aenar. Worene gave a low, frightening feline growl and pounced on the white Naazh, while th'Clane moved in to back her up. The gold Naazh merely stood there, shrugging off Nizhoni's renewed fire.

Miranda Jones's voice came over his wrist communicator, and he heard an echo of it from Kirk's. *"Captain, this is Ambassador Kollos. My habitat is outside the rec deck, and I have a last-ditch plan."*

Kirk raised the communicator to his face. "I'm listening, Ambassador."

"I wish to enter and let the Naazh see me. Do you understand?"

Chekov saw that Kirk grasped the proposal, and so did he. Kollos clearly hoped that the Naazh would be incapacitated by the sight of a Medusan.

"It's too risky," Kirk said. "We don't know how they'll react—it could make them *more* violent."

"That hardly seems possible, Captain. At least it would disorient them long enough for me to get the Aenar out."

"Assuming their helmets don't filter out the effect."

"Unlikely. Filters have to be designed specifically for that purpose."

"What about sighted personnel?" Chekov asked.

"You'll have to withdraw for your own safety. I assure you, my habitat is robust, and Medusans are difficult to kill. Trust us, Captain. This is the lateral move we need."

Chekov watched the decision play across Kirk's face. But he was James Kirk, so he arrived at his decision swiftly. "All right, Ambassador. Come in." He raised his voice. "All personnel! Retreat and form up on me!"

"Wise choice," the red Naazh said. "I told you the rest of you were free to go."

By now, the Aenar had retreated into the rear corner of the deck, and zh'Lenthar looked outraged and betrayed at their apparent abandonment. But the New Humans held their line. Palur helped the injured Zabish stagger over to Chekov, but DiFalco held his gaze unflinchingly. "We aren't going anywhere," she said. "With your permission . . . we all choose to stay and fight. They're family, sir."

"What about . . . Kollos?" he implored her. The Aenar would be safe from the sight of him, but the New Humans were another matter.

"We'll take our chances. At worst, Doctor Jones can help us afterward, like she did for Spock."

Chekov turned to the captain. Kirk held DiFalco's gaze for a long moment, then nodded, gesturing to Chekov to follow him out. With luck, he'd have the chance to apologize to zh'Lenthar and the Aenar in a little while.

As Ambassador Kollos's habitat hovered into the rec deck, the surviving guards evacuated briskly, keeping up fire on the Naazh in hopes of slowing them down temporarily. The Naazh chuckled as they stood patiently, for they seemed to be getting what they wanted. Chekov prayed this wasn't a mistake.

Palur and Zabish followed Chekov out, and the remaining guards gathered up the wounded Lance, Sakamoto, and M'sharna, helping them out into the corridor along with the others. Doctor Chapel was already on hand with a medical team, and they soon swept the wounded away on antigrav stretchers.

"Now what?" Chekov asked the captain.

"Now . . . we wait. And trust that Kollos knows what he's talking about."

They waited, but for long moments, nothing happened. In time, Doctor Jones emerged from the nearby turbolift and joined them outside the rec deck entrance. "Any word from inside, Doctor?" Kirk asked.

She shook her head. "Kollos is concentrating on his attack. The effect Medusans have on humanoids . . . it's involuntary, but they know how to amplify it if they need to."

Chekov stared. "They have never told us that."

Her icy gaze turned in his direction. "Can you blame them? They're feared enough as it is."

"Let's hope," Kirk said grimly, "that this Medusan lives up to his mythical namesake. And that the Naazh don't have a Perseus among them."

Jones frowned at him. "Are you so sure Kollos isn't the Perseus here? After all, there were three Gorgon sis—"

The deck shook, and a deafening blast sounded within the rec deck. Chekov staggered, and by the time he regained his footing, a decompression alarm was sounding. His first impulse was to rush inside—but if the deck was decompressed, he'd be unable to open the doors.

Doctor Jones gasped. "Kollos!" she cried, then fainted into Kirk's arms.

"Doctor! Miranda!" The captain called her name again, but could not revive her. "Nizhoni, get her to sickbay."

With this done, Kirk raised his communicator to his lips. "Kirk to bridge. Spock, report!"

The Vulcan's voice was uncharacteristically tentative. *"Captain . . . the entire recreation deck has been breached to vacuum.*

The aft windows and hull were ruptured by a massive burst of energy, cause unknown. The energy discharge in proximity to the starboard nacelle's acquisition sink destabilized our warp field and triggered an emergency shutdown. We have returned to normal space."

"Life signs?"

A longer pause. "*Sensors show . . . no life signs, and no bodies. Any . . . remains . . . must have been vaporized in the blast or jettisoned in the decompression.*"

"My God," Kirk breathed, and Chekov understood why. Sucked out into space, and into a collapsing warp field . . . there would be nothing left to identify or bury. Just a trail of molecules scattered across a billion cubic kilometers.

"We've lost," Kirk said heavily. "The Aenar . . . are extinct."

Seven

It took more than a day for the *Enterprise* to limp back to Andoria at low warp, the most its damaged spaceframe could handle. Sector Headquarters offered to send a tug, but Kirk felt it important for morale to bring the ship in under her own power. The crew felt helpless enough as it was.

Spock shared somewhat in the crew's frustration, in large part due to his inability to explain just what had caused the explosion that had destroyed the recreation deck and all who remained within. Whatever Kollos had done to amplify his disruptive neurological effects had disrupted internal sensors as well, and Spock had been unable to extract any useful data from the noise.

"Can you at least speculate?" Kirk asked as he, Thelin, and McCoy stood around Spock's science station on the bridge.

Spock frowned up at him. "You know I dislike speculating."

"Yes, but you have a pretty good record at it nonetheless. So I keep asking."

Emitting a sigh of mild exasperation, Spock leaned back in his seat and steepled his fingers. "It is conceivable that one of the Naazh, rendered mentally unstable by the sight of Kollos, inadvertently or intentionally summoned an explosive device from their extradimensional space."

Thelin frowned at him. "They were so traumatized by the sight of a Medusan that they were driven to suicide?"

"Or they attempted to summon a different weapon and selected the explosive device by mistake." Spock shook his head. "However, it is a problematical conjecture. If they had such a device in their arsenal, why not use it on the Aenar compound in the first place rather than resorting to blades and small arms?"

"I said it before," McCoy said. "Some sick types like to kill for sport."

"I did get that impression from the massacre site," Thelin said. "But that raises the reciprocal question: If hunting their prey individually was their goal, why have such a powerful explosive in their arsenal at all? It is logically inconsistent."

"Maybe it was an accident," Kirk suggested. "The way they were able to materialize armor and weapons at will, from some kind of higher dimension . . . that had to take a lot of energy."

"Their crystals did appear to respond to their intentions," Thelin said. "And our scans of the crystals recorded a psion-particle signature consistent with readings from the massacre site. If they were thought-controlled, then a Naazh suffering from exposure to the sight of Kollos might have inadvertently triggered an overload or self-destruct sequence."

"Granted," Spock replied. "However, their technology appeared quite advanced. It seems unlikely that it would lack basic safeguards to prevent catastrophic failure from user error alone. The steps necessary to create an overload would likely have been too complex for a mentally impaired individual to execute, certainly not before Kollos could have observed it and intervened."

McCoy was skeptical. "Let me remind you that the last time Kollos showed his face—or whatever—to someone aboard this ship, it led to Larry Marvick throwing our engines into overdrive and somehow flinging us clear out of the universe. *That* took some pretty complex steps."

"And I can assure you," Spock replied, "that the ambassador deeply regretted that unintended consequence of his act of self-defense. I am certain he would not have repeated the tactic lightly or recklessly."

"I agree," Kirk said. "Naturally, it was a calculated risk, a desperation move. There were plenty of things that could've gone wrong. But if either Kollos or I had thought anything remotely *this* bad was possible, he never would've suggested it and I never would've approved it." He paused, emotions fulminating behind his eyes. "I *have* to believe that Kollos knew what he was doing. As far as I'm concerned, he was a hero. He sacrificed his life in the attempt to defend the Aenar and the *Enterprise*, and that's how he should be remembered."

The memorial service was difficult for Hikaru Sulu. He had been close to both Marcella DiFalco and Hrii'ush Uuvu'it in different ways, and all he wanted was to weep for them and lean on his remaining friends for support. But as second officer, it was incumbent upon him to support the rest of the crew, to speak to them of the fallen and help them process their own grief. It was a struggle to find the right words, and to say them without breaking down.

"Marcella was always the kind of person who got carried away with her enthusiasms," he said to the gathered crew in the arboretum. "I admit, I found most of them kind of frivolous—and I'm one to talk, I know." The comment spawned more laughter than it deserved; the crew needed the release. "So the truth is, I never took her belief in the New Human movement all that seriously. No denying, she did develop some esper skills, but I figured it was just another fancy that would pass in time. Even two years later, I just thought of it as an eccentricity, a sort of game she played with the other espers."

He stopped talking, and it was a few moments before he could start again, his voice trembling. "But I did her, and the other New Humans, a disservice. What they shared wasn't a game—it was a way of life. And when it came down to it, they showed the depth, and the courage, of their convictions. They stayed and fought for their fellow telepaths, even knowing that they would probably die or be driven mad. They acted without thought for themselves . . . because they truly believed they had become part of something greater. Part of a cosmic consciousness that transcended their individual selves." He lowered his head. "I hope they were right."

Talking about Uuvu'it came more easily somehow, even though Sulu had probably been closer to him than to DiFalco these past two years. The Betelgeusian had been an uncomplicated sort, a being of clear ambitions and goals, and one had always known where one stood with him. "I always felt responsible for Hrii'ush and the other 'Geusians. You probably don't know this, but the Betelgeusian exchange program with Starfleet was kind of my idea—or at least, I suggested it in passing to the head of a 'Geusian argosy a few years back, and they liked the idea and made it happen. I'd always liked their people ever since I first encountered them, and I was glad to see them take an interest in Starfleet.

"And I think Hrii'ush took to it better than most. His relentless competitiveness could be annoying, but once you got to know him, you realized that challenging people was his way of making friends with them—and that he'd challenged himself to befriend everyone in the crew. He may have felt jealous later on when Chavi'rru and Shuuri'ik both won the right to go back to the argosies and start their own prides before he did, but I always felt he stuck around the longest because he was in no hurry to leave." He directed a supportive glance toward Worene, who stood with her copper-haired head lowered and her arms and tail wrapped around herself protectively.

"And he, too, gave his life freely when the time came. He was always fearless, embracing his impulses without hesitation—often without thought. But it wasn't selfishness or vanity. Above all else, he was driven to *earn* his successes. To prove himself worthy of a home and family to call his own.

"All Hrii'ush sought was a place where he belonged . . . and so he dedicated himself to protecting the places others belonged. I hope that, at the end, he realized that *we* were his pride all along."

With no New Humans left alive among the crew, it was up to Ensign Palur to attempt to address their loss from a telepath's perspective. "In my people, the empathic gift is rare and jealously guarded. For many Argelians, it is not a trait they would wish to share, for we are a people who pride ourselves on our lives of love and peace, and we believe that knowing the darker sides that others lock away would only create needless strife. But Marcella, Edward, Jade, and Daniel believed that knowing one another's minds gave them greater peace, and greater love for each other. Some may have thought they set themselves apart from humans without their gift, much as my priestess ancestors once did. But I know that they all felt that their gift was evidence of the limitless potential of *all* humans, and it made them feel closer to the rest of you, not more distant. I wish more of us had understood that while they were among us." She wept as she returned to her seat, where Chief Onami embraced her comfortingly.

Commander Thelin spoke only briefly about the fallen Aenar; going into too much detail might seem accusatory toward the crew, so that was best saved for the services on Andoria. Instead, he focused on the courage of their defenders, and expressed his gratitude toward them for choosing to remain in harm's way to allow his daughter a chance to escape. "That selflessness in defense of others was a quality they shared with this vessel's crew," he said, "and I believe that in those final minutes, we and they found a truer understanding than ever before."

Not all of the lives lost had been veteran members of the crew. By all accounts, Specialist T'Nalae had been one of the first casualties, killed in the attempt to protect the Aenar from the gold Naazh. Few of the crew had really known T'Nalae, but Spock spoke movingly of her sacrifice nonetheless.

"T'Nalae believed strongly that all beings should be true to their inherent natures," he said to the gathered crew. "I feared that she interpreted this principle too narrowly, and I expected to have my work cut out for me as a teacher in order to broaden her perspective. But at the end, she greatly exceeded my expectations, and proved that her own truest nature was nobler than she, perhaps, had believed."

Spock also spoke on the loss of Ambassador Kollos, for with Miranda Jones still recovering from their forcible separation, he was the one who had known the ambassador most intimately. "There was much I perceived during my brief joining of minds with Kollos that I could not begin to comprehend, or to express in any language I know. Yet I clearly perceived his essential qualities: his intelligence; his optimism; his joyful curiosity toward all beings, especially the ones most unlike himself. We may rightfully lament that the unknown aggressors that he sacrificed himself to defeat could not share the same joy in infinite diversity. But I can say, at least, that knowing Kollos has given me an improved understanding . . . of the concept of beauty."

"Thank you for your words at the memorial, Spock," Miranda Jones said from her sickbay bed. "I'm sorry I couldn't be there myself."

"You were in no condition to attend," Spock replied. "I regret only my own limited ability to do justice to the ambassador's memory."

Jones was quiet for a time, her expression introspective. This ward was empty aside from them; M'sharna and Sakamoto were still recovering in the opposite ward, but the other injured personnel had all been treated and released.

"I honestly don't know what I could've said if I had been there," she eventually told him in a quiet voice. "I can barely process the idea of Kollos as someone separate from myself.

I . . . I'm a stranger to myself right now. I'd lost track of . . . which parts of me were Miranda and which were Kollos. I'll have to . . . to rediscover that. I feel for something in myself and it isn't there . . . Oh, I thought I knew loneliness before."

Spock gazed at her with sympathy. "I confess I can barely comprehend your experience, for my own merger with Kollos was quite brief," he said. "Still, I may be the one person who has any direct insight into what you have lost. As such, I place myself at your disposal. Whatever you may need, Miranda, I shall endeavor to provide."

She shook her head. "I have no idea what I need. No idea what could help."

He cleared his throat faintly. "There are Vulcan techniques for assisting those who have experienced the death of a bondmate. They involve the use of a mind-meld to allow the bereaved party to draw on another's mental stability and strength. It is not the same, but the methods may be adaptable."

She was silent for a long moment, growing even more still and withdrawn. "No," she said at length. "I can't."

"You need not suffer alone, Miranda. Nine years ago, when I was the one lying in sickbay, you melded with me and helped me fight my way back to sanity. I ask that you allow me to repay the favor."

"Forgive me, Mister Spock," she replied with some bitterness. "But it is not *your* state of mind that concerns me right now. I cannot tolerate sharing my mind with any other but his. Not so soon."

The disadvantage of Spock's choice to acknowledge his emotions was that it left him vulnerable to having them hurt. But he still had his Vulcan disciplines to draw on, so he tempered the feeling, reminding himself of the far deeper pain Jones must now be enduring. No doubt she was retreating behind her old barriers of aloof reserve as a defense mechanism, as she had been prone to do when Spock had first known her.

"I understand," he said in an even tone. "And I apologize for the suggestion. But if there is anything else—"

"All I need right now is to be left alone. Let me sleep."

"Very well." He turned and walked away. He knew she would be no more inclined to accept any empty words wishing her a good rest than he was to offer them.

He noted Doctor Christine Chapel standing in the doorway to the examination room, watching him and Doctor Jones. Nodding at her, he followed her through the exam room into the lab outside the CMO's office. McCoy was currently off duty, recovering from his efforts on behalf of the wounded the previous day, so the office was empty.

"I confess," Spock said once the doors had closed between them and the ward, "I do not know how I can help her."

The brown-haired assistant CMO touched his arm lightly. There was nothing behind it save friendship, for Chapel had long since outgrown her infatuation with Spock. "It's for her to decide what help she needs, and from whom. Don't try to make it your responsibility. That won't help her *or* you."

He nodded, taking in her words. "I understand, Christine."

"What she needs is someone who can help her cope with a fundamental change in her life. Honestly, I'm not sure any of us around here are really qualified for that."

He furrowed his brows. "What is your basis for that skepticism, Doctor?"

Chapel gave a slight chuckle. "The fact that we're all still here." She sighed. "You remember that talk we had a few years back, when I decided I needed to leave the *Enterprise* if I ever wanted to get out from under Leonard's shadow?"

Spock nodded. "I do."

"I said it wouldn't be right away, but soon, once the time felt right. But one thing after another kept coming up, so I kept putting it off. And before I knew it, a year had passed, and then another, and eventually I just resigned myself to seeing out the rest of the five years along with everyone else." She frowned. "No, not 'resigned.' I realized that I was content here, with my friends, more than I might be somewhere else. That having to keep reminding Leonard that I wasn't his head nurse anymore was a small price to pay for what I could achieve aboard the *Enterprise*." The frown became an affectionate smile. "And to his credit, he did get the hang of it in time."

"You suggest that our contentment with our status quo aboard the *Enterprise* has made us complacent, and thus resistant to embracing change."

"That's one way of looking at it, I suppose."

Spock raised a brow, gazing thoughtfully toward the sickbay ward beyond the closed doors. "By happenstance, both Doctor Jones and Commander Thelin have recently raised a similar subject with me, concerning why I have not yet sought command." He turned back to Chapel. "I recall that in the aforementioned conversation four years ago, you were the first to suggest the possibility to me."

She shrugged. "I had change on my mind. Even months after V'Ger, I still didn't believe Admiral Nogura would let Captain Kirk keep the ship—I expected him to get called back to the admiralty at any time. It seemed . . . logical . . . that you might be offered command in his place." She smiled at Spock. "I seem to recall you saying that you weren't in any rush—that you were still savoring your new path. Maybe that helped me change my mind about rushing to leave. There's still time to explore other paths, after this mission is over."

Chapel studied him. "And what about you? Have you given any more thought to exploring the path of command?"

"The matter has been on my mind of late, due to the frequency with which it has been raised in recent days. However, that coincidental convergence is not sufficient in itself to motivate me to make such a decision. For the moment, my attention remains on the Naazh situation and the investigation of the remaining mysteries regarding the affair."

"I'd expect nothing less," Chapel said. "But once the affair is over, what then?"

"Like you, I am content to complete the remaining months of our tour under Captain Kirk's leadership. As for my subsequent choices . . . I shall consider them when the time comes. There is still no need to rush."

Chapel smiled. "That's what I told myself four years ago. Try not to get too comfortable thinking that way."

The next morning, the *Enterprise* docked at Sector Headquarters' orbital spacedock, where it would be berthed for the next two weeks while its entire recreation complex and the damaged portion of the exterior hull were rebuilt. Commander Thelin took his leave then, along with his daughter. Spock saw them off at the main gangway hatch. "It has been a privilege to make your acquaintance, Commander. I regret that our meeting did not have a more positive outcome."

"I am attempting to focus on what positives there are, Mister Spock," Thelin replied. "If nothing else, the threat appears to be ended. The Naazh, for whatever reason, only seemed to target pure Aenar. And the majority of the killers are dead. Kollos achieved that victory, at least. Revenge may not be the Starfleet way," he added, "but the Andorian in me is not ashamed to take some comfort in it. My people will honor the ambassador's sacrifice."

Spock studied him and his child, though Cheremis stood quietly behind him, subdued in the wake of her ordeal. "What do you imagine the legacy of the Aenar will be? Will the surviving hybrids assimilate into Andorian society, or will they attempt to preserve what they can of their unique culture and history?"

Thelin sighed. "I shall strive to preserve whatever *I* can, certainly. I am already planning to petition the government to declare the Aenar compound a historic site, so that the atrocity committed there is never forgotten. If any pro-terraforming factions see the Aenar's effective extinction as free rein to melt the icecaps and see the last of the Aenar's homeland washed away, they will find themselves facing a battle."

"I imagine there will be little sympathy for their position. It is unfortunate that so many humanoids must experience the loss of something before they understand the importance of preserving it. Only in rare circumstances do they have the opportunity to . . . go back . . . and set it right."

Thelin tilted his antennae quizzically. "One day, Mister Spock, I hope you and your captain are free to tell me what it is about me that has occasioned so many meaningful looks and loaded pauses. I presume it involves some classified matter, but I cannot imagine why it would involve me."

Spock almost smiled. "You may trust, Mister Thelin, that any connection of the matter to your life is only . . . at second hand. And it is a matter of the past, resolved many years ago."

"Very well," Thelin replied. "I will pry no further."

"A wise decision." Spock gazed at Cheremis again, and this time he did ever so slightly smile. The smile he received from the girl in return was quick and brilliant. "You have your own future to build, Commander. And I will leave you to it." He raised his hand, fingers split. "Live long and prosper in your world, Commander Thelin."

Thelin furrowed his brow, still confused, but returned the gesture with thanks. "And you in yours, Commander Spock."

Kirk gazed out the tall windows of the officers' lounge, watching the flock of work bees and repair drones installing new hull plates at the rear of the *Enterprise*'s saucer. While he was glad to see his ship's full functionality—and beauty—restored, he found the sight unsatisfying, for in many ways, the wound remained open. He would always regard the loss of the Aenar as one of the greatest failures of his career, even though he could not think of anything he could have done differently. But as long as the Naazh remained a mystery—remained phantoms—his questions and his doubts would linger in his mind.

"Captain," came a familiar voice. He turned to greet Miranda Jones as she emerged from the entry foyer. "I was told I could find you here."

She was quieter, more solemn, than the Jones/Kollos fusion he had come to know over the past two weeks, yet without the prickly pride of her younger self. Still, it was a relief to see her up and about. After two days in sickbay during which she had mostly slept, she had spent another day and a half locked away in her VIP cabin, admitting no visitors.

"How are you feeling?" he asked tentatively, reaching out a hand to guide her down the steps into the seating area before the windows. The old Miranda Jones would have seen it as condescension, and perhaps then it would have been; but now, she welcomed the offered contact.

"That's a hard question to answer, Captain. I'd first have to define who 'I' currently am." She shook her head. "For so long, the two of us were a single consciousness. Kollos and I retained ourselves, but we were blended, the sides of a coin. I barely remember what it was like to be . . . just me." She lowered her head. "Except that it never made me happy."

Kirk took her hand. "I only knew you briefly before you were joined to Kollos," he said. "At the time, I was too young, too blinded by the superficial, to truly appreciate your strengths. I've rarely met anyone with such firm conviction about who they were, in defiance of all others' expectations of who they should be.

"From where I stood, what it was like to be Doctor Miranda Jones . . . was to be radiant."

She gave him a skeptical look. "Trying to flatter me again, Jim?" But her fingers clung to his, and he could sense how much she craved a connection to someone beyond herself.

"After the way you shot me down the first time?" Smiling, he shook his head. "I know better now than to think I could get away with any insincerity around you, Miranda. You're one of the most perceptive individuals I've ever known—extrasensory or otherwise."

Nine years ago, he would have tried to kiss her. In fact, he had, only to get pushed away. Now, he would never try to impose in that way on someone so vulnerable.

So it came as quite a surprise when she kissed him.

"Surprise" was underselling it. The kiss was everything he had imagined back then—and surely would never have gotten from her at the time. It was passionate, warm, open, hopeful, trusting . . .

Vulnerable.

Kirk let himself enjoy the kiss for several moments before working up the self-discipline to push her away. "Miranda . . ."

She flushed, drawing back. "I—I'm sorry, Jim. Captain. That was inappropriate."

"No," he said gently. "I understand why you needed it. And that's . . . why I can't. Not yet. Like you said, you need to find yourself first. Once you know what you want, then . . . Well."

She gave a small, grateful smile, then cleared her throat. "Yes, well. In any case, I can't stay long. I've decided . . . I'm going to Earth. I want to work with the New Humans there. With the way their psionic powers have been growing, maybe . . . they could help me to cope. Fill the void in some limited way. And if I could, I'd like to try to help them cope with the loss of some of their own. As you can imagine, they're an exceptionally close-knit community."

Kirk nodded. As much as he wished he could be her white knight, he knew her fellow telepaths would be better for her.

They could understand her needs in ways he never could. "Of course. I know the New Humans aboard the *Enterprise* held you in the highest esteem. I'm certain they'll welcome you."

Jones straightened her shoulders. "Jim . . . Starfleet should be vigilant. There are still at least two Naazh unaccounted for. The Aenar might not have been the only ones on their hit list."

"I agree," Kirk said. "And so does Admiral Morrow. Rest assured—we will be watching for future attacks."

After a concerned pause, she replied. "I know you'll be watching, Jim. I just pray that you'll be ready."

INTERLUDE

and head them off early, and a turbulent but fulfilling love affair with his fellow flag officer Lori Ciana. But ultimately, he had felt stifled and restless, ill-suited for the role. He had been so desperate to escape it that he had exploited the V'Ger crisis to extort Nogura into giving him the *Enterprise* back, at the expense of his own chosen successor, Will Decker. While he regretted the way he'd gotten the ship back, his uncharacteristic behavior at the time had only proven how desperately unhappy he had been behind that desk. It had only been out on the frontier, protecting the Federation's borders and exploring the strange new worlds beyond them, that he had become himself again, and he had been certain he would never want to give it up.

This time, when Starfleet had called him home after five years, he had been tempted to argue once again. The refitted, upgraded *Enterprise* had been virtually a brand-new ship, its state-of-the-art systems designed for greater longevity, so the five-year maximum was no longer a necessary policy. The Starfleet Corps of Engineers' request to conduct a detailed, months-long diagnostic assay of the ship's prototype systems to assess their long-term performance was not unreasonable, but the timing seemed arbitrary, a relic of outmoded conventions.

Yet when the order to return home had come, Kirk had thought it over and decided not to object. The ship may have been able to handle another several years before needing a refit, but the crew was another matter. The painful losses sustained in the Aenar tragedy seven months before had taken their toll. The crew had lost a fair number of its own over the past five years, an unavoidable hazard of starship life—though fortunately a good deal fewer than on the previous five-year tour, thanks to improved defensive and medical technology, Kirk's greater experience at recognizing and preparing for danger, and Chekov's fierce protectiveness of the people under his care as security chief. But the crew could feel that most of those people had given their lives for a purpose—that their sacrifice had made a difference. That could not be said of the victims of the Naazh. Moreover, the violence had struck painfully close to home. The rec deck had been the spiritual heart of the ship's community, the bustling hub of its social life, where personnel from an unprecedented variety of different species had intermingled and grown closer, the essence of the Federation in microcosm. Losing it, and half a dozen of their shipmates with it, had been a wrenching blow to the crew's morale, robbing them of their safe space. The engineers at Andorian Sector Headquarters had built a fully redesigned and upgraded entertainment center in its place, yet the crew had barely used it, instead choosing to congregate in the arboretum and swimming pool on T deck, in the various observation lounges around the ship, or in makeshift ball courts in the cargo bays.

Indeed, more than a few personnel had already transferred off ahead of schedule, preferring to move on with their lives and careers. M'sharna had been badly enough injured to be mustered out anyway, while a number of other enlisted personnel had simply resigned and gone back to civilian life. A few had chosen to cope with the tragedy by pursuing more positive goals; Shantherin th'Clane had transferred to Andorian Sector Headquarters, hoping to follow Thelin's lead in making a positive difference for his people, while Crewman Worene had decided to enroll in Starfleet Academy and become the first Aulacri officer in the fleet—her way of carrying forward Hrii'ush Uuvu'it's relentless drive to improve and raise his status. Even Doctor Chapel had finally decided it was time to move on, accepting a research post at Starfleet's Sector HQ in the Regulus system.

Thus, while Kirk was still determined to retain a starship command, he had accepted that it did not have to be with this crew, or even aboard this ship. Thirteen years ago, when he had been transferred to the *Enterprise* from the *Sacagawea*, he had been sure that he would never find a ship he loved as dearly as that stalwart little scout. But he had discovered an even deeper love for the *Enterprise*, and if that had happened once, maybe it could happen again with yet another ship. Or maybe he would simply command some other ship on a short-term mission, then return to the *Enterprise* when she was deemed ready for her next tour. But the rest of the crew deserved their chance to move on.

As the *Enterprise* sailed through the Spacedock doors at last, Kirk rose from the command chair, and Spock and McCoy moved into their accustomed places at his side. *"As if you've always been there, and always will,"* a cherished voice said in his memory. He smiled at them both, and met the eyes of the rest of the bridge crew in turn.

"My friends . . . welcome home. And thank you all for your service."

McCoy took a deep, satisfied breath. "Home at last. We could all certainly use the rest." He then turned a wary eye on Kirk. "Just promise me that this time you've learned your lesson. That we'll be back out here in a few months, once the engineers have gotten their fill."

"Don't worry, Bones," Kirk assured him. "This time, things will be different."

Starfleet Headquarters, San Francisco

"The Academy?" Kirk stared at Harry Morrow across the latter's desk, stunned by the admiral's words. "Nogura wants me to be the commandant?"

"I know it's not what you hoped for, Jim," Morrow said with a shrug. Behind him, the Golden Gate Bridge slowly emerged into view as the sun burned the morning fog away. "But Charlie Plaine's sudden retirement was unexpected. The Narumiya Science Institute on Aldebaran III needed a new director, and he couldn't pass up the opportunity to run his alma mater, to repay them for all they gave him."

Kirk nodded. "I can understand that."

"I'm glad to hear that, because you're basically getting the same opportunity. Along with a promotion back to admiral, now that Charlie won't be using his bars anymore." Morrow's fingers idly brushed the rank pin on the shoulder strap of his maroon uniform tunic. Kirk wondered why Starfleet's quartermaster corps could never seem to stick with a uniform design for longer than a single five-year duty tour. He kept coming back home to find himself behind the fashion curve.

"But why me?"

"It's not like you haven't taught at the Academy before, Jim."

"Briefly, as a lieutenant."

"And effectively. I was in the same class as Gary Mitchell, remember? I took your course, and it was more challenging than most of the ones from veteran instructors."

In his mind, Kirk heard Gary Mitchell putting it more bluntly, as he always had: *A stack of books with legs . . . In his class, you either think—or sink.*

Morrow leaned forward. "So just imagine how good you'd be now, after ten, twelve years as a starship captain."

"Close to fifteen, counting the *Sacagawea*."

Morrow waved it off. "The numbers don't matter. The point is, you've achieved more in that time than many captains achieve in their entire careers. You have a wealth of experience to share with the next generation of officers. You could help shape the future of Starfleet."

Kirk had to admit to himself that the idea was intriguing. He hadn't taken to administration the first time, when he had been making decisions about ships, resources, and personnel at a distance. But being the Academy's commandant—essentially its dean of students—could be more hands-on, a post where he could work directly with the faculty and the cadets in their charge. It would be more like commanding a starship crew, but on a larger scale—and with far fewer funerals for the people under his authority. That part appealed to him greatly.

The thought sobered him, and raised a question in his mind. "Is that all Nogura has in mind, Harry? The last time, he had me promoted for political reasons. Are you sure this isn't about what happened with the Aenar and the Naazh?"

Morrow's gaze was steady. "You're not being punished for that, Jim. If the Medusans had blamed you for the loss of Ambassador Kollos, you would've heard about it months ago. They were remarkably understanding about the whole affair. And I think the Andorian government mostly blamed itself for neglecting the Aenar—or rather, the electorate blamed them, and voted out any officials who'd try to put the blame on you to protect themselves."

The admiral stood and came around his desk, leaning on its forward edge and folding his hands before him. He smiled at Kirk. "Trust me, Jim, nobody's punishing you for that incident except yourself. It was a heavy loss, sure, but one of the few among five years of remarkable successes—V'Ger, Lorina, Empyrea, Yannid VI, the Vedala incident . . . do I need to go on?" Kirk shook his head.

"Bottom line, Jim, your orders have already been cut. You get six weeks' leave, and then you report to the Academy as its new commandant. I know it's not the starship posting you wanted, but orders are orders." He shrugged. "If you're really hell-bent on staying out there, you could always retire, like Charlie Plaine. I bet the Narumiya Institute would welcome an experienced captain for one of its research vessels."

The suggestion held little appeal for Kirk. He could imagine Spock being content doing pure research as a civilian, but Starfleet was in Kirk's genes, going back to his great-grandparents aboard the *Pioneer*. He couldn't imagine walking away from it. But he couldn't imagine spending the rest of his career on the ground either.

Fortunately, he'd had five years to think about what he'd do if he ever found himself in this position again. This time, he had a counteroffer ready. "I think there's a better option, Harry. A way Nogura and I can both get what we want. But I may need your help to sell it to him."

Earth Spacedock

"I knew it!" Leonard McCoy shouted. "This is Nogura's revenge for the way you defied him five years ago. I knew he'd find a way to get you back behind a desk eventually."

"Easy, Bones," Kirk replied. The two of them and Spock were in the upper level of one of the multistory lift cars that ran through Spacedock's central travel core like oversized glass elevators. The five-kilometer-high, mushroom-shaped orbital station was so huge and busy that even the extensive network of normal turbolifts within it was not sufficient to accommodate the movement of its staff and visitors between its vertically stacked sections. The three of them were lucky to have this level of the car to themselves for the moment, but that could easily change.

"Nogura can be demanding," Kirk went on, "but he's not vindictive or arbitrary. Whatever decisions he makes, they're in the best interests of Starfleet as a whole."

"But not in the best interests of individual officers. Jim, we went through this the first time you were promoted. I *resigned* over it then! You'll wither away behind a desk. You'll never be happy without a starship to command."

"Bones." His tone was firm enough to halt McCoy's tirade. "Give me some credit for learning from experience. This isn't like the last time. Yes, I'll be an admiral again." He smiled. "But the thing about flag officers is . . . we get to have flagships."

Spock raised an eyebrow. "Intriguing. 'Flagship' is normally a temporary designation for the vessel from which a flag officer commands a squadron of ships. Are you proposing a more permanent assignment?"

The lift chimed to signal their arrival at their destination. The doors opened, and the three men strode out into the executive office complex that surrounded the travel core shaft. "Harry Morrow and I have already sold Nogura on the idea, though it took some doing. For the duration of my tenure as Academy commandant, the *Enterprise* will be attached to the Academy as the flagship of its contingent of training vessels, and therefore as my own flagship."

"Big deal," McCoy said, still unconvinced. "So the *Enterprise* gets a fancy new title attached to it and sticks close to home, while you still sit behind a desk. How is that any different from before?"

Kirk led the others through the exit into the large, domed recreational area beyond. This vast open space, more than a kilometer in diameter and nearly as high, was landscaped to resemble a variety of Earth terrains, with the sections subdivided by market streets representing a number of Earth's major regional cultures. It might have seemed redundant for a station in Earth orbit to go to such lengths to duplicate Earth, when the real thing was just a transporter beam away. But the facility was for the benefit of wayfarers who were stopping off at Spacedock for brief periods and were unable or unwilling to go through the necessary customs and medical checks to be cleared for travel to Earth's surface. As such, it was a version of Earth tailored for the expectations and convenience of offworld tourists—which could be endlessly amusing for an Earth native to experience.

More to the point, the attempts of alien entrepreneurs to approximate terrestrial dining experiences in a manner suited to their species' palates had occasionally spawned some intriguing fusion cuisines. Ever since Kirk's old science officer Rhenas Sherev had introduced him to the phenomenon, Kirk had always taken the opportunity to sample Spacedock's culinary scene whenever he returned to Earth after years away.

For now, though, he simply strolled along the paths of the too-perfect pseudo-Earthly landscape, watching the way the alien tourists and itinerants around him drank it up like some exotic wonder, and enjoying the role reversal. "The difference," he finally got around to explaining to McCoy, "is that neither I nor the *Enterprise* will stay idle. I've proven that I can do Starfleet more good in the field, and Nogura's accepted that. So I'll still be taking the ship out on periodic missions."

"Like what?" McCoy asked. "You mean like Academy training cruises, combat simulations, that sort of thing?"

"Occasionally, but not just that. If I see a situation that needs to be addressed, a problem that needs a special touch or a particular expertise, then I'll assemble an appropriate crew and command the mission. For instance, if there's a medical crisis, I could call on you, Doctor Chapel, and other medical experts as needed. If it's a delicate interspecies negotiation, I could bring Uhura and a team of top diplomats. Supported by a crew of upper-class cadets as part of their field training, as long as the mission isn't too hazardous." He tilted his head. "It won't be quite the same as having all of us together on an ongoing basis, but it's a chance for us to keep working together periodically on the *Enterprise*, with the flexibility to pursue other missions, or other interests, in the interim." He gestured toward McCoy with an open hand. "You could work out of Starfleet Medical, Bones, and only go out on the ship when I needed you. No more drudgery of routine crew physicals, and you could go home to your cabin on weekends."

"It's not me I'm worried about, Jim. This arrangement sounds good on paper, but how do you know Nogura will live up to his end of it? Or how do you know you won't get so bogged down with grading exams and making lesson plans that you don't have time to be a, a roving troubleshooter?"

Kirk grinned at him. "For one thing, because I have faith that you'll be there to drag me out of my office if I start to spend too much time there. For another, I have Harry Morrow on my side. He'll be keeping an eye out for missions to send my way. And as commandant, I'll get to restructure the Academy's training protocols, so field assignments like these can be built into the curriculum. I'll be doing both my jobs at once."

McCoy fell silent, appeased for now, but he still looked skeptical. Kirk was counting on that skepticism to keep him honest, as he always had.

They soon reached the restaurant Kirk had been hoping to try, a Saurian take on Indian cuisine, reportedly so intensely spicy that human diners took their lives and sanity into their hands. McCoy griped about Kirk's need to test himself to his limits even on leave, and settled for the salad. Kirk dared to sample their most infamous curry dish, which was so intense and consciousness-altering that he thought he had a momentary flashback to his time under Tristan Adams's neural neutralizer. When he recovered, he saw Spock placidly consuming his with little more than a raised eyebrow and a verbal estimate of Scoville Heat Units.

Afterward, as Kirk soothed his taste buds with a generous piece of Goan coconut cake topped with *gatsu* nuts from Sauria's Vasakleyro rainforest, Spock returned to their earlier discussion. "One matter remains unaddressed. If the *Enterprise* is to be a flagship under your authority as an admiral, it will still require a captain of its own. Does Admiral Nogura or Admiral Morrow have a candidate in mind for that position?"

Kirk smiled at him. "Getting to handpick my own captain is part of the deal. And I'm convinced there's only one man for the job." He held Spock's gaze meaningfully.

Finally the Vulcan caught on and pulled back in surprise. "You refer to me, Jim?"

"I do, Spock. I want you to be captain of the *Enterprise*."

After a few moments of stunned silence, McCoy spoke up. "Well, don't just sit there like a stone idol, say something, Spock!"

Folding his hands before him, Spock replied slowly. "I will admit that I have been considering the possibility of late. While I have never sought command for myself, it was pointed out to me some months ago by Commander Thelin that command is not something we do for ourselves, but for others. I concede that there would be value in using my experience and knowledge to guide others—and in moving forward in the Starfleet hierarchy so that I do not impede others' advancement." He frowned. "But surely I could achieve that goal as an instructor at the Academy, for example. I would be more comfortable in a position that allowed me the opportunity to teach and to conduct research, rather than contend with the administrative and policy responsibilities of a starship commander."

"That's the beauty of it, Spock. With the *Enterprise* attached to the Academy, you could do both. The special missions would only be occasional, on an as-needed basis. The rest of the time, the *Enterprise* could serve as a research and training vessel. The majority of the time, you could be a scientist and a teacher—while on special missions, you'd be under my command again, running the ship while I ran the mission. Not so different from being my first officer."

"Superficially, perhaps. Nonetheless, it *would* be different, in ways I cannot yet anticipate." He gave a small sigh. "The truth of it is, I am content where I am. After my epiphany within V'Ger, I attained a new level of peace and personal enlightenment. I finally reconciled with the emotions I had struggled with for so long, and it was with the support of you and the rest of my crewmates that I was given the space to cultivate my new insights. While the past five years have not been without hardship and loss, they have been the greatest period of contentment and personal fulfillment in my life to date. While I intellectually understand that we have arrived at the end of that period in my life, I am irrationally reluctant to see it end."

Kirk and McCoy exchanged a look, unsure how to react.

Even though Spock had come to accept his emotional side, it was still unusual for him to speak of it so openly.

Finally, Kirk leaned forward to catch Spock's eye. "I appreciate what you're saying, Spock. I'm glad that I—that we were able to be a part of that safe environment for you, and I hate to see it come to an end too.

"But consider this: You were able to achieve that contentment after V'Ger because you opened your mind to new options. As a result, you were able to grow and find a new, better equilibrium. So who's to say that, if you take another chance on something new, you won't find yourself even happier as a result?"

Spock took in his words while Kirk finished off his coconut cake. "Very well," he finally said. "I can think of no rational reason to refuse the promotion. Indeed, it could prove to be a worthy challenge. And it would allow us to continue our successful partnership."

"So that's a yes?"

"Indeed. Yes, Jim. I accept command of the *Enterprise*."

McCoy shook his head. "Will wonders never cease? Well, congratulations, you old devil. You've come a long way since that little shuttlecraft on Taurus II."

Spock raised a scathing brow. "Indeed. Though I trust that I will have a more supportive crew than I had then." McCoy winced, his silence conceding the point.

Kirk chuckled and offered his hand to his former first officer. "Yes, congratulations—*Captain* Spock. Trust me: command will change your life in ways you can't imagine."

Western Mediterranean

The New Human enclave was idyllic even by Earth standards. As Spock climbed the path from the seaside shuttle landing platform toward the central villa at the peak of the diminutive private island, he observed numerous humans of a wide range of ages and ethnic subtypes mingling in close-knit groups, engaging in recreational activities or merely communing together in meditation, but all of them engaging in less raucous verbalization than was typical for socializing humans. In this warm Mediterranean climate, most were clad in light, gauzy robes in a variety of festive colors—though a number wore little or no clothing, their undress taken in stride by those around them. His own black Vulcan robes absorbed considerable heat from solar radiation, but that merely made him feel less chilled than he usually did in Earthly climes.

One group walked alongside a pair of horses with small children riding them bareback, and another frolicked with several large, shaggy canines. Spock noted that the animals were without bridle or leash, appearing to respond to mere glances or head turns from the humans.

As Spock passed, a number of the island denizens greeted him with smiles or expressions of polite curiosity and acceptance. Some raised hands in the Surakian salute, while a few put their fingers together in the egg symbol of One, which had been popular in the previous decade among transcendental or countercultural movements such as that of Doctor Sevrin. The New Human movement was, in part, an outgrowth of such groups, which naturally had attracted espers even before the coming of V'Ger and its resultant impact on human spiritual movements.

Spock found Miranda Jones in the courtyard of the main villa, at the center of a group of humans seated lotus style on the ground in meditation. He noted that she was attired only in light robes like the others; her sensor web was not in evidence. Nonetheless, she raised her head and smiled at his approach.

"Welcome, Mister Spock," she said, rising gracefully to her feet and stepping toward him, the group parting around her as she did so. "Or should I say 'Captain Spock'? I suppose congratulations are in order."

"There is little to congratulate," Spock demurred, "for the position was chosen for me through the decisions of others. I see it merely as a career adjustment."

"I congratulate the career that made you worthy of the choice, Spock. I remember commenting not that long ago that you could easily have earned a captaincy well before now."

She began to stroll around the courtyard, with Spock accompanying her. "And Cap— *Admiral* Kirk? How is he taking to his 'career adjustment'?"

"It is too early to tell, for we are both taking leave before beginning our new positions. However, he seems to welcome the challenge of administering Starfleet Academy. I believe he will excel at it."

"Of the two of you, I would've expected you to be the one taking a scholarly path."

"James Kirk never ceases to be a man of surprises."

"So I've found." She tilted her head. "When we first met, I found him superficial, arrogant, and manipulative. When Kollos and I melded with you, we saw another side to him through your eyes. We were grateful for the insight. We . . ."

She trailed off, and Spock sensed the depth of the loss that still preoccupied her. "I apologize. I have reminded you of a source of pain."

Jones smiled up at him sadly. "No, it's all right, Spock. I miss Kollos deeply, but the last thing I want is to stop thinking about him. After nine years together, there is still much of him in me, and I want to preserve that as much as I can."

Spock nodded gravely. "I believe I understand."

"Although being among the New Humans has been a godsend. They really have made remarkable strides in developing their telepathy. It's like they're starting to evolve toward a communal consciousness, something like the corporate intelligence of Kollos and myself. It's not as strong, not a complete union, but it's a very real connection nonetheless. It's helped me feel like part of something greater again, and I've needed that." She sighed. "Going back to Medusa would've just been too painful a reminder, so I'm grateful I have them. And I've been able to help them in turn, to cope with their grief at the loss of their members aboard the *Enterprise*, and the loss of the Aenar."

"Then I am gratified that you—and they—have found that source of comfort."

They had reached a path along a craggy cliff that overlooked the Mediterranean below, with the coast of North Africa visible on the horizon. At the base of the cliff, plainly visible through the clear, pure water, several nude humans frolicked with a small pod of dolphins. Curiously, he extended his psionic senses, catching an echo of communication between the two species. "Fascinating. They have achieved telepathic communication with cetaceans."

"Oh, yes, the dolphins. They have such . . . lyrical minds. Although they can be startlingly feral, and have little respect for boundaries."

"It is quite remarkable how far the New Humans have come in advancing their telepathic proficiency in only the past few years. Has there been any progress in determining an explanation for the phenomenon?"

Jones shrugged. "The prevailing theory, as you know, is that V'Ger's ascension somehow jumpstarted their psychic evolution."

"Which seems unlikely," Spock replied. "Similar increases in telepathic rating among human populations have been reported on multiple planets in the Federation, not merely on Earth."

She gave him a skeptical look. "Didn't you feel V'Ger's mind calling out to you when it was still dozens of parsecs away? You know as well as anyone that some forms of psionic communication are independent of distance, based in nonlocal quantum entanglement."

"That is true. But then, why does the effect only manifest in humans?"

"Perhaps Willard Decker's involvement had something to do with it."

"Perhaps. But it is still puzzling."

"I prefer to call it wondrous." She smiled. "At last, I don't have to feel like the only one of my kind."

Spock studied her, absorbing her words. "In that case, Doctor Jones, I am gratified for you. And it will be intriguing to see how the New Human community continues to evolve."

Once Miranda Jones saw off Spock's shuttle a short while later, Arsène Xiang approached her. *"Some of us wish he could have stayed longer,"* the tall, gray-haired New Human communicated to her silently. *"His mind is strong and serene. We could learn much from him."*

She smiled at him. Xiang had little to learn; he was almost as powerful as she was by now. Indeed, she had chosen him to travel to Regulus and help organize the sizable New Human population there as she had done for the Earth community.

"We could," she sent back. *"But he's too curious about the mystery of New Human abilities."*

"Is that so bad?" Xiang challenged. *"It would be wise to recruit more allies. And fellow telepaths—"*

"This isn't their struggle," Miranda told him. *"Besides . . . would Spock even* be *an ally if he knew the truth about us?"*

2279

Nine

Starfleet Academy, San Francisco
Three months later

"All the comforts of home," Leonard McCoy said as he surveyed the Mark IV bridge simulator, which Kirk was showing off to him after its latest upgrade. "It looks just like the *Enterprise* now. Feeling homesick?"

Kirk smiled, one hand resting casually on the back of the command chair. "Don't forget, I still have the real thing at my beck and call. This is for the cadets. Since they'll be doing field training on the *Enterprise* under Spock, they should be familiarized on an equivalent bridge. Among others, of course." He gestured vaguely toward the other simulator rooms that shared this wing of the Starfleet Training Command building's second floor, each customized to represent a different bridge configuration.

McCoy shook his head. "Spock as a teacher. Those cadets are in for a rough ride."

"Just the way it should be," Kirk snapped with a gleam in his eyes. "You can't bring out the best in people by going easy on them."

"Think or sink, right?" McCoy said. He'd heard the stories about Kirk's Academy lectures as a lieutenant.

"Exactly. Space won't go easy on these kids, so we can't either."

McCoy peered warily beneath the consoles. "So does that mean they still have live charges for the *Kobayashi Maru* test?"

Kirk smiled. "They're holographic now. Mostly."

The doctor peered at him sidelong. "Knowing how you've always felt about that test, I'm surprised you haven't gotten rid of it."

The admiral grew more serious. "If I were the dictator instead of just the commandant, I would. But I'm answerable to the superintendent and Starfleet Command. And given how . . . infamous . . . my own history with the *Kobayashi Maru* is," he went on with a shrug, "any argument I made in favor of changing or eliminating it would be unlikely to go over well."

"So you're just gonna roll over and help administer a test you think is wrong?" McCoy studied him closely. For all of Kirk's insistence that he'd arranged things more to his liking this time, McCoy remained skeptical that a man like him could ever be true to himself in an administrative post, even with the occasional special mission to break the monotony. So the idea that Kirk would merely play along with a policy he disagreed with, rather than finding some way to bend the letter of the law until he could convince his superiors to rewrite it, struck him as cause for concern.

"For now," Kirk replied, not exactly reassuring McCoy. "I think it does have its uses. After all, I found a way around it once. It's only a matter of time before some creative young cadet finds a new way to beat it." He smiled. "Why shouldn't they have the same chance I had?"

The doctor looked at him askance as Kirk worked the control to open the sliding panel at the front of the simulator, then led McCoy out into the access corridor beyond. "So the commandant in charge of student performance and discipline is saying he's in favor of cheating. I may not be crazy about you having this job, Jim," he said as he followed the admiral down the few steps to the exit door, "but there are better ways to lose it."

"I would never endorse cheating," Kirk replied lightly. "Except for a good cause."

The heavy double doors slid open and they exited into the corridor beyond, the bright blue sky through the windows startling the part of McCoy's subconscious that had been lulled into believing he was back on the *Enterprise.* As they reached the elevator lobby—an inviting atrium lushly adorned with vegetation and antique celestial spheres and maps from the Federation founder worlds—they were intercepted by a striking, dark-haired woman in her late thirties, wearing commander's bars on her shoulder strap. "Admiral Kirk! I've been hoping to have a talk with you."

"Certainly, Anjani." He turned to McCoy. "Doctor Leonard McCoy, this is Commander Anjani Desai, professor of ethics. Commander, my dear friend Doctor McCoy."

She shook McCoy's hand and offered a quick, dazzling smile, but the dazzle was incidental; she quickly turned back to Kirk and addressed her concern. "I've been wondering about these new problems you proposed for discussion in Command Ethics. They're a bit . . . abstract."

"In what way?" Kirk asked.

"Well . . . a command officer being flung back in time and having to decide whether to allow the death of an innocent whose survival would lead to Hitler or Ferris being victorious? Or encountering an alien intervention in Earth's past and having to decide whether it had been necessary to bring about known history?"

Kirk's gaze was cryptic. "You don't think they're challenging enough questions?"

"I don't think they're situations our students have any realistic chance of encountering," Desai argued, though her tone toward Kirk remained amiable—not an unusual phenomenon among women speaking to James Kirk, McCoy had noted with some envy over the years. "After all, this is Command Ethics, not pure philosophy; my job is to prepare future officers for situations they could realistically encounter. But these scenarios are more like the stuff of fiction. I mean, sure, I've heard Captain Xon's physics lectures about how any faster-than-light drive is also potentially a time machine, but I know there are also prohibitive practical obstacles to surviving a temporal warp. Any crew that did get caught in one would have to worry more about being vaporized by runaway Hawking radiation than by whether or not to shoot baby Hitler or whatever."

McCoy blinked at the commander's words. He sometimes forgot that the reality of time travel was still classified—that for most people outside the admiralty and the civilian Department of Temporal Investigations, the prospect of hopping back through the centuries was still a matter of conjecture rather than the veritable routine it had become for the *Enterprise* crew over the years. After all, if more people knew it was achievable in practice, it would create more risk of people traveling back to remake history to their liking.

Of course, Kirk gave away nothing of this. "Anjani, *we* may not know how to overcome those obstacles, but the galaxy is full of civilizations far more advanced and ancient than we are. There's always the possibility that a crew could run afoul of the artifacts of such a civilization and find itself dealing with that seemingly impossible situation—and the impossible choices it forces them to make."

Desai nodded thoughtfully. "When you put it that way, Admiral, I can see the value. It's a reach, perhaps, but it's a good point that we should be prepared for the effects of technology beyond our own state of the art."

"I'm glad you understand."

She narrowed her big, dark eyes, tilting her head at him. "Still . . . a couple of those examples you proposed were oddly specific."

McCoy cleared his throat. "Jim's always been an avid reader. Like you said, it's the stuff of fiction."

That seemed to satisfy her; she thanked Kirk and stepped into the lift. The admiral and McCoy gazed after her for a few moments. "I think she likes you, Jim," the doctor said. "Hell, she could've just sent you a memo."

Kirk gave him a sour look. "She's under my command, Bones. It wouldn't be appropriate."

"That's a fair point," McCoy conceded. "Still, now that you're more settled, Jim, you should give some thought to things other than work. Putting yourself back in circulation, finding that special someone."

"Bones, you're a doctor, not a matchmaker."

"I'm just saying—we're in San Francisco. It can't be that hard to meet single women. You could join a club, meet people who share your interests. Find a book club, or go horseback riding."

Kirk pondered. "I *have* been thinking of taking up mountain climbing. Or orbital skydiving."

McCoy rolled his eyes. "Damn it, Jim, I'm trying to arrange a date, not a funeral."

U.S.S. Enterprise
In orbit of Vulcan

"So now that you have your own ship," Saavik asked, "that means you can come to visit me whenever you want?"

Captain Spock studied his protégée as she peered over the railing of the upper level of the *Enterprise*'s main engineering complex, observing the bustle of the technicians working below to install new consoles along its formerly bare walls. He was unsure whether the illogical premise Saavik posited was motivated by genuine need or was an attempt to indulge in humor. She was sixteen standard years of age now, still a child in Vulcan terms but old enough to have mastered basic reasoning. However, the chaotic formative years she had endured on the abandoned Hellguard colony had delayed her education until Spock had rescued her and taken responsibility for her rehabilitation. She had come far in the five years since, but echoes of that fierce, lonely child on Hellguard still emerged in her every now and then.

He chose to fall back on answering the question as literally posed. "It does not, Saavikam. The *Enterprise*'s service to Starfleet Academy and its special assignments for Admiral Kirk make only intermittent demands on our time. In the interim, we operate as a pure research vessel or as a testbed for prototype technologies. It is in that latter capacity that we have come to Vulcan."

She pointed below. "Those are the prototypes you will test?"

"No; the new consoles are redundant manual monitor and control systems for cadet training purposes. In normal practice, a modern starship's automation can achieve most tasks with far more efficiency than living beings, so control interfaces for the crew can be simplified. However, that does not provide cadet crews with adequate training in basic procedures."

Saavik was skeptical. "Why train them for what they won't need?"

"As preparation for emergencies when the automation fails. Or for circumstances where it may be necessary to crew a less advanced starship, whether an older Starfleet or civilian craft or one of non-Federation manufacture."

Spock reflected on Commander Scott's tirade against the despoiling of his beautiful engine room with these bulky workstations, lamenting at seeing what he had characterized as "a regal lady gussied up like a cheap showgirl." The engineer had also soundly ridiculed the retrofitting of the torpedo room with an antiquated manual loading system as an alternative to its normal automated loading, insisting that it was one step away from reverting to gunpowder cannons and round shot. Perhaps Scott's displeasure at the alterations to the *Enterprise* was the reason for his recent transfer to the *Asimov*, though Spock was certain he would return once that ship's research mission was complete and Scott's temper had cooled—though Spock could not reliably estimate which of those events would occur first.

Saavik appeared similarly unconvinced, and he wondered if Amanda was coddling her too much (something Sarek would certainly never do). "I would have expected more sympathy from you, Saavikam. You have always taken pride in the strength and resourcefulness you retain from your upbringing in decidedly primitive conditions."

The girl's expression grew sour. "I *had* to. And all I wanted was to get out. But when people never had to live that way, they always think they want to, and they invent cleaned-up versions that let them pretend they're tough." She allowed an ominous smile to show on her face. "Once I'm a cadet, I'll show them real toughness."

"I have no doubt you will," Spock said. "But please try to make allowances for their fragility."

"I promise nothing."

As Spock led Saavik around the narrow balcony to the turbolift doors, he said, "In fact, the primary upgrade we are testing is a prototype for a new defensive shield system, replacing the current force-field coils. It is intended to combine the thorough coverage of the force-field envelope with the strength of a standard deflector grid, allowing a single system to do the work of both."

Saavik frowned up at him as they entered the lift. "That's stupid. It's better to have two layers of protection than one."

"The new system is believed to have sufficient redundancies to compensate. It also requires significantly less power than the current dual system, making it easier to maintain in battle." Seeing her continued skeptical expression, he added, "For now, at least, the *Enterprise* will be retaining its standard deflector grid underneath the upgraded shield envelope. What humans refer to as a 'belt and suspenders' approach—an antiquated metaphor for redundancy."

Spock directed the lift upward through the connecting dorsal toward the saucer section. Saavik gave him an inquisitive look of a kind he had seen on her many times before. "You seem satisfied with your current position here. Teaching cadets, conducting research and experimentation."

"Indeed. I had always resisted command, for I believed its responsibilities would preclude me from doing the work I consider myself best suited for. I am grateful to Admiral Kirk for arranging a position that allows me to continue doing that work in a new capacity."

"So you will be there as my teacher when I get to the Academy."

"Naturally." The lift shifted forward, toward the upgraded research laboratory complex that was the next stop on their tour.

"But what about after that?" Saavik pressed. "When I graduate the Academy, will you never be my captain again?"

He addressed her seriously. "Saavik, you can only remain a student so long. In time, we all must grow beyond our teachers."

Her eyes flashed with impatience, as they often did when she felt he had missed her point. "It wasn't me I was concerned about, Spock. Should you not grow as well? If you expect me to grow beyond you, should you not endeavor to grow beyond Admiral Kirk? He is only human, after all," she added. "You can expect to outlive him by a century or more."

Spock straightened his shoulders. "In which case, there is abundant time before I must consider further change. For now, I am content to be a teacher."

Saavik held his gaze. "I can attest that you are a fine teacher. But there were times, with me, when you doubted it, did you not?"

After a moment, Spock nodded, admitting, "Yes. It was a learning process for me as well."

The lift doors opened. Saavik stepped forward, but turned to block the doorway. "Then I make a request of you, my teacher. Let captaincy be your next learning process. Allow yourself the opportunity to master it." She tilted her head forward challengingly. "Perhaps even to surpass the captains you learned from. After all, is it not the hope of every teacher to be surpassed by their pupil?"

Spock remained motionless in the lift for several moments after Saavik exited. He allowed himself a feeling of satisfaction that Saavik might have already begun to fulfill that hope in him.

San Francisco

"Have you seen these?"

Sulu grinned as he passed a civilian data slate across the restaurant table. Uhura leaned in to read over Chekov's shoulder as the younger man picked it up and read the title displayed on it in a boxy, slanted font: *STARFLEET: THE ENTERPRISE CHRONICLES.*

"Ugh, is this that adventure sim series they based on our missions?" Chekov asked with a grimace. "I've seen a few episodes. When Admiral Kirk called it 'inaccurately larger than life,' he was being generous. My accent is nowhere near that exaggerated! And my hair looks nothing like that."

Uhura looked at him sidelong. "At least your character gets plenty of lines. And the occasional love interest."

Sulu gestured in agreement. "Yeah, what about that?"

"Now, I liked the older sim about Captain Garth," Chekov insisted. "It helped inspire me to join Starfleet. It's a shame they pulled it from circulation after his . . . breakdown at Antos IV."

"Honestly, this one isn't that bad, if you step back and look at it objectively," Uhura observed. "I wish they'd focused more on the junior officers' contributions—and thrown in fewer gratuitous fistfights—but there's some genuinely good writing. And they capture the importance of the work Starfleet does, the dangers and the benefits, quite well." She shrugged. "Allowing for what they had to fictionalize to obscure the classified details."

"My hair is not a classified detail, Nyota."

"Well, kids love it," Sulu said. "Demora's addicted to it, though I worry that the violence is too adult for her."

Uhura smiled. It had only been a couple of months since Sulu had decided to stay on Earth to raise his seven-year-old daughter following the death of her mother, passing up a first-officer posting on the *Bozeman* in favor of a groundside posting as an astronavigation instructor at Starfleet Academy. He had struggled with the choice at the time, considering himself more suited to piloting than parenting, but Uhura was unsurprised at how naturally her friend had taken to fatherhood. His dedication, compassion, and irrepressible good spirits had been just what Demora had needed after the loss of her mother. And the decision might have saved Sulu's life too, as the *Bozeman* had not been heard from for more than a month, since it had entered an uncharted region called the Typhon Expanse.

Sulu gestured to the data slate. "Anyway, turns out the sim series is just the tip of the iceberg. There are tie-ins too."

"Tie-ins?" Chekov asked. "What in the world is a tie-in?"

"You know, side merchandise created to supplement the main series. Ever since we stopped V'Ger from wiping out Earth, the public's been hungry for more stories about the 'heroic' crew of the *Enterprise*. So besides the sim series, there are prose novels, graphic fiction, games . . . there are hundreds of installments."

"Hundreds?" Chekov protested. "But Starfleet has only cleared incidents from our first five-year mission, and not even all of those."

"That's the point," Sulu said, his grin widening. "The main series adapts our real missions—mostly—but the tie-ins go further afield. Sometimes they do stories that are loosely based on uncleared missions, using what they can reconstruct from news reports and such. But a lot of the time, they completely make things up. Go on, take a look—this stuff is crazy."

Uhura leaned closer and read over Chekov's shoulder as he

paged through the illustrated serials on the data slate, reacting with startlement and laughter to what they beheld.

"They just annihilated those plant creatures! No attempt at communication!"

"Is that a papier-mâché Eiffel Tower?"

"The bottled emotions of ancient Vulcans? I really don't think that's how it works."

"Good Lord, are those gnomes?"

"And these characters look even less like us than the ones in the sim!" Chekov cried.

"At least they didn't make you a blonde," Uhura countered.

"Cheer up, Pavel," Sulu said, patting Chekov on the shoulder. "I'm sure you'll get a starring role in the inevitable *Reliant Chronicles* spin-off."

"That's right!" Uhura said, squeezing his other shoulder and beaming broadly. "Second officer at last! At this rate, you'll beat Sulu in the first-officer race for sure."

Chekov flushed. "Well, only because he stayed to raise Demora."

"Hey, don't think I won't be envying you, Pavel," Sulu said. "Those light cruisers get all sorts of interesting missions."

"True. And I'll be able to come back and visit you and Demora more often than on a heavy cruiser." *Miranda*-class vessels like the *Reliant*, Uhura knew, tended to be workhorse ships, sent on short-term missions of various types as needed and otherwise staying close to home, as opposed to the *Enterprise*'s long-term patrol and exploration tours.

"She'll be glad of that. She really likes having you around."

Chekov sighed. "But it will be an adjustment. Very few familiar faces."

"Didn't you arrange to bring Mosi Nizhoni aboard as security chief?" Uhura asked.

"Yes—she's earned it. And John Kyle's aboard too."

"Kyle!" Uhura grinned. "I haven't seen him in years."

"Well, you'll be pleased to hear he's followed in your footsteps. He's *Reliant*'s communications officer now."

"Really! Be sure to pass along my congratulations."

Sulu smiled at her. "Aren't you due for congratulations too, Nyota? Scotty tells me you're joining him on the *Asimov* as chief science officer."

Chekov grinned in surprise. "Science officer? Is there no end to your talents?"

Uhura lowered her eyes demurely. "It's only because the *Asimov*'s mission requires expertise in subspace radiometry. We'll be charting subspace density anomalies that could potentially be used for gravitational lensing. It's a technique developed by the Agni, a way to amplify subspace sensor and communication beams to allow greatly enhanced range and precision."

"Don't be modest," Sulu said. "I studied the Agni incident—weren't you the one who found the key to establishing communication with them?"

"I was just part of the team," she replied. "But yes, that was the beginning of my interest in their communication and detection methods. It should be useful on the mission."

"The *Asimov*," Chekov mused. "That's an older ship, right? *Malachowski* class?"

"Another light cruiser," Sulu said. "Compact, maneuverable . . . a classic."

"Well, we're not likely to see a lot of action charting subspace anomalies. And Scotty's had nothing but complaints about the antiquated systems and all the repairs and overhauls he'll have to do on the fly." Uhura grinned wider. "He couldn't be happier."

The three commanders laughed together, continuing to compare ship specs and mission plans and hopes and dreams. They all knew that this would be the last time they would get to do this for a while. Missions would come and go, to be sure, and they would have their share of downtime between them; but the *Enterprise* family was starting to branch out in different directions, and Uhura, Sulu, and Chekov all knew that was likely to continue. They had managed to stick together for a dozen years, on and off, but now they were starting to grow up and leave the nest.

Uhura glanced at Sulu's data slate and the colorful fantasy version of the *Enterprise* that it portrayed. In fiction, if you wanted more adventures of the same cast of friends and heroes, you could keep them together indefinitely, installment after installment, for as long as the audience's interest remained. But real life tended to be more impermanent. What they had shared on the *Enterprise* was special, something that came along once in a lifetime—and they had managed to have it twice already.

What were the odds that it would ever come again?

Ten

***U.S.S. Reliant* NCC-1864**
Two months later

Captain Clark Terrell leaned back in his seat at the head of the long briefing room table and grinned. "We're going to Dog Territory," he said.

Chekov asked the question before he could stop himself. "Dogs, sir?"

Inwardly, he winced. In the six weeks since he'd come aboard the *Reliant* as its second officer and science officer, he'd already gained a reputation as a humorless Herbert, as his old flame Irina would have put it. Not only was he insecure about his new responsibilities, but he was still learning to adjust to Captain Terrell's laid-back, occasionally whimsical command style and playful camaraderie with his crew. Captain Kirk had been anything but a grim martinet, of course, but his humor had been more tempered, balanced by a strong sense of discipline and command authority. Terrell, while a big, intimidating man in appearance, had a more avuncular command style that somewhat reminded Chekov of Commander Scott, and the established command crew shared a camaraderie that made Chekov feel like an outsider, even though none of the others had deliberately created that impression. Indeed, Terrell's first officer,

Commander Rem Azem-Os—a mature Aurelian with resplendent green-and-gold plumage, diminutive for her people and thus about average humanoid height—had figuratively taken Chekov under her literal wing from the start, making it clear that she planned to retire within the next couple of years and was grooming him as her replacement (*not* literally, fortunately, since her beak and talons looked alarmingly sharp). Having Nizhoni and Kyle on board alongside him also helped keep him from feeling completely isolated.

But Chekov was still searching for his balance with Captain Terrell. Their careers had nearly intersected once before, at the climactic battle with the Tholians over the now-destroyed Starbase Vanguard, but it was hard to make that a basis for casual conversation when nearly everything about it was classified. The fact that Terrell had earned his captaincy of the *Sagittarius* in that battle through the death of its commanding officer also made it seem like a topic best avoided.

In any case, Terrell and the rest of the department heads around the briefing room table seemed no more than mildly amused by Chekov's naïve question. The captain shrugged as he went on. "Well, that's what Chinese astronomers called the region, anyway. The eighth mansion of their zodiac. European astronomers called it Terebellum, and it's the home of the Omega Sagittarii star system." He showed no outward reaction to the coincidental reminder of his first command. "Terebellum's also the name of the colony on Omega Sagittarii II, which was started some sixty years ago and is home to about ninety thousand settlers, mostly human, Arbazan, and Suliban."

"Suliban?" The question came from Lieutenant Commander Ralston Beach, the chief helmsman and assistant science officer. "Weren't they hostile to humans about a hundred years ago?" the jowly, dark-haired man continued in a strong New York accent. Chekov respected that the man made no effort to hide his regional origins in the way he spoke.

"Now, now, Stoney, don't generalize," Azem-Os chided gently, crossing her spindly arms over the front of her modified uniform, a backless halter designed to accommodate her impressive green-gold wings. "As I recall, they were a refugee people, driven from their homeworld by war and wandering the galaxy. It left one faction of them vulnerable to radicalization, and they were genetically augmented by a terrorist leader whose identity remains unknown to this day. But most Suliban were peaceful wanderers just looking for a place to live and be accepted."

"And Terebellum has been such a place for them," Terrell added. "But lately there's been unrest, and it's apparently coming from the human side."

Beach looked abashed. "Not over old grudges, I hope?"

"More like something new. Specifically the New Humans. Terebellum has become one of their primary enclaves, but there have been a number of recent disputes between them and the rest of the colony." He turned to his second officer. "Mister Chekov. I understand you were involved in the incident last year that's provoked the recent changes in the New Human movement."

Chekov was startled, but not truly surprised. He had been expecting something like this. "Yes, Captain. I lost several crewmates who were associated with the movement."

Terrell nodded gravely. "I appreciate your loss, Pavel. But since you're familiar with the movement, maybe you could offer some perspective on what's been going on with them this past year."

"Well, sir . . . in the year since the extermination of the Aenar and the sacrifice of the *Enterprise*'s esper personnel in their defense, the New Human communities on Earth and other human-populated worlds have grown more organized, more consolidated. They've gathered together and worked harder to cultivate and strengthen their psionic powers. I understand they have made significant gains."

The *Reliant*'s chief medical officer, Doctor Bianca Wilder, leaned forward, her cornrowed black hair brushing against her shoulders. "And in the process, they've become more insular, setting themselves apart from other humans. Even most of the espers in Starfleet have resigned their commissions to join the movement. I got into it with a good friend of mine when she decided to resign. She said she thought Starfleet was too backward, too focused on the physical. That she'd rather focus on 'evolving to a higher level of consciousness.' "

"Can you blame them, Doctor, for wanting to band together after what happened to the Aenar?"

Wilder's striking African features softened marginally. "The loss of the Aenar was tragic, Mister Chekov, and I sympathize that you had to be involved with it. But there's no evidence that their killers were reacting specifically to their telepathy. After all, no other telepathic individuals were targeted in their attacks—except for those among your own crew who got between them and the Aenar," she finished gently.

"Be fair, Bianca," Terrell said. "Despite all that, seeing another telepathic minority exterminated, along with some of their own, must have hit them hard. We all cope with tragedies on that scale in our own ways. Sometimes by drawing closer to those who can understand what we're going through."

"Yes, exactly," Chekov said. "Thank you, sir."

Terrell caught his eye. "On the other hand, sometimes people react to tragedy by acting out in harmful ways. Which sounds like it might be the case on Terebellum. So we need to keep an open mind either way, right, Commander?"

Chekov nodded. "Yes, Captain. To be honest, I've expected some kind of tension to arise between the espers and other humans. I wasn't sure which direction it would come from, though." After a moment, he made a pointed addition. "And we *still* don't know. I presume the call for Starfleet assistance came from the non-esper colonists."

"A fair point, Mister Chekov. Naturally, we'll go in with open minds and hear both sides. So far this doesn't seem to be anything more than some neighborly squabbles and civil unrest," Terrell pointed out. "Our job is to patch things up before it gets any worse."

Azem-Os shook her feathered head convulsively and snuffled through her beak. "Family squabbles can be the worst of all. I don't expect this to be easy."

Terebellum Colony, Omega Sagittarii II

"These charges of 'disruption' are nothing but an attempt to discredit us," Leilani Sungkar protested in calm, controlled tones.

Clark Terrell considered the New Human community's regal, gray-haired leader as she spoke. Sungkar sat on one side of the rectangular, open-centered conference table, flanked by two of her fellow espers, Ravi Mehrotra and Maya Arias. While they did not dress in the same sheer robes that were fashionable among New Humans on Earth, they wore loose, low-cut tunics in similarly bright colors. They sat close to one another and projected a sense of serenity that reminded him of the Deltans he'd met, though that smooth surface was marred by ripples of submerged anger and distress.

Much of that anger seemed directed toward the three Terebellan officials seated opposite them, flanking Terrell and Chekov on the narrow end of the table. Governor Kisak, at the center of the trio, was a middle-aged Suliban female whose bald, rounded head reminded Terrell of nothing so much as a cantaloupe with a face. (He knew it was a rude thing to think, but he couldn't help it; that was what she looked like.) On her left was Councilor Agkan, a sour-faced Arbazan male who appeared human aside from hairless brows and a high forehead with subtle Y-shaped ridges. On Kisak's right, at the forward corner of the table beside Chekov, was Security Director Haru Yamasaki, a lean-featured Japanese man with a calculating expression.

"We merely wish to explore and advance our abilities," Sungkar went on, "but we have been met with growing fear and intolerance."

"Because we commune telepathically with the native giant corvids," Mehrotra said, "we have been blamed for their attacks on livestock that was allowed to wander too far."

"Because some Arbazan adolescents chose to voyeurize some of our more . . . private acts of union," Arias added with a flush on her striking Filipina features, "their families have accused us of corrupting their youth."

Sungkar picked up the thought again. "We have even been blamed for telekinetically causing accidents, such as the fall of an old tree onto Councilor Agkan's skimmer." Terrell cleared his throat to stifle a laugh.

"It's nothing but a witch hunt," Mehrotra added. "Singletons fearing what they don't understand." The others threw him a look, and Sungkar placed her hand on his. He bowed his head. "Forgive me. The term was inappropriate."

"I'd say it was most appropriate," Yamasaki replied in precise, polished tones. "It's important that we all speak frankly of our true beliefs, don't you think, Captain Terrell?"

"I'm more interested in facts than beliefs, Director," Terrell replied, refusing to take the bait. "Is there any hard evidence to link the New Humans to any of these incidents?"

"How can there be?" Agkan asked. "They can conspire undetectably, influence objects and leave no trace."

"That's not correct, Councilor," Chekov spoke up. "Psionic energies do leave detectable signatures." He turned to Yamasaki. "Do you have the means to scan for them here?"

"Our equipment is state-of-the-art," Yamasaki replied primly. "I myself earned my degree in criminology from the University of Altair IV."

"And have you found any psionic signatures connected with these events?" Terrell asked.

Yamasaki paused. "The results were . . . inconclusive. There is a fair amount of psionic background noise due to the frequent mental activity of the New Humans."

"Then isn't it possible this is all just a misunderstanding?"

Governor Kisak finally spoke up. "Our people's concern toward the New Humans' growing abilities—along with their growing tendency to set themselves apart from us—is not unjustified," the heavyset Suliban woman said. "Keep in mind, Captain, that all our peoples have good reason to be suspicious of those with enhanced abilities. My own people were terrorized by the genetically augmented Cabal, yet blamed and persecuted for their actions. Most of our original human colonists came from peoples who had been ruled by Khan Noonien Singh during the Eugenics Wars, and who retain long memories of their history. And our original Arbazan settlers were refugees from the genetically augmented tyranny that ruled their entire world until forty years ago."

"I sympathize with your concern about Augments," Chekov told the Terebellan leaders. "But I don't understand how that applies here. The recent surge in human esper ability appears to be a natural evolutionary leap."

Yamasaki studied him curiously. "Naturally, Mister Chekov, I defer to your scientific expertise. It's always been my understanding that evolution is a gradual process—occurring from generation to generation, rather than within single individuals in the course of just a few years. Perhaps you could explain the basis for my misapprehension." For all the deference in his words, the polished snideness in his tone was unmistakable.

"The potential has always been within us," Sungkar interposed. "That has been known for generations, and some few of us, like Doctor Miranda Jones, had already unlocked our full potential. All we needed was a catalyst to unlock it in more of us. V'Ger's ascension was that catalyst."

"Yes," Yamasaki muttered. "You consider yourselves the children of V'Ger, don't you?"

"In a sense," Arias conceded.

"Forgive me, but . . . didn't V'Ger attempt to destroy all life on Earth? If it *was* responsible for your . . . amplification . . . isn't that all the more reason to question your intentions toward the rest of the human species?"

"All we wish," Sungkar countered in less serene tones than before, "is to be permitted to explore our mental unity in peace."

"An odd definition of 'peace,' given that you've telepathically or telekinetically assaulted several citizens."

"In self-defense," Mehrotra said.

"They were threatening us," added Arias.

"And no actual harm came to them," Sungkar finished.

"The law defines any unwanted or offensive contact as battery," Yamasaki countered. "That has been ruled under Federation law to include telepathic contact. Psionic fields and particles are physical phenomena, after all; therefore, psionic influence on another's mind is a form of physical contact. It doesn't have to do damage to be a criminal act."

"You see?" Governor Kisak said. "Wherever their enhancements come from, the impact is the same: superior power breeding a sense of entitlement and the willingness to impose upon others. As your own people say, Captain, power tends to corrupt. The rest of us do not feel safe—*will* not feel safe—as long as we must share our world with these espers."

"This is our home," Sungkar protested. "As much as it is yours. You and I were born in the same town."

"And you have made it quite clear that you consider yourselves to have evolved beyond your origins. That you no longer need any connections save to each other. You have alienated yourselves from our world. All we ask is that you complete the process and leave Terebellum once and for all."

Terrell traded a look with his second officer. Like Chekov, Terrell could sympathize with the colonists' fears of powerful telepaths. His own experiences aboard the *Sagittarius* in the

Taurus Reach had involved encounters with species of extraordinary psionic power, from the Shedai to the Tomol. But it was one thing to fear powerful beings with clear aggressive intent. It was another to presume hostility just because someone was different.

These were *humans*, after all—new or otherwise. Surely that had to count for something.

Chekov and Lieutenant Nizhoni had been coordinating with Haru Yamasaki on security arrangements when the call came in: A fight had broken out between a group of New Humans and some of their neighboring farmers. Shots had been fired, and telekinesis had been used in response. Yamasaki had just been talking about the inevitability of violence erupting between the groups; as his team headed for the site alongside the *Reliant* personnel, Chekov noted that the Terebellan security director seemed more satisfied than concerned, as if glad to be proven right.

By the time the security teams arrived, the fight had settled down into a stalemate, with both sides waiting tensely to see if the other would make the next move. They stood down readily when the authorities showed up, as if they were grateful for a chance to end it. Chekov took it as a good sign that the colonists still saw each other as neighbors rather than enemies.

Still, both sides defended their actions with righteous indignation when Yamasaki questioned them. "They trespassed on our compound carrying phasers," insisted Ravi Mehrotra, evidently the informal leader of the group of New Humans involved in the quarrel. "We were protecting ourselves. Our children."

"*Your* children?" countered Girsu, the burly, long-haired Arbazan farmer who spoke for the rival group. "You've been giving *our* children nightmares! Agitating our *besuin* so they don't give milk!"

"Our communion has no such effect," objected the olive-skinned, dark-eyed woman at Mehrotra's side, who had introduced herself as Niloufar Darvish. "It's only for us to share."

"Really," Yamasaki said. "Then your telekinetic surges that threw Girsu's farmhands into a ditch and broke one of their wrists . . . those were intended for your own people and . . . misaimed?"

"They stormed in waving phasers around," Mehrotra insisted. "We could feel the imminent violence from them. We were entitled to defend ourselves."

"And the strength of your . . . defenses . . . continues to escalate. Surely you can see how that could be alarming to those of us without your . . . gifts."

"We mean no harm to anyone. Haru, you know me. We went to the same school."

"Yes, I remember," Yamasaki said. "I remember the pride you took in your esper abilities—that something extra none of the others had. Oh, though I assure you, I never gave credence to the rumors that you used your powers to improve your grades—or to make girls like you."

"That's a vile accusation!" Mehrotra took an angry step forward, and Yamasaki and his accompanying troops started to raise their phasers. Darvish touched Mehrotra's arm, and he calmed after something passed between them. "You haven't changed one bit, Haru. You've always envied others' achievements, though you've never had the guts to come out and say it."

"It's the way of singletons," Darvish added. "Envy, mistrust, self-absorption. Pieces afraid to form a whole."

"You see?" Girsu spoke up. "That's all we are to these people. 'Singletons.' Inferior beings to be treated like . . . like livestock."

"I've listened to your livestock," Darvish told the Arbazan farmer. "Don't project your own contemptuous treatment of them onto us."

"There, she confessed! They have been disturbing our livestock. Our children too!"

"We've done nothing to either of them," Mehrotra insisted. "They're responding to *your* anxiety, the atmosphere of tension you're creating out of fear."

"Is that fear really so unjustified," Yamasaki said, "when you speak of us as 'singletons,' as lesser beings than your enlightened whole? Is it so hard for you to understand why your neighbors no longer recognize you as human when you seem to have renounced the label yourselves?"

"Humanity is a concept with room for growth and evolution. We're New Humans, not post-humans."

"The Augments called themselves human. The Cabal called themselves Suliban. They still set themselves above the rest of us." Yamasaki stepped forward. "If you wish to convince us that's not your intention, then I advise you to stand down and allow us to take you in . . . along with the trespassers, of course. We'll let the justice system sort this out. Assuming you still consider yourselves subject to our laws."

After exchanging a few more silent looks, Mehrotra, Darvish, and the rest of their group agreed to surrender to custody, along with Girsu, his farmhands, and the other trespassers. It seemed like a fair outcome, but Chekov was concerned that Yamasaki's sympathies were so clearly with those who feared the New Humans.

Granted, Chekov could understand the Terebellans' fear of Augments. He had been a junior engineer when Khan Noonien Singh and the rest of the Eugenics Wars superhumans rescued from the *S.S. Botany Bay* had taken over the ship. He and a handful of others had been trapped in the engineering section with Khan's people when the emergency bulkheads had sealed it off, and his youthful enthusiasm and indignation had driven him to act more recklessly than his fellows, leading them in a resistance effort against the Augments . . . until Khan had personally hunted him down amid the bowels of engineering and overpowered him with relentless ease, demanding only his name and then commending him for his courage before rendering him unconscious. Despite his enemy's gracious words, Chekov had rarely been so terrified in his life.

Yet it seemed unwarranted to direct the same suspicion toward natural-born espers. DiFalco, Logan, and the others on the *Enterprise* had never acted superior. They had been a little weird, maybe, but well within the range of diverse behaviors and worldviews found within that ship's crew, a microcosm for the Federation as a whole.

So why was it that a Federation that accepted so much diversity of thought, custom, and ability between different species had so much trouble with a new form of diversity within humanity?

Captain Terrell had found his visit to the New Humans' main compound quite agreeable. He and Lieutenant Commander Beach had been greeted warmly enough by Leilani Sungkar and her fellow espers, who had granted them full access to observe the New Humans' activities and confirm that there was nothing aggressive or untoward going on. Certainly the vibe had been quite placid and positive. A number of the espers communed in silent meditation, while others worked harmoniously to tend the gardens and harvest fresh vegetables. A trio of them had even been gathered around a *haipa*, a large indigenous felinoid with blue-and-gold fur, a serpentine tail, and large red eyes underneath winglike antennae. The animal rumbled happily as they stroked its fur and cooed endearments at it, though Beach assured Terrell that the *haipa* were not a domesticated species.

The dining experience was also excellent. With their permission, the resident chef had read Terrell's and Beach's thoughts of their favorite foods and had done an excellent job re-creating their flavor and presentation. "Best meal I've had in ages," Beach commended him. Turning to Sungkar across the table, he said,

"You know, you should invite the governor and her people to dinner. Nothing brings people together like a good meal."

"We have tried," Sungkar said. "At first, they appreciated it, but then the novelty wore off, and the problems didn't fade." She shook her head. "An invitation to dinner would not have smoothed things over with the farmers yesterday."

Terrell was well aware that this invitation had been largely meant to win his sympathies so that he would intervene on behalf of Ravi Mehrotra and those arrested with him. But there was only so much he could do. Their fate was in the hands of the local authorities and laws; the most he could do as a Starfleet captain was to provide oversight and ensure those laws were being enforced fairly.

Next to Sungkar, Maya Arias frowned. "The problem is that we continued to grow and they didn't. Just because they're trapped in their own heads, they assume the worst about others' motives. It's always been an intrinsic flaw in humans, a cause of unnecessary fear and conflict. Why can't they see that we're the solution to that flaw? All that we are about is love and peace. It comes naturally to us, because we can truly understand each other and know not to fear."

Terrell spoke gently. "I think that potential's in all of us. Even without psionics, humans have always had the capacity for empathy—for imagining what other people feel, even if we can't know directly."

"Mirror neurons," Beach said. "He's right. The humanoid brain processes the emotions we see in others with the same equipment it uses to process our own feelings. To the brain, it's all the same. Psionics add something extra, but our eyes and ears can do the job too."

Terrell nodded at Beach's words. "True, sometimes we imagine the worst. Sometimes we mistake our fears for others' feelings. But that basic ability to identify with others, to feel their joy and pain as if it were our own, is the basis of our civilization—and if you ask me, it's our greatest defining trait as a species.

"We may lack the ability to share every thought in our heads," Terrell went on, "but that lets us show compassion in another way—by filtering our thoughts and protecting others from the opinions and impulses they might find hurtful."

"Oh, yeah," Beach said. "Sometimes it's better not to share everything you think. Just ask my ex-wife."

"Doesn't that just demonstrate baseline humans' inability to completely accept one another?" Arias asked.

Terrell thought it over. "I don't see it that way. If anything, I'd say it's what enables humans to engage in diplomacy with other species—to engage with outsiders before total understanding has been gained."

"What do you mean?" The striking Filipina woman appeared puzzled, unaccustomed to not immediately grasping another's thoughts.

"Well, if the only beings you know how to engage with are those you're already one with," Terrell asked with a gentle smile, "then don't you lack a necessary skill for engaging with the rest of the universe? What you have between yourselves is amazing, even enviable in many ways. But you're always going to have blind spots toward the rest of the universe. Not all species' minds are susceptible to telepathy, or willing to open to it. So that ability to reach out to those whose thoughts you can only imagine is still important.

"Maybe if you keep that in mind," he said, holding Sungkar's rich brown eyes, "you'll be better able to imagine where the other colonists are coming from."

"We are not the ones who need to change our behavior," Arias protested.

Sungkar placed a hand on hers. "No, of course not, Maya. But perhaps a better understanding of their behavior will help us find ways to de-escalate it, to guide them toward greater understanding. Think of how we get along with the *haipa*. We don't try to tame them; we merely respect their ways and reassure them we pose no threat. As long as we don't push them where they don't want to go, they have no reason to push back."

Terrell found it an unflattering comparison; it implied that Kisak and the others might have been right about the New Humans seeing them as lower life-forms. Then again, maybe it was the other way around; he got the impression that the New Humans saw animals as deserving just as much respect as so-called sentient beings.

In any case, it was a start, however imperfect. At least it meant the New Humans wanted to find a peaceful settlement. Terrell just had to build on that and bring both sides to the table.

Haru Yamasaki had to admit that Captain Terrell was a fine negotiator. The captain had not only convinced Governor Kisak to come to the table opposite Sungkar once more, but had made a case for peace and unity that was at once impassioned and reasonable. With the concessions Sungkar had offered, the governor had agreed that the charges on both sides of the recent confrontation should be dropped as a gesture of good faith. Yamasaki had calmly, courteously accepted the consensus, agreeing that the most important thing was restoring the peace of the community.

In private, though, he erupted in rage and screamed into the couch pillows—at least until he flung them across the room and knocked over a lamp and his second-place spelling trophy from middle school. On reflection, he was glad to see the trophy broken; he'd always hated it, a constant reminder that he'd fallen short of perfection in others' eyes. It had been the fault of that damned pronouncer anyway. "Ultimo" should have been a simple enough word to spell, but he couldn't be blamed that the old woman had overpronounced the first syllable so artificially that it had sounded more like "altimo." He should have protested at the time, but he had been too numbed with shock. It had been the first of many times that his chances for achievement had been undermined by others' folly.

And this negotiation was another. The espers had always thought they were better than him, better than everyone. They had only gotten worse in the past five or six years, since whatever freak phenomenon had triggered this new mutation, this dangerous amplification of their unfair advantage. Now they'd manipulated Terrell into taking their side.

"Why can't he see?" Yamasaki muttered to himself as he swept up the remains of the broken trophy. "Negotiating with them isn't compromise, it's a concession to the enemy. They're an aberration. They shouldn't even exist! Humans should remain human!" He went out back and dumped the debris into the recycler. "It's just not fair."

"No, Haru Yamasaki. It is not fair."

Yamasaki was a trained security officer, so when he heard the voice of an intruder in his yard, he spun, ready to defend himself with whatever was at hand, even if it was just a dustpan.

Before him stood a being in scarlet-and-black combat armor with claw-like adornments on its blank, opaque visor.

He yelped, fell backward to the ground, and stared up at it in fear. "What . . . what do you want with me?"

"We want what you want. For humans to remain human. For the alternative to exist no longer." It offered him one gauntleted hand. "We sense that you believe in this principle as strongly as we do. And we need your help to enforce it."

Yamasaki was intrigued. At last, someone appreciated what he had to offer. He took the armored humanoid's hand and let himself be pulled upright. "Tell me more," he said, grinning.

Eleven

Resolving the dispute between the Terebellan factions proved less challenging than Pavel Chekov had feared. It turned out that the majority of the population was humbled and troubled by the fighting that had broken out, unaware that tensions had gotten so bad between the New Humans and their immediate neighbors. For every human colonist whose view of humans with enhanced abilities was colored by fears handed down since the Eugenics Wars (which, admittedly, had been a very long time ago), there were others who still gave more weight to the "Human" than the "New" and began asking why members of their own species were being treated as hostile.

Thus, Governor Kisak and the council under Agkan found themselves facing political pressure from a hitherto-silent majority to drop their hard line and reconcile with the New Humans. In turn, Sungkar and her people made a renewed effort at public outreach to reassure those who still mistrusted them—like having their telekinetic healer speed the recovery of the farmhands who had been telekinetically injured, and offer similar healing services to others in need, sophont and livestock alike. Or using their connection to the *haipa* cats and giant corvids to encourage them to hunt farther afield from the Terebellans' farmlands and leave their livestock alone.

By the second day of negotiations, Sungkar and Kisak were laughing together like the old friends they had once been, and the remaining points of contention were being resolved in quick succession. The only hitch in the proceedings was that Haru Yamasaki had called in sick that morning, leaving the security arrangements in the hands of his deputy and Lieutenant Nizhoni. "If things are going so smoothly, you'll have no need of me anyway," the security director had told Chekov over his communicator. As usual, though, he was not as good as he seemed to think he was at masking the passive-aggressive hostility beneath his deferential words. Yamasaki was clearly a man who resented losing or being outperformed at anything. It was no doubt why he disliked the New Humans so much. But in Chekov's estimation, he was still an intelligent and rational person. Hopefully that meant he would come around in time, as most of his fellow colonists now had.

All in all, Chekov was confident that a settlement would be signed by lunchtime, and *Reliant* could be on its way.

Until two whirling shimmers of light suddenly appeared on either side of the New Human contingent and resolved into a pair of chillingly familiar, faceless armored figures.

The Naazh had returned.

Before Chekov could react, the one on the left—an unfamiliar Naazh in heavy, clean-lined blue-and-silver armor—drove a buzzing, vibrating toothed blade through Ravi Mehrotra's heart from behind. Beside him, Leilani Sungkar and Maya Arias let out choking gasps and convulsed in pain, and Chekov realized that the telepaths must have felt their companion's death within their minds.

As the gathered delegates screamed and scrambled for the doors, the second Naazh, wearing scarlet-and-black armor that Chekov recognized from the *Enterprise*, closed menacingly on the staggered Sungkar. Nizhoni's phaser beam struck it from behind a moment later, and a pair of the Terebellan security officers fired on the blue one. Neither Naazh was affected by the fire.

Did the Naazh survive the explosion? Chekov wondered. *Or is it another in duplicate armor?*

Recovering, Maya Arias moved in front of Sungkar and extended her hands. She roared in anger, and a telekinetic surge pushed the red Naazh back with surprising force.

"Not this time," the Naazh said as it struggled against the surge. It certainly sounded like the chilling voice from the *Enterprise* attack, though it was hard to be certain through the filtering. It held its hand before the red crystal on its belt, then flung the hand forward. A bright flare of red light surged from the crystal and staggered Arias. A second later, the Naazh's armored hand closed around Arias's neck and crushed it.

By now, the *Reliant* and Terebellan security personnel had succeeded in spiriting Sungkar and the remaining New Humans out of the room. The red Naazh strode after them, casually shaking off fire from multiple phasers. "You can't run forever, deviant," it declared as it followed them through the exit.

The blue-armored Naazh shook Mehrotra's lifeless body off its whirring short sword and turned to Chekov and Nizhoni. "We have no quarrel with you," it said. "Just leave us to our work."

"Why are you doing this?" Chekov demanded. "Is it because the New Humans defended the Aenar against you?"

The featureless blue helmet held on him for a moment. "It is because they should never have existed." It touched its belt crystal and disappeared in a flash of dimensional energies.

Nizhoni had already drawn her communicator—a return to the old flip-open design, since the wrist communicators had proven awkward to use. "Nizhoni to *Reliant*," the security chief said. "The Naazh have attacked the New Human negotiators and killed two of them."

"*This is Azem-Os,*" the first officer's breathy, owlish voice replied. "*We're getting reports of more Naazh attacking the New Human compound. Multiple fatalities already.*"

Nizhoni caught and held Chekov's gaze, and he nodded. The two of them had always known this day might come again, and this time, with help from Starfleet Security's research labs, they were more prepared. "Beam us up, Commander," Chekov told Azem-Os. "And tell security to initiate the Phantom Protocol."

When Chekov rematerialized in the New Human compound alongside Nizhoni's security squad, they found themselves in the midst of chaos. Several human bodies littered the ground, all mutilated horribly. The surviving New Humans had gathered together in one mass, with the children and older or weaker members being guarded by brightly attired adults with hands extended defensively—no doubt more telekinetic adepts. But Chekov was heartened to note that, in addition to a squad of Terebellan security officers, a number of the compound's neighboring farmers and townsfolk were on the defensive line as well, protecting their fellow colonists with whatever weapons or farm implements they had available.

Even so, they hardly seemed adequate to face down the four Naazh who advanced relentlessly toward them, unaffected by phaser fire or plasma rifle discharges, and only briefly staggered by telekinetic surges. Chekov recognized the blue-and-silver one who had killed Mehrotra, along with the white-armored, antennaed Naazh from the *Enterprise*, or another in matching armor. Could the different designs represent specific units or specializations rather than unique personalizations? Or were the Naazh just impossible to kill?

The other two hunters were new: one in black-and-brown armor styled almost identically to that of the white Naazh, the other in dark green armor with gold trim, its smooth visor topped with three sharp spikes and adorned with gold tracings that conveyed the vague impression of a fanged mouth on its lower half. Though they were heavily outnumbered by those they faced, they strode forward with easy confidence, and the green one was even laughing in anticipation. Clearly they believed that their opposition was no match for them.

Chekov intended to prove them wrong this time.

At Nizhoni's signal, two of her security troops, Scott Crick and Tong Chi Kiang, moved out behind the Naazh carrying the large device they had beamed down with, while the rest of her team and Chekov moved in to confront the armored attackers, drawing the special weapons they had brought to supplement their heavy-duty body armor.

Chekov found himself confronting the blue Naazh again, and the sleek-armored killer studied him curiously. "I told you to stay out of this."

"I don't serve you. I serve them." He tilted his head back toward the New Humans and the other Terebellans defending them.

"Your choice," the Naazh said, lunging at him with its whirring short sword.

Chekov blocked the sawlike blade with his duranium baton, its shaft crackling with a nadion charge that surged into the Naazh's blade. The foe grunted in surprise and reeled back as Chekov pressed the attack, getting in a pair of good blows that discharged energy into the armor. Finally, breathing hard, the Naazh managed to recover from its surprise and begin blocking his swings. But all those years fencing with Sulu had taught Chekov well, and he held his own. The batons had been Sulu's idea, back in those last months on the *Enterprise* when the crew had brainstormed anti-Naazh tactics in case they ever returned. Phasers were terrific at a distance, but in close-range melee combat, they were difficult to aim and provided no defense against a blade. Contrary to the old saying, bringing a knife to a gunfight could be highly effective if you were close enough to reach your enemy before they could aim and shoot—or if you had armor that was immune to their fire.

Since the Naazh favored melee weapons, they had to be fought with melee weapons.

Soon the blue Naazh gave Chekov an opening and he stabbed the tip of the baton at one of the seams in its armor, above the silver belt-like strip around the waist. An intense energy discharge was released from the tip, drilling into the armor's weak point, and the Naazh cried out in pain and fell back. Once it had some distance, it touched its sapphire-blue belt crystal with its free hand, then reached it out as if waiting for a sidearm to materialize in it.

But nothing happened.

The Naazh stared at its hand in apparent surprise, and Chekov grinned. Crick and Tong had done their work well. The device they had activated was a modified communications beacon, of the type designed to be seeded in deep space in order to boost subspace signals' range and speed. They were thus capable of emitting powerful subspace fields. Spock and Chekov had carefully studied the recorded sensor readings from the Naazh attack on the *Enterprise*'s rec deck, analyzing the energies of their dimensional transporters in order to determine what subspace frequencies and field geometries would inhibit them. Now it looked like Spock's theories had been proven correct, as they usually were.

Chekov closed in on the blue Naazh, noting that the other three armored warriors were also reacting to their sudden inability to summon new weapons and armor. Nizhoni and Crewman Sanzio had managed to snarl the black-and-green Naazh with bolas made of fullerene-reinforced cable, strong enough to be used in a starship grappling line from the old days. The green one was struggling, its arms bound to its sides, but the black one, whose legs had been hobbled, had rolled deftly into a sitting position and was already beginning to slice through the durable cable with its sword.

Nizhoni's voice emerged from the speaker in Chekov's security helmet. *"Commander! Colony security reports that the red Naazh has teleported away. Ms. Sungkar is safe for the moment."*

"Acknowledged," Chekov said. "But that means it will be coming here. All teams, watch the perimeter of the damping field!"

He lunged at the blue Naazh with the tip of his baton, hoping to do more damage, but the enemy knocked the shaft aside with its short sword. As they circled each other, Chekov saw that Nizhoni and Sanzio had ganged up on the bound green Naazh with their own batons, and it convulsed and fell under their combined attack. However, the black Naazh had cut itself free and was joining its white-armored twin in a renewed charge at the New Humans and their defenders. The white one had summoned its sidearm before the damping field had risen, and it aimed coldly and fired on the defenders, taking down one of the telekinetics as well as an Arbazan security officer and a Suliban farmer.

Then, astonishingly, the next plasma bolt *splashed* off thin air. Chekov had to parry another thrust of the blue Naazh's blade, but after a moment he spotted the gathered telekinetics holding their ground, eyes shut and bodies trembling in intense concentration as more bolts scattered against the psionic barrier they had erected. It was as if the danger had awakened some new escalation in their abilities.

Bolts of sizzling plasma now shot forth from the other direction. *"It's the red Naazh,"* Tong called. *"It's trying to take out the beacon! Shield is holding . . . returning fi— Aaahh!"*

Compartmentalizing his concern for Tong, Chekov pressed his assault on the blue Naazh, determined to end this before the red one managed to take out the damping field. They ended up locked in a slow, fatal dance as they strained with all their might to hold off each other's weapons. The Naazh's strength considerably exceeded Chekov's, but the continuing discharge of the energy baton into its armor was hurting it, canceling its advantage.

The dance turned Chekov far enough around to see the red Naazh continuing to fire at the beacon, bolts smashing into its deflector shield and making it flicker visibly. Crick had retreated behind the shield, dragging the injured but moving Tong beside him, and was firing back on the red Naazh with little effect, unable to get clear to use his bolas or near enough to deploy his baton. It was only a matter of moments, Chekov estimated, until the field collapsed and the Naazh would be free to summon more, deadlier weapons out of thin air.

What happened next was almost too fast for Chekov to register. There was a piercing cry from above and a streak of gold, and then the red Naazh was dragged skyward with such force that it dropped its sidearm. Craning his neck, Chekov saw that it was being carried off in the talons of one of Terebellum's giant golden corvids, whose mighty wings gleamed in the sun.

In moments, the huge bird was high enough that Chekov could barely see the red-and-black figure in its grip struggling. But then the red shape parted from the gold, plummeting toward the ground. Just before it reached the upper perimeter of the damping field, though, it was engulfed in a spherical flicker and vanished. One foe had left the battlefield.

Now a pair of *haipa* cats were racing toward the white-and-black Naazh. Like the corvid, they were coming to the aid of the New Humans they had communed with. But they lacked the advantage of surprise now, and Chekov feared for their safety as the white Naazh turned its sidearm on them.

But the telekinetics had learned from their avian friend. Concentrating as one, they stared at the white Naazh, crouched down with fists clenched before them, then flung their arms skyward with a roar. The antennaed warrior was hurled dozens of meters into the air. It, too, teleported away before it hit the ground.

The black Naazh and the green one followed it soon thereafter, the former as it came under fire from Crick wielding the red Naazh's fallen plasma blaster, the latter after being rendered effectively helpless under Nizhoni and Sanzio's attack. Apparently it was easier for their dimensional technology to take things out of the field than draw them into it. That was fine with Chekov.

Now only the blue Naazh remained, standing there startled at the sudden collapse of its forces. "Give up now," Chekov panted, "and you won't be harmed."

That just seemed to make it angry. "Arrogant interloper!" it cried, confusingly, and lunged at him with its blade held high. It left itself wide open for Chekov to jam the baton into its shoulder joint, the energy discharge weakening its arm and allowing the *Reliant* officer to wrench the short sword from its grip.

"Last chance! Surrender!" Chekov cried.

"I won't lose to you!" It lunged, arms reaching for his throat.

So be it, Chekov thought, and stabbed the tip of the sword right into the large blue crystal on its belt.

The stone cracked, and a blast of energy knocked both combatants backward. The Naazh screamed in pain.

Chekov sat up to see the blue Naazh sprawled flat on its back, its belt crystal flaring and sparking. Nizhoni and Sanzio moved in around him to help him to his feet, and they watched in disbelief as the armor glowed, lost its color, turned translucent, and then vanished . . . leaving its very human-looking wearer helpless on the ground, his face exposed at last.

It was Haru Yamasaki.

As Sanzio dragged the Terebellan security director to his feet, Chekov stared at him in disbelief and betrayal. "You are one of the Naazh?"

That drew a quizzical look. "Is that what you call us?"

"How? *Why?* To murder your own people . . ."

"They are not my kind. Nor are they yours."

"Look!" Chekov dragged him over to behold the fallen bodies of his own security officers and the Terebellan farmers who had fought alongside them. "This is your doing! Why? What did they offer you to join them?"

Yamasaki smirked. "Only the power to protect pure humanity against corruption." He looked over the shocked New Humans in contempt. "Your scourge will not be allowed to continue evolving. The hunters *will* see to that. If not today, then soon enough."

U.S.S. Reliant

Captain Terrell stared at Governor Kisak's mottled green visage on the bridge viewscreen. "Yamasaki *disappeared*?"

"Right out of his hospital bed," the matronly Suliban confirmed. *"And the captured Naazh sidearm vanished at the same time. My scientists report detecting spikes of extradimensional energy at both sites."*

Terrell and Chekov traded a look of deep concern. "And the New Humans?" Chekov asked from where he stood at the right flank of Terrell's command chair.

"Safe for the moment. They're aware of the risk, but after today, they believe they can defend themselves. We stand with them now, and the techniques you showed us should help if it becomes necessary. Thank you."

"Starfleet will always be at your disposal," Terrell told her.

She lowered her head in dismay. *"I can't believe Haru was capable of such violence. Such cruelty and hate. I know he could be difficult, competitive, but he never would have been entrusted with keeping our peace if there had been any signs of such . . .* savagery *in his psych profile. Do you think . . . did these Naazh do something to him?"*

"Unfortunately, without getting to question him, we can't answer that."

"We know one thing, though," Commander Azem-Os fluted,

ruffling her wings as she stepped down from the aft upper deck to stand by Terrell's left. "The Naazh, at least some of them, are not invaders from outside . . . but members of our own communities. If Yamasaki is any example, possibly people whose mistrust or hostility toward telepaths has been radicalized."

The governor frowned sadly. *"I did not want to think it was connected, but the farmer Girsu has been missing since before the battle. He has gone off on his own before, but . . . he was probably the most vocal opponent of the New Humans. If the Naazh have recruited from within us, then perhaps he was one of them as well."*

Beach looked back from the helm station. "But why target telepaths? Or I should say, why just *these* telepaths? Just Aenar and New Humans, not Vulcans or Deltans?"

"Only the minorities," Azem-Os replied. "The exceptions to the species norm."

"But when the Naazh attacked the *Enterprise*," Chekov said, "they showed no hostility toward the Argelian empath in our crew. Only the Aenar." He sighed. "And maybe the New Humans among us. We thought they were just caught in the explosion because they chose to stay and fight. Maybe they were targets all along."

Terrell crossed his arms and spoke grimly. "Something tells me we'll get more answers soon enough. Unfortunately, we won't get them until the next Naazh attack. And now we know that it could come from anywhere—and from any*one* in the Federation. One of our neighbors, our friends. Someone whose fear and animosity toward certain kinds of people are stronger than any of us knew."

He shook his head. "How the hell can we hope to see that coming?"

Twelve

New Human enclave
Western Mediterranean

Admiral Kirk found the New Humans' small island a much less idyllic place than Spock had described several months ago. Starfleet and Earth Security forces roved across the island and patrolled its perimeter. Emergency medical shuttles rested near the central villa, and one took off and flew toward the nearby North African coast as Kirk neared the building. The villa and its surrounding grounds were in a sorry state, with sizable portions of both apparently torn apart by energy blasts or more exotic forces.

Miranda Jones came out of the villa as he approached, striding straight toward him, even though she was without her sensor web for the first time in his experience. She looked sadder and wearier than Kirk had ever seen her. Although he still found her beautiful, especially in the sheer, flowing green tunic she wore, he could actually tell for the first time that she wasn't as young as she had been a decade ago.

"Admiral Kirk," she said as she drew near, a smile briefly forcing its way through her pall of solemn grief. "It's gracious of you to check in on us."

"I'm sorry I didn't come sooner," Kirk said as he clasped her hands in greeting and commiseration. "My duties at the Academy and on the *Enterprise* have kept me very busy."

"It's all right, Admiral. I can't blame you for not wanting to be reminded of last year's tragedy. Unfortunately, none of us have that luxury any longer."

She led him over to a surviving bench beneath a pair of mostly undamaged trees. "You can still call me Jim," he told her.

"I know," she replied with a smile. "I'm just getting a feel for your new title."

"You and me both." They laughed.

Taking a seat alongside her on the bench, Kirk said, "I've been briefed on the attack, but I'd like to hear it from you, Miranda. If you don't mind."

She grimaced. "I don't mind telling you, Jim. I mind very much that it happened.

"There were six of them this time," she said in a cold, level voice. "Six genocidal killers, right in the heart of the safest planet in the Federation. They included three we've seen before—the gold one and the antennaed white one from the *Enterprise*, and the black one from the Terebellum colony." Kirk didn't ask how she knew their colors. She had either been briefed by the sighted New Humans or had seen it directly through their eyes.

"So they escaped the explosion on the *Enterprise* after all," Kirk said.

She furrowed her brow. "You don't buy the theory that they're duplicate armors?"

He shook his head. "We've only ever seen one of each at a time. And that armor could resist point-blank fire from multiple phaser rifles with barely a scratch. The force of the explosion wouldn't have been enough by itself to kill them. We assumed they were sucked out and disintegrated in the collapsing warp field, but now it seems they were able to teleport out first."

She clenched her fists. "They're like monsters from a horror story—impossible to kill, impossible to beat because they always adapt. They didn't mess around with knives and swords this time, not after their defeat last week. They came in with disruptors blazing.

"Four of us died before we could mount enough of a telekinetic defense to fight back. And when we did, they were able to counter it with that . . . belt-stone flash of theirs. We had to improvise new defenses the best we could. We lost three more before Starfleet Security arrived with their anti-Naazh devices."

"How did they get past the shields?" Kirk asked. As soon as the *Reliant* had reported the attack on Omega Sagittarii a week before, Starfleet had equipped the island with deflectors and subspace disruptor beacons.

"They had a mole," Jones replied, seething with anger. "A woman named Francesca Vassallo, who flew in from Rome once a week to bring us fresh food and wine. We knew her, trusted her." Her fists clenched in her lap. "Now they tell us a search of her computer logs revealed that she was affiliated with anti–New Human groups, people who equated our emergence with the rise of Augments and saw us as a threat to the peace. She'd been spying on us for months, gaining our friendship, our complacency. It let her gain access to sabotage the disruptor beacons."

Jones shook her head. "Normally, we would have sensed something. We don't actively intrude on others' thoughts, but there are unconscious emotional cues that leak out when someone is planning violence."

Kirk nodded. "I remember—ten years ago on the *Enterprise*, you sensed Marvick's homicidal feelings toward Kollos."

"But not clearly enough to realize in time that he was the source," she said ruefully. "This time, we were all on our guard after Terebellum. And all our minds are open to each other. So if Vassallo had given off any such violent urges, we *should* have been able to recognize them."

Kirk touched her shoulder gently. "It's just more proof that the Naazh can shield their minds from telepathy. All it means is that they don't need their armor to do it. It doesn't mean you let your guard down, Miranda."

"I appreciate it, Jim." She placed her hand on his, and though she didn't cling to it as needily as she had last year on the *Enterprise*, she let the contact linger, gentle and warm. "The first sign we had of anything wrong was when the shields fell. That's when we finally sensed what Vassallo had done. At that point, I suppose, she *wanted* us to know it had been her.

"So some of us confronted her. I perceived it through their eyes. She laughed and placed her hand over her waist, and the Naazh armor materialized around her as they watched." She winced. "And then she started killing them. And then the others came."

Kirk clasped her hand in both of his. "Still . . . it's remarkable that you were able to fight back so effectively. You drove them off, even took two of them down." One, clad in orange-and-black armor, had been identified as a human, Stewart Tsai, who had evidently been a fellow member of Francesca Vassallo's extremist group. The other, the one with antennaed black-and-brown armor, had been Satakeshi th'Kenda, an anti-Aenar agitator from Andoria, whose whereabouts during the massacre in the Aenar compound could not be verified. It was now believed that he was one of the two unaccounted-for members of the five-Naazh group that had committed that atrocity. Unfortunately, Tsai had been teleported away before he could be questioned, and th'Kenda had taken his own life when the New Humans who overpowered him had attempted to probe his mind—a violation of their normal telepathic etiquette, but deemed necessary in the heat of the moment.

Jones nodded. "We've found that our powers are amplified when we gather in groups. It's part of the reason we've congregated into these enclaves in the past year. We suspected this might be coming."

The admiral stared at her. "Did you have reason to believe the Naazh would target you as well as the Aenar?"

She hesitated. "Call it a precaution. An awareness of the risk. The Naazh's motives for exterminating the Aenar were never understood. Until now. For us, it seemed safest to assume the worst." She gestured around them. "As you can see, it proved a wise choice. We have the means to fight back now."

"But at the same time, by gathering into these enclaves, you're making yourselves clearer targets. Other New Human enclaves have been attacked on Alpha Centauri, on Aldebaran III, on Deneb V. Spock and the *Enterprise* are at Centauri now, providing relief."

Jones rose and began to pace around the bench. "Believe me, Jim, we're very aware of the problem. And steps are being taken to address it." She turned to him. "As long as there are extremists within the Federation who hate New Humans to this degree—as long as they could be living among us, wearing the faces of friends and neighbors, perhaps even authority figures—we can't be safe here.

"But we have another option. The Medusans have offered us asylum in their space, and we've accepted."

Kirk rose to his feet and faced her. "The Medusans? Miranda, are you sure?" The thought that she might go back to them was more alarming than he had expected. He still remembered the intensity of the kiss they had shared . . . and he had not been oblivious to McCoy's words about trying to find someone.

She smiled. "Don't forget, I lived with them for nearly a decade. And there are other humanoids living in their space, serving on their ships, sharing minds with them as I . . . did with Kollos. There are proven protocols in place for keeping them safe from accidental visual exposure." A pause. "Besides, the Medusans still feel an obligation to try to make amends for their inability to save the Aenar. They want to do what they can for the Naazh's current targets."

"It just . . . seems rather drastic. To leave behind your homes, your lives . . ."

"Believe me, we've already debated that extensively among ourselves. We don't all think alike—many of us still had strong ties back home and were reluctant to move into the enclaves. But they understood that it was better to leave their loved ones than to risk seeing them hurt or killed in a Naazh attack. What's drastic is what those monsters are doing to us."

She tilted her head. "Is this really concern for us, Jim, or does it wound your pride that Starfleet can't protect us?"

He flushed, hesitant to admit his more selfish motives. "Starfleet has made a difference. On Omega Sagittarii and here."

"Not enough of one. And who's to say there aren't Naazh in your own ranks?"

It was a moment before he replied. "I can accept—barely—that there could still be some humans intolerant enough to be vulnerable to radicalization by a group like this. But Starfleet screens its recruits carefully. It selects for people who celebrate difference rather than fearing it."

Even as he spoke, though, he remembered Lieutenant Stiles's kneejerk bigotry toward Spock after discovering that Romulans were a Vulcan offshoot. Even the best screening could have blind spots.

Jones sensed his hesitation and nodded. "You can't entirely deny the possibility, can you?"

He sighed. "No." He clasped her shoulder. "But even so, most of us in Starfleet are on your side. Sworn to protect all Federation citizens, all innocents, from this kind of atrocity."

Her smile returned. "I know that, Jim."

"Then at least let me arrange a Starfleet escort to Medusan space. Bring in the *Enterprise*, and whatever other ships I can convince Starfleet to spare. Being an admiral has its advantages." When she hesitated, he went on. "There are enclaves of your people on nearly a dozen worlds. Who else but Starfleet has the reach and the speed to gather them all up quickly, and the power to defend them against the ongoing Naazh attacks? You can't expect us to just sit back and let the Medusans defend our citizens for us. At least not while they're in Federation territory."

She sighed, visibly conceding the point. "Very well. I'll recommend it to the others."

"Do you think they'll agree?"

"I'm confident of it. After all," she finished with mild amusement, "we do tend to be of one mind."

He nodded and started to turn away. But she smiled, took his hands, and pulled him back down to the bench. "You don't have to go just yet, Jim."

"I, ah, I'm sure we both have responsibilities to get back to."

"Remember what I said about strong emotions leaking out? I can sense the real reason you're reluctant to see me leave."

He shook his head. "I can't think of my own desires in the middle of a crisis like this."

"Jim—I have desires too. Living among the New Humans has helped me learn to be more frank about them with myself—and with others."

She kissed him once again, and though it was not as desperate as their first kiss, it was just as warm and open, and much more confident. When it was over, he needed a moment to catch his breath, giving her time to continue. "I know you're ambivalent about this because of your behavior ten years ago. But we've both matured since then, in judgment and in empathy. I can trust you now in a way I couldn't then. So forget about the past." She kissed him once more, briefly.

"It's more the future I'm concerned about," Kirk replied. "If you're leaving for Medusa . . ."

"All the more reason to seize the opportunity while we can," she said. "With the losses I've sustained this past year, I've come to appreciate the value of making the most of the time we have with someone. The fact that it will end is all the more reason to embrace it in the moment."

That was a sentiment Kirk understood far too well. For all

that he longed for something more lasting, for all the times he'd mourned a love taken too soon, he still cherished the time he had spent with each woman.

He smiled and stroked her hair. "If you're sure it's what you want . . ."

"Have you ever known me to be indecisive, Jim?" She dragged him to his feet. "Come on. There's a lovely secluded spot on the beach. We can watch the sunset."

"It's hours until sunset."

She gave a mischievous smile. "I know."

He let her pull him along, but one concern remained. "On an island full of telepaths, is any place really private?"

"Oh, don't be modest, Jim. Just because they can feel our emotions doesn't make them voyeurs. Think of it like living in a dorm with thin walls."

He ran with her hand in his, laughing. It was remarkable to see this side of her. He had assumed before that the more exuberant parts of her erstwhile corporate intelligence had come from Kollos's side. Maybe she retained some of that joyousness after the ambassador's death, a legacy he had left her. Or maybe it had been inside her all along, just waiting for her to feel confident and trusting enough to let it out.

Either way, he felt he was finally seeing her true beauty for the first time.

Starfleet Sector Headquarters, Andoria

Thelin th'Valrass slammed his hands down atop Admiral zh'Menlich's desk. "But we *have* to join in the defense of the human telepaths!" he told her. "We owe these Naazh a blood debt. They struck on our very soil. We must be part of the fight against them now."

"Is it really our fight, though?" Majurisa zh'Menlich countered. "Their quarrel was with the Aenar, and now with humans. A breed of humans who set themselves apart, as the Aenar did."

"That does not negate the ties of kinship," Thelin insisted. "Not only the kinship of blood and species, but of our chosen family, the Federation. The Naazh are invaders attacking Federation citizens."

The heavyset, middle-aged *zhen* leaned back in her seat, antennae curling skeptically. "Some of them *are* Federation citizens."

"Subverted by some alien force that hides its true face. Committing acts of terrorism and genocide against other Federation citizens. How is this not Starfleet's purview?"

"Starfleet has multiple ships assigned to the effort already."

"And it needs more. The targeted humans are spread across multiple worlds."

The admiral peered up at him. "Are you so certain, Thelin, that *they* aren't the ones we should be worried about? Growing so quickly in power in just a few years, gathering together in organized groups?"

Thelin glared back, controlling his anger at her insinuation. "They have harmed no one. The Naazh have been slaughtering them, as they did the Aenar. Know their motives through their methods, Admiral."

Zh'Menlich sighed. "I don't mean to be insensitive, Thelin. I know you lost family. But I have to be objective, and consider the larger interests of Andor."

Thelin chose his words carefully. "I know that the trend of the past century has been to draw inward—to focus on our own problems and allow the humans and Vulcans to deal with the rest."

"Those problems are considerable. Even existential."

"Granted," Thelin said, though he suspected zh'Menlich was overstating the case; the terraforming was more a matter of economic convenience and comfort than survival, and surely

Federation science would find a solution to the Andorians' current reproductive decline before it became critical. "But Starfleet has always stood ready to come to our aid. Have we become so passive that we cannot repay them in kind?" He leaned forward. "Remember how it was a century ago, when the Andorian Guard was the linchpin of Starfleet's defense force. Our ancestors fought fearlessly in defense of those not our own, whether Federation citizens or not. They stood against the Ware, against the Klingons at Ardan IV, against Maltuvis at—"

"All right, all right," zh'Menlich said. "You had me at Ardan IV." Thelin smiled inwardly. He had known the admiral's ancestor had commanded the *Docana* in that conflict. "The *Charas* is nearly done with repairs; you can take it out as soon as you assemble a crew."

Thelin absorbed the admiral's words. The *Charas* was a fairly small vessel, but fast and well armed. With a skeleton crew, it could hold a fair-sized contingent of New Human refugees, and contribute meaningfully to their defense if—

Then the rest of her words struck him. "As soon as *I* assemble a crew?"

She smirked. "It's your mission, Commander, so you might as well command it. I'll put you in for a field promotion to captain. Isn't that what you always wanted, Thelin?"

He stood there mildly stunned as the promotion sank in. Of course, it was a promotion in little more than name; a ship the *Charas*'s size could easily be helmed by an officer of commander's rank. But Starfleet tended to treat ranks as something more like job titles, so officers assigned to ship commands tended to be formally given captain's rank regardless of strict matters of officer grades and promotion schedules.

Still, technicalities aside, Thelin now had his own starship to command. It had been his ambition for so long, but he had given up on it almost as long ago, contenting himself with a more domestic path. Now his old wish had been abruptly granted due to an awful situation. He honestly did not know how to feel about that.

But of course, his feelings were not the important consideration. He straightened to attention. "Thank you, Admiral. I'll assemble a crew immediately."

"And I'll notify Starfleet Command that we're joining the party," zh'Menlich said. "Congratulations—*Captain* Thelin. I hope you get your vengeance."

"My first priority is to protect Federation lives," he said. "But if I can avenge the Aenar in the process . . . so much the better."

Kardia, Regulus III

Arsène Xiang lowered his hands from Reiko Onami's head and opened his eyes. "I'm sorry, Reiko. I fear there's nothing within you I can help you to unlock." The gray-haired, strong-featured New Human took on a tone of gentle apology. "To be frank . . . the esper testing protocols that were used until recently were highly prone to . . . false positives."

"So I'm not a telepath after all?" Onami asked.

Xiang smiled at her. "What I sense from you, Reiko, is that you possess deep empathy for others and a truly open mind. Maybe those are what the tests registered."

Onami barked a laugh. She rose from her chair and moved to lean on the railing of the balcony where they sat, looking out over the clean-lined towers of Kardia, one of the largest cities on Regulus III. In the street below, an eclectic mix of humans, Vulcans, Arodi, Caitians, and others bustled among the multiple vendor booths and food carts of the monthly street fair. It reminded her of her childhood home on Nelgha, except there were far more humans here, including the New Humans who ran most of the booths and carts, inviting the fair patrons to take advantage of their psionic gifts for advice, tailored cuisine, or just entertainment. The New Humans here had congregated in their own neighborhood of Kardia, mingling freely with their neighbors, rather than setting themselves apart in more isolated enclaves as on other worlds. But then, Regulans had always—with some exceptions—been a welcoming people. According to Xiang, this was the busiest the fair had ever been, as it was the last one before the local community boarded the *U.S.S. Palmares* and joined the New Human exodus.

"Deep empathy, huh?" she repeated after a moment. "I'm not sure about that. I can hardly stand most humans. Always got along great with nonhumans, but my own species?" She made a rude noise. "They drive me crazy."

The older New Human chuckled. "Of course. They're your family. No one frustrates us so much as the people we love the most." He put a hand on her shoulder. "Just embrace what you already have. That should be enough."

She blushed a bit. The kindly old guy was threatening to make her change her mind about humans. "You're really sweet, Arsène, but don't worry. I didn't really have some deep driving need to be a New Human. I'm just curious about, ah, New Humanity as a phenomenon. The emergence of a whole new culture—it's really caught my interest."

"Of course. To a student of different species and their interactions, it's quite the opportunity."

She leaned back on the railing and studied him. "You aren't offended? Don't mind that I'm here to put you under the microscope?"

Xiang chuckled. "I was in Starfleet once myself. Enlisted, like you, with a specialty in history and xenosociology. So I understand that compulsion to learn and explore."

He spread his arms. "Besides, we have nothing to hide. Indeed, we *want* others to learn more about us. To understand what New Humans really are, and that we pose no threat to them."

Onami heard the solemn undercurrent. "After this past week,

I can understand why you think that." She frowned. "But does it matter? If you're all fleeing to Medusan space, doesn't that eliminate the problem?"

Xiang shifted in his seat, steepling his fingers in a gesture that reminded her of Spock. "If you had to run and hide from a threat, would you be content to hide forever? To make that your permanent way of life, always in retreat from those who would never accept your existence? Or would you hold on to hope that you could change that status quo, by changing enough minds that there would no longer be any reason to fear?"

"I see what you mean." She studied him. "You seem like you've given this a lot of thought, considering that it's only been a week since we learned your people were targeted."

He cleared his throat. "Well . . . the fact is, we've faced suspicion and intolerance from other humans since we started to grow in ability after V'Ger. Many people still focus on the danger V'Ger posed rather than the transcendence it allowed us to glimpse, so our association with V'Ger—or at least the perception of same, whether it's real or not—makes many people wary of us. The enduring fear of Augments plays into that as well, as Terebellum showed."

"But you couldn't have expected a response this violent."

He sighed. "I'm a historian, my dear. One thing I've learned is that people rarely recognize how bad such threats are until the killing has already begun."

Haru Yamasaki seethed at the sight of all the New Humans in the booths and carts around him, blithely showing off their psionic powers as if they were harmless entertainments for the Kardian public. The Regulans were too trusting, letting such threats into their backyard all too readily.

He turned to Mahar Anaza, amazed that his recruiter into the cause was able to watch all this so calmly. Of course, the

Romulan was pretending to be one of Regulus's many Vulcan citizens, but nonetheless, he was a hunter to the core, his passion for justice and retribution as fierce as that which had burned in Yamasaki's heart since he had accepted the dimension stone Anaza had offered him back on Terebellum.

It had been a surprise to learn that his recruiter had been a member of a Federation enemy, but Anaza had made it clear that he recognized the Aenar and New Humans as a threat transcending politics, one his own superiors in the Romulans' Tal Shiar intelligence agency had dismissed. Like Yamasaki, he had been stymied by his own nation, unable to take any action against the threat until the opportunity to join the hunters had been given to him. He had been one of the Lords' first recruits, the effective leader of their small but efficiently deadly corps of hunters, and thus it was strange to Yamasaki that he could be so stoic in the midst of their prey.

"*Why are we not armoring up?*" he demanded silently, sending his thoughts through the mental connection the dimension stones provided. He could feel the stone calling to him through the entanglement link from the dimensional pocket where it was stored, ready to be summoned with a thought. "*All these psionic freaks together in one place, off guard and in the open. This is the most target-rich environment I've ever seen!*"

Anaza put a cautioning hand on his arm. "*I share your fire, hunter, but contain yourself. We both saw their strength in numbers on Terebellum.*" The Romulan winced; his back was still strained from being carried off by that giant corvid ten days before. His scarlet armor had saved him from being gored or crushed by its talons, but the sheer force of being yanked skyward by his arms and upper torso had been damaging enough. "*And here they will have the Regulan police and defense forces on their side, as well as Starfleet. The time is not right.*"

"*When, then? We need to wipe them out before those Starfleet traitors help them escape to Medusa!*"

Anaza chuckled. Yamasaki looked around, but no one in the crowd seemed to notice the un-Vulcan reaction.

"*Don't worry,*" Anaza sent to him. "*As effective, and cathartic, as our usual methods are, there are other ways to hunt. Goading them into flight has always been the plan.*"

The Romulan smiled. "*And our golden young firebrand is in position, gathering the knowledge we need to make our next strike the most devastating yet.*"

Thirteen

U.S.S. *Asimov* NCC-1652

"Come quickly! They're killing us! They're trying to blow the warp reac— Aaahh!!"

Nyota Uhura winced as the terrified voice screamed and fell silent. More screams could be heard in the background of the open channel as the *Asimov*'s captain, Erin Blake, leaned forward urgently. "*Yggdrasil*, do you copy? *Yggdrasil*, come in!" The dark-haired young captain turned to her chief engineer. "Mister Scott, can you get any more speed out of the engines?"

"I'm giving her all she's got, Captain," the grizzled, mustached engineer replied, a refrain all too familiar to Uhura's ears. "But she's not as young as she used to be. It's a struggle to keep her warp polarity in alignment. Any faster and the frame-dragging will pull us off course."

Blake sighed. "Just . . . do what you can, Mister Scott." Uhura could hear in the captain's warm but professional voice that she was familiar enough with Scott's reputation to know what that meant. Uhura sympathized; ever since she'd boarded the *Asimov* as its science officer, she'd felt safer knowing that Scotty was along with her.

Unfortunately, this was not the kind of mission they had signed on for. By the luck of the draw, the midsized research vessel's pursuit of subspace density anomalies had made it the nearest ship available to rendezvous with the *Yggdrasil*, the civilian transport that the New Human community on Deneb Kaitos IV had launched to join the convoy to Medusan space. Admiral Kirk, coordinating the task force from the *Enterprise*, had asked the group to stay at Deneb for their own protection until the *Asimov* could reach them, but they had believed they would be safer in transit—a belief that had now proven to be a mistake. According to their panicked reports, some Naazh agent on Deneb must have sabotaged their shield grid and subspace damping beacon before they launched, the failure timed to leave them helpless in open space, too far from rescue. The *Asimov* was just minutes away now, but it would be minutes too late.

An energy spike from the *Yggdrasil* caught Uhura's eye. "Captain—their warp core is starting to destabilize!"

"*Yggdrasil*, do you read?" Blake shouted. "You need to jettison your warp reactor now! Please copy—"

She broke off, for a piercing pinpoint of light flared briefly on the main viewer, alongside the undeniable energy readings on Uhura's science console. "The ship is gone, sir," she confirmed, dutifully but redundantly.

"Ahh, damn the Naazh," Scott muttered. "You don't suppose the explosion took them with it, do you?"

"We thought the explosion on the *Enterprise* did them in, but they apparently survived it," Uhura said. "And I have no doubt they set this one off on purpose. So it's a safe bet—" She broke off, relieved to spot scattered life readings as the radiation cleared. "Captain! I'm reading thirteen escape pods. Estimate one to two life signs in each."

Blake sighed in relief. "Thank the Great Bird. That's close to half the contingent. How soon can we rendezvous?"

Uhura gasped as the life signs in two of the pods fluctuated. First they increased in number, simultaneous with a subspace energy spike in each . . . then the numbers rapidly diminished to one per pod, then to zero after a second spike. "Oh, no. Two Naazh are teleporting from pod to pod, killing the occupants one by one."

Blake turned to Scott. "Same question, more urgent."

"Still a minute away, sir," Scott said heavily.

"Uhura, do they have a minute?"

"No, sir. Four pods are now lifeless." The readings changed. "Make that five." A tear rolled down her cheek. "We'll never make it in time."

Scott brightened. "Maybe we can, lass—if we don't slow down first. In fact, we should go faster, and the hell with the warp polarity."

Blake stared. "But we'll go right past them."

"If this works, Captain, we can go back for them. But I'll have to time it just right."

The young captain wasted no time, trusting in Scott's experience. "All right. Mister Schnell, maximum warp on Mister Scott's command."

"Aye, Captain," Daryl Schnell replied from the helm.

By now, two more escape pods were under Naazh attack, their biosigns dwindling. In mere moments, the Naazh would teleport out of them and into the next two pods. Uhura wished she knew what Scotty was planning. She had enormous faith in him, but under the circumstances—

"Punch it!" Scott commanded. Schnell pushed the manual override throttle to the limit.

The energy spikes of Naazh teleportation appeared and faded in the now-lifeless escape pods. The *Asimov* flew right through the pack of pods, seemingly with no effect. Then the energy spikes appeared on Uhura's sensors again, and the Naazh reappeared—

—in empty space, hundreds of meters behind the escape pods.

"Sir!" Uhura cried, setting the main viewscreen to focus on the Naazh flailing in space.

Blake shot to her feet. "I see them! Schnell, drop to impulse, come around, and fire on those Naazh. Transporter room, lock on to escape pods and prepare to retrieve survivors."

Uhura began to have an inkling of what had happened, but she just hoped it would throw off the Naazh's targeting long enough. Fortunately, their convulsions of surprise had put them into slow spins around their centers of mass, which must have made it hard to reorient themselves as they drifted farther away from the escape pods at an angle to their course. Soon enough, the *Asimov* had swung around and opened fire with its phasers. Astonishingly, the armor suits withstood even direct hits from starship phasers, but the readings showed they had sustained damage. It wasn't enough to prevent them from teleporting away—but this time, they did not return.

Once Uhura had reported this, Blake ordered her crew to retrieve the survivors from the remaining six pods. Then she turned to her engineer and said, "Mister Scott, now that we have a free moment, maybe you could tell me how the hell we just saved those people, so I can sound like I know what I'm talking about in my log."

Scott grinned. "Like I said, Captain, going faster caused the warp polarity to go out of alignment—and I gave it a little extra boost in the wrong direction right as we went past. We needed to increase the frame-dragging as much as possible."

Blake frowned. "But that's . . . the gravitomagnetic effect, right? Like around a rotating black hole."

"It's the same principle," Uhura told her. "The relativistic effect of the moving mass tilts the axes of space and time, essentially dragging them out of alignment." She smiled. "It's like we twisted space just a little bit as we went past."

Blake nodded. "And since you did it *during* the Naazh's teleport . . ."

Scott nodded. "Their coordinates were already set, so they couldn't compensate for it. I figured that since it's an interdimensional jump, whatever other continuum they're passing through wouldn't be affected by a twist to *our* four dimensions." He chuckled. "Like pulling the rug out from under them."

The captain shook her head. "And all because our ship is old and out of calibration."

The engineer stroked his graying mustache. "Well, you know . . . age does have its compensations."

U.S.S. Enterprise

Admiral Kirk still found it odd to step onto the *Enterprise* bridge and see another captain occupying its center seat. The fact that it was Spock made it palatable. This was their third special mission over the past several months since their respective promotions, and Spock had easily lived up to Kirk's expectations of his fitness for command. But Kirk was merely human—*of the old persuasion*, he added in his mind, *and getting older*—and sometimes he wondered if he would ever truly be able to see someone else in that chair, even his best friend, without some degree of envy.

It helped that he had decades of experience subsuming his emotions beneath duty and discipline. Maturity may have loosened him up from the self-consciously serious "stack of books with legs" he had been in his younger days, but he was still able to call on that restraint when he needed it.

"Status, Captain Spock?" he asked as he stepped down into the command well.

The Vulcan rose from the chair to face him. "All surviving New Human populations are now in transit," he reported. "The *Potemkin* has evacuated the enclave on Aldebaran III and shall reach Medusan space ten hours ahead of us. The *Asimov* reports that the survivors from Deneb Kaitos IV are stable, and they are eight hours from rendezvous with us. The *Palmares* is inbound with the Regulus contingent, scheduled to rendezvous half an hour later. The *Reliant* has retrieved the New Human community from Delta IV without incident, and is en route to collect the fifteen New Humans who managed to survive the assault on Altair IV—though with the survivors from Omega Sagittarii already on board, that will leave them somewhat overcrowded. It will still be at least two days before they can rendezvous with the convoy."

"Acknowledged." Kirk felt a twinge of regret at that. Currently, besides himself and Spock, the *Enterprise* carried Doctor McCoy, Commander Sulu, and a few other familiar faces, such as the newly promoted Lieutenant Palur at the bridge science station. With Scotty and Uhura hours away on the *Asimov* and Doctor Chapel helping to escort the Regulan New Humans on the *Palmares*, that left only Chekov, Kyle, and Nizhoni from *Reliant* to complete the set, as it were. Kirk believed his selection of ships for the New Human task force had been based on his knowledge of the selected personnel's abilities and experience, rather than a sentimental desire to get the old crew back together. Still, he found it agreeable that the two goals aligned, and if there had been some bias in his selection, so be it; the reason this crew had stuck together so long in the first place was because they had all proven themselves to be superlatively skilled individually and to work even better as a team.

At the helm, Sulu turned around to face Kirk and Spock. "It's going to be pretty crowded around here before long."

"Our facilities should be more than adequate," Spock reminded him, "thanks to your efforts in converting the cargo bay."

Even with a reduced crew complement clearing up space in the residential quarters, it had still been necessary to equip the *Enterprise* with extra dormitory facilities for the New Human refugees, as some of the incoming ships were too small to accommodate them for long. The vast cargo storage facility that occupied much of the secondary hull's volume had been the ideal site—particularly since no one had much desire to see the Naazh's current targets put up in the recreation deck. For the duration of the mission, the rec deck was being used for spare cargo storage to clear up more room below.

"I've done my best," Sulu said. "We have enough cots and facilities in place—it's a good thing the New Humans don't feel much need for privacy or personal space."

"But something still concerns you?" Spock asked.

Sulu grimaced. "I just hope the shields and dampers around the cargo bay are effective. The Naazh seem to be adapting to our defenses almost as fast as we develop new ones."

"The Medusans will be joining us soon enough," Kirk reassured him. "From what Doctor Jones tells me, they have countermeasures of their own that they believe will be effective."

"I hope so, Admiral. I know Medusans are capable of some amazing things, like how Kollos got us back from that . . . continuum we were stuck in. But the Naazh . . . they're just so relentless. So savage. They just keep coming. And we still don't know why."

"Regrettably," Spock replied, "history is replete with groups motivated by violent hatred toward others for arbitrary or incomprehensible reasons. For some, the mere fact of difference, or the mere existence of competitors for their accustomed power and privilege, has been perceived as an existential threat requiring violent response."

"That's what worries me," Sulu said. "That there may be no hope of compromise. No way to change their minds and end this fight."

"Indeed. Altering the viewpoints of those invested in extreme beliefs is exceedingly difficult. But it is sometimes possible. If and when we manage to capture and interrogate a Naazh, we may find some key to halting the violence."

"Do you really think that's possible, sir?"

Spock folded his hands over his waist. "The savagery of the

Naazh, while formidable, is no worse than that of the Vulcan people nineteen centuries ago. Yet Surak succeeded in bringing peace."

Sulu stared. "Only after he gave his life for it."

"Yes," Spock replied gravely. "That is sometimes the price that must be paid."

Leonard McCoy found Miranda Jones in the *Enterprise*'s spacious cargo storage complex, where she had been spending most of her time since she had come aboard. The lowermost cargo floor on S deck was about the size of two adjacent basketball courts, much of it taken up by cots, tables, food synthesizer stations, and portable refreshers. Many of the side bays had been emptied of their usual cargo containers in order to convert them into additional, slightly more private (though compact) dwelling spaces. Overhead, *Enterprise* security personnel armed incongruously with energy batons and bolas stood guard on both of the upper catwalk levels along the side walls of the three-story space. To aft, the huge segmented doors that divided the cargo bay from the shuttlecraft landing bay were open, which was usually only the case when the ship was loading or unloading cargo; now it was because the lowered shuttle elevator platforms at the forward end of the hangar level were being converted into extra dormitory space for the refugees still incoming from the *Asimov* and the *Palmares*. Gazing up toward the rear of the landing bay some distance away, McCoy felt relieved that at least the clamshell doors were shut, so that there was more than just an invisible force field separating all these people from the vacuum of space.

The open portion of the cargo bay floor was currently being used by about a dozen and a half of the New Humans for some kind of telekinetic defense drills. McCoy watched in amazement as the telekinetics sparred without touching, thrusting out hands to knock each other back with invisible bursts of force, to attempt to levitate each other, to hurl or deflect objects, and so forth. McCoy repressed a shudder; he and his crewmates had been the victims of telekinetic attacks on so many occasions—Gary Mitchell, Charlie Evans, the Platonians, and so on—that it was hard to get used to the idea of those powers being used on the side of the good guys. *Pure hocus-pocus if you ask me,* he thought—and he hoped that nobody was listening.

The bigger surprise was that Doctor Jones was one of the telekinetic combatants. She'd always been just about the strongest human telepath ever recorded, but this was a new addition to her repertoire. As McCoy watched her push herself, he feared that it was taking its toll.

After a few more moments, she told the others to take five, strode over to the sidelines, and began to wipe her sweat with a towel. McCoy made his way over to her, and she called out before he could. "Doctor McCoy! Are you enjoying the show?"

He waited to speak until he was alongside her. "It's impressive, I have to admit."

"Glad to see it on your own side for a change?" she challenged.

He stared. "You weren't listening in on my thoughts just now, were you?"

She touched his arm reassuringly. "Never, Doctor, I promise. But there are other ways to read people. And it's a sentiment we've heard before."

He looked her over. "I see you're wearing your sensor web again." The diaphanous garment over her workout clothes had been re-tailored from a flowing gown into a more figure-hugging form, no doubt for freedom of movement.

"If we come under attack, I want every advantage," she replied. "I can perceive much through the others' eyes, and through my own psionic insight, but the sensors fill some gaps here and there."

He furrowed his brows. "I'm concerned you may be overlooking one sizable gap, Miranda."

"And what's that?"

"Yourself. You're fighting so relentlessly for everyone else that I'm concerned you're ignoring your own health."

"I'm fine, Doctor."

"Are you sure? As a gentleman, I'd never impugn a lady's appearance, but as a doctor, I have to express my concern about the level of fatigue you're showing. You seem drained, overtired. And . . . not to be indelicate, but a touch of premature gray here and there, while certainly dignified, can be a sign of excessive stress hormones."

She glared at him. "You haven't changed. Still overly concerned with beauty and youth."

"My dear lady, a true beauty like yours improves with age, like a fine wine. I'm simply concerned for your health."

"Flattery aside, my people need me, Doctor. The Naazh could attack at any time."

"All the more reason to make sure you don't collapse from exhaustion at a key moment." As she turned to toss the towel into a recycler, he moved in front of her. "Just come to sickbay for a quick check. It won't take fifteen minutes."

"In my experience," she said with a sour expression, "when a doctor says it'll take fifteen minutes, I'll spend at least an hour waiting for it first. Since you went to the trouble of making a house call, can't you check me out here?"

McCoy rolled his eyes. "You're as bad as Jim. No wonder you two finally got together."

"Call it an occupational hazard of leadership."

He grumbled at that, then said, "I can do a basic scan, but I'd prefer to get you on the diagnostic table. There's still so much we don't understand about the amplification of your mental powers. I want to make sure they aren't having a harmful effect on your brain and nervous system."

"I really don't have time for that, Doctor. These people depend on me—emotionally on top of everything else. We've grown very close. We don't like to be separated more than we have to."

"You can bring some with you if you like. The more samples we can study to build our baseline, the better."

Jones gave a heavy sigh. "If I say I'll think about it, will you just give me a quick scan for now, maybe a vitamin shot if you think it'll help?"

He thought it over. He wasn't crazy about the compromise, but at least it was some progress. "All right. *For now.* As long as you really think about it instead of just brushing me off."

"You have my word, Doctor McCoy."

He accepted it at that and proceeded with the tricorder scan. He did indeed give her a vitamin shot and prescribed fluids, a meal, and sleep, which seemed medically adequate for the moment. It was the kind of compromise he was all too used to making with Kirk and Spock, and indeed with most commanding officers he'd served with in his career.

But he couldn't shake the feeling that Jones's resistance to an examination had something more behind it. He just wished he could begin to imagine what it was.

Fourteen

By the time the *U.S.S. Palmares* arrived, the *Enterprise* had been joined by the *Asimov* and the Medusan diplomatic transport *Chrysaor*. The latter was actually one of several antiquated Federation vessels that had been traded to the Medusans to facilitate their interactions with more corporeal species, a squat gray toad of a ship with a spherical forward hull for its humanoid crew and an oddly shaped aft section modified for its Medusan occupants, like a metal eggplant skewered by ten long rods. The Medusans had come to provide support and defense to the convoy as the New Humans were delivered to their space, but the *Chrysaor* kept its distance for now, to avoid spooking any New Humans (or Starfleet personnel) who were still intimidated by the risks of contact with Medusans.

But while the *Asimov* had come bearing only eleven survivors of the Naazh's attack, enough to beam aboard the *Enterprise* quite easily, the *Palmares* had a considerably larger contingent of New Humans from the populous Regulus system. The *Soyuz*-class starship was large enough to hold most of them, particularly since it was traveling with a skeleton crew of sixty; but to facilitate the interaction of the two groups of refugees, the *Palmares* had drawn in alongside the *Enterprise*'s secondary hull and extended a docking tunnel from its portside gangway hatch to the starboard docking port that opened onto the larger starship's main cargo bay. Admiral Kirk was there with Captain Spock to greet the contingent that came across from the *Palmares*.

Kirk smiled as he shook the hand of the tall, mature Arkenite who boarded first. "Captain nd'Omeshef," he said warmly. "It's been a long time since Starbase 24."

Jaulas nd'Omeshef's pupil-less green eyes crinkled beneath his large, hairless cranial lobes and the inverted black *U* of the *Anlac'ven* headband that adorned it. "Not that long, Admiral—but you have risen quite far in that time."

"We've both traded up from the scout ships we started with," Kirk said. "Gained in experience and responsibility."

"Yet here we are on a joint task force once more. With you in command, I have faith that this one will be more successful than our last."

Kirk winced at the reminder of the mission that had nearly cost him his first command less than a year after his promotion to captain. He'd forgotten what a killjoy nd'Omeshef could be.

He changed the subject by introducing Captain Spock and Miranda Jones, and exchanging further greetings with Christine Chapel, who had boarded along with nd'Omeshef, as well as Arsène Xiang, the gray-haired leader of the Regulan New Human community—and another familiar face he had not expected. "Chief Onami," he said, greeting his former xenopsychologist with a warm handshake. "This is a surprise. Are you with the *Palmares* now?"

The dainty but tough petty officer shook her head. "No, sir. I'm on leave, studying the New Humans. I happened to be on Regulus just before they moved out, and . . ." She shrugged. "Well, I decided I wasn't finished learning about them."

Jones looked impressed. "Even given the danger involved in associating with us?"

Onami shrugged. "If I had a healthy sense of self-preservation, would I have joined Starfleet?" Jones laughed.

"Her company has been most charming and welcome," Xiang

said, making Kirk wonder if this was the same Reiko Onami he'd known, essentially a junior McCoy with a fraction of the tact. "From what I hear, you led her well for five years, and you kept her safe. For that, Admiral—and for your efforts above and beyond in organizing this task force on our behalf—you have my deepest thanks."

Once the greetings were out of the way, Jones took Xiang and Onami down in the turbolift to meet the other New Humans two decks below, and to show them the arrangements that had been made for the other incoming refugees. "Doctor Chapel," Kirk said, "I wonder if you'd be free to join Captain Spock, myself, and the senior staff for dinner tonight. Scotty and Uhura will be coming aboard from the *Asimov*."

Chapel beamed. "Almost the whole gang. The admiralty has its privileges, I see."

"I simply made sure to call on the best."

The dark-haired doctor looked around, frowning. "Leonard's still well, I trust?"

"Indeed," Spock said. "The doctor is aboard and fulfilling his usual shipboard function." A brief pause. "Whatever that may be."

"Well, in that case," Chapel said irascibly, "I'm going to track him down and give him a piece of my mind for not being here to greet me." She headed off with an eager grin that belied her words.

"If I may drag you back to business," nd'Omeshef said to Kirk and Spock, "the science staff at Regulus Sector Headquarters provided us with some experimental anti-Naazh ordnance that they think will aid us in the next attack. May I bring it aboard, Captain Spock?"

Kirk deferred to Spock for this; while the admiral commanded the mission, the ship itself and who or what was allowed aboard it was always the captain's responsibility. "Certainly," Spock replied. "I am interested to learn what avenues they have pursued."

The *Palmares* captain gestured toward the security personnel who had been waiting at the far end of the docking tunnel, and they crossed over with several carrying cases. Nd'Omeshef opened the first and took out one of the weapons within, handing it to Kirk. It resembled an old-fashioned riot control gun with a short, wide cylindrical barrel. The mature Arkenite also showed Kirk one of the puck-like cartridges that fed into the barrel. "The *Reliant*'s team had some success with bolas to restrain one of the Naazh, but were unable to prevent it from teleporting away. The Regulus science team's thinking was that the Naazh's control crystals appeared to be neurometrically or telepathically controlled, since they only needed to hold their hands over the crystals without any manual or verbal command entry."

"Logical," Spock replied.

"So this adheres to the Naazh's armor and deploys cables to wrap around it and immobilize the wearer—but the cartridge contains a miniaturized version of Doctor Tristan Adams's neural neutralizer mechanism, in order to suppress brain-wave patterns."

Kirk stared. "That technology was restricted over a decade ago. On my recommendation."

"We got special dispensation for the sake of the emergency. My science officer Selek'held collaborated with the team that developed it, and he's confident it can work."

Kirk was distracted by Spock's intense attention toward a member of the *Palmares* security team, a short-haired Vulcan woman with her head lowered. Kirk did not recognize her, but something about her apparently made Spock concerned. No, not just concerned—if Kirk was any judge of Spock's expressions, he had just had a hypothesis confirmed.

Spock moved forward abruptly and clenched the woman's forearms, pinning them to her sides and making her drop the case she was carrying. "Spock to bridge," he said. "Intruder alert in cargo bay."

Nd'Omeshef stared. "What is the meaning of this?" As he spoke, the intruder alarm began to sound, and the security personnel on the catwalks around the bay straightened to attention and drew their energy batons.

Instead of addressing him, Spock spoke to the Vulcan woman, who stared at him with cool contempt. "You have disguised yourself well, Specialist. But once we learned that the Naazh included Federation citizens motivated by xenophobia toward telepaths, I began to suspect that your death was not as it appeared. I did not wish to impugn your memory without evidence, so I kept my suspicions private. But I have been anticipating your return . . . T'Nalae."

Kirk stared, but his understanding came close on the heels of his shock. Now that Spock had pointed it out, he could recognize the young *V'tosh ka'tur* despite the surgical alterations to her features. "Of course," he said. "You led several others into the side lounge to escape the red Naazh . . . then the gold Naazh appeared inside and started killing them. We thought you were one of its victims, but—"

She laughed. "Yes. You wondered how we penetrated the shields? I was already inside, the anchor who brought the others through."

Kirk grabbed the neural neutralizer cartridge from nd'Omeshef, loaded it into the gun, and aimed it at T'Nalae. "Why?" he demanded with cold fury. "How could you hate these people so fiercely that you'd commit such slaughter?"

She chuckled. Her new face was more angular than the old, harder and more fitting for her true self. "You have no idea what you're dealing with, Admiral Kirk. The creatures you defend so nobly are the real evil here, an aberration that threatens the proper order of things. The Naazh are champions of justice, putting an end to their perversion."

"You'll have no chance to hurt them, T'Nalae. This bay is surrounded by subspace damping fields. You won't be able to summon your armor or call for reinforcements."

T'Nalae laughed louder. "Primitive fools. You think your

petty four-dimensional tricks can stop us? I've studied all your defenses. And I've spent a year honing my skills, upgrading my armor. I need no assistance this time." Her smile grew smug and sinister. "I don't even need to use my hands."

She looked straight ahead and shouted one word in Vulcan: "*Mesuvulau!*"

Spock was thrown back as a swirling sphere of energy formed around her. A second later, it faded, and the gold Naazh was revealed. Her armor was more elaborate now, with heavier torso plating and more pronounced hornlike protrusions atop the featureless golden visor.

Kirk immediately fired the neutralizer cartridge. Almost faster than he could see, the cartridge shot out its cables and wrapped around T'Nalae, binding her arms. He heard a chillingly familiar hum as the miniaturized neural neutralizer engaged. But she had already moved a hand over her belt crystal and activated it, the neutralizer having no apparent effect. Another swirl of energy surrounded her, and when it faded, the cartridge and cables had vanished, presumably into whatever extraspatial realm the Naazh used to come and go.

"New weapons aren't much use against someone who infiltrated the design team," T'Nalae pointed out, her smugness not concealed by the helmet's voice filtering.

On the main cargo floor below, Kirk saw, the New Humans had already jumped into action, with the telekinetic adepts forming up around Jones and Xiang while the rest retreated toward the portside cargo enclosures. But T'Nalae ignored them, turning and running aft along the catwalk. The two nearest guards in that direction met her and struck with their energy batons, but the weapons had no effect; T'Nalae must have adapted her armor to them as well. She knocked one guard into the outer bulkhead and the other off the catwalk railing; one of the telekinetics reached out and slowed that guard's fall so she made a safe landing.

A third guard, thinking fast, closed the double pressure doors separating the cargo bay catwalk from the landing bay. T'Nalae leaped off the catwalk and arced several meters aft, alighting onto the shuttle elevator platforms that had been converted to extra berthing space. Kirk wondered why she was running *away* from the New Humans that were her targets.

Spock cried out the answer just as it started to coalesce in Kirk's mind. "The landing bay doors!" They exchanged a look. If T'Nalae shot out the clamshell doors and the atmospheric containment field across them, she would vent the entire vast space to vacuum.

"Secure the bay access doors!" Kirk ordered. While most of the guards on the platform level closed on T'Nalae, the guard nearest the control console ran to it and entered the command to begin closing the wide, two-deck-high segmented doors between the cargo and landing bays. Meanwhile, Kirk, Spock, and nd'Omeshef ran aft along the upper catwalk. The guard who had shut the catwalk doors before had already reopened them and preceded the command officers through. Kirk recalled her name—Emily Jackson—and resolved to give her a citation for quick thinking.

As Kirk ran along the catwalk directly above the elevator platforms, he saw the guards hurling their bolas, attempting to ensnare T'Nalae. The cables that wrapped around her upper torso had no effect, for her armor blades sliced through them with a single flex of her arms. But one cable wrapped around her legs and made her tumble. By the time she began to cut her legs free with the blade on her forearm, the guards had closed in with batons, ramming their tips into her armor like cattle prods. They had little effect, and after a moment, she broke free and shot upward in an improbable spinning leap, her slashing blades felling at least two of the guards and slicing a third guard's baton in two.

With another prodigious leap, T'Nalae reached the guard

at the door console, grabbed the edges of his breastplate, and hurled him into the path of the closing bay doors. He scrambled to get free of the support channels for the massive metal doors, but T'Nalae entered the command to reverse their closing, then smashed the console with her armored fists.

By now, Kirk and the two captains had reached the forward edge of the landing bay floor, where they formed a defensive line alongside several guards armed with batons and phaser rifles. But before T'Nalae could resume her run toward him, a group of New Human telekinetics leaped into view from the cargo floor, their jumps almost as prodigious as T'Nalae's. As they landed on the elevator platforms below him, Kirk saw that Miranda Jones and Arsène Xiang led the group. He suppressed a surge of fear for Miranda's safety. Whatever they now shared, it didn't make her helpless. With her abilities, he reminded himself, she could defend herself as well as anyone on the *Enterprise*.

The New Humans formed an arc around the gold Naazh and struck at her with telekinetic surges. T'Nalae reeled back only slightly, then used her belt-stone flash to disperse their psionic fields. They fell back, and she summoned a firearm from dimensional space, opening fire on the telekinetics with plasma bolts. One woman was struck in the arm, screaming in agony as she fell, but the others dodged with preternatural speed, as if sensing the bolts in advance. The *Enterprise* guards merely waited until the battle had moved forward, then came to the aid of the fallen woman. They recognized that the fight had escalated beyond their level.

What happened next stunned Kirk. As T'Nalae continued to fire, Xiang grabbed a heavy blanket from one of the cots set up on the elevator platform and tossed another to Jones. Wrapping the blankets around themselves, they closed their eyes and concentrated . . .

. . . and with a quick flash and shimmer, the blankets transformed into silver armor!

Rather than the faceless, insectile suits of the Naazh, the New Humans' armor and helmets left their faces bare. Xiang's was stylized to resemble the lamellar armor of a Tang-dynasty infantryman, while Jones's had more of a European look, its chestplate bearing an impressionistic relief carving of Medusa's head, like the aegis of Greek myth.

"Fascinating," Spock breathed. "Direct transmutation of available matter!"

As primitive as it looked, the transmuted armor was effective, deflecting T'Nalae's plasma bolts. The remaining telekinetics fell into formation behind the two armored leaders for protection. T'Nalae cupped a hand before her belt stone and drew from it a long sword with a glowing, energized blade, a trick that amazed Kirk just as much as when he'd seen the red Naazh do it a year before. Did the belt stones link directly to the other-dimensional space they used?

But the surprises weren't over yet. Xiang and Jones reached out, and two fallen energy batons flew off the deck and into their hands. With another shimmer of energy, the batons transmuted into swords that the two armored figures used to engage with T'Nalae. Whatever the blades were now made of, they were strong enough to match the Naazh weapon. *How could Miranda have gained this kind of power?* Kirk wondered.

Thunder sounded, and the deck heaved beneath Kirk. He almost fell, but Spock caught him. The fighters below, already off-balance from their clash, were knocked down.

"Bridge to Captain Spock," came Sulu's voice. *"We're under attack by a Federation scout ship that appears to have Naazh enhancements."* Another blast rocked the ship. *"Powerful ones."*

"Engage and evade at your discretion, Commander," Spock instructed him, even as nd'Omeshef drew his own communicator and ordered the *Palmares* to retract the docking tunnel and clear for maneuvering.

The attack had allowed T'Nalae to break free of the scuffle

below, and she ran straight for Kirk, who fired futilely with his phaser while the guards joined in with their rifles at full power. The barrage slowed her only marginally, but it was enough for the telekinetics to regroup and hit her from behind with another psionic surge, making her tumble into the shuttlecraft storage and maintenance hangar underneath the bay floor where Kirk and Spock stood. They and the guards spread out and moved aft, trying to stay ahead of the sounds of the fierce battle beneath their feet. Kirk heard groans, scrapes, and thuds suggesting that entire shuttlecraft were being dragged across the deck and thrown at T'Nalae.

My God. What have we gotten in the middle of?

The report of a Naazh plasma pistol sounded again several times, and a hole was blown in the deck a few meters in front of Kirk. The sounds of the battle came through more clearly now, and occasionally another shot came through to enlarge the hole before the New Humans presumably impeded T'Nalae once again. "They won't hold her long," Kirk said to Spock. "And I don't know what we can do once she gets up here."

"I may have an idea, Admiral," Spock said, nodding toward the side of the bay. Kirk followed his gaze and grinned.

Each side of the landing bay contained small hexagonal docking ports for three work bees—boxy yellow Cargo Management Units just large enough for a single operator, used for hull inspection, maintenance, or cargo hauling depending on what attachments were used. The CMUs were hardly combat craft, but they were sturdy and significantly bigger and heavier than a suit of armor.

Kirk had barely managed to unplug the work bee from its charging boom and extend it on its docking sled by the time T'Nalae's armored form leaped up through the hole in the deck. He popped the canopy and climbed into the bee's control seat, an awkward fit for an operator without an EV suit. A shot from T'Nalae's weapon grazed the canopy as it shut, damaging it enough to prevent a secure seal. But she had fired in passing as she made her way toward the clamshell doors, evidently not believing Kirk could pose much of a threat. He silenced the pressure alarm, engaged the work bee's antigravs, and fired its maneuvering thrusters to join the fight.

By now, Jones and Xiang had also emerged from the hole and were charging at T'Nalae once again, Miranda firing psionic surges while Xiang went at her with his sword. But another blow from the attacking ship outside staggered the New Humans again, whereas T'Nalae held her ground, having braced herself an instant before as if she'd sensed it coming. She drove her sword through Xiang's gut with a savage yell, then let him fall to the deck with the energized blade still inside him. Then she stepped toward the clamshell doors and opened fire at the containment-field emitter strips along its sides. Their violet light flickered, the field starting to break down. If she managed to blow a hole through the doors next, the bay would depressurize explosively within seconds.

Then Spock slammed into her with the nose of his work bee.

It knocked her down hard enough that she skidded several meters across the deck, but it appeared to do almost as much damage to the CMU, which flailed and scraped against the deck, its forward headlight cracked and its nose crumpled. T'Nalae recovered from her tumble and fired her weapon at Spock's canopy, cracking and blackening it with her first shot. A second would surely get through.

So Kirk spun his own bee around to point its rear particle-beam thruster directly at T'Nalae and fire it at full power, while simultaneously firing his forward reaction-control jets to counter the forward thrust. The jets were too weak to counter the main thruster, so his bee accelerated forward and crashed into the bees' attachment storage bay nose-first. But the collision spun the bee around enough for him to see through the side window that T'Nalae had been knocked down by the particle beam, which had left some mild carbon scoring on her armor. She was on her hands and knees on the deck, shaking her head and reaching for her dropped firearm.

But Jones had now been joined by the rest of the telekinetics, two of whom had the wounded Xiang's arms over their shoulders, carrying him forward. As one, they reached out to the dazed T'Nalae and flipped her onto her back, pinning her to the deck as she struggled. One of them flicked a hand and sent her sidearm flying. Jones then strode forward determinedly, raised her sword, and drove it into T'Nalae's belt crystal, shattering both sword and crystal with a blinding burst of light. By the time the light faded, Jones was on her back, dazed, and T'Nalae lay exposed on the deck, the last glint of her armor fading.

As Kirk climbed out of his work bee, the ship shook from another salvo. Spock, having extracted himself from his own CMU, jogged up to him. "We should get to the bridge, Admiral."

"What about T'Nalae?" Kirk asked as he moved over to help Miranda to her feet. "I don't want her to get away this time."

"Don't worry," Jones said from the deck as she reached for Kirk's hand and let him pull her up. "My people are holding her in place. The interference should stop them from taking her."

It was only then that Kirk saw her eyes clearly for the first time since the start of the battle.

Eyes that glinted like polished silver.

He pulled his hand away, stepping back in shock and betrayal. He remembered Gary Mitchell's eyes gleaming at him that way, his best friend's warmth and humor replaced with cold, steely contempt as he used his exponentially growing psionic powers to play with Kirk sadistically before crushing him like an ant underfoot . . .

"What *are* you?" he demanded of her.

The ship rocked again. "Nothing you need to fear, Jim," she told him, her voice seeming to echo in his head, as if he were "hearing" her words telepathically as well as aurally. "Trust me on that. The immediate threat is outside."

That, at least, was undeniable. *One problem at a time*, he thought. "Spock, to the bridge." He held Miranda's gleaming eyes—briefly. "You too. With me."

As soon as Kirk reached the bridge, it was clear that the battle was not going well. On the main screen, the *Palmares* was trailing plasma, its starboard shuttlebay was breached, and several of the slender, fragile subspace antennae protruding from its specialized long-range sensor pods had been broken off, along with the entire starboard pod. From the way its impulse vents were guttering, it looked like its main energizers had taken damage.

Glancing at the damage-control station, Kirk saw multiple orange and red damage lights along the *Enterprise*'s aft secondary hull, starboard warp nacelle, and impulse engines. "Aft dorsal deflectors at twenty-one percent," reported S'trakha, the Saurian lieutenant at the weapons/defense station. "Force field holding at seventy-six. Overload to forward phaser power accumulators. Targeting is on manual."

The *Chrysaor* had taken fire too, but the blobby Medusan craft was a diplomatic transport with minimal armaments, unable to do anything beyond trying to stay out of the way. Only the *Asimov* seemed to be holding its own; though it was an older vessel, its shields seemed to have weathered the attack better than those of the other two ships. Kirk reminded himself with a slight smile that Montgomery Scott was serving on that ship at the moment.

"Hostile ship on viewer, Mister Sulu," Spock ordered.

"Aye, sir," Sulu acknowledged from the helm. "She's coming back around now."

The incoming ship was of a Federation class Kirk recognized, a sleek civilian passenger liner with a red-and-black nose and a silver body with close-mounted, elongated warp engines trailing back behind it. But the Naazh had modified it in some way, covering it in plated armor whose patterning suggested horns and bones. Fierce, blinding bolts shot out from the prow and flanks of the normally unarmed liner, and the *Enterprise* rocked again. Sulu returned fire, joined by the *Asimov*, but the phasers were as ineffectual against the liner's armor as hand phasers had been against the Naazh's personal armor.

"She's circling behind us," Sulu said. "Targeting the landing bay."

"Trying to finish what T'Nalae started," Kirk said to Spock.

"Evidently without concern for her survival," the Vulcan captain replied.

Captain Blake brought the *Asimov* in to defend the *Enterprise*'s rear, but even its sturdy shields could only take so much; one bolt got through and struck its boxy port nacelle, causing its lights and shields to fluctuate. "Enterprise, *we can't hold out much longer,*" Blake reported.

"Jim." Miranda's hand touched his arm, and he turned to face her. She had dispersed the transmuted armor at some point, but her eyes still glowed, and she seemed to have more gray hairs than he'd noticed an hour before. "You can't hold out against them. There's only one option. Move in close around the *Chrysaor*. As tightly as possible. Quickly!"

He narrowed his eyes. "I respect your concern for the Medusans, Doctor Jones, but a close formation would put them in more danger."

She gasped slightly at his impersonal address, but she went on regardless. "There's no time to explain, Jim. I know you don't feel you can trust me right now, but we need you to. All of us." She clutched his hand. "Please, Jim."

He felt the same vulnerability, need, and trust from her that he had known since their first kiss. That, at least, did not seem to have changed. Again, he remembered how cold and superior Gary had become when his eyes had glowed like that . . . but then he remembered how Elizabeth Dehner's eyes had glowed too, and how she had retained her compassion and humanity in spite of it.

Maybe it had just been Gary all along.

He turned to Spock, who nodded in acceptance. So he spoke. "Admiral Kirk to all ships. Take up close formation around the *Chrysaor*, minimum safe range."

The captains acknowledged, and Sulu began bringing the *Enterprise* in close to the Medusan ship while the *Asimov* and *Palmares* made best speed to join it. All four ships took additional damage from the Naazh liner, for their direct movement made them predictable targets. Kirk just hoped Miranda's plan would be worth the cost.

Once all three Starfleet ships had matched velocity with the far smaller *Chrysaor* and drawn as close around it as they feasibly could, Jones said, "Brace yourselves. This could be a bit bumpy." Kirk was confused, but he put a hand on the bridge railing nonetheless.

"Captain!" Palur called from the science station. "Some kind of dimensional distortion is forming around the *Chrysaor*!"

Even as the young Argelian spoke, Kirk saw a ripple and flicker of light around the Medusan ship. It surged outward to engulf the other three ships, and the *Enterprise* rocked slightly, light flashing within the bridge from no apparent source. Kirk felt a wave of extreme sensory distortion, as if all the shapes around him were dissolving into a haze of nameless colors, and himself along with it.

Just as suddenly, the sensation cleared; Kirk felt intact again, and the bridge appeared normal. He looked at the viewscreen—

—and the stars were gone.

In their place, surrounding the four ships, was a field of swirling luminescence. It had a strange duality to it; at one moment, it looked to him like shimmering, waving streaks of red and violet, while at the next, it seemed like a mottled, fractal field of blues and greens. But there was no moment at which it changed from one to the other; his mind simply changed its opinion about what he saw when his gaze shifted, as it would with an optical illusion.

The one thing he knew for sure was that he had seen it before.

Spock had risen from his command chair, and his words confirmed Kirk's perception. "Admiral, this is the same extra-dimensional continuum we were flung into ten years ago by Lawrence Marvick's tampering with our engines." He turned to contemplate Miranda. "At least . . . we *believed* it was Marvick's doing at the time."

Jones sighed heavily. "It wasn't," she confessed. "But this is going to be a very long explanation."

Fifteen

"So let me get this straight," Captain Erin Blake said. "This was the *third* time the *Enterprise* left the galaxy?"

Admiral Kirk looked around the briefing room table, taking in the reactions to her question. He, Captain Spock, Doctor McCoy, and Commander Sulu had been joined by Commanders Scott and Uhura from the *Asimov*, along with its captain, the *Palmares*'s Captain nd'Omeshef and his first officer Naomi Vega, and Miranda Jones, who spoke for the New Humans while Arsène Xiang was treated for his injuries in sickbay. The human *Enterprise* veterans looked almost sheepish at Blake's question, as if not wishing to upstage their fellow officers.

"Not exactly, Captain," Spock replied. "While we were technically no longer in this galaxy, neither did we leave it in the conventional way."

"Instead," Commander Vega said between sips of her coffee, "you ended up in an extradimensional continuum like the one we're in now."

"Yes," Spock replied. "When Doctor Lawrence Marvick was driven into mental instability by the sight of Ambassador Kollos, he tampered with the *Enterprise*'s engine controls in a way that threw them into an exponential acceleration." Commander Scott lowered his head, looking ashamed. Kirk knew he had always blamed himself for letting his hero worship of Marvick, one of the designers of the *Enterprise*, blind him to the evidence of his instability.

"Even though our instruments showed conventional warp factors," Spock went on, "later analysis showed that the effective velocity equivalents we achieved were far higher."

"Yes," nd'Omeshef said. "As I recall, the Corps of Engineers took quite an interest in the 'transwarp' configuration that Marvick achieved. They've been trying to duplicate it ever since."

Scott snorted. "A fat lot o' good it'll do them. It nearly tore us apart and plunged us into who knows where."

"Except, Mister Scott, apparently it was not Marvick's tampering that was responsible for our entry into this continuum." Spock turned to Jones. "At the time, we hypothesized that the continuum was a dimensional pocket within the negative energy barrier that we had encountered twice before along the nearest border of this region of the galactic inner disk, or else the result of the barrier interacting with the transwarp field to create a dimensional displacement. We had been accelerating in the direction of that barrier, and though our instruments did not show us actually reaching it, we were unable to verify their results due to the observational distortions created by the transwarp effect. But since we were dealing with an unexplained phenomenon, we concluded that it was likely associated with the other unexplained phenomenon we had been approaching, which had created similar sensory distortions.

"However, Doctor Jones has now belatedly informed us that this was not the case."

All eyes turned to Jones, who took a deep breath and sighed. Her eyes still glistened silver, but the effect seemed more translucent than before. "This is difficult to admit," she began. "Kollos carried a great deal of guilt for deceiving you all, and for the consequences it had for Spock in particular. But he had no choice—or at least no time to choose a better option.

"As you said, Captain Spock, we were heading for the barrier.

And Kollos knew what effect the barrier would have on me if he allowed the ship to cross it."

Vega's coffee cup froze just short of her lips. "Yes—I remember now. The report from the *Enterprise*'s first barrier crossing. All the espers in the crew were killed by the barrier passage. Somehow it burned out portions of their brains."

"Not . . . *all* the espers," Kirk said. "The two strongest ones—my second officer, Lieutenant Commander Gary Mitchell, and a medical specialist, Doctor Elizabeth Dehner—survived the barrier passage . . . and were changed by it. They developed exponential increases in their psionic ability."

"But only for a little while, if I recall," Vega said. "Eventually their brains burned out from the strain."

"It was . . . more complicated than that." Kirk, Spock, Scott, and Sulu traded heavy looks. They had kept certain details out of the official logs for fourteen years, but Kirk knew the current circumstances no longer allowed such discretion. "In Mitchell's case . . ." He hesitated. "It seemed to be too much for him. The shock, the temptation . . . he became unstable. Dangerous. It became necessary . . ."

Spock took over the story, his deep compassion audible only to those who knew him best. "I persuaded then-Captain Kirk that Mitchell had to be put off the ship on the nearby Delta Vega mining planetoid, an uninhabited outpost. Though it was a difficult decision, the captain acted for the greater good of the ship."

Next to him, McCoy's eyes widened at his unflinching account. The doctor and Mitchell had served together for a time aboard Kirk's previous command, the *Sacagawea*. Once McCoy had joined the *Enterprise* crew, Kirk had told him the truth about Mitchell's recent demise; but it must still have been unnerving to hear Spock reiterate the incident and his part in it. At the time, McCoy had been outraged that Spock—whom he had only just met—had seemingly argued in favor of killing Mitchell, in defiance of the Vulcans' professed nonviolence.

Kirk had corrected his misapprehension: Spock had actually been arguing for stranding Mitchell alive, making his case by pointing out that it was the only viable alternative to execution. But McCoy had been unconvinced, and Spock had reciprocated his initial hostility. They eventually learned to trust and respect each other—but by then, they'd come to enjoy their bickering too much to stop.

In any case, the distinction between stranding Mitchell and executing him had turned out to be moot, as Spock went on to explain. "However, Commander Mitchell then escaped, killed our helm officer, and apparently persuaded Dehner—now manifesting her own psionic abilities—to join him. But Captain Kirk prevailed upon Dehner to remain loyal, and she assisted him in containing Mitchell. Regrettably, both Mister Mitchell and Doctor Dehner lost their lives in the resultant conflict."

"If we're putting all our cards on the table," Kirk said heavily, "let's not mince words. I killed Gary Mitchell. Dehner had weakened him enough to give me an opening, and I dropped the side of a mountain on him with a phaser rifle."

Into the grave he had dug for me, Kirk recalled. It was that act of theatrical cruelty that had hardened Kirk's heart against his old friend enough to let him go through with it. And to do what had needed to be done next: exhuming what had been left of the body to make absolutely sure that Mitchell's powers had not allowed him to survive. At least Doctor Piper's postmortem had confirmed that the end had been quick—though the remains had then been cremated and dispersed across Delta Vega just in case.

Now he met Miranda Jones's glowing eyes—which locked on his directly as if she were not blind—and spoke. "He was my best friend, yet his power made him a monster. Tell me, Miranda—is that what the Naazh are so afraid of?"

"It's not like that, Jim. In fact . . . the monster may not have been Gary Mitchell at all. Not entirely, at least."

Kirk stared back, stunned. "Explain," he finally said.

Jones fidgeted, as though struggling to work up the courage to speak. After a moment, she turned to the *Enterprise*'s current captain. "Tell me, Spock—didn't you ever wonder why the barrier burned out the brains of the human espers on board, but didn't do the same to a telepath as formidable as you?"

Spock straightened, both eyebrows shooting up in surprise. "I have never been able to verify a hypothesis. I initially suspected it was related to the difference between human and Vulcan neurology. But once we appeared to pass through the barrier with you aboard—and without the shield modifications the Kelvans made to block the barrier's neurological effects during our second passage—it had no evident effect on you either. So I hypothesized that we might have been protected by the Vulcan training we both received—that the ability to shield our minds from others' thoughts and emotions might also have shielded us from the barrier's effects."

Jones gave him a wistful smile. "In a sense, Spock, you were right the first time. It was because you weren't fully human—or rather, not a human esper. It was because . . . your telepathy came to you naturally."

Spock furrowed his brows, and Kirk could practically see the wheels turning behind his eyes. "It *has* long been a mystery how human telepaths, as well as Aenar, were able to manifest psionic abilities without the paracortex or equivalent neurological formations found in other telepathic and empathic species."

A new calm came over Jones, a sudden shift reminding Kirk of the transitions between herself and Kollos. But surely that couldn't be; Kollos had died a year ago.

"The simple fact of the matter is, they can't," she said coolly. "Their psionic powers—*my* powers—do not come from the human brain at all."

Beside Spock, McCoy stared at Jones with wide-eyed disbelief. "My God, Miranda, what are you saying?"

She crossed her arms, choosing her words. "More than a millennium ago, a group of incorporeal psionic life-forms from a higher-dimensional subspace domain were driven from their home continuum by the genocidal regime that ruled it. For convenience, call their race the Spectres.

"The outcast faction had been declared heretics because they developed the ability to travel to other dimensions, other planes of existence, in order to make contact with the life they found there. This was a violation of the purist, authoritarian doctrines of their domain's rulers—call them Lords. These Lords saw contact with the corporeal life of other planes to be an abomination, a perversion of the highest nature. The explorers fled from their home plane, but that was not enough for the Lords; to preserve their authority, their absolute domination, every single being who defied their dogmas had to be hunted down and exterminated, as cruelly and painfully as possible, as a warning to others who might follow their example."

Jones's silver eyes met those of the others around the table. "And so, in order to elude the hunters, these political refugees needed to find a place to hide. A place where they could lay low as long as the threat remained."

"My God," McCoy gasped. "You're saying they hid inside humans?"

"They needed sentient brains to occupy—neural substrates complex enough to host them and active enough to mask their presence. They chose the Aenar first," she said. "While Aenar brains didn't have paracortices per se, their structure was more receptive to symbiosis than that of the other Andorian subspecies—and their history as an outcast minority on Andoria made them more sympathetic to the rebel Spectres. They consented to allow them to live within their brains. They called them *thetad*—'sleepers.'"

"Fascinating," Spock said. "And, in exchange, these Spectres gave the Aenar telepathic ability?"

"It was an unavoidable side effect of the sleepers' presence,"

Jones told him. "They could cloak their own characteristic mental signature, but even in a dormant state, they charged the Aenar's brains with raw psionic energy, making them capable of telepathy. Luckily for the refugees, this galaxy contains enough naturally telepathic species—some in which telepathy is a rare or discouraged trait, as with the Argelians or Arkenites—that the Spectre Lords hunting them couldn't tell the difference."

"That still doesn't explain where human telepaths come in," McCoy said, "or what any of this has to do with how we ended up in this weird universe either time."

"Unfortunately, the Aenar population was small," Jones said. "With telepathy had come pacifism, for the Aenar could not bring themselves to harm those whose pain they could feel for themselves. But on those rare occasions when they came into contact with the Andorians whose civilization was expanding across their planet, they were feared and persecuted for their abilities, which seemed like witchcraft to a civilization at that level with no history of telepathy. Since they were no longer willing or able to fight back, the Aenar learned to retreat when the Andorians came—to avoid contact as much as possible. They retreated into smaller and more inhospitable territories, and their population declined. Climate catastrophes and fertility problems compounded the population loss until they were in danger of extinction—along with the Spectres who shared their bodies. Even a fully awakened Spectre can't easily separate from a host, so the death of the host will usually kill the Spectre as well, unless it has enough advance warning to sever the link.

"So the sleepers began seeking new hosts that they could inhabit. Ideally ones whose brains would not resonate so well with their psionic fields, so that they would be less likely to give their presence away by inducing strong telepathy in their hosts. They found the ideal candidates on the third planet of a yellow star not particularly far from Andoria.

"They found humans."

McCoy spoke angrily. "Tell me this, Miranda: Did you know this? Did Gary? Or DiFalco, or Logan? Did any of you know?"

Jones was slow to answer. "You must remember—the Spectres were hiding from a genocidal foe that would stop at nothing to see them exterminated. Secrecy was essential to their survival."

"So they didn't know! You and every other human esper—all of you were possessed without your consent!"

"The first generation *did* know," Jones said. "As I said, the Aenar consented to the arrangement. The first humans the Spectre refugees approached did so as well. But in both cases, they agreed to the provision that their memory of the merger would be suppressed afterward. They would have no awareness of the sleepers' presence within them, except through whatever psionic abilities they developed, or perhaps in dreams that faded when they awoke."

McCoy was not mollified. "But you developed your telepathy in childhood, Miranda. That means there had to be a Spectre occupying your brain before you were old enough to give consent!"

"Yes," she replied, maintaining her cool reserve. Kirk wondered if it was really Miranda Jones who was speaking. "The Spectres are able to translocate within parent and child at the same time. It's how they survive through the generations. My father's Spectre passed to me when he died. My mother's had also coexisted in me until then. Perhaps it was that combination of factors that endowed me with such strong telepathy."

"Don't you see how they used you, Miranda?" McCoy demanded. "Violated your mind, your body, without giving you a choice? My God, they've done this to dozens of generations of two different species that we know of!"

"Do you think *they* had a choice? They were hiding, desperate. They understood the ethical dilemma. They hated being forced to use the beings they had hoped to contact and befriend.

"And so they adopted their own version of the Prime Directive," Jones continued. "To remain forever dormant within their hosts. To live passively, generation after generation . . . existing only as observers and never intervening directly in their hosts' lives, except through the unavoidable psionic spillover."

"Then that makes them voyeurs. Watching your entire lives unfold for their entertainment."

The defiant anger she displayed was pure Miranda. "Do the natives of a pre-warp planet consent to being infiltrated and watched by Starfleet observation teams? At least the sleepers were *forced* to make this choice by the threat to their survival. But to avoid execution, they willingly accept imprisonment. They condemn themselves to an almost totally dormant existence, trapped inside shells of flesh, observing but never acting, rather than impose upon their hosts' freedom to live their lives.

"Does that seem selfish or exploitative to you, Doctor McCoy? Could you condemn yourself to such an existence for centuries on end out of deference to others?"

McCoy, at last, had no reply. Jones looked around at the others. "It was when I melded with Kollos ten years ago that I finally became aware of the Spectre masked within my mind. Kollos informed me of its presence, and I allowed it to awaken, to communicate with it." She smiled. "It was a shock at first, but I did not consider its presence a violation. Indeed, once I knew my . . . passenger . . . was there, I realized that I had always been subliminally aware of it. I just thought it was a part of me—a part I cannot imagine being without. Can something be an invasion if it's always been a piece of who I am?"

Kirk leaned forward, catching her argent gaze. "You say Kollos *informed* you of the Spectre's presence—not that he discovered it. Do you mean the ambassador was already aware that you had a Spectre within you?"

She nodded. "I have to confess another deception now, on the Medusans' behalf." She steepled her fingers on the table before her. "What you have to understand is that Medusans are also higher-dimensional beings. The part of them that exists in our three-dimensional space is just a cross section of their true selves."

"Indeed," Spock said, not sounding surprised. "That would explain much. If observers who witness a Medusan are perceiving a being of multiple dimensions, their brains would be unable to process the information."

"That's somewhat correct," Jones said, "though it would take another hour and several hundred equations to put it more precisely."

He raised a brow. "I look forward to that opportunity."

Sulu looked equally intrigued, and he spoke up now. "It also explains the Medusans' navigational expertise, doesn't it?" he asked. "If they can perceive our three-D universe from a higher-dimensional level, it's like . . . like being able to look at a garden maze from above and see the escape route in its entirety, while the people stuck inside it have to figure it out the hard way."

"Exactly," Jones replied. "And the Medusans were able to use that to their advantage. When they made contact with the Federation, they were able to sense the sleepers' presence in certain humans, and in the Aenar as well. They sensed that the Spectres were in distress, and that they were occupying unknowing hosts in order to survive. So they wanted to find a way to reach out and offer them assistance."

"The navigation program," Spock said. "Their proposal to meld with humanoid telepaths for navigational purposes was a cover for making clandestine contact with the dormant Spectres. This is why they pursued the Aenar first, and then human telepaths."

Scott gave a snort of frustration. "No wonder the program never panned out. No wonder we got the navigational advances with new equipment, no telepaths needed. It was never really about navigation in the first place."

"That's right, Mister Scott," Jones said. "The Medusans' goal, ideally, was to offer the refugees an alternative—a way they could be safe from the Lords' hunters without having to settle for a waking death, to live openly and freely without needing to possess other beings. They wanted to free both the sleepers and their hosts. But they had to do it clandestinely, for fear of alerting the Naazh."

"The Naazh are the agents of these Lords?" Captain nd'Omeshef asked.

"That's right." She grimaced. "The sheer hypocrisy of it is, while the Lords profess to despise Spectres who interact or merge with corporeal beings, they do the same thing themselves in order to hunt us down and murder us. They recruit humanoids who feel hostility toward telepaths—who see us as a threat, or who envy our advantage, or who believe that we're an affront to their ideas of species purity. They play on these people's xenophobia and insecurity, encourage their worst fears and resentments, and offer them the power to defeat what they fear."

"So let me get this straight," Sulu said. "The good Spectres are sleepers, and they're inside the Aenar and New Humans. The bad Spectres are Lords, and they're inside the Naazh."

"Too many names," Commander Vega said, getting up from the table. "Anyone else need more coffee?"

"It has to be more than simple recruitment," Uhura said to Jones. "When T'Nalae was aboard, she expressed dislike for the New Humans, yes, but it wasn't violent or extreme. She never would've passed her first Starfleet evaluation if she were that psychopathic."

"Once the Lords possess their hosts and turn them into Naazh," the telepath explained, "they manipulate their minds, their emotions. They amplify their fears . . . tease out their darkest hidden feelings of resentment and rage and unleash them. They destabilize their neurotransmitters, deaden their empathy and impulse control, intensify their paranoia and cruelty. They exploit and abuse their hosts in exactly the way the sleepers strive so hard to avoid."

"And it comes with a cost, doesn't it?" Kirk realized. He peered at Miranda's gray hairs, remembering Gary's. "It drains you. Ages you."

She nodded. "It's another reason the sleepers stay dormant. Having an active Spectre within you, using its powers to their full extent, takes its toll on the metabolism. It shortens your lifespan." She paused, then went on with a grimace. "Yet another thing the Lords don't tell their Naazh servants. They hate corporeal beings as much as they hate the refugees, so they see them only as tools to be used up."

"Is that what happened to Gary and Doctor Dehner? Did the barrier . . . awaken their sleepers?"

"More than that," she answered. "It supercharged them, caused their powers to escalate exponentially, beyond what was normal even for a Spectre." She shook her head. "From what you tell me, the shock of the forced awakening must have deranged Mitchell's Spectre, or Mitchell himself, or both. I doubt either of them can be considered responsible for their actions. Mitchell surely didn't understand what was happening to him, hearing this other voice speaking ever more loudly inside his head. He didn't have a Medusan to make the introduction for him."

Kirk sat back, stunned. All these years, he'd believed Gary had simply been drunk with power—that his own erratic personality, his hedonism and lack of discipline, had been corrupted into something far worse by the temptation of his growing abilities. He had resigned himself to the fact that the good in his friend had died before Kirk had been forced to kill what remained.

Had he been wrong? Had Gary been a victim all along, overwhelmed and in pain, asserting his power to compensate for his growing loss of control? Had he still been Kirk's friend right to the end?

Jones looked at him sympathetically, no doubt sensing his

emotions. She spoke gently. "Your official account wasn't that far from the truth, Jim. Given enough time, with the way their Spectres were draining them, both Mitchell and Dehner would have burned out and died anyway. They probably would have suffered far worse madness and torment before the end, as would their Spectres." Kirk held her gleaming gaze, nodding his thanks.

After a moment, Spock eased the conversation onto another tack. "I take it that we have finally arrived at the explanation for our entry into this pocket dimension."

"Yes," Jones said. "When Larry sent the *Enterprise* into—what did you call it—transwarp, we hadn't reached the barrier yet, but we were heading faster and faster in its direction. Kollos had made enough contact with the Aenar's Spectres that he knew what had happened with Mitchell and Dehner at the barrier. The psionic surge in their Spectres was powerful enough for the others to feel a thousand light-years away.

"So Kollos knew that he couldn't allow me or my Spectre to pass through the barrier. Not to mention any other espers who might be on board, without the Kelvan shielding to protect them."

"I take it Medusans don't just *sense* higher dimensions," Sulu said.

Jones nodded. "They manipulate them too. Kollos . . . 'lifted' the *Enterprise* out of normal space into another domain the Medusans have access to. He let you believe you'd entered some kind of pocket within the barrier, rather than reveal the full extent of his abilities."

McCoy looked indignant. "You mean Kollos could've taken us back to normal space at any time? He didn't need to meld with Spock and almost drive him permanently mad?"

"As I said, Doctor, Kollos greatly regretted the unintended consequences of his deception. But secrecy had to be maintained to protect the sleepers from annihilation—not to mention the threat to the Medusans if the Lords found out they were helping the sleepers. So Kollos had to go through with the charade that melding with a humanoid was necessary to navigate the ship to safety."

"It is all right, Doctor McCoy," Spock said. "I reconciled myself to the incident long ago. As I have remarked before, I consider the blame to be at least as much mine as Kollos's. And I do not begrudge Kollos his decisions in the name of protecting a threatened people. The needs of the many outweigh the needs of the few, or the one."

"Only if you choose to be the one yourself," McCoy countered, "instead of making it somebody else." He turned back to Jones. "You talked about how the Lords use their hosts, age them and burn them out like riding a horse to death. Look at yourself, Miranda! How is what this Spectre's doing to you any different?" He narrowed his eyes. "Or am I talking to the Spectre after all?"

She remained calm. "My Spectre and I have been one for as long as I can remember. I see even less of a distinction between us than I saw between myself and Kollos when we were melded."

"So there were *three* of you in there all along?" Naomi Vega asked, her eyes wide. "That's quite a party."

"To answer your first question, Doctor McCoy," Jones continued, "I've chosen to let my Spectre stay active for the duration of the crisis. It's a sacrifice I'm willing to make to protect my fellow New Humans. The Naazh attacks just keep getting more relentless, and I won't drop my guard until the sleepers and their hosts are safe."

Kirk saw a realization strike Spock. "The increase in New Human power levels over the past six years . . . the banding together of human telepaths to hone and strengthen their abilities . . . was it a response to the Naazh threat?" the Vulcan asked.

"In a way, yes. The belief that the power increase was triggered by V'Ger was indirectly true." Jones spread her hands.

"When V'Ger merged with Willard Decker and transcended our plane of existence, it was like a telepathic flare shining across the dimensions. The sleepers feared—correctly, as it turned out—that it would attract the Lords' attention to Federation space, to the sectors containing Earth and Andoria. That forced them to—not to take control of their hosts, Doctor, if that's what you're thinking," she told McCoy preemptively. "But to stir themselves out of dormancy—put themselves on standby, if you will, so they'd be ready to awaken fully and respond if they were attacked. The incidental result of that was an increase in their hosts' psionic powers. The Aenar had such an increase too, but they kept to themselves, so it went unnoticed.

"But the Aenar were found first, by unlucky chance. Or, more likely, the Naazh chose to attack them first because they were weaker and more isolated—because they wouldn't fight back.

"Once the massacre happened, it was the New Humans' own choice to band together and develop our defenses. I admit, I encouraged it, because I was aware of my Spectre and of the threat from the Naazh. I approached the strongest telepaths, like Arsène Xiang, and introduced them to their Spectres, as Kollos did for me. Although the sleepers' secrecy needed to be maintained, we needed a few New Humans aware of the whole truth so we could ready the others."

"If your Spectres were active all this time," McCoy asked, "why didn't your eyes start glowing until the fight?"

"Because they haven't remained active. Once we made contact, they returned to relative dormancy so as not to place a strain on our bodies. They awaken fully only when we need to exert more psionic power than we can harness on our own—as we did down in the cargo bay."

She sighed tiredly. "When I was with Kollos, I was able to coexist safely with my active Spectre, because Kollos was able to shoulder the burden and cushion me from its effects. It's been a strain to carry it all by myself for the past year.

"But we're safe in this pocket space, for now. The Medusans are protecting us." She smiled. "Soon we'll all be in a safe place. And then I—and my Spectre—can finally rest."

"Were you ever going to tell me?"

Kirk and Jones were alone in the former's quarters, letting him give voice at last to the feelings that had been churning inside him since he had first seen her silver eyes. Now those eyes remained unwavering as she faced him. "Surely you understand why I couldn't."

He stared at her. "All this time, I was worried about taking advantage of you. Now I find you've been the one lying to me."

"Not 'lying,' Jim. Keeping secrets. There's a difference." Her gaze narrowed. "Are you shocked to learn that the woman you made love to had a nonhuman sentience sharing her body? I thought you'd grown past such small-mindedness with Kollos."

"I've got nothing against . . . variations on the theme," Kirk said. It certainly wasn't his first time with two partners at once. "I do have a problem with not being asked for my consent first."

She sighed and rolled her eyes. "Didn't you hear me in the briefing room? My Spectre and I have been one person for as long as I can remember. To me—to *us*, if you prefer—the distinction between us is irrelevant, almost nonexistent. Perhaps that was why I took so readily to merging with Kollos."

"Kollos already knew before you melded. Didn't I deserve the same consideration?"

Her smile was sardonic. "Not to be indelicate, Jim, but what's in my mind is rather less relevant to what you and I share."

Kirk paced. "It's about more than just you and me, Miranda. You say that Kollos told you about the Spectres ten years ago. That means you've known from the beginning who the Naazh were and why they were after the Aenar. You knew they *would* go after human telepaths next. If you'd told us what you knew—"

"I couldn't take that chance! We didn't know for sure if the Naazh were aware of the sleepers' presence in humans. If I'd told you, it could have exposed them to Naazh attack even sooner. The secret had to be kept, long enough to give us the chance to gather the New Humans and prepare them clandestinely for the coming assault."

"You could have told *me*. I know how to keep classified information secure."

"It wasn't my secret to share. Not until I had to."

"Didn't you say your Spectre is as much a part of you as your human half?"

She winced, and the part of him that wasn't angry at her regretted his pettiness. "My Spectre wasn't the only one in danger," she explained.

He couldn't counter that, so things were quiet for a moment. "I'm sorry, Jim," she finally said. "I never meant to mislead you or take advantage of you. I did what I had to—and between us, I did what felt right, what I thought we both needed. I take my Spectre side so much for granted that I didn't consider it to be an issue. I failed to consider how you would see things differently."

Kirk pondered her words for a time, and again it was Jones who broke the silence. "So where do you and I go from here?"

"I'm . . . not sure yet," he said slowly. "We'll have to wait and see." He studied her silver-eyed visage. "But I need to know . . . is there anything else you're not telling me?"

She smiled, as if remembering someone dear to her. "Well . . . there is one more secret I've been keeping. But I think you're going to like this one."

Sixteen

U.S.S. Reliant

"Still no word from the *Enterprise* and the other ships?"

Looking up from the bridge communications station, Lieutenant Commander Kyle shook his head in response to Clark Terrell's question. "Negative, Captain. Nothing since the report that they were under attack." Terrell could hear the worry in John Kyle's voice. He remembered that the goateed Englishman was an *Enterprise* veteran, though not as recently as Chekov and Nizhoni.

Terrell turned and moved aft to the science station, where Chekov was running a radiometric scan. "Anything showing up on long-range sensors?"

Chekov worked the controls to refine his wave analysis, conferring briefly with the crewman at the telemetry subsystems monitor beside his station to verify that the subspace sensor antennae were functioning optimally. "At this range, I can't read anything for sure. But there's no subspace pulse or radiation signature consistent with an energy release massive enough to destroy four whole vessels at once."

"They mentioned only one fairly small Naazh ship," said Commander Azem-Os, who stood in the command well on the other side of the bridge railing, looking up at Terrell. "Hard to believe it could take out even one starship, especially one commanded by the likes of nd'Omeshef or Spock."

"Both are impressive officers," said Thelin th'Valrass, leaning forward on the aft bridge rail. The newly minted captain of the *U.S.S. Charas* had come aboard to arrange for the transfer of several dozen New Human refugees to his ship so as to relieve the crowding aboard the *Reliant*, but then the distress signal from the *Enterprise* had put that on hold. "But it took only a handful of Naazh to exterminate the entire surviving population of pure-blooded Aenar, despite the best efforts of many of Starfleet's finest. If their individuals are able to wreak destruction in such extreme disproportion to their numbers, it would be unwise to underestimate their starships."

Terrell held out his hands. "Now, let's not go jumping to conclusions just because of a comm blackout. Like Chekov said, there's no evidence of destruction. Maybe the Naazh are jamming the signal so the convoy groups can't coordinate."

"What about the *Euryale*?" Azem-Os asked, referring to the Medusan diplomatic transport that had joined them not long before the *Charas* had. "We know the Medusans' navigational sensors surpass ours—maybe their other sensors and communications do as well."

"Good idea," Terrell said. "Kyle, hail the *Euryale* and see if they have better luck. In the meantime, Chekov, I want continuous local sensor sweeps for any hint of subspace distortions or dimensional rifts. Anything that might be a Naazh battleship."

"Aye, sir," Chekov replied, with only a hint of dismay at being ordered to find a kind of ship he'd never seen before.

A few moments later, Kyle reported their answer. "All they'll tell me is that they're confident whatever danger the other ships were in has passed, sir. They suggest we continue toward Medusan space as planned."

"That's very vague," Terrell said. "You couldn't get any specifics from them?"

"They're a cryptic lot, sir. Probably comes from living alongside Medusans. Must change one's perspective quite a bit."

Terrell frowned. If the Medusans had some extra source of knowledge of the other ships' situation, whether through advanced sensors or by psionic means, then that was really something they should share with the rest of the class. "I'm always up for broadening my perspective, Mister Kyle. Hail them again and tell them I want to speak to—"

"Sir!" Chekov called as a detection alarm sounded. "That dimensional rift you wanted? It's opening nearly on top of us!"

Why do I never get service that fast when it's something good? Terrell wondered. "Red alert. Shields up." As Terrell moved to his chair, he noted Thelin speaking into his communicator, giving the equivalent orders to the *Charas* crew.

The Naazh ship on the viewer looked like a commonplace Class-J transport—a small civilian runabout with a gray-hulled, teardrop-shaped fuselage and a pair of nacelles slung underneath on angled pylons. But this one had been heavily modified, plated in chitinous armor and crystalline encrustations that looked like weapon ports.

Indeed, the crystal protrusions flashed with plasma fire barely after Terrell had the thought. To his surprise, though, the fire was directed at the *Euryale*, strafing it along its aft dorsal hull—the Medusan habitat section.

"Why are they after the Medusans?" Azem-Os wondered. "They've never shown them hostility before. And the *Euryale* poses them no threat."

"Never mind why," Terrell said. "Nizhoni, target the hostile ship and engage, free fire. Whatever it takes to neutralize them. Beach, move us in, try to keep us between them."

As his officers acknowledged, Thelin ordered his own bridge crew to harry the Naazh ship as well. But even though both ships were heavily armed, their combined fire barely made a dent in the modified transport's armor. And the Naazh had boosted the small ship's speed and maneuverability as well as its strength. It was able to swoop around their interference and counter their fire, inflicting damage on both ships. In the meantime, it continued laying down fire on the *Euryale*, striking its warp nacelles and ventral sections hard.

"Sir," Kyle reported as *Reliant* rocked under a forceful hit, "the *Euryale* is reporting an imminent reactor breach. They're requesting evacuation for their humanoid crew, twelve in all."

Terrell turned to stare at the dapper blond officer. "What about the Medusans?"

The Englishman struggled to maintain his stiff upper lip. "They report . . . there are no longer any Medusans on board to save."

Terrell allowed himself only a moment to take that in. "Bridge to transporter room. Lock on to all remaining personnel aboard the *Euryale* and beam them aboard."

"McNair here, Captain. Half the beam conduits are out and the pattern buffers are losing synchronization. We need time to reroute and rebalance the system."

"I can't give you much time, Tom," Terrell told the transporter chief.

"Sir," Chekov said, "I can reroute manually from the transporter room."

The captain nodded. "Go." Chekov rushed from the bridge like the eager boy he still so often seemed to be, and Terrell hoped his confidence was warranted. The people remaining aboard the *Euryale* were depending on it.

Because of the damage to the conduits and buffers, the large emergency transporters would take too long to restore to functionality, so Chekov had chosen to split the twelve evacuees between the main transporter room and the one adjacent to it within the G-deck transporter complex, slaving the other room's platform to his console with the transfer controls.

"Molecular synchronization still fluctuating," called Chief McNair from the circuitry bay adjacent to the transporter platform.

"Reset and cross-circuit to D," Chekov instructed as he fine-tuned the vector settings, using a few tricks he'd picked up from his early engineering apprenticeship under Montgomery Scott.

Finally, the synchronization lights on the operator booth's overhead panel all lit up. "Target lock on!" Chekov called. "Energizing!"

It seemed he had inherited Scott's gift for dramatic timing as well, for no sooner did he get confirmation of twelve successful dematerializations than the vector panels all flashed red and the malfunction warning indicators lit up. As he wrestled with the feedback surge in the confinement beam, Terrell's voice over the bridge channel told him what he could already see: *"Chekov, the* Euryale *is gone! Did you get them?"*

"They're in the buffer, sir! Stabilizing now!"

The energy surge had corrupted much of the pattern data, but fortunately, all twelve signals in the buffer retained enough coherent qubits for quantum error correction to reconstruct the rest. It took a few more seconds to complete the syndrome measurement, and then the transporter platform lit up with six beams of snowy shimmers that resolved into humanoid figures, crouched down and covering their heads.

The two in the front straightened up, and Chekov saw they were of an unfamiliar bipedal species, dressed in simple gray jumpsuits. Their heads were eyeless, covered in pale blue fur, and they had multiple slitted nostrils as well as large, intricately ridged shell-like ears. The one on the right, apparently male, reached out his furred hands nonthreateningly. "Do not be alarmed. I am Eren, commander of the *Euryale*. My people, the Reon-Ka, are members of the Medusan Complex."

Chekov stepped out from the booth to greet him and the others. "Welcome aboard the *Reliant*. I'm Lieutenant Commander Pavel Chekov, and—"

He broke off at the sight of the other four *Euryale* crew members who had now come to their feet. Two were of another unfamiliar species, bearish bipeds with slitted, red-tinted visors securely affixed over their eyes. But the other two . . .

The other two were Aenar.

As Chekov stared dumbstruck, a rational part of his mind offered up the logical explanation. The Medusans had dealt with the Aenar more than a dozen years before, attempting to recruit some for their navigational program. While that apparently hadn't worked out, perhaps some Aenar had gone to live with them for some other reason. They were a private people, so perhaps they had wished to keep this to themselves—especially after the rest of their kind had been slaughtered on Andoria and aboard the *Enterprise.*

But at the thought of that horrible day on the recreation deck, Chekov realized that he *recognized* one of the Aenar. Kinoch zh'Lenthar, the fiery political activist, had been a frustrating guest during her brief time aboard the ship, so Chekov had a vivid memory of her face—a face that was unmistakably gazing back at him now. Her eyes seemed different, not just pale but seeming to have a silvery glow. But he couldn't concern himself with what was probably a trick of the light. A more important thought dominated his mind.

If the Naazh survived that blast . . . then maybe . . .

He barely remembered to say "Excuse me" as he dashed out the door and across the corridor to the opposite transporter room. Coming down from its platform were three more Reon-Ka, two Aenar . . . and one human woman.

Because of her glinting silver eyes, it took him a moment to recognize her.

"Marcella?" he gasped.

Marcella DiFalco smiled tightly at him. "Great to see you again, sir. We've got a lot to talk about, but right now we need to get to the bridge before the Naazh blow up this ship too."

With the Naazh's seemingly unmotivated destruction of the *Euryale* now complete, the modified Class-J transport had redirected its attention to the *Reliant*. Terrell clamped his seat arms securely over his legs to hold him in place as the ship rocked and the orange and red lights continued to multiply on the damage and repair station's analysis screens.

At the recessed tactical station near the front of the bridge, Mosi Nizhoni yelled and ducked as sparks erupted from the power supply access panel behind her. For all that Starfleet strove to harden its power conduits against surges, there would always be weapons and cosmic phenomena of sufficient power to jump across any circuit gap or burn through any insulation, and the Naazh's weapons were probably the most powerful ones Terrell had seen since his time in the Taurus Reach. "Lieutenant?" he asked.

"Just startled, sir," Nizhoni replied. "But we've lost the force field, along with the ventral deflectors."

"Stoney, don't let them get below us," Terrell told Beach. He turned to Azem-Os, who was handling the engineering station. "Rem, can we break to warp?"

"Negative, Captain," the Aurelian replied sadly. "There are burnouts in the control circuits and one of the flow regulators is fractured. Repairs would take hours."

"The *Charas*'s engines are disabled as well," Thelin reported, his antennae curling back in frustration.

"We can help with that," came an unfamiliar voice from behind Terrell. He spun to see Chekov emerging from the turbolift with two others, presumably evacuees from the *Euryale*. Both newcomers' eyes had a silvery shimmer. One was a brown-haired human woman, and the other looked Andorian, but paler and with a higher forehead. At Thelin's shocked gasp of recognition, Terrell realized she must be an Aenar.

A similar gasp came from Nizhoni at tactical. "Marcella?"

The ship rocked from another volley of Naazh fire. "If I may, sir," the silver-eyed woman said, not waiting for Terrell's permission before striding across the bridge to the tactical station. Giving the wide-eyed Nizhoni a reassuring smile, she fearlessly placed her hands on the still-sizzling power supply panel and concentrated. Electricity flickered around her body, and she grimaced and grunted but seemed essentially unharmed.

Nizhoni's attention was torn between the inexplicable sight and the sudden status updates from the tactical console. "Captain! The . . . the force field is back to full power . . . *twice* full power! And increasing!" The thunder of the Naazh bombardment began to subside. The enemy ship's fire was intensifying, if anything, but less of its effect was getting through.

Chekov had returned to the science station. "Sir . . . the field generators have been charged with massive amounts of psionic energy. Chief DiFalco must be somehow . . . tapping into the natural psionic fields around us and drawing their power into the ship." Terrell appreciated that he'd managed to introduce the woman in the course of his explanation.

Thelin stared. "Are you saying she's given the *Reliant* a telekinetic shield?"

The Russian shrugged. "Essentially."

"Chekov, is this woman a New Human?" Terrell asked. "How does she have so much power?"

"She is, but she wasn't this powerful before she . . . died. Or seemed to."

The female Aenar spoke angrily. "Can't you tell she's suffering? We have to get your ships out of here."

Azem-Os began, "Our engines are in no condition—"

"We're aware. We can deal with that too." The silver-eyed Aenar stepped toward the Aurelian and reached for her head. Azem-Os reared back, splaying her taloned hands and spreading her wings in an intimidation display. "Oh, for— There's no time for your timidity!"

"Forgive me," Terrell said, "but I've encountered beings with powers like yours before, and they were not benevolent."

"We're not the ones trying to blow you up, you flatheaded fool!"

"Please, sir," Chekov urged. "The Aenar are pacifists—despite Ms. zh'Lenthar's manner. And I trust the chief." He glanced toward DiFalco, concerned at her visible and audible distress as she continued to shield the *Reliant* against the Naazh's fire.

Terrell sighed. "All right, Rem, let her do . . . whatever."

With an unhappy ruffle of her green-gold feathers, Azem-Os relented. The Aenar—zh'Lenthar—put one hand on Azem-Os's crested head and the other on the circuitry panel of the engineering station. "Show me the damaged components in your mind. Imagine their proper structure and function. Concentrate."

The first officer complied, and she and zh'Lenthar stood together silently for several moments, their breathing becoming synchronized—and accelerating. Chekov worked his console. "Captain . . . I'm reading more psionic energy from her and from the other Aenar we beamed aboard, in resonating patterns."

"I suggest you bring the other ship inside your shields and dock with it," zh'Lenthar said. "We can't repair both ships in time. DiFalco will let them through her shield."

Terrell nodded to Thelin, who raised his communicator and gave his ship the order. After a moment, Commander Goetch reported from main engineering. *"Captain! Somehow the damaged flow regulator is . . .* healing *itself. I don't know any other way to describe it. The warp control circuits are coming back online as well, all by themselves. This is impossible."*

"Take the gift horse, Jim," Terrell replied. "And get ready to ride it out of here, best warp speed, at my order."

"Aye, sir."

"Matter transmutation," Chekov murmured. "The power required would be incredible! How can they channel it all?"

A gentle bump shook the hull. "*Charas* is docked, sir," Beach said.

"Mains are back online," Azem-Os and zh'Lenthar said in eerie synchronization.

"Punch it!" Terrell ordered.

The *Reliant* shot to warp, accelerating swiftly. "We've lost them, sir," Beach reported a few moments later. "No sign of pursuit."

"Drop shields," Terrell ordered. "Divert power to main engi—"

He was interrupted by the sound of DiFalco and zh'Lenthar collapsing heavily to the deck.

"So the explosion that destroyed the rec deck . . . it was a cover?" Chekov asked.

From her bed in the *Reliant*'s sickbay, DiFalco nodded. "Kollos knew the only way to save the last of the Aenar was to make the Naazh think they'd succeeded in killing them. When he showed them his appearance, he knew it would only temporarily disorient the hosts, since the Lords inside them would shield them from madness, as our Spectres did for us. But it gave him enough time to spirit us and the Aenar away with a dimensional warp, then trigger the explosion to cover the evidence. He had to make it look like we'd all been vaporized in the blast or sucked out into warp space, so the lack of remains wouldn't be suspicious."

"And just to be clear," said Captain Terrell, who stood nearby with Doctor Wilder, "when the *Euryale* crew reported there were no Medusans left aboard to save, they didn't mean that they were all dead, but that they'd already escaped the same way Kollos saved you?"

"Exactly, sir."

Chekov's mind reeled at what DiFalco had told him about the Spectre Lords and sleepers and the true nature of human and Aenar telepaths. Nearby, though, Commander Thelin just looked relieved as he stood by Kinoch zh'Lenthar's bed, holding her hand. Chekov empathized with his joy that the Aenar were not extinct after all. It was a weight off of his own conscience as well, knowing that they had not been exterminated on his watch. And apparently the survivors from the *Enterprise* were not the only ones. The two Aenar ships believed destroyed during the first wave of Naazh attacks—the diplomatic mission and the group searching for a new homeworld—had both been teleported to safety by the Medusans as well.

"So naturally," zh'Lenthar said to the assembled officers, "we must request that you keep our survival completely confidential. In fact, Captain, I request permission to suppress the memory of our presence in your crew's minds before we leave. It is imperative that the Naazh and their Lords not become aware of our continued existence."

"I'll agree to classify your survival," Terrell replied. "I'm not ready to authorize mental tampering, though. I trust my people."

The activist sighed. "You're lucky we're pacifists. We could just do it without asking, you know."

"You're not making a compelling case, *Zha*."

"Kinoch," DiFalco said gently, and the Aenar sighed and fell silent.

"Frankly, I'm more concerned about these 'Spectres' you say you have living inside you," Terrell went on. "You're telling us that every human esper for centuries has had an incorporeal alien of enormous psionic power living inside them without their knowledge."

"Not *every* esper," DiFalco said, sounding rueful. "At least, not most of the latent ones. The esper tests were based on the Vulcan model, on the assumption that telepathy was innate to human brains. So the tests produced a lot of false positives. People without Spectres inside them, just with brain structures that made them passively receptive to certain psionic effects, like the Vulcans' esper testing devices or the energies of the barrier on the galaxy's edge." She looked at Chekov. "When the *Enterprise* passed through that barrier in 2265, it killed all the crew members with those sensitive brain structures, all the false-positive espers. But two others in the crew did have dormant Spectres within them, and the barrier awakened them and supercharged their abilities. It made them like us, but they were overcome by the shock of the sudden awakening and didn't have control of their powers."

DiFalco gestured to the silver-eyed Aenar on the other beds. "But when the Medusans took us in, they told us about our Spectres and showed us how to communicate with them, allow them to awaken. We've spent the past year learning to commune with them, to harness their powers safely and controllably."

Chekov couldn't contain his curiosity any longer. "Can I ask about the eyes? What makes them turn silver like that?"

Doctor Wilder spoke before DiFalco could. "I wondered that myself. My scans show that it's some kind of biofluorescence of the electrolytes in their aqueous humors. The excitation must come from the intense psionic energy radiating out from their brains." She tilted her head, causing some of her long cornrows to slide off her shoulder. "That's why it manifests in the Aenar too. It's only a surface effect, independent of the optic nerve. Oh, and I think the psionic energy bleaches the hair pigments too. That's why they turn gray so fast, before the hairs have time to grow out."

DiFalco sighed. "The stigmata of an active Spectre, awake and exerting its energies."

"Can you even see through that?" Chekov wondered.

"As long as the light's good. Sort of like mirrored sunglasses. And . . . the Spectre shares its senses with me. I can perceive things we don't have words for."

He touched her hand. "You . . . don't seem thrilled by that."

The glint in her eyes shifted, and he realized why when a tear rolled down her cheek. "Oh, Pavel, I feel like such a fool. I was so . . . fervent about this new evolutionary stage in humanity. This unlocking of our untapped potential, elevating humans toward a new spiritual level." She shook her head. "But it was all a lie. My powers were never mine. They were just . . . spillage from the sleeper inside me stirring out of dormancy. An intruder hiding inside my body since I was a child." She shuddered.

"I've told you before," zh'Lenthar said. "If it's always been part of you, it makes no difference. It's symbiotic, not parasitic."

"Symbiosis is consensual!"

"Did you consent to have mitochondria in your cells?"

"Mitochondria have been part of cellular evolution for billions of years," Wilder reminded the Aenar activist. "From the chief's account, these Spectres began inhabiting humans only a few centuries ago."

"Exactly," DiFalco said. "All those old tales of psychic and supernatural abilities in humans—they were just superstition and myth. For all we know, real psi abilities didn't start to appear in humans until a generation or two before the Vulcan contact." She lowered her head. "The potential was never ours to begin with."

Terrell crossed his arms. "Chief DiFalco, are you telling us you don't agree that the Spectres' presence within the New Humans is benevolent?"

She thought it over, grimacing slightly. "I understand why the refugees were forced to do what they did. I've gotten to know my Spectre well enough to know how much of a sacrifice it made, choosing to stay permanently dormant to ensure my freedom of choice. I know they only did it to hide from the Naazh. And . . . I've accepted having the Spectre awake inside me so that we can fight together to defend the Aenar—and now the New Humans. The refugees don't deserve to die for what they did, and their hosts certainly don't deserve to die for something that was done to us without our knowledge."

She looked up at Terrell with resolve in her eyes. "But I still feel betrayed and violated, and I'm not the only one. Some of the New Humans who know the truth are fine with it—like Jade," she said to Chekov, who appeared to recognize the name. "But the rest . . . we want it to end." She took a determined breath. "We'll keep fighting as Spectre hosts for as long as it takes to stop the Naazh. But once the refugees and their hosts are no longer in danger . . . then I want mine gone. These powers were never mine, so I don't want them anymore.

"The hell with 'New'—I just want to be human again."

Seventeen

U.S.S. Enterprise

A second Medusan ship had joined the convoy in the pocket continuum, and Jim Kirk was pleased when Miranda Jones brightened and informed him that Ambassador Kollos wished to beam aboard the *Enterprise*. Miranda had told him the night before that Kollos's death had been feigned as part of the cover for the Aenar's survival, but it seemed that her sorrow at his loss had not been entirely an act. She had known all along that he was alive, but he had been far enough away—in more than three dimensions of space—that their intimate link had been severed, with only the faintest psionic thread remaining to connect them. The loneliness and need that had led her to seek comfort from Kirk had not been feigned, and she had thanked him for the emotional support and companionship he had provided. But at the moment the Medusan ship was in range again, Kirk could see the return of the contentment that Miranda had radiated ever since her original meld with Kollos, and he wondered if she needed him anymore.

Of course, Kirk was glad that the ebullient Medusan diplomat was still alive—especially as it came with the assurance that the Aenar and New Humans supposedly lost in the destruction of the recreation deck were still alive and well, teleported to safety by Kollos under cover of the blast. All aside from the unfortunate Edward Logan, who had been one of the first victims of the gold Naazh.

Also known as Specialist T'Nalae.

Once the *Enterprise* had entered the pocket continuum, it had apparently cut T'Nalae off from the separate pocket dimension that the Naazh drew their armor and weapons from. She was still possessed by a Lord, but it was helpless, unable to fight or to teleport her away. At last, it had been possible to capture and hold a Naazh. And there was no other Naazh that Kirk was so eager to interrogate.

Now he stood in the brig along with Spock, McCoy, Jones, and the brig's guard on duty, with Kollos's mobile habitat hovering silently behind them. As he stared at T'Nalae through the force screen of her cell, seeing the shimmering silver eyes that had been hidden behind her blank gold visor, he thought back to how casually Gary Mitchell had reached out with his mind and strangled his friend Lee Kelso to death, when they had been laughing and joking together just days before. According to Miranda, the Spectre inside Gary had most likely been panicked, hyperaggressive, and borderline psychotic from its forced awakening and power amplification, like a human suffering from a cordrazine overdose. By contrast, the Spectre Lord possessing T'Nalae's body was a hunter, acting on a genocidal agenda and using her as its instrument. Kirk wanted to believe she was not responsible for Logan's death any more than Gary had been for Kelso's.

T'Nalae, though, seemed determined to take full credit for the murders she had committed. "Whatever Jones and her mental *ménage à trois* told you is a lie, Admiral Kirk," snarled the short-haired young Vulcan—no longer so young in appearance as before, and not just from the cosmetic surgery. "We hunters are not victims or slaves, the way the hosts of the renegades are. I freely chose to allow my Lord to enter me."

McCoy winced. "Did you *have* to phrase it that way?"

Spock addressed her sternly. "To clarify, Specialist: Do you freely confess to the murder of Crewman Edward Logan and several Aenar, to being an accomplice to the murders of Crewman Joshua Vidmar and Petty Officer Hrii'ush Uuvu'it, and to participating in the terrorist attack on the New Human compound on Earth?"

She winced. "The guards were not our quarry. They just got in the way. As for the others, they were not what they pretended to be. Logan was not human anymore, if he ever truly was. The infiltration of your species had to be halted."

"By killing its hosts?" Kirk demanded. "You're trying to make it sound as if they were victims of the Spectre refugees. So why kill the hostages along with their hostage-takers?"

"You don't understand. There is no difference between the two. The hosts are one with the so-called sleepers that possess them, their minds incurably corrupted from birth as their masters desired. There is nothing in them worth saving, and it would endanger far more lives if even one were allowed to escape."

"You Naazh have the same creatures inside of you," McCoy challenged. "So doesn't that make you just as corrupted?"

"No, Doctor. That is why we hunters depend on the dimension stones, and on the extradimensional source of matter and energy from which we draw our armor and weapons. The crystals provide a filter, preventing us and our Lords from being tainted by a full merger. They protect us and let us remain ourselves."

Jones stepped forward and spoke contemptuously. "Or maybe they just don't trust or respect you enough to teach you to share their true power. You're just foot soldiers using the weapons they place in your hands. No, you *are* the weapons. Your hatred and fear toward us make you easy to manipulate into mindless killing machines."

T'Nalae stared back with hate. "My Lord and I share a common purity of vision, of purpose. It came to me and revealed what the *Enterprise* was harboring in the guise of the Aenar survivors. It saw that I recognized their intrinsic wrongness, and that of the human espers as well.

"At its request, I let it join with my mind and share its knowledge of the long struggle. Of the perverted and unnatural experiments of the extremist faction you call 'refugees,' hybridizing corporeal and incorporeal forms from different universes in search of a chimeric blend with the power to conquer both. Just as humanity fought the Augments, so the Lords fought to eradicate these dangerous fusions before their corruption could spread through both domains of existence. But they escaped to this domain and began their long infiltration, breeding their chimeras for generations until they were ready to awaken and conquer. V'Ger was their cover story, their excuse to begin their emergence."

She took a step toward him, undaunted by her proximity to the force field. "You have seen the enormous power that these hybrids can wield in our plane of existence. Their ability to harness vast amounts of psionic energy, to manipulate and transmute matter into whatever forms they wish. You know how deadly that power is, how defenseless you are against it. You should understand the great danger it poses to our plane. You should stand with us, Admiral. We are Federation citizens fighting to protect our homeworlds from invasion. That's supposed to be Starfleet's job!"

Kirk studied her for a moment. "It's hard to believe in the Naazh's benevolence," he said, "when you go out of your way to kill so personally, so bloodily. To terrorize and stalk your victims, and take pleasure in the kill."

"We hate what they have done to themselves. What their insurrection did to the Lords' domain, and what they will do to your domain if allowed to spread. They are deserving of hate, not of sympathy. We take pleasure in ending their scourge."

Kirk crossed his arms. "Let me tell you why I don't believe you. Right now, there are a few hundred New Humans and over a dozen Medusans sharing this continuum with us, and they have you at their mercy. As you said, they're powerful enough that I and my crew couldn't stop them if they wanted to do to you what you've done to the Aenar and to many of them.

"But instead of hunting you down with swords and daggers—instead of murdering the part of you that's still T'Nalae out of hatred for the entity possessing her—they intend to do something you've apparently never bothered to try." He smiled darkly. "An exorcism."

T'Nalae pulled back, eyes widening. "What?"

Jones smiled graciously, speaking with a mix of Kollos's insouciance and her own righteous indignation. "We're going to treat both you and your resident Spectre far more gently than you've treated us. With the help of the Medusans' psionic and hyperdimensional abilities, we're going to excise the Lord from your body and send it back to its home domain." Her smile turned grim. "Frankly, more than a few of us would be willing to see you dead for what you've done to us. But that would be sinking to your level."

"Sometimes the best revenge is to be better than your enemy," Kirk said. "To deny them the pretense that they're just doing what anyone would do."

T'Nalae was shaking her head, horrified. "No. No, you can't do this! Admiral, you speak of morality, but I consented to this joining! How many sleeper hosts can say that? It was my free choice to accept this power, and taking it away from me by force is a violation."

Spock replied gravely. "You forfeited the right to that power, T'Nalae, when you used it to kill others." He stepped closer. "Last year, you came to me seeking insight on how I mastered my emotions. I have ruminated since then on how to answer that question, and I can now say that I have done so by understanding that the power of emotion—like any other power—is not a license, but a responsibility. I hope that you, too, will come to understand that once you have been freed from your possessor. I will be here afterward if you need me."

He moved back along with McCoy and Kirk, who nodded to Jones. She moved closer to the brig door, her eyes flaring brighter silver as Kollos's habitat moved in alongside her.

T'Nalae shook her head. "No. No, don't take it from me!" Then she stiffened, eyes wide, and began to scream.

"Please stop fighting it," Jones said through clenched teeth. "You're making it harder than it needs to be!"

"I'll . . . never . . . stop fighting!"

She strained, fists clenching, but her groans intensified, accompanied by the occasional gasp of exertion from Jones. Kirk saw McCoy looking on in horror and Spock in unconcealed regret.

Finally, T'Nalae flipped back and hovered in midair for several moments, convulsing as if she were drowning. Was the Spectre Lord trying to kill her rather than let her go? Or was it her own refusal to let *it* go that was killing her?

Then she convulsed one last time and fell to the deck. Jones slumped as well, and the manipulator arms on Kollos's habitat caught her tenderly. Kirk nodded to the guard to lower the force field, and McCoy rushed in to check on T'Nalae's vitals. "She's stabilizing," he reported after a moment.

But Kirk had already discerned that, for T'Nalae was sobbing. "Nooo," she moaned weakly. "I'm alone. So alone . . ."

He looked down on her in pity. "I hope someday you understand, Specialist. It's not about fighting for its own sake. It's about having something worth fighting for."

Now that T'Nalae's Lord had been successfully excised and forced back to its native realm, the Medusans were finally able to bring the Starfleet convoy out of the pocket dimension—which had simply been a quarantine area to prevent the Lords from discovering their real destination. Kirk had assumed that the Medusans had intended to settle the New Humans on a planet within their territory. He had been correct as far as that went—but he had been mistaken to assume that the Medusans' territory was limited to his home universe.

What he saw now on the bridge's main viewscreen, as the *Enterprise* and the other two Starfleet ships maintained tight formation between the two Medusan craft in order to be carried along with them, was almost beyond his comprehension. The space they passed through seemed to ripple, distorting the images of the other ships so that sometimes they appeared far more distant, or facing the wrong direction, or duplicated out to infinity, or even turned inside-out so that he could see their interior compartments and crew. Sometimes their engine glows and running lights seemed to be refracted by the surrounding space itself, warped into kaleidoscopic blobs and rippling rings of interference.

"This is the real Medusan Complex," Jones told him while she and Kollos's habitat flanked him where he stood at the aft bridge rail, behind Spock in the command chair—an arrangement Kirk still struggled to get used to. "As in a complex transdimensional manifold, an interphase space connecting multiple spatial and subspatial domains."

"Interphase," Kirk said. "Like the interphase space I was once trapped in on the Tholian border. But it was . . . not at all like this. It wasn't like anything."

"You were merely adrift in one portion of it, Admiral," Spock replied. "You would not have seen much."

"I remember how empty it felt. As if I were . . . between universes."

"You probably were," Miranda said. "But the Complex intersects several universes—subspace domains large and small, some with more than three spatial dimensions, some with different physical laws from our own."

Kirk could believe that. At one point, they passed through a blindingly bright universe where space itself seemed dense and almost fluid. At another, they sped briefly through a network of wispy strands of energy resembling the roots of a fungus. One spatial domain looked fairly normal at first glance, but the perspective of the planet they flew past shifted strangely, as if its surface and clouds were flowing through themselves and cycling out the other side. "Fascinating," Spock said. "A five-dimensional hypersphere."

Kirk stared. "You're sure it's not four?"

Spock gave him a patient look. "There are no stable orbital configurations for a planet in four-dimensional space."

"Right. Silly me."

Finally they arrived in a domain that looked far more familiar—like normal space, but with fewer stars. The star they neared was a cool orange dwarf, and sensor readouts showed a Class-M planet in a relatively tight orbit. "That's our destination," Jones said. "This domain has physics almost exactly like our universe—it's just a great deal smaller, with a different dark-energy ratio compensating for the much lower mass. So it can support habitable planets like this one, which we call Ceto.

"Most importantly, it has a high enough psionic particle density to sustain Spectres quite comfortably, making it easier for them to exist and wield their powers outside of corporeal hosts."

"This is where the Aenar now reside?" Spock asked.

"That's right. And where the New Humans can take up residence, safe from the Naazh. It's more than big enough for both groups. All three, really." She sighed. "I'm happy to stay bonded with my Spectre, but some of the others haven't been thrilled to learn the truth—including your former navigator, DiFalco." Kirk nodded. Miranda had already informed him that DiFalco was assisting the *Reliant*, while the other New Human survivors from the *Enterprise*, Jade Dinh and Daniel Abioye, were helping to guide other ships in the convoy toward Medusan space. The New Humans the *Potemkin* had brought from Aldebaran III had already been ferried across dimensions by the Medusans and were below on the planet, and the others would begin to arrive within the day.

"So once they're safely settled on Ceto, the Spectres will no longer have to hide within humanoid hosts. They won't have to stay joined if they or their hosts don't want it. Or they can join only part of the time, if they prefer. But from now on, it will be a free choice for both Spectre and host."

"I'd like to see the planet for myself," Kirk said. "Talk to the Aenar who are here—and to the Spectres, if I can."

Kollos's mischievous smile came onto Miranda's face. "Still don't quite trust us, Captain?"

"I have an obligation to make sure, Ambassador. I'm responsible for the New Humans' safety, so I have to exercise due diligence."

"Of course," Kollos/Jones said, taking no offense. "You and your officers are more than welcome on the planet." Their smile widened. "We so rarely have guests from your neck of the woods."

Ceto

The Aenar and New Human settlements were in a beautiful part of Ceto, a temperate coastal area filled with pristine forests of slender, towering trees bracketed by low, rolling mountains on one side and a picturesque coastal inlet on the other. The forest floor was dotted with whimsical-looking plants—freestanding purple growths that spiraled in on themselves, large flowers that looked like pumpkin-headed dandelions, pitcher plants with bioluminescent tendrils dangling from them. Around the trunks of the trees grew lush vines from which dangled fruits that looked like red onions but smelled far sweeter. The gravity was a shade lower than Earth's, making Kirk feel light on his feet as Miranda Jones and Kollos led him, Spock, and McCoy to visit the settlement being constructed for the New Humans.

When they arrived in the broad, gently sloping river valley where the town was being constructed, they saw a number of Aenar there—a group of about a half dozen, holding out their hands and materializing a moderate-sized single-story dwelling on the lot where their silvery eyes were directed.

"When we brought in the first group of Aenar, the ones from the ships we rescued," Jones said, "they initially built their dwellings in a cave nearby, one we helped them to enlarge to approximate their original compound. But over the past year, as they've gotten used to the fact that they're safe here, they've ventured farther out into the world. They don't need the sunlight to see by any more than I do, but we enjoy the warmth of it on our skin, and the touch of a cool breeze. We enjoy the chance to exercise, to explore . . . to commune with the animals of this world."

The Aenar dwellings they walked past were interestingly different from the ones in the Aenar compound on Andoria. Those structures had been designed and built by Andorians with the needs of sighted beings in mind, with windows and interior lighting. The dwellings here were different; instead of windows, they had thin walls made of something like rice paper and wide openings covered in curtains, presumably to let sounds and scents in from outside. Seeing this made Kirk realize that the building under psionic construction had been of a more familiar, human-friendly design, presumably meant for the incoming New Humans.

Another trio of Aenar were walking slowly past now, reaching out before themselves and creating a paved path to the riverbank as they advanced. Kirk stared. He had faced several beings with transmutation powers of this magnitude before, but he had rarely seen them use those abilities for anything so mundane and functional.

"It's surprisingly low-key," McCoy said, echoing Kirk's thoughts. "With abilities like you people have, I'd expect to see diamond waterfalls and castles in the sky."

Jones chuckled. "Despite appearances, what the Spectres can do isn't magic, Doctor. Even in this domain with its rich psionic fields, exertions like these take a great deal of energy."

McCoy stared. "I thought you said these Aenar were melded with Medusans, like you are. That they're protected from the burnout effect from an active Spectre."

"Oh, they are, Doctor. But even incorporeal beings can wear themselves out by working too hard. As much as the Spectres here enjoy the chance to wake up and use their abilities after centuries of dormancy, they still need to pace themselves."

"I find it interesting," Spock said, "that your own Spectre persona never seems to speak through you as Kollos does."

She shrugged. "As I said before, Spock, my Spectre and I have always been one. Even when it was dormant, I felt its presence as a part of my own identity, without realizing it was something separate. It's already part of who I am, so there is no difference." She looked around. "Most of the Aenar I've talked to feel the same. Their telepathy has been part of their nature throughout their lives, throughout most of their recorded history. It's part of who they are. So they have no wish to be separated from their Spectres."

"And the humans?" McCoy challenged. "You said they'd be free to separate if they wanted."

"And so they are," she replied firmly. "We're taking you to see them now."

She led them to a fair-sized building that was marked as a medical clinic. "Why are they here?" McCoy demanded.

"Just a precaution," Jones assured him. Her expression grew abashed. "I may have glossed over the difficulty of my own experience with my Spectre's awakening. Even though Kollos prepared me—even though I was already comfortable with the idea of sharing my consciousness with another—it was a shock to discover that something I thought was a part of myself had been an outsider my whole life. Imagine if your left hand suddenly started speaking to you and acting on its own. It would not be an effortless adjustment."

She led the group in through the clinic doors, with Kollos's habitat taking up the rear. Inside, Kirk noted Arsène Xiang conversing with the leader of the Aldebaran New Humans. Xiang looked almost completely recovered from his brutal stabbing in the *Enterprise* cargo bay less than thirty-six hours before—more a testament to his Spectre's telekinetic healing abilities than McCoy's skills. Chief Onami was nearby, speaking calmingly to several members of their group, evidently a pair of mothers and their preadolescent son. It seemed that being among the New Humans had benefitted Onami, Kirk thought, even though her own esper rating had apparently been a false positive.

"At first, I felt angry," Jones went on. "Violated. Against Kollos's advice, I forced the Spectre from my mind and body—and I passed out from the strain, much like T'Nalae did." She paused. "When I awoke, I thought I'd feel free, but instead I felt incomplete, like less than my full self. I resisted for a day or so—you know how stubborn I am—but finally I realized I couldn't be myself without the Spectre part of me." She went on with irony. "The hard part then was convincing the Spectre. I'd hurt it by forcing it out. It hadn't been on its own for more than two centuries, and even with the Medusans there to give it comfort, it was afraid and confused. Just as much as I was.

"We worked it out, of course. We merged again and became complete—more complete than before, since now my Spectre half was awake and known to me."

Xiang came over, still moving slowly and wincing a bit from his healing injury, and put an avuncular arm around Jones's shoulders. His eyes gleamed in more ways than one. "I'm grateful to Miranda for introducing me to my Spectre as Kollos did for her."

"Arsène was the strongest telepath I met on Earth," Jones said, "which suggested a strong affinity with his Spectre, even without conscious knowledge of its existence. Unlike me, Arsène embraced his passenger without protest. But then, he's far kinder than I've ever been."

Xiang chuckled. "Kindness had nothing to do with it. I retired from Starfleet over fifteen years ago, Admiral, and nothing in my life since then has offered the same opportunity for discovery and wonder—until my esper abilities started to grow a few years ago. Meeting my Spectre was like making first contact inside my own skull." He beamed, his smile brighter than his silver eyes. "We explore the new and unknown because we hope it will change us for the better. For me, that's finally happened. It's been a delight to rediscover myself—and my new best friend," he finished, tapping his head.

Jones and Xiang led them into a ward where Kirk saw several humans, no doubt from the Aldebaran refugee group delivered by the *Potemkin*. They were reclined on diagnostic couches and tended to by bipeds of an unfamiliar species, ursine and gold-skinned with red-slitted visors that seemed permanently affixed to their skulls.

"Of course, not everyone handles it as well as Arsène," Jones went on. "So we've worked out a more careful process for introducing hosts to the Spectres within them, and guiding them through the discussion of whether to remain joined. The medical precautions are part of it, but they're rarely needed anymore."

She placed a hand on the furry shoulder of one of the visored ursines, who looked at the new arrivals and nodded gravely before returning his focus to his patient. "These are the Kinaku. They're natural telepaths who form corporate intelligences with Medusans, as I have with Kollos. They're how the Medusans interact with the humanoids on Ceto and elsewhere, to protect them from the sight of the Medusans' natural forms."

"Interesting," Spock said. "Why do the Medusans not employ them as diplomatic liaisons with the Federation, then?"

The Kinaku looked up again. "We're very shy."

Xiang chuckled. "The Spectres and their hosts aren't the first telepathic species the Medusans have given refuge to, Admiral. The Kinaku were almost exterminated by the empire that conquered their world over a millennium ago, in a part of the outer Alpha Quadrant we haven't reached yet. So they're content to live in the Complex's pocket domains."

"Pardon me," the visored ursine went on. "We are ready to separate."

McCoy peered at the delicate-featured, black-haired young woman on the couch, who seemed to be in a semiconscious or meditative state. Kirk noted that her chart was labeled WU, MEIHUA. "She's decided she doesn't want her Spectre?"

"It is mutual. Excuse us."

The observers stepped back and watched as the Kinaku placed his bulky hand on Wu's forehead and concentrated. Kirk initially feared the separation would be as convulsive as it had been with T'Nalae, but instead it proceeded far more gently, presumably because it was consensual. Wu's diminutive frame moved only slightly, stiffening, and her breathing intensified. Her eyes shot open, gleaming silver, and then a similar shimmer formed around her head and spread over her body, rising up and outward from her. The sparkling aura was more colorful than her eyes' glow, like an aurora, as if the psionic energy being released were exciting the molecules in the air to iridesce.

Finally the glow lifted off Wu and moved to hover in the air. At the same time, the young woman relaxed and let out a long, slow sigh. Her now-dark eyes widened and a mix of emotions played across her face—confusion, discovery, fear, relief, sadness. Her eyes looked around and locked on Kirk, probing for a moment. "I can't sense your thoughts," she said. "It's just mine again." She smiled in relief, but at the same time, a tear trickled down her cheek.

The Kinaku physician stood. "Let her rest now."

He started to lead them away, but Jones reached out to the auroral glow in the air. "These gentlemen would like to speak with you, if you're up to it," she said to the disembodied Spectre in a soft, reassuring tone. "Follow us, please."

"Don't worry," Xiang added. "You'll soon get the hang of moving on your own again." He grunted and put a hand on his abdomen. "Not unlike me."

The two powerful Spectre hosts led them out into the rear courtyard of the clinic, where several humans sat or strolled in the gentle orange sunlight, some with Aenar or Kinaku attendants. They found a quiet spot for their conversation and waited for the freed Spectre to join them. After a moment, the shimmer of light emerged through the closed door and drew toward them, beginning to take on a semblance of a humanoid form. "It's a telepathic illusion," Jones explained. "The easiest way for a disembodied Spectre to speak to us. It may take her a while to get the hang of it, though."

Kirk soon understood her choice of pronoun, for the form the Spectre was trying to project was a simulacrum of Meihua Wu, made of translucent silver-white light with wisps of auroral color clothing it. The image flickered and multiplied as it moved, as if jumping quickly back and forth between overlapping moments and alternatives. At one point, it broke apart and shifted vertically, momentarily settling into a bizarre configuration with its upper torso gliding along the ground at waist level while its legs walked on air above its head. *"Be patient,"* a replica of Wu's voice echoed in Kirk's head. *"Spatiotemporal (be) geometry (patient) is challenging (be patient)."*

The image's two halves converged and passed through each other, finally settling into a reasonably normal image of Wu, albeit translucent with silver-white hair and still with a degree of chronological stutter. She looked like a woman made of moonlight, reflected in a rippling pool. *"I hope you (an agreeable form) you will find this (engage with) an agreeable form (this) to engage with."*

"Indeed," Kirk said to the Spectre's angelic countenance. "Quite a beautiful form, in fact." Jones threw him a look—*Really?* He cleared his throat. "But that's not important. What matters to us is the chance to communicate directly with a Spectre—to confront you about how you've . . . involved yourselves with humans all this time."

"You mean (used) how we have used humans, Admiral Kirk (humans)," the Spectre said, her image and voice overlapping themselves slightly less now. *"You are entitled to say so. It was not a course we took without argument (we took) among ourselves. What began as a temporary measure in desperation (trap) became an accustomed habit (desperation), a trap for ourselves.*

"Our wise elders argue that the brutality of the Naazh has proven the need (brutality) for our concealment," the Spectre went on. *"But our lives of enforced passivity were hardly better than extinction. And we have now cost the lives (selfish) of many of our hosts through our selfish presence. I, for one, am glad I no longer endanger Meihua (no longer)."*

"What was she to you?" McCoy challenged. "What are we to your people? Disguises that you wear? Pets? It's hard to call it a partnership when one partner knows nothing about it."

"Do you expect me to disagree, Doctor McCoy? But Meihua was no pet. She was (protector) my home, my protector. Through her, I experienced singing. Through her mother, Jasmine, I knew the life of a police detective. Through her grandmother, Mana, I felt what it was like to master cuisine and run a successful restaurant. I (shared in) could not live for myself, so I shared in their lives. It was hard to be passive through all of it (their lives)—to experience it as a living dream. But their joys and successes brought compensation."

"So glad you found us entertaining."

The gleaming face grew wistful. "*We saw your hardships too. We saw you struggle with hatred, violence, near-annihilation (devastated us). At times, it devastated us not to intervene. But we could not, for bringing you to the Lords' attention would have been far worse (could not).*

"*The Aenar were good shelter—quiet, hidden, barely noticed. Living in humans was riskier. Many of us were killed in your wars; even awakening enough to protect our hosts risked drawing the Lords' attention (were killed). When we could stir enough to communicate, we debated (other hosts) whether we should find other hosts, a safer haven. But we still sensed potential in you. More of you fought to protect than to destroy (potential).*" The image smiled. "*And so you saved yourselves, and us. The good in you prevailed, and you ascended to the stars and built a union based on peace and partnership. And we felt safer (peace and) than we had since the Lords first took power in our domain.*"

"What was the nature of your conflict with the Lords?" Spock asked. "Or can it be expressed in our terms?"

"*It was not so unlike the conflicts you have in your reality,*" the Spectre said sadly. "*We sought to seek out and encourage different ways of being, of thinking (enrich us). We believed they would enrich us, enlarge our existence. The Lords saw difference as a threat, new ideas as a pollution of (existence. They) their purity.*

"*We found a way, with only a simple adjustment of our psionic matrices, to transcend our domain and cross to others. We discovered life made of matter, of fermionic particles rather than psionic field resonances. It astounded us with its diversity (transcend our), with the vastness of the universes it occupied. It pleased us greatly to discover that matter could organize into patterns with intelligence like our own (despite)—minds we could connect with and learn from, despite being so extraordinarily alien (connect) (pleased).*

"*But to the Lords, corporeal life was an unconscionable horror, a mockery of true life. They discredited our exploration with lies, claimed that we had been corrupted by corporeal entities to be their agents, invaders (lies) set on destroying our domain. They played on the fears of our people to solidify their power, to restrict freedom of thought and choice.*

"At first, they merely contained us—segregated us from the community. The means they used to isolate us were harsh, damaging. This was presented as a necessary evil for the good of the majority. When we began to die from it, the Lords rationalized it as accident (harsh), then as our own fault for resisting. In time, the masses were inured enough to our deaths that the Lords were free to inflict them with intent.

"But we had allies on the outside—a resistance that still believed in us and planned in secret. Once the purge was underway, they took action to free us, sacrificing many of their own in the process. But they broke containment and allowed us to flee."

The Spectre lowered her simulated head. The image was steady now; her chronological stutter seemed to have faded with practice. *"At first, we sought to live among the people we had contacted in your universe. But there were those among them who feared us, much as the Lords had feared corporeal life. The Lords hated us enough to swallow their own bile and recruit those fearful humanoids as their instruments. They were the first of the hunters you call Naazh, and they slaughtered our protectors in their community in their effort to eradicate us. The Lords heightened their rage and cruelty, encouraged them to kill us using the primal weapons of corporeal species. This served their purposes, for it let them blame the Naazh's sadistic methods on the intrinsic savagery of corporeal life, distancing themselves from responsibility. But it also sent a message to our allies in our home domain and in yours—a warning of the terrors that would befall them if they attempted to help us.*

"We tried to settle on primitive worlds with no sentiences to endanger, bonding with simpler forms of life. Their individual

brains were too small to house us, but we could translocate across many in a distributed network. But the amount of psionic communication needed to maintain that connection was too easy for the Naazh to detect, and they found us there and killed more of our number.

"So our only choice was to use corporeal brains for concealment—and to conceal ourselves from those hosts, for their own safety. The rest you know."

"I'm sorry."

It was the same voice, but Kirk heard it through his ears rather than in his mind. Kirk turned to see Meihua Wu up and about, listening to her former sleeper's account. "I'm sorry I couldn't be a more welcoming host to you, after all you've been through. But I still feel . . . violated."

The moonlight face turned toward its living mirror. "*You owe me nothing, Meihua. I have taken far too much from you—your privacy, your certainty, your safety.*"

Wu shook her head. "The Lords took that—from both of us. I don't blame you for doing what you had to do." She turned to Kirk and the others. "I'm just glad it's over. I'm not sure quite who I am now. I'm different . . . but it's like I'm finally who I always thought I was. Just a normal person." She breathed a faint laugh. "Having psychic powers was fun at first, but now that I know where they really came from . . ." A shudder ran through her dainty frame. "Maybe if I'd had the choice, I would've been okay with it. But it's just too much."

She stepped closer to Kirk and Spock. "Now that I'm just me again—no Spectre, no powers, just a girl who loves to sing—can I go back home to Aldebaran?"

Kirk put a hand on her shoulder. "Soon, I hope. Once we can be sure there's no more danger." It was possible that the Naazh would not be able to determine, or would not believe, that a former New Human was now free of Spectre possession. Perhaps they would kill a former host as punishment for having harbored a sleeper. He didn't want to frighten Wu by saying as much, though, so he simply said, "For the moment, you're safest here on Ceto."

When she finally made contact, T'Nalae suppressed a laugh. She didn't want to alert the brig guard that anything was amiss; it might spoil the surprise.

Once the Medusans had forced her Lord from her body and banished it, they had believed she would no longer be able to serve as a beacon—that it would be safe for them to bring her to the renegade Spectres' haven without risk of discovery. But they had forgotten one thing: that Vulcans, unlike humans and Andorians, were innately telepathic. And that a Vulcan's telepathic bond with another being could be permanent and nonlocal, an entanglement surpassing time and distance.

They had broken her Lord's grip on her . . . but she retained her own latent link to it, too passive and faint for them to detect until she reactivated it. It could not reach into this space to find her—but she could still reach out.

Eighteen

U.S.S. Enterprise

The auditory ambience of the *Enterprise*'s bridge had evolved over the decades that Spock had served within its various iterations, as equipment function had advanced and aesthetic tastes in auditory status indicators had evolved. However, one component of that ambience that had remained irritatingly consistent over the majority of the past fourteen years had been the grumblings of Doctor Leonard McCoy. The doctor rarely entered the bridge without promptly making his presence known through distracting and generally uninformative banter.

This time, at least, McCoy had come to the bridge to report something useful, albeit with his wonted lack of clarity. "Well, that's the last of 'em. So we can all stop watching what we think now."

Spock signed the data slate he had been reviewing, handed it back to the yeoman, and glanced over at the doctor. "Have the New Humans settled in adequately on Ceto?"

"Settling in will probably take a while, but they all made the trip in one piece, at least. Enough that Jim ordered me back to the *Enterprise* to get some rest." The surgeon put his hands on his back and stretched theatrically. "I've rarely been so happy to follow an order. I'm not as young as I used to be, you know."

"Yet your predilection for stating the tautological remains evergreen, Doctor."

McCoy glowered at him. "It may be mathematically obvious, Spock, but it's a fact we humans tend to let ourselves forget until it sneaks up and surprises us." He sighed. "My problem is, I'm getting to the point where the reminders start coming closer and closer together."

"I take it the admiral has remained on the surface, then?"

"It'll be a while before age starts to catch up with that man," the doctor said with envy. "Yeah, Jim wanted to stick around and help the New Humans get settled. This relocation is his show, after all, and you know how he gets when he feels responsible for something."

"Indeed."

"Christine's still down there too, finishing up at the clinic. She'll be coming up with Jim when he's done, joining us for that postponed dinner. You're welcome to come, if you like."

The thought of renewing acquaintance with Doctor Chapel, now that they had both taken steps to move beyond the career stasis she had remarked on the year before, was agreeable to Spock. "I shall attend if my duties permit."

McCoy frowned at the sparse array of stars on the main viewscreen. "Well, I hope Jim can keep the speechifying to a minimum for once and get back here soon. It feels wrong, not being in our proper universe."

Spock quirked a brow. "The physical constants of this universe are essentially identical to our own, or else we could not exist within it. There is no difference that the human sensorium is capable of detecting."

McCoy rose to the bait with satisfying predictability. "It's not about sensing, Spock, it's about knowing! Just the *idea* of being outside our native universe feels unnatural. Nothing familiar out there, no way to find our way back home. It's a frightening thought."

"This is hardly your first time occupying a continuum other than our own, Doctor. Unlike our time in Elysia, for example, or yours in the quantum timelines of the Terran Empire and the Vulcan Consortium, in this instance we are fully aware that we shall be able to return home, as soon as the Medusans escort us back."

"And that's just why I'm so eager to get on with it, Spock!" He grimaced. "Whereas I suppose you'd like to stick around and explore the place. Not that it looks like there's a whole lot to explore," he added, waving at the screen.

"Indeed—it would be an intriguing opportunity. However, I still have responsibilities to Starfleet Academy and its cadets. I, too, will be gratified when we return."

After a moment, he realized that McCoy was studying him solicitously rather than continuing their banter. "You got quiet all of a sudden. Something bothering you?"

"It merely occurred to me to contemplate what must become of Specialist T'Nalae upon our return. She will have to be prosecuted for the murder of Edward Logan and several Aenar aboard the *Enterprise* and multiple New Humans on Earth, and as an accomplice in additional homicides committed by the Naazh. Indeed, she may very well be charged with treason and war crimes."

McCoy frowned, reflecting his seriousness. "Was she really responsible, though? She was possessed by one of those Spectre things, or Lords, or whatever."

"It is true that the Lord within her heightened her aggression and paranoia. But by her own admission, T'Nalae consented to become a Naazh, evidently with full knowledge of what that would entail."

"I guess that must've been when she passed out in the shower the night before the attack," the doctor muttered. "I feel like a fool. I saw the heightened psionic charge in her paracortex, but I thought she was just reacting to the Aenar being aboard. I was looking right at the Spectre in her and I didn't even realize it. If I had . . ."

"Doctor," Spock said, the firmness of his tone drawing McCoy's attention away from his burgeoning guilt. "Were my mother here, she would likely respond by saying, 'If wishes were horses, then beggars would ride.' My father, on the other hand, would point out the illogic of basing conditional statements on impossible conditions.

"You detected a psionic signature that generations of human, Vulcan, and Andorian scientists before you have universally mistaken for innate telepathic activity. Since your training in psionic medicine was predicated on that conventional wisdom, and since you had no knowledge of the Spectres' existence at that point, you could not have interpreted T'Nalae's readings in any other way."

McCoy's vivid blue eyes held his. "Spock . . . I appreciate—"

An alarm interrupted him. "Captain!" Palur called from the science station. "Reading multiple dimensional incursions in low orbit."

"Deflectors and subspace dampers have autoengaged," Lieutenant S'trakha added from tactical.

That told Spock that they were not Medusan signatures. McCoy approached the same conclusion more gradually. "Is it the Naazh? How the hell did they find us?"

The *Enterprise* shook under several powerful blasts. McCoy grabbed the aft railing to stabilize himself. "Confirmed," Spock said. "Doctor, report to sickbay and prep for casualties."

McCoy was already on his way to the lift. "Yes, sir, *Captain*. You just try and make sure my preparations won't be needed!" The doors closed before Spock could offer a riposte.

But his attention was needed elsewhere anyway, as a second barrage reminded him. He activated the intercom on his armrest. "*Enterprise* to Admiral Kirk. We are under attack from hostile spacecraft, presumably of Naazh origin. They may attempt to attack the population on the surface."

"*They won't need to, Spock,*" Kirk's voice came back. "*Because more than twenty Naazh just materialized on the surface, armed for bear.*"

Ceto

Over the past year, Kirk had seen the arms race between the Naazh and their quarry escalate anew each time they had clashed. Now, with more Spectre hosts gathered in one place than ever before, the Lords had responded with a commensurate increase in numbers. A horde of Naazh had materialized around the village all at once, surrounding it on three sides, with the mountains penning the villagers in on the fourth. They showed more variety in armor design and colors than Kirk had seen before, and in body size and shape as well.

But they were armed consistently this time. Rather than targeting their prey one at a time with daggers, swords, or armored fists, the entire horde of Naazh carried plasma rifles. More than a dozen New Humans and Aenar were struck down before the trained telekinetics could rally a defense.

Kirk rushed to the aid of a group of villagers, but the rapid crescendo of an engine whine drew his gaze upward, barely in time to see another Naazh piloting a small hovercruiser, closing on him swiftly with one hand on the aerial bike's handlebar and the other firing a plasma weapon, strafing the ground as it closed on Kirk and the villagers with him. He had no time to dodge.

"Sir!" Something invisible shoved Kirk aside. He rolled with it and came up on his feet, turning to see a familiar figure—a slender woman with silky, waist-length black hair, holding out one hand to shield Kirk and the villagers with a telekinetic barrier and using the other to hurl debris at the Naazh on the hovercruiser, driving it off.

"Crewman Dinh!" he called out once the immediate threat was past.

Jade Dinh turned and smiled at him, her eyes gleaming bright silver. "Capta— *Admiral.* Good to see you, sir."

"You too," he said sincerely. He'd heard she was still alive along with DiFalco and Abioye, but seeing her here was another matter. "The others?"

Dinh stepped toward him, swiftly and efficiently bundling her meter-long hair into an impossibly compact bun at the nape of her neck. He would have thought she was using her Spectre powers to pull it off if he hadn't seen her do the same a few times back on the *Enterprise.* "Just me, sir. Abioye's ship is in orbit, and DiFalco's still on *Reliant.*"

The other telekinetics had rallied to shield the villagers, so he took the opportunity to scan the armored hunters arrayed beyond. In addition to the two dozen or so Naazh on the ground, he counted at least six more flitting overhead on hovercruisers. The majority matched the eyewitness accounts and visual records of the attacks throughout the Federation. "Looks like they've gathered most of their forces here for a final assault."

"But how did they find us?" Dinh wondered.

"Good question, Crewman." Kollos and Miranda had been convinced that the Naazh within T'Nalae had been banished, the connection completely broken. Was there another Naazh spy in their midst? Or had they missed something in T'Nalae?

Explanations would have to wait. The assembled Naazh were using the anti-psionic flares from their belt crystals to break down the telekinetics' defenses, and several of the defenders fell to plasma fire. "Excuse me, sir," Dinh said resolutely, her voice echoing as she strode forward to face the enemy. "Please get the others to safety. We'll handle this."

As Kirk aided the villagers in their retreat, he saw Miranda, Arsène Xiang, and a few silver-eyed humans and Aenar advancing confidently to join Dinh. Xiang and Jones had manifested the same transmuted armor they had worn on the ship—Tang infantry for him, a stylized aegis in silver for her—and several others had done the same. Unlike the Naazh, all had chosen armor that showed their faces, in designs that reflected their heritage or aspirations. They looked like mythic champions rather than impersonal predators.

As Kirk watched, the simple jumpsuit Jade Dinh wore glowed and metamorphosed into a brighter, grander version of Starfleet security body armor. He smiled.

The Naazh gathered up and charged at the defenders, firing fiercely. The silver-eyed Spectre hosts spread their hands and lifted solid barriers from the ground, transmuted from its matter.

"They won't hold long, Jim," Miranda's voice sounded in his mind. *"Only a few of us have active Spectres; even fewer are trained to fight with them."*

"Can the Enterprise *help?"* Dinh's voice asked.

"Negative," he replied aloud. "The ships in orbit are under Naazh attack too."

"The caves," Xiang suggested to them mentally. *"The first Aenar settlement. We can shelter there."*

"How far are they?"

"Not far. We should be able to keep us all covered long enough."

Kirk frowned. "Miranda, you said too much of that would exhaust a Spectre—and its host."

"Remember, I have Kollos with me too," Jones replied. *"And for those without Medusan bonds, the strong psionic fields here will ease their efforts. Don't worry about us."*

"Acknowledged," Kirk said. But he still worried.

U.S.S. Reliant

The Aenar (or the Spectres within them) who had telekinetically repaired the *Reliant*'s warp drive had also been able to give it an extra boost of speed when they concentrated together, enough to bring it and the repaired *Charas* to the Medusan border a day earlier than anticipated. The plan—worked out between Terrell and Captain Eren, the Reon-Ka commander of the erstwhile *Euryale*—had been to transfer the New Human passengers to Medusan transport ships that would then take them to a secret location within the Medusan Complex—and Terrell now knew, thanks to Eren's explanations, that said location was a planet in some parallel dimensional plane that the Complex intersected with.

But rather than the Medusan transports, the *Reliant* was met at the border by the *U.S.S. Potemkin*. The *Constitution*-class starship's captain, Hannah Schwarzschild, now appeared on the *Reliant*'s bridge viewscreen. *"Something's happened,"* said Schwarzschild, a robust dark-haired woman who looked half her age. *"Apparently the Naazh have somehow located the haven planet the Medusans had arranged for our passengers. The Medusans have redirected their ships to assist. I'm told the* Enterprise *and two other Starfleet ships are already on hand as well."* She shook her head. *"Leave it to Jim Kirk to end up in the middle of things, am I right?"*

"I couldn't say," Terrell responded. "The admiral's path and mine have yet to cross."

"I'm afraid they still won't, Clark. At the same time the haven world was attacked, the Medusans reported that their homeworld was under attack as well."

Captain Eren gasped in horror, multiple nostrils flaring on his eyeless blue face. "No! My home."

Terrell traded a look of concern with Chekov. "No good deed goes unpunished," the second officer said. "The Lords must have had their fill of the Medusans protecting the Spe—their targets."

"Attack in what way?" Azem-Os asked. "More Naazh ships?"

"From what the Medusans say, they seem to be under direct invasion by the extradimensional aliens they call the Lords. The specifics were unclear, though."

"One incorporeal race attacking another?" Nizhoni put in

from the tactical station. "I can see how that would be hard to explain in our terms."

"One thing's clear enough," the captain told her, rising from his chair. "We might be looking at the start of an interdimensional war. Let's just hope it doesn't spread beyond incorporeal species."

"I fear the corporeal denizens of Medusa would be no safer," Eren said. "If not our bodies, then our minds could be devastated. And I fear the Medusans would divide their energies to protect us, to their own detriment."

"In that case," Terrell said, "we need to get to Medusa and help if we can."

"We barely even understand the nature of the combatants," the *Potemkin*'s captain replied. *"What can we possibly do to help?"*

"At the moment, I'm not sure. But I've seen Starfleet crews go up against powers like this before, and they've generally managed to come through in the end."

"Captain," Eren said, wringing his blue-furred hands, "your compassion is moving, but you do not need to risk your ship, your crew. This . . . this is a conflict far larger than you or the Federation. It is beyond what you could cope with."

Terrell stepped closer to face him, though the Reon-Ka had no eyes he could meet. "That may be true. The full scope of this fight is bigger than I or my crew can even grasp, let alone affect. I've been involved in a similar conflict once before. There wasn't much I could do to change the bigger picture. But there were still ways I could help, with the immediate problems within my reach."

He put a hand on Eren's shoulder. "That's all you can really ask of anyone—that they try to help as far as their hands can reach. If enough of us do that, it adds up."

Eren bowed his head in gratitude. "Thank you, Captain Terrell. I and my crew are at your disposal."

Schwarzschild sighed. *"Unfortunately, we're eleven hours away at the* Potemkin*'s best speed. We might be too late to do anything but pick up the pieces."*

Terrell perked up at that. "As it happens, Hannah, we've temporarily gotten an extra speed boost, courtesy of our passengers. We and the *Charas* will go to Medusa and deal with the Naazh attack. You catch up when you can."

Schwarzschild's eyebrows rose. *"Those New Humans have no end of surprises. I guess that's why the Naazh are so afraid of them."*

Oh, Hannah, Terrell thought. *You have no idea.*

U.S.S. Enterprise

While sensors showed only four relatively small Naazh ships in Ceto's orbital space, they were as powerful as Spock had come to expect. They had struck hard and fast at the three Starfleet vessels, which had been in parallel forced orbits several hundred kilometers above the settlement, in order to remain in easy transporter and communication range. With no more New Human passengers aboard, the three ships were again reliant on the technological defenses Starfleet had devised against the Naazh.

Unfortunately, the Naazh had continued to upgrade their offensive capabilities, and all three vessels were struck hard. "Torpedo loading system is offline," Lieutenant S'trakha reported from tactical.

"Switch to manual," Spock instructed. Though slow and inefficient, the manual loading system might still suffice as a backup if the crew's training had been adequate.

After another blow struck, S'trakha reported, "We're losing warp power to phasers. Engaging auxiliary power." That particular backup had been installed six years earlier on Kirk's orders, shortly after the V'Ger incident. It would render the phasers thirty-four percent less potent, however.

"*Asimov* to *Enterprise*," came Captain Blake's voice. "*We've taken heavy damage to the impulse engines, and our forced orbit's starting to decay. We'll have to thrust out into a natural orbit while we make repairs. We'll keep supporting you with torpedoes as long as we can.*"

"Acknowledged," Spock replied. He effortlessly calculated how much RCS thrust the *Asimov* would require to increase its orbital velocity to cancel Ceto's gravity at this altitude, as well as how quickly it would take the ship out of effective combat range.

He opened a preset channel on the armrest intercom. "*Enterprise* to *Palmares*. Captain nd'Omeshef, the Naazh appear to be focusing on a single critical system on each vessel."

"*I noticed, Captain Spock,*" the Arkenite commander replied. "*Our own shields are taking quite a pounding. Subspace dampers too.*"

"Mister Sulu, move to support the *Palmares*," Spock ordered. "Mister S'trakha, fire at will upon their attacker. We must prevent them from—"

"*Too late, Spock!*" cried nd'Omeshef. "*Shields are breached.*"

"*A Naazh has appeared in the engine room!*" Commander Vega cried over the open channel. "*The warp core is under fire!*"

"*Initiate core shutdown. Prepare to eject antimatter bottles. Sound evacuation order.*"

"Mister S'trakha?" Spock asked.

"No effect with phasers. Torpedoes still loading."

The *Palmares* began to expel the antimatter bottles from the ventral side of its rear section, but it was too late. The explosion that erupted from the *Soyuz*-class starship's engine section was smaller than it would have been if all its antimatter had been released, but more than adequate to tear its hull apart from the inside. The cool, calculating part of Spock recognized that even the release of the smaller amount of matter-antimatter plasma within the intermix chamber would have created enough heat to vaporize most of the surrounding engine room to plasma temperature, with the catastrophic thermal expansion propagating outward through the rest of the ship's atmosphere and superstructure.

Spock had learned to embrace the portions of himself beyond that cool, calculating part. But it was the only part of his mind that he wanted to contemplate the death of the *Palmares*'s crew at this moment, until he had the luxury to deal with his emotional response. But he allowed himself a fleeting moment of relief that Christine Chapel had made dinner plans aboard the *Enterprise* this evening. Doing so had probably saved her life.

"Shield status, Mister S'trakha?" he asked, in order to focus the young lieutenant's attention back onto his duties.

"Uh, holding, sir."

"Captain Spock," Sulu said from the helm, "we're not under attack anymore. The Naazh ships have moved off."

"Sir," added Lieutenant Palur from the science station, "while we were . . . preoccupied, one of the Naazh ships seems to have placed something in forced orbit above the colony."

"On screen," Spock ordered.

The object was a large crystal, much of it encased in what appeared to be the same pseudo-organic material as Naazh body and spacecraft armor. The exposed portion was conical and oriented toward the planet. "Looks like it could be a weapons platform," Sulu observed. "The crystal tip is probably the emitter."

"Targeting the settlement?" Spock asked.

Palur frowned. "Near there," the Argelian said. "About twenty kilometers off. Maybe it's misaligned?"

"Asimov *to* Enterprise," Blake called over the still-open channel. "*We've detected a second Naazh ship planting another orbital device matching the one you're observing. Also aimed near but not directly at the settlement.*"

Moments later, both ships were able to observe the placement of the third device as it happened—the Naazh ship generated a dimensional rift from which the satellite emerged, then moved on. Sulu looked up at Spock with concern. "This is starting to look like a pattern."

"Indeed—perhaps a most unfortunate one." Spock returned to his command chair and opened another channel. "*Enterprise* to Admiral Kirk."

Ceto

"All right, Spock, keep me posted," Kirk said into his communicator after Spock had filled him in on the situation in orbit. He pushed aside his grief at the loss of his old comrade nd'Omeshef and the nearly sixty others aboard the *Palmares*; he would need to maintain his focus if he wanted to limit the number of additional casualties that would join them over the next few hours. "Whatever they're doing up there, it hasn't stopped the Naazh from attacking down here."

"Are you in imminent danger, Admiral?"

"We've retreated to the Aenar's old cavern settlement," Kirk said, looking around himself at the spacious enclosure—an almost spherical space carved from the living stone of the mountain, with the Aenar's dwellings affixed to its walls like shelf fungi on the trunk of a tree. The Aenar had installed little in the way of illumination, but the hosts with active Spectres had transmuted portions of the cave walls and ceiling into luminescent materials, suffusing the cavern with an eerie blue glow that reduced the apparent difference between the frightened human and Aenar faces he surveyed. "The opening is defensible, and the strongest telekinetics in the group are holding them off." For a moment he envied them, remembering the satisfaction he had felt on Platonius when his kironide-enabled telekinesis had let him put the sadistic Parmen in his place and save his crew from slavery. Then he remembered the days of nasty aftereffects from kironide poisoning and chelation therapy, and his envy evaporated into nausea.

"Are you expecting reinforcements from Medusa?" Spock asked.

"That's what Kollos and Miranda are trying to find out right now. Leave it to us, Spock—you focus on the situation up there."

"Acknowledged. Enterprise *out."*

Kirk checked in with the defenders at the cave entrance. Led by Arsène Xiang, they had nearly finished transmuting a solid wall across the opening. "Takes less energy to maintain than psionic shields," the gray-haired, Tang-armored New Human told Kirk.

"But will it hold?" Kirk asked, hearing the ongoing barrage of Naazh plasma fire striking its other side.

"It buys us time, Admiral," Xiang replied gravely. "Hopefully enough time to figure out what to do next."

Thanking the older man, Kirk moved on to the Aenar settlement's main communications building, finding Miranda Jones and Jade Dinh emerging from the single-story structure. "Bad news, I'm afraid." Jones spoke in the tones Kirk had come to recognize as Kollos's, but with less enthusiasm than usual. "The Lords are mounting a simultaneous assault on Medusa. The homeworld can't spare any defenders—we'll have to make do with the forces on hand."

The admiral grimaced. "Obviously what they intended. Cripple or destroy our ships in orbit, attack the homeworld so they can't send help."

"We've lost several of the Medusan ships in orbit too," Dinh told him. "The rest, including Abioye's, have gone to ground or retreated into space. The Naazh seem content to let them go as long as they don't interfere with their satellite planting."

Jones's regal face took on a frown. "Do you believe the satellites are weapons?"

"When have we ever seen the Naazh whip up anything but

weapons?" Kirk asked. "The question is, why mount both a ground assault and an orbital assault?"

"To keep us busy until they're ready to fire?" Dinh proposed.

Kirk studied her. "Would active hosts like you be able to stop those satellites from the ground?"

"With the defenses they probably have, I doubt it."

"Then something doesn't add up yet, and it worries me."

"I'm more worried at the lack of coordination," Kollos/Jones said. "The Medusans aren't experienced at combat, Jim. We're a peaceful people as a rule, and when we have needed to defend ourselves . . . well, let's just say we've managed to get by on our looks."

Kirk nodded, remembering how Kollos had saved himself from a murderous Lawrence Marvick merely by allowing himself to be seen. It was a hell of a natural defense mechanism. "But that's no use on the Naazh," he said.

"Not with their Lords shielding them."

"We still have Spectres on our side."

Dinh shook her head. "The sleepers have always survived by flight and concealment. We've fought when cornered, like now—but our track record isn't promising."

Kirk stared at her choice of pronoun, and the silver-eyed science specialist smiled and nodded slightly to confirm his realization. Unlike Meihua Wu, and like Jones, she had fully accepted her Spectre as part of her identity.

Miranda's hand touched his. "We need a general, Jim. Or rather, an admiral. An experienced military mind to direct our defense. Are you willing?"

Kirk hesitated only briefly. Part of the reason he had always resisted flag rank was that he never liked to sit back in safety while issuing orders that sent others into danger and death. He had always preferred to lead from the front lines.

But in a situation like this, with inexperienced defenders facing an assault on multiple fronts, there was a need for someone to stand back and survey the entire board while others did the work on the ground. That was an admiral's place—and like it or not, he was an admiral now.

"All right," Kirk said, moving into the communications shack. "First off, let's get those ships back in the fight. If the Naazh are so protective of those satellites, we need to intensify our efforts to take them out . . ."

Nineteen

U.S.S. Reliant

Several of the Aenar had transported aboard the *Charas* with Captain Thelin, modifying its warp drive to let it keep pace with the *Reliant*'s Spectre-augmented speed. However, the two ships did not make it very deep into Medusan space before they came under attack from a trio of small but powerful Naazh ships. Chief DiFalco and the Aenar did their best to reinforce the ships' shields against the Naazh's weapons, but the Aenar's pacifism meant they had trained to use their powers only for defense. The ships withstood the barrage of exotic weapons fire from the Spectre-enhanced vessels, but despite the best efforts of Beach and Nizhoni to make an end run around the Naazh, the enemy ships proved too fast and maneuverable to let them break past or get far enough from their bombardment to form a stable warp field.

Clark Terrell looked up at DiFalco, who stood behind the ensign at navigation as if tempted to reclaim her old Starfleet responsibilities. But the chief had a larger role to play now. "Any more tricks up your Spectres' sleeves?" Terrell asked her.

She turned and shook her head, her silver eyes downcast. "There are steps we can take if we reach Medusa, in concert with its people. Out here, though, there's little we can do."

"Even with all the New Humans we have aboard?"

"New Humans with dormant Spectres, untrained in harnessing their powers. I'm afraid they can't help."

Terrell rose from the command chair and straightened his uniform jacket. "Well, maybe there's something I can do. Mister Kyle, hail the Naazh vessels."

The blond Englishman stared at him. "Sir?"

"You heard me, John."

"They've never been willing to listen before, Captain," DiFalco said with some heat.

"We're still Starfleet, Chief. We have to try."

"Ready, sir," Kyle said.

Terrell cleared his throat. "Hostile vessels. This is Captain Clark Terrell of the *U.S.S. Reliant*. I'm a citizen of the United Federation of Planets—and I know that most or all of you are probably Federation citizens as well. You may have given yourself over to the incorporeal beings known as Lords, but I plead with you to remember your allegiance to the Federation and halt your attacks on your fellow citizens, and on our Medusan allies. Whatever grievances you have, surely your parents raised you better than to believe this kind of violence was the way to resolve them. Please respond so we can find an alternative."

At first, the only response was more weapons fire. But after a few moments, Kyle reported with some surprise, "Reply coming in, sir."

"On screen."

The main viewer lit up with the image of a familiar set of blue-and-silver Naazh armor. *"Captain Terrell. Still idealistic to a fault, I see."*

Terrell stared, recognizing the haughty tone of voice despite the filtering. "Haru Yamasaki, isn't it? You're a long way from Terebellum."

The blue Naazh laughed, and after a moment, his helmet

glowed, turned transparent, and vanished, revealing the former Terebellan security director's prim, narrow face—and eyes with the same silver gleam as DiFalco's. *"I go where I'm needed to defend humanity."*

"The people you've killed are still human, Yamasaki. No different from you or me. In fact, much the same as you are now."

"You evidently know about the Lords. Then you should know that a hunter came to me the night before the peace talks. He and the Lord within him revealed the truth about the New Humans and the Aenar." His cool, calculating expression grew colder, his voice tinged with disgust. *"As I knew all along, their mutations were not natural. Just like the Suliban Cabal, they were experiments, genetic augmentations created by an enemy power to undermine the Federation from within.*

"Created by the Medusans," he finished.

"What?" DiFalco shouted. "That's insane!" Terrell touched her shoulder, and she fell quiet, reminded of her place.

Yamasaki frowned at her. *"Your eyes . . . but you're not one of us."*

"I'm one of your Lords' targets. Inhabited by an incorporeal being of the same species as the Lords—but hunted by them, persecuted and murdered as political dissidents. Forced to flee to this universe and hide within corporeal brains to protect themselves from extermination."

A disbelieving smirk formed on Yamasaki's face. *"You can't possibly think that lie will sway me. I share my consciousness with my Lord. We have no secrets from each other, only total truth. It's very refreshing."*

"Do you really think beings who call themselves 'Lords' would be so egalitarian, Haru?" Terrell asked. "How do you know you're not only hearing the thoughts it wants you to hear?"

"Haven't you felt how your Lord is draining you?" DiFalco

challenged. "Aging you by forcing you to use its powers constantly?"

"Judging from your eyes, your . . . occupant is doing the same. I consented to it for the sake of our mission. I'm willing to pay any price in the defense of humanity."

"The difference is, I had to convince my Spectre to stay active. It didn't convince me." She shook her head. "Look, I'm not crazy about the fact that it was hiding in me my whole life, making me think its powers were mine. But after seeing the brutality of your Naazh buddies toward the Aenar—after seeing them murder my friends, my crewmates—I understand why it had no choice but to hide. Your Lords are genocidal monsters, and they'll tell you whatever lies will convince you to let them use you. Trust me, they won't stop until it kills you."

Yamasaki shook his head. *"All you're doing is convincing me I was right. Let's stipulate, for the sake of argument, that you're telling the truth. I'm a fair man, so I'll give you the benefit of the doubt. But if that's so, doesn't that mean you're* still *a product of alien intruders altering humans into something unnatural and dangerous? Either way,"* he went on with smug self-satisfaction, *"whether you're the creation of the Medusans or of these 'Spectres,' doesn't that still make you a danger that I cannot allow to exist?"*

Chekov rose from the science station. "It won't be that easy, Yamasaki. We have the means to defend ourselves. And we have the will."

Yamasaki laughed. *"I admire your conviction, Commander Chekov. Really, I do. But you have only the barest inkling of the Lords' power. I'm afraid you're ten thousand years too early to take them on."*

"Nice to hear," Terrell said. "I always like being ahead of schedule."

Yamasaki smirked again. *"Very well."*

His helmet rematerialized, and his voice went on through its filtering, finally void of its usual pretense of courtesy. *"Then you will be glad to know the date of your death has been moved up."*

U.S.S. Enterprise

"Captain Spock?"

All Lieutenant Palur had to do was call Spock over to the science station and gesture at the simulation on its upper display screens. It took him only moments to digest the results, which confirmed what he had already suspected. Nodding to the Argelian lieutenant, he returned to stand by his command chair and opened the channel to the surface. "*Enterprise* to Admiral Kirk."

"Kirk here."

"Enough of the Naazh satellite array is now in place that we can determine their likely number and effect. The pattern being formed is most consistent with an array of twelve emitter satellites arranged as a spherical dome centered on a position sixteen to twenty kilometers underground, directly below the settled portion of Ceto."

Kirk sounded puzzled. *"Why so far below the surface?"*

"Given the power readings of each satellite and the likely magnitude of the dimensional disruption they could create, the discrepancy would hardly matter. Simulations show that the disruption will be sufficient to destroy everything within a spherical volume approximately two hundred kilometers in radius around the focal point."

It was a moment before Kirk spoke again. *"You mean they're going to tear a chunk out of the planet?"*

"If we are unable to halt the completion and activation of the satellite array, Admiral. Five satellites are already in place. Fortunately, there are only four Naazh ships emplacing them, and they divide their time between assembling the grid and fending off our vessels. Whenever we have attempted to destroy or displace one of the satellites, its onboard defenses and at least one of the Naazh ships have prevented us."

"Intensify your efforts, Spock. We have to keep them from completing that formation, no matter the risk."

Spock's lips compressed as he contemplated the likelihood that Kirk's order would mean sacrificing some lives to save others. Vulcan sayings about the needs of the many offered little solace to the commander ordering the few to their deaths. As McCoy had said in the briefing room the other day, it was less morally challenging to choose to be the one sacrificed than to choose others for the role. This was one of the aspects of command that had deterred Spock from pursuing it for so long. But he reminded himself that it was the Naazh who were forcing the choice—and that everyone in Starfleet had chosen to accept that risk when they had joined the service.

However, more pragmatic concerns occurred to him. "Doing so will be difficult, Admiral. The *Enterprise*'s weapons are only partially repaired. Mister Scott has restored the *Asimov* to full mobility, but its armaments are less than ours. And the Medusan craft have little offensive capability."

"I have some ideas about that," Kirk replied. *"If the Medusans are willing to lend their skills, we may be able to use some of the Naazh's own tricks against them."*

U.S.S. Asimov

"Ah, it's no use," Montgomery Scott groaned as he fine-tuned the tractor beam controls on the *Asimov*'s bridge engineering station. "No matter what I do, I just can't get a lock on this blasted satellite. It's using some dimensional trick to refract the beams around it."

"So towing it away is out," Captain Blake said as she paced the front of the bridge, "and blowing it up is out." The armored portions had regenerated after every phaser bombardment and torpedo hit, and the crystal portions had simply swallowed up the weapons fire like an open door. By now, the Naazh had emplaced eight of their satellites and not one had been destroyed or knocked out of formation. "What's left?"

Scott pondered the question unhappily. There was nothing he loved more than a good engineering problem to solve, but he wished the universe wouldn't keep sticking them in the middle of time-sensitive, life-or-death struggles. It took the joy out of them.

Still, it did have a way of focusing the mind. "If they can use their dimensional warps against us, maybe we can use a modified warp field against them. Configure the shuttles' engines to generate a field to disrupt the satellites' dimensional distortion, remote-pilot them into place."

"Wouldn't the Naazh just shoot the shuttles down?" Uhura asked from the science station.

"If we had enough of them, and kept up covering fire . . . No, it'd take too long to configure that many."

"Any way we could project the disruption field from here?"

After a moment's thought, he smiled. "Aye, lass . . . maybe if we rig the deflector dish, we could do something similar."

Blake nodded. "Get on it, Mister Scott. Commander Uhura, brief the other ships on the plan. If we all do this, maybe we can stop enough satellites to save the planet."

"Aye, Captain."

Scott blinked. He'd gotten so used to working alongside Uhura as the science officer on this mission that it was odd to see her performing something like her old communications role. But it made sense for the science officer to brief the rest of the defense fleet on the specifics of the procedure they would be attempting.

Scott programmed in the first draft of the modifications, starting a simulation to model results and refinements, while Uhura briefed the *Enterprise* and the Medusan defense ships to stand by for his numbers. Moments after she finished, she touched a finger to the receiver in her ear—a familiar gesture that warmed Scott's heart—and turned to Blake. "Captain, the *Stheno* is incoming on vector seventy-one mark nineteen and requests we divert to give them a wide berth. Their Medusan personnel are attempting a maneuver suggested by Admiral Kirk."

Blake's bright eyes turned to Scott and widened inquisitively. He shrugged, having no idea what the Medusans could do. Certainly they had an impressive ability to transfer ships between dimensions, but only at close range. He doubted they could withstand the Naazh ships' fire long enough to get close enough to one of the satellites.

Still, Blake ordered the helm officer to move the *Asimov*, while Uhura put the *Stheno*'s incoming trajectory on the main screen. As the squat, sphere-headed Medusan ship barreled toward one of the satellites at high velocity, Scott briefly wondered if it was attempting to get past the Naazh with sheer speed and *chutzpah*. It seemed like a suicide run.

But then a cloudy dimensional distortion formed around the *Stheno*, expanding outward several hundred meters . . .

. . . and when it faded, there was a decent-sized asteroid in its place!

The *Stheno* veered off as the asteroid plunged the final few hundred kilometers to its target satellite, barely giving the Naazh ships enough time to target it and open fire. Their shots only grazed it, failing to knock it sufficiently off course before it struck its target satellite and vaporized in a quick, bright flash and a swiftly dissipating cloud of dust and debris. Once sensors reacquired the satellite, Scott saw it tumbling, its armor half-vaporized and its crystal cracked and flickering.

"It's starting autorepair," Uhura reported after a moment, "but it can't maintain altitude. I don't think it'll be able to repair itself before it crashes."

"Target zone?" Blake asked.

"Fourteen hundred kilometers downrange, Captain. No danger to the settlement."

The bridge crew cheered, but Blake made a tamping gesture with her hands after a moment, quieting them. "That's one win, but we need more. We don't know how many spare satellites they have, or how many gaps it will take to cripple the array. And Mister Scott's disruption beam is only a defense, not an attack." She clapped her hands together. "So let's keep looking for creative solutions, people!"

Scott chuckled to himself. *My favorite order.*

Ceto

Something seemed wrong.

Kirk was gratified to see that the Spectres, Medusans, and other defenders were holding their own against the Naazh. The cavern entrance was a nicely defensible position, a high ground and a bottleneck at the same time. The transmuted barriers were holding, and the telekinetics had managed to bring down part of the mountain face on the Naazh horde—an unpleasant reminder of Kirk's final battle with Gary Mitchell, but undeniably effective. The small avalanche had buried three of the Naazh and inflicted heavy damage on two more.

The Medusans were doing their part as well. Their ships in orbit had taken out two Naazh satellites and seriously damaged or displaced two others with asteroid attacks—though at the cost of attracting a fiercer response from the Naazh ships, with the *Stheno* having been destroyed and two other ships badly impaired with multiple casualties—including more than a dozen

Medusans, who had refused to retreat from this fight even at the cost of their lives. Here on the surface, the Medusans had unleashed a chilling multidimensional attack on several of the Naazh hovercruisers. Kirk had not been able to watch the Medusans in action, of course, but he had seen the aftermath—the bikes' remains twisted and warped as though turned inside-out in multiple dimensions. The bloody fragments of Naazh armor around one pile of wreckage suggested its pilot had met the same grisly fate. It was never in Kirk's nature to take pleasure in a sentient being's death, but he found himself unable to mourn the Naazh's suffering. Whoever had worn that armor may well have been a Federation citizen, but they had voluntarily renounced everything the Federation stood for and chosen a path of hate and murder.

Even the disembodied Spectres had gotten in on the action. It was hard for them to focus their psionics to manipulate physical objects without sharing the nervous system of a corporeal host, but they had attempted to target the Naazh mentally instead, projecting illusions to confound their senses. One Spectre had succeeded in turning two of the Naazh against each other, making each believe the other was a New Human; only one of them had survived the fight, but not without injury. Another Spectre had telepathically persuaded a swarm of small local flying creatures, resembling oversized rhinoceros beetles with dragonfly wings, to converge around the Naazh's hovercruisers by the thousands, blinding their pilots and forcing them to crash.

All in all, the battle was going slowly, but well. "But something's still wrong," he told Spock over his communicator. "The Naazh are taking heavy casualties, but they aren't retreating. They're digging in for a long siege. Why would they do that if they plan to blow apart this whole chunk of the planet with their satellite array? Why not just teleport away and cut their losses?"

"A good question, Admiral. Our progress at disabling the array has not been sufficient to require them to rely on their ground forces as their primary strategy. Indeed, they have succeeded in repairing or replacing two of the satellites, while we have only succeeded in taking out one more, and at this rate we may not have enough ships remaining to implement Commander Scott's disruption field when the time comes."

Kirk frowned. "We've seen the Naazh survive explosions before. But there's no way they could withstand destruction of that magnitude, is there?"

"Given that the disruption would disassemble local bulk spacetime at a fundamental level, nothing possibly could," Spock replied. *"Jim . . . are you proposing that this is a suicide mission?"*

Kirk shook his head, though only for his own benefit. "I don't see fatalism in the Naazh's attitudes. If anything, they're enjoying this." He shrugged. "And why would they even need to send more than thirty Naazh to fight us? There's little we could've done against the satellites from down here. And it wouldn't take this many to keep us busy. This is a wholesale extermination force—but that's redundant if the Lords are planning to devastate the whole area with one shot from those satellites."

Even as he laid out the problem, envisioning its facets in his mind, it all came together. "That's it, Spock! Not a suicide—a sacrifice."

"I see. You believe that the Lords intend to eliminate the majority of the Naazh along with the Spectre refugees and their hosts."

"Of course," Kirk replied bitterly. "They're just tools to the Lords—inferior corporeal life-forms. Once they've served their purpose, naturally their masters would throw them away."

"But the Naazh in the ships emplacing the satellites—"

"May not even have been told about the Naazh on the surface. The Lords may have another plan in mind for disposing of them."

"Perhaps if we inform them of the Lords' duplicity . . ."

"We could try, but I doubt they'd listen. The Lords have corrupted them, turned them savage and irrational. In my experience, people blinded by hate are the hardest ones to convince of anything, even when they don't have aliens altering their minds from within. They'd never believe us."

Spock was quiet for a moment. *"There may be one person we have a chance to convince,"* he said. *"And if my suspicions are correct, she could offer us a way to reach the others."*

Twenty

U.S.S. Enterprise

T'Nalae crossed her arms and stared at Spock through the force field of her cell. "I don't believe you."

"Is it so unlikely that the Lords would dispose of their corporeal agents as ruthlessly as they have had you extinguish the sleepers' hosts?" Spock countered.

"The ones you so benignly call 'sleepers' exploit their hosts as mere vessels. Our Lords gave us the choice, and they gave us the crystals and armor to protect us from the damage of a full merger."

Spock peered at her. "Doctor McCoy's examination of you following your capture showed evidence of accelerated aging and neurological deterioration. This is a consequence of having an active Spectre exerting its powers within you. Your crystal interface did not protect you from that." As she absorbed that, he went on. "But it did protect the mental privacy of the Spectre Lord. Without a complete merging of minds, it would have been able to conceal its true intentions and goals from you."

T'Nalae rallied her defiance. "I wasn't the only one in that cargo bay with graying hair. Doctor Jones showed signs of the same deterioration."

"Recently, yes. But not during the first forty-three years of her life. You met her when she came aboard last year, so you surely recall that, if anything, she looked young for a human of her age. How do you reconcile that with your Lord's claim that her Spectre was actively influencing her throughout her lifetime?"

She shook her head. "You're trying to deceive me."

"I am pointing out a logical contradiction in your own stated knowledge and beliefs. If you refuse to acknowledge that contradiction, you only deceive yourself."

"The renegades are the ones who live through deceit and concealment! Who spent centuries pretending to be indigenous telepaths, refusing to reveal the truth about what they were."

"Who spent centuries condemning themselves to permanent dormancy, unable to pursue their own lives, rather than infringe upon the freedom of choice of the humanoids within whom they were compelled to hide for their own survival."

"Why are you so convinced they're telling you the truth? Aren't you outraged by the violation they've inflicted on thousands of humans and Aenar?"

Spock frowned. "Again you contradict your own position. It is difficult to project a convincing stance of sympathy for the very individuals that you and your associates have hunted down and slaughtered with extreme brutality."

T'Nalae looked away. "That was . . . I've explained that. They were too far gone. Whatever appearance they projected, there was nothing left of them to save. Only the predators that the demons within them had turned them into."

After a moment's thought, Spock nodded to the guard to lower the force field and stepped inside, in order to compel the former astrophysics specialist to look at him once more. "I find it regrettable, T'Nalae," he said as the field snapped back into place behind him, "that you persist in failing to interrogate the obvious flaws in the rhetoric you parrot from your Spectre masters.

"You are aware that I have melded with Miranda Jones's mind in the past, when she restored my sanity after my exposure to the sight of Ambassador Kollos. You are aware that such a healing meld is deep and strong, a complete fusion in which nothing can be concealed. And during that fusion, I sensed no deceit or corruption within Doctor Jones, no malevolent alien presence engaged in infiltration or slow conquest. There was anger in her, yes, but it came from her own experiences as a human with abilities and challenges that few around her could comprehend or assist her with.

"That, T'Nalae, was a state of being that I could easily relate to—and it is one that you should understand as well. You and I were both outcasts on Vulcan, scorned and devalued by the less wise and tolerant members of our own people—those who paid lip service to Surak's teachings without truly understanding their intent. It filled us both with profound loneliness, a deep need to find some place where we would belong, where we could be true to ourselves without penalty.

"I found that here on the *Enterprise*. Doctor Jones found it with Kollos and the Medusans." He tilted his head forward to peer more closely into T'Nalae's eyes. "And I presume that you believe you have found it with the Naazh. That your desire for it was what the Lords played on in order to recruit you."

Her expression grew sullen. "There is a certain satisfaction in being among people who will not shame you for saying what you honestly think. Who do not use tolerance as a bludgeon to punish unpopular beliefs."

"No," Spock replied dryly. "They simply use *actual* bludgeons to fracture the skulls of those they do not tolerate. Obviously that is far less cruel."

She winced, which Spock took as a sign that there was still hope for her. But he would have to resolve this quickly, before the Naazh could complete the satellite array.

"You condemn the 'renegades' for their deception and concealment. But have you not needed to hide your true self the same way, for fear of the persecution you received on Vulcan when you openly expressed emotion? The dissidents are the same as you, T'Nalae. They were the victims, not the predators. They were hunted and executed merely for seeking *contact* with corporeal life, which the Spectre Lords found repugnant and a threat to their doctrines of purity. They hid within unknowing minds because it was the only way to conceal themselves from extermination."

He stepped closer, sharpening his tone. "An extermination the Lords are now on the verge of achieving—thanks to you, T'Nalae. I know it must have been you who directed the Naazh here, that you must have retained a latent telepathic link through your own innate gifts once the Lord within you was expelled. Thousands of Aenar, New Humans, Medusans and their allies, and your fellow Naazh are about to be exterminated in one cataclysmic blow—and you will be the one responsible for every single death. Including the death of Admiral Kirk," he finished, not without an audible tinge of anger.

T'Nalae shook her head fiercely. "I don't believe you! My Lord could not have hidden all this from me!"

"You do not have to believe me," he told her, softening his tone again. "If you are confident that truth cannot be concealed between joined minds, then allow me to meld with you—Vulcan to Vulcan, a complete union of minds, with no crystal filter between us."

She narrowed her eyes. "You know I do still have a link to my Lord, even though it is not inside me. If you try anything, it will protect me."

Spock did know that; indeed, he was counting on it. "Then let it make its case, as I shall make mine. And the choice will be yours."

After another moment, she nodded. "Very well. I give you leave to meld with me."

Spock had always had a natural talent for melding, able to initiate a mind link with minimal preparation, whereas the majority of Vulcans required lengthy meditation to prepare. This ability had benefitted the *Enterprise* crew on multiple occasions when time was of the essence.

But Spock had rarely found it so easy to achieve a meld as he did now with T'Nalae. It seemed that, in the wake of having her fusion with the Lord forcibly severed, her mind yearned for a connection to fill the void, leaving her unusually receptive. And yet, as their thoughts and emotions swiftly blended into one, Spock realized that T'Nalae's own yearning for him as a mentor and guide was equally strong. He had not realized the degree to which she had idolized him as an exemplar of what she wished to become, a Vulcan who embraced and mastered her emotional side. She had been disillusioned to learn he still followed Surak in his own way, but her mind still craved the ideal mentor—and surrogate parental figure, perhaps—that she had mythologized him to be before they had met.

Spock found himself strongly reminded of Saavik, who would become his student at the Academy before much longer. When that time came, it would be incumbent upon him not to fail Saavik the way he believed he had failed T'Nalae. Thus, he felt a special obligation to redeem that failure and bring T'Nalae back to a beneficial path.

A surge of emotion—T'Nalae's—nearly overcame him in response to the analogy. He had thought—*she* had thought—that Spock had rejected her. That he had misunderstood her like all the other logic-obsessed followers of Surak, closed his heart to the possibility of a connection. To find that he likened her to his own *t'kam'la*, a student as close as family—that he feared failing her, rather than merely failing to convince her—was overwhelming. That such compassion, such potent bonds, could exist in the same mind with Vulcan logic and discipline . . . it threw all of T'Nalae's certainties into a whirl.

Without certainty, all that T'Nalae had left were questions—and questions opened the door to answers. New truths flooded into her mind—the memories of Spock, of Miranda Jones, of Kollos, and more. The proof of everything he had said about Jones's nature, her profound loneliness and need for connection . . . and the part of herself that had always been there, dormant and passive, not a malicious puppeteer but merely a background hum—like the sound of the *Enterprise*'s engines, a constant presence conveying enormous power deep below, but so steady and unobtrusive that it went unnoticed until it ceased.

Yet there was more. Spock could not have perceived it during his meld with Jones; nor could she at the time, before she had been aware of the renegade Spectre within her. But T'Nalae knew the mind of her own Spectre, so she could parse the overtones in that subliminal hum—the self-imposed quiescence, the wariness of pursuit. The temptation to intervene when the host was frightened or in pain, and the anguish of having to do nothing instead.

The touch of that sorrow was enough to unleash a deeper sorrow, a profound guilt that threatened to overwhelm both minds in the meld. *It's all true.*

I was lied to

I'm a murderer

Aenar screaming, not fighting even as the blade swings

I was used

Logan's blood, the betrayal in his eyes

I'm a monster!

A vortex of grief, fury, and self-hate drew their minds down. Spock reasserted his distinct will, drawing on his meditative disciplines to anchor him and reach out to T'Nalae. *Do not succumb, T'Nalae. These emotions are true. They are of value. But only if you master them.*

I cannot live with this pain!

The pain is a part of your life. A part of your being. As much as a limb or a sensory organ. It exists to support you, to be harnessed by you. The mind can govern it, direct it constructively. But first you must accept it. Both the strength of the emotion and the discipline of the intellect. Both are required to achieve completion and positive action.

How can my existence achieve anything positive? The lives I've ended, the people I've betrayed . . .

That is the past. It has already occurred. Its only existence now is as a source of wisdom and motivation. Learn from your pain, your guilt toward your past actions. Let it guide your choices in the future.

It took time to calm her and repeat the lesson enough for it to begin to sink in. Some part of Spock was aware that their time was almost up; Sulu was calling from the bridge and reporting that the satellite array was nearly complete and beginning to power up.

T'Nalae registered it at the same time he did. *The other hunters . . . the admiral, everyone below . . . are they really going to kill them all?*

Ask them, Spock told her. *Use your residual link. Turn the tables on the Lords* and make *them tell you the truth.*

I'm not strong enough.

Reach outward. Sense the strength of the psionic field in this universe. It will give you the power you need. I will support you.

He sensed her agreement, first tentative, then more resolute. Together, they reached out, tapping into the psionic field, feeling its power, then guiding it through her latent entanglement link with her expelled Lord. As T'Nalae pressed it for a deeper connection, one that would allow no deception, it began to resist.

But Spock was reaching out in another direction, taking advantage of his own residual entanglement with Kollos and Miranda to connect with their shared mind, and that of the Spectre who was part of Jones. Once they sensed what he intended, they lent their strength, and reached out to the wider Medusan and Spectre group consciousnesses. As one, they tapped into the pocket universe's psionic field, using it to connect, to reach out for the Naazh. The Lords had prevented that contact before, but T'Nalae's open link to her Lord gave them a back door they could exploit. As T'Nalae probed past her Lord's defenses, demanding the truth, Spock felt the Naazh being joined into the communion as well.

Whatever truths T'Nalae unearthed, all the Naazh would know.

Ceto

Stewart Tsai reached out an orange-and-black glove and helped pull Girsu to his feet, using the armor's strength to drag the Arbazan farmer out from under the massive tree that one of the enemy Augments had dropped on his legs. Girsu thanked him with a nod of his fearsome, spiked green helmet. Tsai wished he had possessed enough imagination to allow his Lord to draw such an effectively intimidating armor design from his mind, rather than the fairly basic armor he wore. He didn't even particularly like orange.

After all, the armor the hunters wore served both to strengthen their resolve and to dishearten their foes. The rise of a new race of Augments had to be stopped at all costs, and an ordinary man from Earth, or a farmer from Terebellum, needed every available edge to stand against them. The faceless armor made it easy to divorce the violent acts his mission required from his own life and identity, his wife and daughter, his work as a prosthetic surgeon. It let him cease being Stewart Tsai and simply serve as the vessel for his Lord's fury.

Without that ability to surrender his will, Tsai would never have had the courage to stand and fight here on Ceto, even with nearly the entire cadre of hunters by his side (while the remainder, according to his Lord, were picking off the New Human stragglers still en route and keeping the Medusan homeworld from interfering with the extermination). The battle had been fierce and more than a few of his fellow hunters had been lost or severely injured. Going up against the New Humans had been bad enough, but now they fought alongside formidable allies—Aenar, Medusans, even the renegade members of the Lords' species who had created both breeds of telepathic Augments. Yet the Lords were committed to their responsibility to undo the damage created by others of their kind, and so they had stood their ground. Tsai admired them for that, and so he found the courage to stand and fight with the rest of the hunters. He trusted the Lords to keep him safe.

That trust carried him forward as the battle raged, as the hunters wore down the enemy's defensive line and shot holes in the transmuted wall protecting their cave retreat. Tsai and the Lord guiding his body thrilled together at the prospect that they would soon break through and have their enemy at their mercy, conveniently bottled up for the slaughter.

Suddenly, new ideas and memories began flooding his mind, through what he thought of as the mental "channel" to his Lord. It was as if the Lord was opening up to him more fully than ever before, letting him share completely in its vast, alien thoughts, a nearly overwhelming experience. Yet at the same time, it was as if the Lord was fighting the revelation, unable to resist some outside compulsion to share it.

He and Girsu halted their charge up the slope. They turned to face each other, seeing nothing but their opaque visors, but their shock came through nonetheless.

Then, together, they and the rest of the hunters looked skyward.

There was no doubt. As soon as their attention turned toward orbit, they found themselves looking back down through the eyes of their fellow hunters in space, sensing their thoughts as

the Aenar was a Federation lie, a cover for a clandestine program to breed the powerful telepaths as a fighting force. Their pretense of pacifism could not be real, he had insisted; no species would passively allow itself to go extinct, rather than fighting for survival with any means at its disposal. Anaza's superiors had believed the Federation too feeble and timid to pursue such a devious endeavor, but Anaza's studies of the Federation had revealed the existence of an intelligence organization known as Section 31, specializing in extreme actions and officially disapproved activities. Indications were that the group had been dissolved nearly a decade before the Romulan Star Empire had ended its isolation and begun to clash directly with the Federation once again, but Anaza knew that nothing was as it seemed with such a group; more likely, it had merely gone underground, its extinction as much a ruse as that of the Aenar it cultivated.

His determination to prove his theory—his "obsession," as his superiors would have it—had led to his dismissal as an intelligence analyst and his assignment to a remote military post, where he had spent years nursing a grudge against the Tal Shiar and the Continuing Committee, drowning himself in drink to avoid facing his inability to fight the threat posed by the Aenar, and by the human telepaths that had begun to emerge after the mysterious cosmic event known as the V'Ger incident.

When his Lord had sought him out, confirmed the truth of his worst fears, and offered him the power to personally destroy the enemy that only he had seen, it had literally saved Mahar Anaza's life. He had been weeks away from seeking his escape through his ceremonial dagger rather than his liquor cabinet. But the power he had felt when he had accepted his dimension stone and let his Lord merge with his mind had been more intoxicating than all the ale on Romulus, and more productive as well. He had finally had the power to become a warrior, to terrorize and slay his enemies. His Lord had even allowed him to practice the use of his armor and weapons by killing the Tal

Shiar assistant director who had cost him his career and his dignity. After all, she had been a threat to the safety of the Empire.

The ensuing battles had been glorious, a series of brutal strikes against the Federation's secret weapons. Anaza had seen the Aenar as his primary enemy, but when his armor had first formed, its pattern drawn from his subconscious notions of what would most effectively intimidate his foes, he had found it to be colored primarily red, like the blood of humans and most other Federation species. He must have always expected that the greater battle would come to be against human telepathic adepts. The Lords had agreed, but had insisted on biding their time until Starfleet's guard had fallen before striking at the New Human population.

Anaza had been injured in that struggle, plucked into the sky by a Terebellan giant corvid and barely able to teleport away in time to escape a lethal plummet. It had been an ignominious defeat, but it had all been part of the Lords' plan to trick Starfleet and the Medusans into gathering the quarry in one place where they could be taken out with a single blow. Anaza had admired the intricate elegance of their scheme.

But now he realized that the targets he and his orbital team were about to destroy with the array of dimension-stone satellites included the vast majority of the hunters. And those hunters' Lords had just fled from this miniature universe, leaving them defenseless.

Anaza hated being toyed with.

"It doesn't matter," Chiranaso th'Miruch said from his own ship. The white-armored Andorian had always been the most extreme of the hunters, a member of a fringe sect that glorified their people's warrior past and despised the pacifism of the Aenar subspecies. Right now, he was swooping past the *Enterprise* on another strafing run, eating away at the last of its deflectors. *"They've played their part. It's the duty of warriors to lay down their lives for victory."*

"But why were they even there at all?" Anaza challenged. "Our enemies below could not have stopped us. The Lords themselves are holding the Medusans at bay in our own universe."

"So?"

"So they were sent down there to die! Our fellow hunters! Who's to say we aren't next?"

"We're the best of the best. The most ruthless, the most effective. That's why we got this job. If you don't want to be discarded with the rest, then prove your worth. Activate the last satellite. Win the war."

Within him, Anaza felt the Lord pressing him to obey, firing up his fury and hate toward the enemy below. All it did was intensify his hate for superiors who jerked him around.

He brought his ship about, accelerated toward th'Miruch, and unleashed a full-power barrage on his ship as it began its final strafing run on the defenseless *Enterprise*. The Lord within him protested, but he could feel that it was under mental pressure from outside forces—a pressure that had increased now that the Lords on the surface had fled, so that the effect had become more concentrated on the few remaining. Thus, Anaza was able to resist the Lord's demands and continue firing on th'Miruch's ship until its core breached and vaporized the ship and its pilot. He sensed that the Andorian's Lord had been equally paralyzed by the outside attack, unable to abandon th'Miruch's body before its immolation. *Good*, he thought.

He reoriented his fighter and began firing on the nearest satellite, using the Lords' weapons to cripple their device. As he headed for the next one, he noted that the other two remaining hunter ships were in conflict. One was also attacking the satellites, attempting to save their fellows on the surface as he was, while the second was firing on the first, attempting to defend the orbiting weapons. He could sense that hunter transmitting the activation codes, hoping that the incomplete grid would be sufficient to destroy the telepaths' settlement and every living person on the planet.

As he flew toward that ship and diverted more power to his weapons, Anaza sent a transmission to the *Enterprise* informing it of a phaser frequency that would disrupt the regenerative ability of the satellites' armor and allow them to be disabled if the fire were held long enough. He doubted the Federation lackeys aboard that ship would understand the honor that compelled him to turn to his enemy to save his sibling hunters, but he knew they would act on it nonetheless, for it would serve them as well.

Then he issued a challenge to the remaining enemy hunter. "I won't be a pawn in anyone else's game anymore," he cried as the enemy's fire began pounding his ship's armor. He laughed as he charged directly into the fire, returning it in kind and gambling that his drive to win was stronger.

"I will decide my own fate!"

Medusan space, home universe

"It's over, Yamasaki," Captain Terrell declared over the speaker in the cockpit of Haru Yamasaki's combat-modified scout ship. *"Your masters deceived you. They set your fellow Naazh up to murder each other, and now they've abandoned you. Your forces are fighting each other, and their attempt to destroy the New Human settlement has failed. It's over, Haru. Stand down."*

"Never," Yamasaki said defiantly. "None of this matters. The actions of the New Humans, the powers they've demonstrated, are proof enough that they're still a threat, just as I always said."

"But you know the Lords tricked you!" Commander Chekov cried. *"Used you! And no doubt still plan to kill you!"*

Yamasaki laughed and shook his head. "I'm too valuable to them. Why do you think they assigned me here instead of the planet? And now they need me more than ever."

"You really don't care about the lies, the manipulation?" Ter-

rell asked, bewildered. *"You don't feel used, betrayed that they were serving an agenda having nothing to do with your goals and beliefs?"*

He chuckled again. "That's where you're wrong, Captain. Specifics aside, our goals still align. We both wish the destruction of the same group. As long as we share that enemy, the rest is irrelevant."

Terrell sighed. *"Good grief. Have you ever admitted to being wrong about anything?"*

"I'm not wrong about this," Yamasaki said confidently. "I know I have the faith and full commitment of my Lord. As long as my determination and intellect are focused on our common goal, we will stand together and continue the good fight. The path to victory is—"

He faltered as his armor dematerialized, dropping him a centimeter into his pilot's seat. A wave of pain and nausea swept over him; when it cleared, the cockpit's alarms and status displays showed him that the scout ship's armor and crystal weaponry had disappeared as well—along with the presence of his Lord in his mind. The sudden absence took a moment to register. Once it did, he refused to believe it. There had to be an explanation. He could not have been so wrong.

He just couldn't.

When Thelin th'Valrass saw the shields and armor fade from Yamasaki's ship, he immediately handed the conn of the *Charas* off to his first officer and ran to the transporter room. At last, he had his chance to get revenge for the slaughtered Aenar—to take on one of their butchers face-to-face and settle with them in a fair fight, with no hyperdimensional tricks to protect them.

True, Yamasaki had not become a Naazh until recently, so he had not been involved with the Aenar massacre. But he had willingly aligned himself with the creatures responsible for that atrocity, and had wholeheartedly joined in the effort to inflict another like it on members of his own species, making him a traitor by blood as well as politics. Such a person was a true monster, deserving no mercy. He would be a fitting target for Thelin's vengeance.

When Thelin materialized in the cockpit of the drifting scout ship, phaser in hand and set to kill, he found Haru Yamasaki curled up under the pilot's console, weeping inconsolably. "No! It's not fair! Don't leave me! You were the only one who understood me! Tell me it's not true! Tell me I wasn't wrong! Please—I'll do anything you say, just take me back!"

After a few moments, Thelin returned the phaser to his belt, dragged the unresisting, sobbing wreck of a man to his feet, and ordered the *Charas* to beam both of them back. Yamasaki would have to spend the rest of his life facing who he really was. Surely that was revenge enough.

Twenty-One

Ceto

"So Medusa is safe?"

Miranda/Kollos nodded in answer to Kirk's question as they, Spock, and McCoy strolled through the town along with Captain Thelin, who had accompanied the last batch of New Humans to Ceto aboard the *Potemkin* while his own vessel and the *Reliant* were undergoing repairs back in normal space. Around them, assorted New Humans, Aenar, and the shimmers of disembodied Spectres worked together to clear away debris and repair battle damage with their telekinetic powers. "It seems the prospect of facing a united front of Medusans *and* fully awakened Spectres was more than the Lords were ready for. Once their attack here failed, they abandoned their assault on the homeworld."

"So I take it that means Ceto is safe as well," McCoy said, staring in awe at the feats of reconstruction being performed around them. "Just imagine . . . this is what they can do when they've only been active for days. Once they're fully trained . . ." He shuddered. "I've said it before—I'm just glad the folks with magic mind powers are on our side for a change."

"Yes, Doctor," Miranda/Kollos said, "we should be able to defend Ceto if the Lords try again. But it may not be necessary. The Medusans have already received messages from others in the Spectres' home domain—dissidents seeking refuge or aid. Apparently the sleepers aren't the only ones who disagree with the Lords' rule, not by a long shot." They smiled. "Who knows? The Lords' supposedly infallible, unbeatable regime has just suffered a humiliating defeat. That's bound to weaken their iron grip on their people."

"You believe there might be a revolution?" Thelin asked.

"Possibly—with a little help."

Spock appeared skeptical. "From what I was able to sense of the Lords' domain during my meld with T'Nalae, I do not believe that unseating their power will be a simple matter. It could be the work of a generation or more."

"Which, on the scale of Spectre lifetimes, could be centuries," Miranda/Kollos agreed.

Kirk looked around. "Which means, I suppose, that it's best if the Aenar and New Humans remain here indefinitely."

McCoy stared at him. "You mean never go home again?"

"I'm fine with that," Jones said—and Kirk could tell now that she was speaking for herself. "I've long felt more at home with the Medusans than I ever did in the Federation. Many of the New Humans I've spoken to feel the same. After all, this is a place where Spectres can live freely, without needing corporeal hosts for anchoring or concealment. They can bond with humans and Aenar when they wish, and exist independently the rest of the time. It will let humans, Aenar, and Spectres share a fully equal existence at last. For those of us who've embraced our Spectres, it feels ideal."

"And then there are the rest of us," came a new voice. Kirk turned to see Marcella DiFalco approaching, along with Chief Onami, who had requested to return with the *Enterprise* now that the New Humans were safe. According to Onami, she still felt she had much to learn, but Arsène Xiang had persuaded her that she'd be better off applying what she'd learned so far to her own life back home. Kirk was glad to have two more familiar faces aboard, though he regretted that Chekov, Nizhoni, and Kyle had been unable to make it for a reunion with the rest of their old shipmates. Still, it was a relief to see DiFalco alive and well—and with her eyes back to their familiar hue.

Noting the same, McCoy moved to her side solicitously. "You've had your Spectre removed?"

"At last, yes," DiFalco said with a sigh. "The fight's finally over. My Spectre and its kind are safe, and I wish them well, but I still can't come to terms with what they imposed on me and my ancestors without our knowledge. I—I just want it to be over."

"Nearly half of the New Humans have made that same choice, sirs," Onami told Kirk and Spock. "There should be enough room on the *Enterprise* and *Potemkin* for their return."

"And the Aenar?" Spock asked.

Thelin provided the answer. "Every last one has chosen to remain here, united with their Spectres. I can understand why. Telepathy has been an inherent part of Aenar society for more than a millennium, inseparably woven into their culture. Their new understanding of its origin has not altered that. With so few Aenar left now, preserving their culture and identity is more important than ever." He looked around at the villagers continuing their telekinetic work. "Who knows? With their transmutation abilities, the Aenar may be able to reverse their reproductive decline and build a thriving population once again. It is only a shame that they will not be able to share such solutions with Andoria."

"Why the blazes not?" McCoy asked.

"Consider it from their position, Doctor," Spock said. "They have been persecuted and threatened for centuries, their species driven nearly extinct by multiple forces. The threat from the Lords is in abeyance, but if you had their history, would you be quick to trust that it was ended?"

"Or indeed," Thelin added, "that no others would ever pose the same threat?"

The doctor grimaced. "I guess you're right. The Naazh we captured after the battle, after the Lords up and abandoned them, came from all over. Andorians, humans, even a Romulan. And T'Nalae too. I can't blame the Aenar for feeling the whole galaxy is out to get them."

"In that case," Kirk said, "it's probably best if the Aenar's survival remains a secret. The galaxy believes they're extinct, and they'll be safer if we don't reveal otherwise."

Thelin nodded. "A wise choice, Admiral. Perhaps one day, they will be ready to reveal themselves, but it should be on their own schedule."

"For that matter," Spock added, "I would recommend classifying the existence of the sleepers. Many would not understand or accept the Spectre refugees' reasons for concealing themselves within human hosts. And recent events have shown that the Federation is not as free of prejudice and paranoia as we like to believe."

Kirk stared. "That's rather cynical of you, Spock. The Naazh were the exceptions, a tiny minority."

"I agree. But history shows that even a small minority of xenophobes can do disproportionate harm if they organize with violent intent."

"Even if none of the Spectres stay in our universe, sir," Onami added, "some people would be afraid that they were still around, still a potential threat. And when the fear of an enemy persists in the absence of a genuine enemy . . . well, the result is free-floating paranoia that can lock on to any convenient target, deserving or not."

"All right," Kirk said, clapping his hands together. "So we'll report that the Naazh successfully drove the Aenar extinct, and that the New Humans were offered asylum by the Medusans and resettled in parts unknown." He glanced at DiFalco. "Explaining how half of them lost their powers—or how you came back from the dead, Chief—will take a bit more creativity, though."

His former navigator sighed. "It's a shame, though," she said. "That humans never really had the capacity for telepathy after all. I really thought we were evolving to a new level. Now human telepathy will be gone forever, at least in our universe."

"Not absolutely," Spock observed. "I myself am proof that part-human hybrids can inherit telepathy from their nonhuman parents. I do not identify as human, but other hybrids may."

"It's not quite the same, Spock," McCoy said.

"It may be to them, Doctor. Many of my childhood peers considered me a fraud for identifying as Vulcan because I was 'impure.' But I *choose* to live as a Vulcan, and my choice makes it real. Would you object to someone identifying as human by choice merely because they shared the genes of another species?"

The doctor fidgeted. "Well, when you put it that way . . ."

"Sir," DiFalco asked Kirk in the ensuing silence, "what about the Naazh? They know the truth about this place, and at least the ones captured on the surface know about the Aenar. So do we just . . . leave them here?"

"Most of them are Federation citizens," Kirk said. "As were their victims. We have a duty to bring them back for trial in Federation courts. We can't deny them the rights they denied their victims. We have to be better."

"Many of the captive Naazh are repentant," Spock said. "They were deceived by the Lords as to the true nature of their quarry, told whatever falsehoods would resonate with their own fears and expectations. Like T'Nalae, they feel shame at the atrocities they were party to, and they wish no more harm to the Spectre refugees or their hosts. Many of the rest still believe they were in the right, but resent the Lords for abandoning them to die. They would most likely agree to keep the secret as an act of defiance toward the Lords."

"As for the rest," Kirk said, "if we classify these events, they'd face added criminal charges for exposing official secrets."

"That seems unreliable," Miranda/Kollos said. "Perhaps we should simply erase their memories of this place."

Kirk frowned, exchanging an uneasy look with Spock. "That's a step we've taken on occasion when circumstances demanded it. But I'm reluctant to go that far if it can be avoided. The Naazh have had their minds violated enough."

Thelin stared. "They are hardly the victims here, Admiral!"

"No," Kirk countered firmly. "But that's all the more reason I won't let them drag us down to their level."

"It is not always possible to cure hate," Spock observed. "But we cannot allow ourselves to abandon the effort to redeem those who remain redeemable. All our species have conquered the hatreds and irrational fears that were once pervasive, choosing instead to favor openness and cooperation. Through hope, persistence, and positive effort, we have changed minds, one by one, until we changed enough of them to redirect the course of entire societies."

"That's right," McCoy said. "Maybe we humans never really had telepathy. But we never needed it—because we make up for it with good old-fashioned empathy."

"So this is goodbye," Kirk said as he and Miranda walked hand in hand through the Cetonian forest. "For good this time."

"I'm afraid so," she said. "The refugees won't be safe in our universe as long as the Lords rule in theirs. My Spectre needs to stay here—and that means so do I."

He was slow to respond. "I knew what we had would be brief. That I'd have to give you up once we got the New Humans to safety. But that doesn't make it easy to let you go."

Jones tilted her head. "I wasn't sure you still felt that way, knowing what you know now about me and my secrets."

"Neither did I—until the time came." He stopped walking and clasped her by the shoulders. "But I look at you now . . . and I never thought shining silver eyes could be so beautiful."

He moved to kiss her, and she eagerly met him halfway. It went on quite a long time, and she was in rare form, almost like a first kiss all over again.

Then Kirk realized this was the first time they'd kissed when Kollos was along for the ride. And Kollos was always enthusiastic about new experiences . . .

After a moment's hesitation, Kirk shrugged and went with it. After all, the last thing he wanted was to lose his spirit of adventure.

U.S.S. Reliant

"Good morning, Captain," Rem Azem-Os said to Clark Terrell as he stepped onto the bridge.

"Morning, Rem. I relieve you." He looked around to see all the rest of the alpha-shift crew already in place, with Doctor Wilder also on hand. *So much for liking to be ahead of schedule,* he chided himself. But he was glad to have a crew more reliable than he was. It gave him something to live up to.

"I stand relieved." The Aurelian relinquished the command chair smoothly. "Engineering reports the mains should be back online by oh-nine-hundred hours. All other systems are restored to nominal function, though we'll need a few weeks in drydock to get the *Reliant* back in top form."

"Well, that just means more leave time before our next mission. Thank you, Commander."

Chekov put his hands on the railing in front of the science station and leaned in toward Terrell. "Too bad DiFalco and the Aenar couldn't stick around to fix the ship for us."

"Yeah," Beach said from the helm, "and too bad they wouldn't let us keep those engine and shield upgrades."

Bianca Wilder glared at them both. "You know how much of a strain those tricks put on their bodies. Emergencies are one thing, but don't get spoiled, boys."

"I'm just saying," Beach went on, "people who can do magic like that are handy to have around."

"Or dangerous," Chekov said. "Imagine if they'd stayed in the Federation, their powers continuing to grow. From what DiFalco told us, even the Spectres didn't have that much power over matter in our dimension until they fused with humanoids. And the refugees could be just as vulnerable as their Lords to the seductions of that kind of power. We could've faced a new Eugenics War one day after all."

"That's a little cynical," Terrell said. "Personally, I think the Federation has lost something now that the New Humans are gone. Their movement may have been based on . . . call it a misunderstanding of their true nature . . . but still, it was a source of hope for many. A promise that humanity was capable of achieving something transcendent. After the time I spent among the New Humans, I have enough faith in their basic humanity to believe they could have kept that idealism intact."

"Forgive me, sir, but I believe that would have changed had their powers continued to grow," Chekov said. "Absolute power corrupts absolutely."

Terrell raised a finger. "You know, they've done a few studies on that. They've generally found that it wasn't true—that how people used power, for good or ill, reflected what their tendencies had already been before they had it. People whose impulse was to do good continued to do good, just more effectively." He gestured at the *Reliant* around them. "Look at us. The power we control would be astonishing to our ancestors. But are we more corrupt than they were?"

"I think I see what Pavel's saying, sir," Wilder put in. "It's not just a matter of raw power, but its proportion. The technology we use is shared by everyone; the power is distributed equally. But if we were the only ones who had it, imagine the temptation to abuse that advantage."

Chekov smiled. "Yes, Doctor, that's it exactly. Thank you."

"But wait, wait," Kyle put in. "If that's the standard, then that's not *absolute* power, it's relative power."

Beach groaned. "Oh, Johnny, don't tell me you're going to be the guy splitting hairs over definitions."

"Excuse me," Terrell said gently. "Don't we have a starship to run?"

The bridge crew murmured apologies and got back to work. But Terrell smiled to himself. The friendly banter was a sign of a healthy crew. Even Chekov finally seemed to feel at home here—and it was probably a good thing to have his cynicism on hand to temper Terrell's idealism, though the captain certainly hoped the reverse would be the case as well. These men and women had bonded into a solid team, one he was proud to command.

He hoped they would stay together for a long while to come.

Epilogue

Eldman, New York

"I finally understand, Gary."

Jim Kirk stood over the memorial plaque that Gary Mitchell's mother and father had erected in the family plot fourteen years before, in the absence of a body to bury. After a moment, he went on.

"What happened to you out there . . . it was never your fault. All these years, I thought you'd gone mad with the temptations of power. I didn't want to blame you for what you were turned into against your will. I never let myself speak ill of the dead—I wanted to protect your memory, for your parents' sake, and for your legacy.

"But on some level, Gary, I resented you for being too weak to resist the power. I never . . . I never had much respect for your impulse control, your self-discipline. I know it was unfair. You were a good officer when it counted. You saved your impulses for off duty—usually. And when you did follow your heart over your orders, like on Dimorus or Nacmor, you did it for a good cause, and you saved me from *my* excesses—my own tendency to be blinded by duty.

"But I knew that discipline didn't come easily to you. You had to work at it. For years, I was convinced that one day your reckless pursuit of your appetites would get the better of you . . . and after the barrier, I thought that was what had happened."

He looked skyward, breathing shakily. "Now I know how wrong I was. When that other mind awakened inside you, screaming in pain inside your head . . . you must have been so frightened. So confused about your own identity. So desperate for control. The Spectre in you probably felt the same way.

"In the end, all you wanted was to create a world of your own," Kirk went on. "A place where you could start anew, where you could have the control you needed. Maybe if we'd let you . . . if we'd tried to understand what you were going through instead of fearing your power . . ."

He lowered his head and sighed. "Well, it wouldn't have saved you. With an active Spectre inside you, its power growing exponentially, you wouldn't have lasted long. But at least, perhaps, you could have felt safe in the time you had left. I'm sorry I couldn't give you that."

Kirk could think of nothing more to say. After a couple of minutes of silent contemplation, he offered his old friend one last silent farewell and turned away, to where Spock had been waiting nearby. "I'd ask if there's anything you wanted to say to him, but I'm sure you'd find it illogical."

"Not at all, Jim. If one needs to work through a personal issue involving a deceased individual, it is useful to have a symbol on which to focus one's thoughts. It is not dissimilar to certain Vulcan meditative practices." He tilted his head. "The loss of Mister Mitchell was the first personal tragedy I saw you endure in our time aboard the *Enterprise*—though far from the last. It helped me to understand you as a man, and as a commander."

Kirk studied him. "It was the first time I heard you admit to feeling for another person. I think that was when I started to see you as a friend instead of just a first officer."

"That was my intent," Spock replied dryly.

The admiral let out a much-needed laugh. "Well, it worked out pretty well, I think." He put a hand on Spock's maroon-jacketed shoulder. "You may not be my first officer anymore,

Spock, but I'm glad we still have a way to serve together. And I think you've taken quite well to command, Captain."

Spock raised his brows contemplatively. "The position has its advantages. Though I still consider myself a teacher first.

"However, you have taken quite well to the position of admiral, Jim. Much more so than you did the first time."

Kirk thought it over as they walked toward the cemetery exit. "That time, I was forced into it by Nogura, limited by his agendas. This time, I get to make the job my own. Plus I still have the *Enterprise*, and you and Bones, and the chance to work with the rest of the family from time to time. It's the best of both worlds. I can handle problems like the Naazh crisis—problems bigger than one starship can handle—but still stay close to the people who matter most to me."

"Indeed," Spock said. "This new arrangement has proven most effective so far. It will be quite interesting to see what other challenges we can solve in the future."

Kirk smiled in agreement, but in truth, he was ambivalent. While he had spoken truly about the benefits of his new post, a part of him would always regret that the center seat was no longer his—that his responsibilities now anchored him to one planet, rather than freeing him to probe ever deeper into the unknown. The extraordinary realms he'd glimpsed on the New Human mission had renewed his hunger for discovery and adventure. Would the occasional special mission between Academy duties be enough to sate that need?

They'll have to be, he told himself. *Spock has earned the* Enterprise. *And we all have to grow up sometime.*

Once they were back on the sidewalk, in a public place where transporter use would no longer be a breach of etiquette, Spock drew his communicator. "If I may, Admiral?"

"Go ahead, Captain."

Spock flipped open the antenna. "Captain Spock to *Enterprise*. Two to beam up."

Acknowledgments

The Higher Frontier is set in the post–*Star Trek: The Motion Picture* continuity I've previously depicted in *Star Trek: Ex Machina* (January 2005), *Star Trek: Mere Anarchy Book 4—The Darkness Drops Again* (February 2007), and *Star Trek: Department of Temporal Investigations—Forgotten History* (May 2012). Specifically, it falls between the 2275 portions of *Forgotten History* and Part Two (2279) of *The Darkness Drops Again*.

The concepts and characters of this novel are drawn primarily from the following episodes:

> *Star Trek: The Original Series*. "Where No Man Has Gone Before" Written by Samuel A. Peeples. *Star Trek: The Original Series*. "Is There in Truth No Beauty?" Written by Jean Lisette Aroeste. *Star Trek: The Animated Series*. "Yesteryear" Written by D.C. Fontana. *Star Trek: The Motion Picture*. Screenplay by Harold Livingston. Story by Alan Dean Foster. *Star Trek II: The Wrath of Khan*. Screenplay by Jack B. Sowards. Story by Harve Bennett and Jack B. Sowards. *Star Trek: Enterprise*. "The Aenar" Teleplay by André Bormanis. Story by Manny Coto.

The New Humans originated in Gene Roddenberry's *Star Trek: The Motion Picture—A Novel*, though the term was not capitalized there, and my version is significantly different. My portrayal of the Andorians and Aenar draws on several other prose works. The *Star Trek: Enterprise* post-finale novels, including *The Good That Men Do* and *Kobayashi Maru* by Andrew Mangels and Michael A. Martin and *The Romulan War: To Brave the Storm* by Michael A. Martin, provided information about the Aenar's senses and their habitat. *Star Trek: Typhon Pact—Paths of Disharmony* by Dayton Ward established that the last known Aenar was believed to have died more than a century before 2382. *The Chimes at Midnight* by Geoff Trowbridge, appearing in *Star Trek: Myriad Universes—Echoes and Refractions*, established the Andorians' twenty-third-century planetary warming program, to reconcile earlier novels' portrayal of a temperate Andor in the twenty-fourth century with *Star Trek: Enterprise*'s portrayal of a glaciated world in the twenty-second. Though that novel took place in the alternate timeline seen in "Yesteryear," it posited that the terraforming effort began ca. 2224, before the death of young Spock split the timelines, so it stood to reason that the terraforming and the resultant controversies also happened in the primary continuity, though I've posited that the specifics unfolded differently after the timelines diverged. Thelin's bondmate Thali is also from *The Chimes at Midnight*, where they had a less happy outcome to their relationship. Andorian Homeworld Security was established in *Star Trek: Worlds of Deep Space Nine Volume One—Andor: Paradigm* by Heather Jarman, which also established Zhevra as the continent housing the Andorian capital city, variously called Laikan or Laibok in other books (even in the same book). Michael A. Martin addressed this inconsistency in *Star Trek: Enterprise—The Romulan War: Beneath the Raptor's Wing* by identifying Laikan as the political capital and Laibok as the industrial center, but that didn't strike me as quite consistent with the references in twenty-fourth-century books. Making them twin cities that merged into one over the centuries is my attempt to reconcile the two.

Star Trek: The Captain's Daughter by Peter David informs the status of Kirk, McCoy, and Sulu following the *Enterprise*'s return to Earth. Doctor Wilder of the *Reliant* was introduced in IDW Comics' *Star Trek—Alien Spotlight: The Gorn* by Scott Tipton, David Tipton, and David Messina. Commander Beach's nickname "Stoney" comes from Vonda N. McIntyre's novelization of *Star Trek II: The Wrath of Khan*. Captain Terrell's history aboard the *Sagittarius* in the Taurus Reach is depicted in the *Star Trek: Vanguard* and *Star Trek: Seekers* novel series by David Mack, Dayton Ward, and Kevin Dilmore. Spock and Chapel's conversation in Chapter Seven references *Star Trek: The Original Series—The More Things Change* by Scott Pearson. Scott wrote his novella to be compatible with my *Ex Machina* continuity, so I'm returning the favor herein.

My depictions of the *Enterprise* interiors are influenced by, but not identical to, the version in *Star Trek: Mr. Scott's Guide to the Enterprise* by Lora Johnson (then known as Shane Johnson), and the phaser rifles described in the text are based on the conjectural design for a movie-era rifle in Johnson's 1983 *Weapons and Field Equipment* fan manual. The refit *Enterprise*'s dual shield/force-field system was alluded to in ST:TMP; the specifics depicted here (and previously in *Ex Machina*) are based on a memo reprinted on p. 50 of *Star Trek: Phase II: The Lost Series* by Judith & Garfield Reeves-Stevens. Andrew Probert's site at probertdesigns.com was invaluable for plotting the sequences taking place in the *Enterprise* cargo/landing bay that Probert designed for *Star Trek: The Motion Picture*, and David Kimble's *Star Trek: The Motion Picture Blueprints* and cutaway poster were also helpful. My description of Earth Spacedock's interior was partly inspired by the "Starbase 79" fan blueprints of Lawrence Miller, and the 1999 *Miranda Class Cruiser General Plans* by Michael C. Rupprecht with Alex Rosenzweig were helpful for depicting the *Reliant*, as were Donny Versiga's CGI fan art re-creations of the *Reliant* bridge and transporter room. Thanks to Michael Okuda for answering my questions about how transporter reassembly works and what traces it might leave.

For Vulcan vocabulary, thanks to the Vulcan Language Dictionary at https://www.starbase-10.de/vld/. The Andorian terms *naazh* (phantom) and *thetad* (sleeper) come from a conjectural Andorian language created by Spence Hill in 1990.

Various conceptual and stylistic elements of *The Higher Frontier* were inspired by the Japanese *Kamen Rider* franchise created by Shotaro Ishinomori, with storylines developed by Toshiki Inoue and Yasuko Kobayashi having particular influence.

Finally, thanks to all the fans who helped me out with donations when I needed them desperately, a number of whom have had characters named after them in the preceding narrative. Thanks to Devin Clancy, Scott Crick, Ricarda Dormeyer, Ross Fertel, Devon Fisher, James Goetch, Ronald Held, Emily Jackson, Casey Lance, Ronald Mallory, Cody Lee Martin, Tom McNair, Michael Narumiya, Marko Nörenberg, Charlie Plaine, Rahadyan Sastrowardoyo, Daryl Schnell, Daniel Schreck, Gavin Sheedy, Jeff Van Beek, Francesca Vassallo, Josh Vidmar, and anyone else I missed. And thanks to cousins Barb and Mark for letting me finish up the manuscript from their home.

About the Author

Christopher L. Bennett is a lifelong resident of Cincinnati, Ohio, with bachelor's degrees in physics and history from the University of Cincinnati. He has written such critically acclaimed *Star Trek* novels as *The Captain's Oath*, *Ex Machina*, *The Buried Age*, the *Titan* novels *Orion's Hounds* and *Over a Torrent Sea*, the *Department of Temporal Investigations* series including the novels *Watching the Clock* and *Forgotten History*, and the *Star Trek: Enterprise—Rise of the Federation* series. His shorter works include stories in the anniversary anthologies *Constellations*, *The Sky's the Limit*, *Prophecy and Change*, and *Distant Shores*. Beyond *Star Trek*, he has penned the novels *X-Men: Watchers on the Walls* and *Spider-Man: Drowned in Thunder*. His original work includes the hard science fiction superhero novel *Only Superhuman* from Tor Books and the duology *Arachne's Crime* and (coming in 2020) *Arachne's Exile* from eSpec Books, as well as various works of short fiction in *Analog* and other magazines, most of which have been collected in the volumes *Among the Wild Cybers: Tales Beyond the Superhuman*, *Hub Space: Tales from the Greater Galaxy*, and *Crimes of the Hub*. More information, ordering links, annotations, and the author's blog can be found at christopherlbennett.wordpress.com.